The Promise

Ruth Saberton

Copyright

The Promise

Published by Millington

All characters, organisations and events in this publication, other than those clearly in the public domain, are fictitious and any resemblance to real persons, living or dead, is purely coincidental.

The opinions expressed in this book are solely the opinions of the author and do not represent the opinions or thoughts of the publisher. The author has represented and warranted full ownership and / or legal right to publish all materials in this book.
The moral right of the author has been asserted.

ISBN: 978 09955901 99
E1.7

For Dad

with love.

CONTENTS

PROLOGUE

Pencallyn
27th May 1944

It was an evening when the world turned slowly, seeking to suspend time. Jazz music drifted on the breeze as the dance hall door opened for couples to slip into the velvet darkness. When the future was uncertain every moment was lived as though it was the last. Promises were given in a heartbeat. As his fingers closed around hers, she knew he was woven through her heart just as the ivy and honeysuckle were stitched through the garden. This man was planted in her soul and rooted there for ever, come what may.

Her fingers answered the pressure of his in the wordless language they spoke so fluently. They'd only known one another a matter of months, but time was irrelevant when you had found your soulmate. Even the war became background noise when all that mattered was being together and dreaming of the future – and there *would* be a future. There had to be, for parting was unthinkable. Without him she would spool into nothingness and the very fabric of her would unravel, for ever unable to return to the form it had taken in the time before he was hers and she was his.

She tightened her grasp on his hand as though he was a Spitfire that might fly away to a place where she couldn't follow. The notion made her heart shiver. How could she tether him? Keep him from harm when none of them were safe these days?

He slipped his hand from hers to pull her close as he dropped a kiss onto the crown of her head. The tender gesture said he understood how she felt; loss and partings were never far from their minds now. How could it be any other way when each day brought news of more deaths? Telegrams splintered lives, and bomb blasts shattered glass and bone. Even here in sleepy Cornwall death was never more than a whisper away. When the bombers flew overhead you held your breath and hoped against hope this was not your time.

How had the extraordinary and the grotesque become normal? Changes that once appeared so shocking had slipped into the everyday landscape just as pillboxes, anti-aircraft guns and the rumbling of armoured vehicles down widened lanes felt as though they had always been present. Brave grasses tufted the scarred earth where roads had been bulldozed through ancient woodlands, and wildflowers freckled newly made banks as though Nature longed to soothe the hurt. There was beauty amid the destruction just as there was love amid the death. That at least was a comfort.

Living this way made everything so vivid. When the luxury of believing time was infinite had gone, the days were thrown into sharp relief – they were all walking a tightrope and once you looked down you could never ignore the void. Death was everywhere and life was precarious. Being young and in love and dizzy with a thousand new feelings was something more precious than any treasure. This spring she had been convinced the sun was warmer, the sky a brighter shade of blue and the world more beautiful, because she was alive as never before. Like Sleeping Beauty, she had been asleep until a kiss had awoken her. Now she was awake she would never slumber again. Everything was totally, utterly and gloriously changed!

There was no going back.

The moment she'd first met him she'd known instinctively nothing would ever be the same again. She'd been waiting for him all her life, and now they'd found one another nothing else mattered. *Nothing.* There was nothing they couldn't overcome. The war seemed like a dream when the sun shone, the swallows darted through the sky and the woods became deep pools of shade where warm skin would cool only to be heated anew by secret kisses. Surely summer would carry on for ever in a dream of lips sugared from doughnuts, eyes dark with desire and a voice which rose and fell with a music all its own. She wanted to hold onto this time as she wanted to hold onto him.

She wanted this summer to last for ever, and she wanted him to never leave, so she'd wandered through the garden to the old sundial to wish for these things. Wishes made there had been granted before, and anything was possible in the magical garden. Perhaps she should try wishing Hitler away? Even that felt possible here in Cornwall, where the mists of time were thin and the old ways just a shadow away. Magic was in the tremulous birdsong that had rippled the air with the same notes ever since time began, magic was in the lichen which spread over the rocks like a sage blush, and magic was in the unblinking shadow of the sun. She needed to wish harder and more often, that was all. She had let the childhood games lapse. Perhaps if she walked through the labyrinth and left a message in the secret place then the sundial would grant her wish and keep him here for ever?

It was how the childhood game had always worked.

Comforted by this plan, she melted against him. The rough fabric of his uniform prickled her cheek but she scarcely noticed because everything about this felt so right. Others might curl their lips and make scathing comments, but she knew the truth; he was her soulmate. On paper it would seem unlikely, and in the world beyond the garden their life together would be difficult, but none of this mattered because they were made for one another.

Dusk seeped from the woods in a violet wash as evening's paintbrush swirled through a palette of a thousand twilight hues. After the storms of the past few days the air was clear and sharp with the scent of wet earth. Above their heads spillikin branches spiked the heavens and the first stars pin-cushioned the sky. But a clear night was dangerous, with the moon's treacherous light giving enemies both across the water and closer to home an advantage. It was not an evening to stray far or to take risks. They'd been careless once before, and tonight she smelt danger in the air.

His arm held her close as they stepped through the gate and into the lush tangle of garden. Once, on a warm night like this, and surrounded by the exotic foliage her father had so loved, he remarked they could be anywhere – South Carolina, Georgia, Virginia – the names on his lips as exotic and exciting as their love affair, and every accented syllable heavy with the promise of adventure and possibility. Life was blossoming for her just as the garden was burgeoning into life. Here, the chimera of war was a child's half-remembered nightmare.

Nothing could touch them because they were young and in love. The gods loved them – of course they did! Why else would they have been brought together? There was no way their lives would have become entwined like this if it wasn't written in the stars. This was meant to be. It was Fate. Destiny. Her reason for being.

She knew he felt the same way. They dreamed about the future and had made plans, bright glimpses of hope to soothe the terror of a war which felt as though it would never end.

"You'll love racing across the lake in my little sailboat," he had said. "And my folks will just adore you."

She'd wondered at the truth of this. There was uncertainty sometimes in his eyes when he spoke of his family, and fear traced a cool finger down her spine because she knew what it was to have to hide your love, and she also knew what his family meant to him. She was not the girl they would have hoped he'd find any more than he was a man her father would welcome. She knew he missed his family. He talked about them often, and so she knew about his kind and capable mother who taught at the elementary school and his handsome father who worked the small five-acre lot and preached at the chapel. She knew about the vast lake which trapped the sky, the swing with the peeling paint on the veranda and the little wooden boat he prided himself on. His world in America was a universe away from blackouts and bombs and felt a little like a story. 'Tell me again,' she would say, and he'd laugh because she never tired of hearing the words and knew them off by heart.

"There's a small homestead set in the hollow of the hills where the sun shines and the crops shiver in the breeze. We'll walk along the dirt road where the crops grow tall, sit on the porch in our rockers and watch the red sun sink low over the ridge. We'll take my boat out onto the lake and fish for our supper and watch the sunset. My mom will teach you to make apple pie, you'll drive my truck down the dirt road and we'll grow old together with all our children around us. We will, I promise," he'd add fiercely. "You're my girl and I love you. There's only ever you. Now, always and for ever."

Now, always and for ever. These were their promised words, and a vow which bound them together for all eternity. It was a promise as binding as any spoken in church, and when they'd whispered them by the old sundial something had listened and had recognised the solemnity. The birdsong fell silent and the air hummed with magic. They were one.

Now, always and for ever.

The swifts were diving for insects and bats flitted above them as deeper night claimed the garden. The music was faint as the path drew them away from the village and urgency closed its fist around them. The darkness seemed to grow thicker and, although she couldn't see them, she knew the black hulls of waiting watercraft were lurking beside the riverbanks, as dark as fallen trees fossilised in mud, like the timber bones of a long-forgotten forest waiting for resurrection. Something dark was building. Something big was coming. It was in the constant rumbling of the vehicles, the opening of concrete aprons over the beach and the gathering of warships. Even in Cornwall the war was catching up with them.

Time was running out.

They were heading to the old farm at the farthest side of the estate. The original dwelling had been abandoned after the last war and had proven to be a wonderful meeting place. When the Cornish rains cloaked the garden, they curled up beneath a blanket and listened to the gentle rhythm of the raindrops hitting the roof. Nobody ever came here and they were safe from prying eyes. The ruined farm was their sanctuary in a world gone mad.

He took her hands in his.

"Marry me," he said.

She couldn't speak. Everything was spinning. Her thoughts carouselled because she knew every moment of her life had led her to this point. Of course she would marry him and they would go back to America together. All the obstacles in their path would be overcome.

He took her delighted silence as shock, and his hands tightened their grasp, those gentle and sensitive hands that could heal and write poetry and fire a gun. Hands that touched her with such love and which made her tremble.

"We haven't known each other long, but I promise there'll never be anyone else for me," he said softly. "I don't have much to offer you, and I know there are other guys lining up who could give you the world with a bow on it, but I swear to God they could never love you as much as I do. I will love you until the end of time."

"Now, always and for ever," she whispered.

"Is that a yes?"

"Of course, it's a yes! Of course I'll marry you!"

He held her tightly then and kissed her, a kiss which spoke of hope and longing and of the dread of an imminent parting. It was a kiss promising a lifetime of love wrapped up in whatever moments they could steal. It was a kiss she would remember for the rest of her life.

"I don't have an engagement ring," he confessed.

"I don't need one."

"You sure do. What kind of guy doesn't have a ring for his girl?"

"One who's miles from home fighting a war!"

"That's no excuse. I can't be giving you Brits more excuses to think badly of us Yanks."

She thought about saying the Brits didn't think badly of the American soldiers who swept through Cornwall like a loud and colourful tide, but they both knew she'd be lying. The girls of Calmouth and Pencallyn might be thrilled with the influx of handsome young men, and the children delighted with sticks of gum, but there had also been much complaining from older folk about the requisitioning of houses and farms, and the barricading of the beaches.

There was the dark side of human nature too. Until he came into her life, she had never encountered it. To stare it in the face and smell its foul stench had shocked her. The ugly looks, the vile words, and the utter dismissal of someone who was worth a million of those who scorned him hadn't been something she had ever expected from her own family or their guests. Or anyone decent. What were they fighting against if not this? She sometimes wondered whose side some people were really on.

"I have something which might work until we find a ring you like," he said slowly.

His fingers slipped into the pocket of his uniform. A small silver crucifix swung on a delicate chain.

"I can't have that. You told me it's your mum's! It's been in your family for years and she gave it to you for protection."

"I know, honey, but I need to know you'll be protected while I'm away fighting. I need my girl to be safe. How can I leave her otherwise?"

She felt a prickle of unease. "But you need it! You're in more danger than me."

"I'm not scared of those Germans. Trust me, they'll run like girls when they see Uncle Sam arriving."

But it wasn't the Germans she had meant, and she didn't know how to tell him what really scared her.

He fastened the chain around her neck and stepped back.

"There. You're safe," he announced. Fanciful as it sounded, she did feel as though she was protected by the simple crucifix as it rested against her breastbone.

"I love you," she said.

He kissed her tenderly.

"And I love you, my beautiful fiancée. I'll spend the rest of my life taking care of you and making you happy, I promise."

But the unspoken words 'however long that may be' hung in the air like a spell cast by a bad fairy at a christening. She was young but she was no fool; she knew the clouds were gathering across the sea. The creeks and estuaries bristled with craft. At night bombers flew over and the sky over Calmouth was lit up with fire. More troops were arriving each day. A camp had been set up for them, the local manor house had been requisitioned, and American officers were billeted at Pencallyn House, too. How she wished this wasn't the case and the officers had never come. Especially the one with eyes like glaciers and a way of appearing from nowhere.

She shivered.

"Cold?" he asked.

She shook her head, unable to explain and not wanting to desecrate the moment by attempting to vocalise her fears. How to articulate a feeling? Describe how a stranger struck dread into you for no reason? It was nothing but foolishness.

"I'm fine," she whispered and lay her head against his chest. The steady beat of his heart beneath the scratchy fabric pushed the stalking fear away. With him she felt brave and strong. She felt whole. All would be well.

The moon was rising. Silver pools of light crept across the lawns and dappled the gardens through the pampas fringes and the gunnera. At night Pencallyn's garden felt primeval, as though a long-extinct creature might burst forth at any moment. She couldn't shake off the sensation that something was watching them from deep within the foliage, and she shivered again.

"My cold one," he murmured, slipping off his jacket and draping it across her shoulders. "It's getting late. Time you went inside and warmed up. I guess it's time I got back to my billet too. Can't oversleep and give the officers another excuse to have a pop at me. I sometimes think they hate me more than those Nazis!"

He said this as a joke but they both knew there was little humour in the situation. Enemies weren't solely above their heads or on the French shore. Some were far closer to home.

Fear was always breathing down her neck. But it was like a game of grandmother's footsteps; when she spun around to confront it there was nothing. Maybe it was her imagination. When you lived in an old house filled with shadows and memories it was hard not to become prone to fancies and strange imaginings. The childhood games played in the garden, the made-up story of the sundial, the frustration and unhappiness in Pencallyn; everything seeped into the very bricks of the place, and the overgrown and neglected gardens became the perfect mirror to reflect the secrets and tangled lives of the people within. The promise of a new life in America with sunshine and oceans of wheat and sailing boats on lakes as big as the sea filled her with joy. She couldn't wait!

Hand in hand they walked through the silent garden. Once they had ventured as close to the house as they dared, they kissed farewell, a tender kiss that spoke of promises.

"I'll see you tomorrow?" she asked, and he smiled, his slow and heart-tumbling smile. He was so, so beautiful. Beautiful, brave, clever and kind – and he loved her and was going to be her husband. The immensity of this good fortune was too much to bear. Whatever had she done to deserve it?

"I'm already counting the hours," he said, tracing the curve of her cheek with his thumb. She loved his hands; the long and sensitive fingers that could tend a wound and make her melt. She was wishing she could turn back time, hide away in the deserted farm and draw him closer and closer until she could no longer say where she ended and he began. She loved him. She *adored* him. It was wonderful – glorious – and she had never felt so alive.

She knew she could never feel like this again. For her, it was him and only him. There would never, ever be another.

"I love you now, always and for ever," he murmured. "No matter what comes next that will always be true. Whatever happens, I'll come back for you and we'll sail away together, for ever. That's a promise."

"Now, always and for ever," she whispered.

"Now, always and for ever. No matter what happens I will come back for you. I'll never be far from you. Never."

She wanted to plead with him to stay just a few moments longer. She ached to cleave to him as the ivy to the old house or the moss to the trees, but these words couldn't be said because duty and war and a thousand other obstacles stood between them.

After one last kiss he melted into the deep gardens as he had done so many times before, and she continued on her way home. Clouds were scudding up to scarf the moon and smother the stars. The greenery beyond seemed to press in on her and she picked up her pace. She knew the air of menace was in her imagination, but even so she wanted to be back at Pencallyn as soon as possible. Without a light from the house to guide her, she trained her eyes on the gravel path, her concentration and focus on making her way quietly home through the blackout.

If the wind had waited for a few moments, or if the moon had peeped out from behind the clouds, the figure creeping past the edge of the house would have been illuminated; but all was velvet darkness. Her head was full of dreams and her heart full of hope. The secret engagement necklace lay warm against her skin, and as she let herself into Pencallyn the Wheel of Fortune clicked on its final, fatal turn.

CHAPTER 1

Nell
The Present

The task ahead is at best daunting and at worst impossible.

Towering piles of boxes are listing like post-quake skyscrapers. Paper mountains are threatening to bury me in an avalanche of documents and ancient memos. All are long redundant but have been held onto for unknown reasons. No surface is left unutilised; from bookshelves to windowsills to the top of the refrigerator, all available space is press-ganged into operation as a dusty home for unread books, empty envelopes and yellowed newspapers. Cupboard doors bulge and threaten to spew forth a tsunami of clutter. The sofa is piled with catalogues and brochures offering goods long since obsolete. The wardrobes are swollen with clothes and shoes saved for best. Then there's the shed, bursting with parts of dismantled lawnmowers, tangled entrails of wire and the treasured screws and bolts my dad thought might come in handy one day.

But that day never came and now it never will.

My throat tightens. There will never be a purpose for this strange treasure trove. Its meaning is utterly lost. Without my father to navigate I'm adrift on an ocean of things he never used but somehow needed. Without him to steer a course I'm drowning, going under, under and under in the storm surge of grief and loss and piles of endless *stuff*. Had he needed three broken radios? A box of vacuum cleaner bags when he didn't own a vacuum cleaner? My nose prickles with the threat of tears, always present lately and constantly taking me unawares at the most peculiar times, because I can never ask him why he had all this. I'll never know what drives a man to hold onto things for his entire lifetime and I'll never be able to ask my father anything again. Not ever. There's no one I can call Daddy. No arms to hold me when I cry. No wise calm voice, no person who knows me inside out and loves me regardless of my flaws and faults, no pleasure at hearing my voice at the end of the phone line. I am nobody's little girl.

I'm all alone.

I pinch the bridge of my nose with my thumb and forefinger and do my best to stem the rising panic. I am in my thirties. I am an adult. And this was not a surprise. How could it have been when I nursed Dad for so long? None of this is unexpected – except, perhaps, the sheer size of the task of packing away a lifetime and the impossibility of knowing what I ought to keep. My father wasn't exactly selective. I guess he either treasured everything or nothing. Which it was is anyone's guess.

Before panic overwhelms me, I push open the back door and step into the garden. Creepers have made a leafy macramé cover across the top of the porch, and late August sunshine casts dapples of shade onto the old rocking chair my father had loved. As a child I had sat on his lap in this chair as he read stories to me or rocked away my tears. Now, to see it motionless and empty, and to know it would never to rock for him again, breaks me.

What will I do with the chair? Do I keep it? Sell it? Chuck it in a skip? What would Dad want me to do? What do I want to do?

I have absolutely no idea. In the eight weeks since my father died, I haven't had a clue what to do with all this stuff. Everything I've done so far has been carried out on some weird kind of autopilot. At some point I must have registered the death and filled in all the countless forms that are necessary, and arranged the funeral too, but I don't have any recollection of doing so. In the past I would have asked Andy to help me sort out the house. I guess I still could, but since we're no longer married it doesn't seem right or fair to lean on him. We said we'd stay friends, but he's busy with work and a new girlfriend so the last thing he needs is a needy ex-wife.

It really is down to me. I only have myself to rely on now.

I turn my attention to another pile of paper. This time it's all the insurance documents, MOT certificates and service details of every car my father owned since about 1975. Honestly. He has kept the lot. I guess I can bin these – or are they important? I don't own a car, so I really have no idea, and I'm nothing like Dad because my instinct is to chuck everything out. I'm not quite in the Marie Kondo league of minimalism but I'm pretty tidy. It used to drive Andy crazy. Maybe I'm the yin to my father's yang? Or my neat freak mentality is some kind of rebellion against his chaos? Is it time I booked myself in for some therapy? I certainly need it after the past couple of years, and doubly so if I'm going to hold onto my sanity while working through Dad's belongings.

Anyway, back to the Liverpool and Victoria Insurance cover note from 1998. Bin or keep? Oh Lord. I have no idea. What was he thinking? Why was he keeping all this stuff? I wish I could ask him, but I'll never be able to ask him anything again. And this sometimes hurts so much I think I could die from it. It's a dull pain deep in my chest, burrowed in somewhere beneath my breastbone and lodged right in my heart, and nothing seems to make it go away. I know all the clichés about time healing, and I'm sure they are true, but my tears are never far away. I cannot, *cannot*, fall apart. There's far too much to do. I need to get this lot sorted and I need to get back to work.

To distract myself from a downward spiral, I call my best and oldest friend. Unlike me, Lou always knows what should be done and the appropriate course of action to facilitate this. I guess it's why she's a junior partner in a top London law firm and I'm a struggling novelist.

"Get a house clearance firm, Nell," is her suggestion. "Your dad's place was quite cluttered when we were kids. I can't imagine what it's like now."

"Ten times as bad?" I offer. Without my noticing, and like a time lapse film, my dad had been filling the house with ever more random items. I'm sure any psychologist would say his stuff gave him meaning and identity, and would conclude that his need to hold onto things was a result of being adopted. All of this is most likely true, but it's little help in terms of sifting through all the stuff.

"Seriously?"

I lean against the porch. "Seriously."

"Didn't you notice how bad it was before he got so ill?"

The truth is until three months ago, when my father had finally told me the truth about having advanced liver cancer, I'm ashamed to say I'd been an irregular visitor to my childhood home. When Andy and I were married Dad would come stay with us in London, but after divorcing I've been house sharing and I rarely travel to Bristol, so there were large gaps in the time we spent together – more bitter regrets for me now, of course. Although he never said as much, I know he was disappointed my marriage was over.

When I finally returned to Bristol to take care of my father, I soon discovered the front door could barely open due to the mound of junk mail and boxes wedged behind it, and that in order to pass along the passageway I had to turn sideways. When the palliative care team moved a hospital bed into the living room, I simply swept everything out the way and cleared a path through the clutter to access the areas we needed. My old bedroom was still clear and, if it was a little odd to wake up in my single bed with Take That beaming down at me from the wall, at least I wasn't at risk of being crushed by falling boxes. As things turned out, Dad didn't stay at home for long and his final days were spent in the hospice, where I camped out by his bed. By then an untidy house was the least of my problems.

"I guess I did notice," I say finally, "but I couldn't give it head space."

"Nell, that's fair enough. You've had the worst few years. Please don't make things harder for yourself than they need to be. Nobody could have done more for your dad than you have."

I hope she's right. I'd done my best, but it was hard when there was only me. Sometimes I'd been impatient, feeling my nerves jangle each time he called for me, and during the final weeks when I was sick with exhaustion I'd snapped at him on several occasions. These moments haunt me, and I hope wherever he is now my father understands I never meant it. I was so tired, and I was grieving before he'd even left me.

I hope he knows how much I loved him.

How much I *still* love him.

Is he looking after my lost baby? The little one Andy and I never met? The thought that they may have found each other is the only comfort I have in all this. There's a boulder in my throat, and it's just as well Lou's speaking because I don't think any words could squeeze past.

"You need to get out and have some fun, Nell. Maybe a holiday?"

If my best friend could see my bank account, she'd not be making suggestions like this. I've hardly written a word in months. My freelance contacts have given up asking for articles and my agent has told me not to get in touch unless I'm ready to show her something – and I don't think a blank screen is quite what she has in mind. Still, I'm not going to tell Lou any of this because, generous to a fault, she'll be booking me on a cruise or something crazy. Like my dad, I'm fiercely independent. It's not great for bank balances, or relationships at times, but it's the way we are. Or should I say the way *I* am, since there's only one of us left? Me. The last of the Summers family.

"Fancy a weekend away? My treat," Lou offers, true to form.

"Thanks, Lou, but I can't at the moment."

"Because of money? Pay me back when you're the next JK."

Since JK Rowling writes massive tomes and I can hardly write a to do list, such a feat looks more and more unlikely every day.

"Lou, no. I can't."

"Well, at least let me do the probate. No arguments, Nell! Write my ex into your next bestseller if you want to pay me back. Make him a serial killer. An ugly one who can't get it up!"

"I write historical romance!"

"Shame. What's the point of being an author if you can't eviscerate total arses in fiction? But seriously, make some time for yourself."

"I will, I promise, once the house is sorted."

"Definitely get a firm in to clear it. Pick out what you want to keep, and let the professionals do the rest."

I look down the garden. At the far end, where the evening shadows are starting to bloom, a beady-eyed robin eyeballs me. Some people believe robins are the spirits of our loved ones returned to say hello. If this is my dad, I'd rather he appeared as something a little more helpful. A removals man, perhaps?

"Clearing the house may take a while. There's over seventy years' worth of stuff here."

"It's weird to think Sam was that old. He never seemed it, did he? I had such a crush on him when we were teenagers. I don't think my taste was bad either – he aged better than Boyzone! But better than that, he was kind. Really kind."

I smile when she says this because although my father was a strikingly handsome man, the sort women look at twice and then again to be sure they aren't imagining things, people were drawn to his easy smile and generous nature just as much as his good looks.

"I miss him," I whisper.

"I know you do, sweets. He was a star. Look, you really don't have to do this on your own. Why don't I drive to Bristol and give you a hand?"

"You don't need to do that."

"I know I don't *need* to, but maybe I'd like to. I can't bear thinking of you there on your own. I know it's a crummy time, but we could have some fun. Fun is still allowed. Sam would hate you to be alone and sad."

"Yes, I know. Thanks, Lou."

"Don't thank me. I want to help. Anyway, what will you do next?"

"I was going to see if I could marry a prince, but that option's gone so I'll have to get off my backside and write a bestseller."

"Any prince would snap you up," says Lou loyally. "You're Finchley's answer to the Duchess of Suffolk."

Now I really do laugh. Catching my reflection in a grimy window, I know although the newest addition to the British royal family might share my café au lait skin and sprinkle of freckles and wear her long dark hair piled up in a messy bun, that's as far as any passing resemblance goes. Bitten nails, scruffy cut-off Levis, oversized polo shirt and a topknot skewered with a Bic is hardly a look fit for a palace. I also have big blue eyes inherited from my mother's side of the family, which makes strangers do a double-take when they attempt to place my heritage without looking obvious about it. I've lost count of the times I've been asked where I'm from. 'Bristol' as an answer confuses certain types even further. Some get quite nasty.

"I'm serious! I have a long list of eligible men who'd love to meet you."

"Flatter away all you like, but I'm not being set up," I warn. "The last thing I need is you playing Cupid. I'm happy being single and you know why."

She backs off at once. "So, back to sorting out the house – I take it you've checked there isn't anything precious under all the crap? Heirlooms? Gold bars? Strange relatives crawling out of the woodwork to claim the estate?"

"The way I feel they'd be welcome to it. The house is rented anyway, so what would they be after? Some old power tools? The contents of the potting shed? The stack of car magazines jamming the back door open?"

"No idea, but people can get funny when things like this happen."

"There's none of Dad's adopted family left."

"Did he ever trace his birth family?"

"I think he might have done something – but he always said he wanted to wait until his adoptive mother, my Nanna Summers, died, and that was only last year."

"Wow. She must have been old."

"One hundred and six."

Nanna Summers, wizened as a raisin and with a shock of white hair, had seen out two world wars, her husband and her daughter-in-law. I sometimes wonder if long life is a blessing or a curse.

"Sort out what you want to keep and let someone else deal with the rest. Don't be too sentimental," is Lou's advice, but I feel sentimental about being the last of my family, having no siblings to share memories and swap stories about our childhood, and being all alone in a world which feels empty and frightening without a parent in it. Who is there now to take care of me? Who will put their arms around me and promise everything is going to be just fine?

A tear slips down my cheek and I brush it away with the back of my hand, glad I haven't used Face Time. If a bereaved daughter cries unseen in an empty house, does she really cry at all?

"So, call the house clearance people today and stand back," says Lou. "Let somebody else do the tough bit. Look, I've got to run, but if you need me ring any time. You promise?"

I promise and end the call, feeling very alone. Lou's life of high-powered legal meetings feels a world away from writer's block, cancer and house clearances. Where would anyone start? How will I know what to keep? Pictures, of course. Countless packets spill photographs onto tables, the mantelpiece and windowsills. There's no order to them and I time travel from gawky teen, to gap-toothed kid to graduate. There are jumbled moments from Dad's life too. There he is on a fishing boat, little more than a teenager, and beaming as he holds up a mackerel. He loved fishing and sailing. There he is on a sailing holiday with my mum before they were married and here's one of me in her arms as a chubby toddler. I iron another crumpled image out with my fingertips and discover my parents' wedding photo. Dad kept this one in his wallet. He held my mother close to his heart all these years. He must have really missed her.

I study the photo. They look so hopeful. My father is proud and formal in his tux and my mother smiles up from a froth of lace. Thank God they'd not realised the swift cruelty with which life could change. Only a few years later on that young wife, my mum, had taken me to playschool with no idea when she kissed her husband goodbye that it would be for the last time.

One speeding driver changed our lives for ever.

I've known other moments like this. Moments when your world changes beyond all recognition. Split seconds in time when you become somebody totally new. An image on a sonographer's screen followed by a soft intake of breath …

I yank my thoughts away. Now is *not* the time for a downwards spiral; there's too much to do. I work my way through fat bundles of letters and notes, written in the distinctive and beautiful cursive which towards the end had slipped into a heartbreaking scrawl, and throw into bin bags the heaps of old magazines and junk mail. Once the floor is clear I move on to the shelves where Christmas and birthday cards going back decades, and written by those who left long before him, are slotted in between the books. One in particular catches my eye because it's tilted at an angle as though my father had been trying to ease it out of its tightly jammed resting place, only to give up when the book remained wedged and his strength failed.

I picture him making the liberation attempt, face crinkled with concentration and tongue between his teeth while he tugs at the spine. Irritation clouds his expression when his fingers lack the strength to pull the book free, frustration swiftly followed by the exhausted hiss of breath as he folds over and into himself, utterly defeated. Watching his strength wane was painful for both of us. The arms that had lifted me easily as a child became thin and poppy-bruised. His broad shoulders were stooped, and the legs that had spent a lifetime powering him along became too unsteady to make it to the bathroom. It was so cruel, and my heart breaks all over again for how exhausted he must have been in those last weeks if even pulling a book from a shelf was too great an effort.

I wonder what it was he'd wanted to look at. Dad had never been a great fiction reader; gardening magazines and sailing biographies had been more to his taste. I'm intrigued.

Hooking my index finger into the spine, I tug the book out, my eyes widening as I liberate a battered and dog-eared guidebook to Cornwall. Why on earth would Dad have been reading a guidebook to Cornwall? Was he planning a trip? Certainly not when he'd last tried to read this book. Making it from the sitting room to the bedroom had been an effort enough.

I crouch down and inspect the bookshelf more closely, but there's nothing more than some outdated engineering manuals from his long career as a mechanic, and a few books on fishing. There's nothing else about the West Country. I'm on the brink of giving up when I notice something else protruding from the back of the shelf. Closer inspection reveals an envelope stuffed behind the row of books. It's trapped against the back of the bookcase by the weight of the volumes pressed against it and so has been totally hidden from sight. There's no way this envelope arrived there by accident. My father must have hidden it where it wouldn't easily be found. This envelope must have been what he'd been trying to retrieve – but if he'd needed it so badly why hadn't he asked me to help him? Why struggle?

I guess the answer is obvious; my father hadn't wanted me to see what this envelope contained. He was trying to hide whatever it contains. Or perhaps he was trying to decide what to do about it. He'd known his time was running out.

I hesitate, torn between wanting to know what's inside and not wanting to know, and filled with a childish sense of wrongdoing. This feels like spying on my father, because whatever he's secreted away is not intended for anyone else's eyes.

"What is it, Daddy?" I say out loud, but of course there's no answer, only the dust settling where weeks before his fingers rested. If I want answers, then I have to look inside the hidden envelope.

I want answers.

With shaking fingers, I extricate my father's final secret.

CHAPTER 2

Estella
The Present

High summer was always beautiful in Cornwall. For more years than she cared to recall Estella had watched the landscape's palette change from the endless greens of hopeful spring to the buttery hues of the over-ripe cornfields. White cow parsley frilled the narrow lanes which wound their way across the countryside, and glimpses of the sea were sapphire slices so bright and blue they made you blink. This was the time when the land was at its most beautiful, plumply rich with nature's spoils and turning to the golds and coppers which slowly spread autumn's burnished hues across the county like marmalade over granary toast. The season was at the tipping point and there was a whisper of cold in the breeze; a gentle reminder the days were counting down to the dying of the year.

"You're not getting chilly are you, Miss Kellow? Maybe you should come inside and wait for your cab?"

Estella looked up, startled by the approach of a young woman dressed in blue scrubs and with an NHS ID badge pinned onto her chest. Staff Nurse Sally Jones apparently. To see nurses without hats and starched white aprons still took Estella by surprise but of course this was a nurse. She was at the hospital, wasn't she? Estella had come here to see the doctor about …

About …

Like a fish flickering beneath the surface of the sea, it was gone. Estella tutted to herself. Well, she'd come to see the doctor about something. It couldn't be that serious if they'd let her out again, could it? As for waiting inside on such a glorious day – absolutely not. Hospitals always made Estella nervous, probably because she'd spent far too much time inside them as a child, and it seemed a wicked waste to be cooped up inside on such a glorious day.

"Is everything all right, Miss Kellow?"

"I'm fine," she said. "I like the fresh air. Far too many germs inside a hospital."

"You're not wrong there," agreed the nurse. "But if you must sit outside, let's get you cosy."

Before Estella had a chance to protest, capable hands were draping a blue blanket across her knees.

"Better, love?"

'Love?' Once Estella would have bridled at such an address but she felt too weary to quibble. How did one reach the impossibly ancient age of ninety-five only to be treated like a child? Had she asked for a blanket? Or to be fussed over? Or to have Social Services organising medical appointments for her? Estella was managing just fine at home, which was exactly what she'd told the doctor. She didn't want a blanket any more than she wanted to be spoken to as though she was an infant, but she was too tired to protest. Now, as in the past, Estella knew which fights were worth pursuing. Besides, the staff here did their best. They were simply doing their jobs.

Blankets arranged to her satisfaction, the nurse moved on, leaving Estella waiting for her cab. She was content to sit and gaze across Calmouth Bay. It was a scene which, to her old eyes, seemed to have barely changed in a lifetime. The town was a grey blur across the sparkling river, maybe spreading out a little more these days in the fashion of someone letting their belt out after a good lunch, but the distant clanking from the docks was the same as it had always been, and the traffic on the water as frenetic. The gulls' cries were unrelenting as they danced high above, and although she could no longer distinguish it she knew the blue flash of a kingfisher's wings would dart along the riverbanks while watchful-eyed herons waited in the shallows as still as standing stones.

Unlike Pencallyn's wilderness this was a tame garden where no trumpet-mouthed gunnera led a charge for freedom or silent ivy snaked its way across forgotten paths. This vista was alien yet familiar, the sea and the river the same as always yet not quite as they had been when Estella had recuperated here as a girl. This paradox thickened the clouds of confusion which had blown across her thoughts with greater and greater frequency lately. Oh! Where was she again?

Estella blinked, the scene shifted, and she was outside Calmouth Hospital. Of course she was. This confusion was utterly infuriating, and frightening too. It was the reason she had seen the doctor today and why she'd visited the Kellow family solicitor last month in order to sign her paperwork. She would get her affairs in order before anyone took it upon themselves to declare she wasn't in the right state of mind to make important decisions. Decisions didn't often come that were more important than making a will, and with no next of kin to inherit Pencallyn House Estella had been forced to think laterally. When the solution had come to her a few weeks ago, and in the dead of night, she had laughed out loud. Of course! It was genius! As soon as the hands of the longcase clock in the hall had crawled to nine o'clock, Estella had telephoned the family solicitor and made an appointment. She was in no doubt she'd made the right decision for Pencallyn's future. Her unsuspecting beneficiary would be a more than capable custodian of the house and long neglected garden.

"You're absolutely certain this is what you wish to do with your estate?" was all her solicitor said when she'd arrived at his office and disclosed her unusual plans to him. "Nobody has coerced you?"

"Young man," said Estella sternly, fixing him with her most haughty expression, "do I look the type to be coerced?"

He shook his head and laughed. "No. Absolutely not."

"Well. There you are. My choice of beneficiary may not make any sense to you, but it does to me, and it will for Pencallyn. So, are we going to sign and witness my new will or not?"

He popped the lid from a Mont Blanc and passed the fountain pen across the desk.

"We are, Miss Kellow."

Estella signed her name with a flourish, and the solicitor and his junior partner witnessed it. Instantly she felt lighter and as though a burden she'd carried for an entire lifetime had been lifted. It should never have been her burden to bear, and if Alex hadn't died Pencallyn would have been his. Or, if things had been different for her, she might have had an heir …

Estella pushed these thoughts away. Things were as they were, and she'd learned a long time ago there was no point wishing otherwise. That way led to madness and despair.

At least her solicitor didn't question her sanity – unlike these damn medics who all thought she was going gaga, Estella reflected as she basked in the sunshine. 'Early stages of dementia' was how the young doctor had put it and, dear of him, he'd looked quite upset as he'd delivered the results of her tests. Estella had thought the diagnosis rather ironic, since she remembered everything from the past with a razor-sharp detail. You could ask her to quote a Shakespearean sonnet, or recount what Alex had once said about the treacle tart which had annoyed Cook so much, and she could comply in an instant. It was only the more recent things which were becoming hazy, and really what did this matter? Was any of *that* important? Who cared what old Estella Kellow had eaten for breakfast, or even if she had eaten at all? Did it matter if she wore odd socks or sometimes got the years mixed up? The present was meaningless anyway compared to what had come before.

Now as Estella watched the river from the bench in the hospital garden, it seemed to her that the years shimmered. In Cornwall time was as full of holes as a fishing net. The old ones had known this and left secret markers:

a weathered granite cross, a green-eyed well or a circle of huddled stones. Sometimes these places were adopted by churches or masked with a garden ornament, but the air around them still shivered with ancient power and you disrespected them at your peril. Nobody knew this better than Estella.

Or Evie Jenkins …

Estella blinked against the glare of the sun. When her eyes opened once again, the decades had slipped and shuffled like a deck of cards in deft hands and she saw the river as it had been long ago. The water was still busy. but with warships and DUKs and patrol vessels. The estuary was forbidden to pleasure craft, and the low-hanging trees close to the guarded riverbanks hid spy vessels which would sneak out under cover of night bound for who knew where. Secrecy shivered with the leaves and sighed in the wind. The wildlife grew bold as it reclaimed the tideline, and otters splashed in the unmolested shallows. Concrete aprons smothered the shore, piers bruised the line of blue, and tangles of barbed wire hemmed the sand. Pillboxes pimpled the cliffs, their presence hinting of danger over the horizon, and at night searchlights swept the sky. Evil waited like a spider poised in a web, and the gathering activity on the river spoke of the growing danger of invasion. Barrage balloons floating overhead were no more surprising than scudding clouds, while the guns, tank traps and humps of Nissen huts became as much a part of the Cornish landscape as rugged cliffs and silver beaches.

Estella longed to walk beside the river once again, to trail her hand in the cold clear water and skim stones, but her body was tired and even short distances were exhausting. Instead she walked there in the magical way of memory. At home when she dozed her spirit slipped out of the window and soared over the water and across the years. She left behind her old, tired body and mind, both of which stumbled so often, and became as strong and clever and quick as ever. After her dreams Estella often woke with tears on her cheeks and spent her day cloaked in melancholy; her night-time life in the past felt closer than the present.

Sometimes Estella found it impossible to know what was real or where she belonged. Deep in the nibbled caverns of her mind, time slipped and blurred. Losses long mourned and passed were fresh as new shell wounds. Tears fell and nobody understood why. How could they? She was crying about events which had taken place nearly a century before. They were all long forgotten. Her past was stuff of history books and documentaries now and she was old. It was a shock for Estella when time moved and slid like this. Who was this old person? Where was the *real* she? Who was Estella Kellow now?

"Where am I?" she whispered, although what she really meant was 'Who am I? What am I? Where does the *I* go when it wanders?' But Estella didn't have the strength to try and answer these questions, and her thoughts drifted with the breeze, running free down the path and away into Pencallyn's garden. She saw two girls standing side by side at the old sundial. Both were young, and their dark heads were so close together it was as though they were Siamese twins, neither ending nor beginning but instead one magical creature fashioned from the same soul. Their hands were clasped, and on the side of the sundial lay a small penknife. The blade was spotted with blood.

"Blood sisters," said one girl to the other. "We're sworn family, and if we ever break that promise we're cursed. We'll die or worse."

"What could be worse than dying?" asked her companion. Her dark brows drew together scornfully. "There ain't nothing worse than dying."

"I don't know, but I think it would be very, very bad. We've used the old magic to make our promise."

"Don't be soft. There ain't such thing as magic!"

"Don't say ain't, Evie! Of course there's such a thing as magic. You don't think the sundial was placed here by mistake, do you?"

The doubter glanced around. "Don't talk daft! That's nonsense!"

"Is it? Break your promise and then see if you don't believe me. My family are unlucky. One of them probably broke a promise made here. Why do you think my brother died?"

"Because the Jerries shot him down, that's why! This is just one of your stories."

"Is it? You believe that if you like, but do you really want to take the risk of being wrong? And the sundial is a symbol placed where the ley lines cross. They go all the way from here to France and beyond. This is Cornwall, where the old magic is strong and it never, ever forgets a promise."

This girl was right; it didn't, and who knew this better than Estella? She needed to warn them before it was too late. They had to understand! The old ways weren't to be toyed with.

Estella tried to run forward, but she couldn't move or make a sound. All she could do was watch the two girls hug and promise to never break their promise. Curses didn't matter to them because they were sisters of the heart, and now of the blood, and they would never, ever let one another down.

Or so they thought.

The scene shifted again, and Estella was back on the bench outside the busy hospital. Doors hissed open and closed, ambulances crawled past and a constant river of humanity flowed by. She looked around for the two girls, but they had vanished decades ago and the bindweed was back in her mind, snaking its way through the gaps and prising the mortar away from the bricks of her memory. Like Pencallyn's garden, Estella's mind was choked with weeds but if she could clear it, beauty and hidden treasure lay within.

You just had to know where to look.

And you had to *want* to.

The doctor had been kind, but he was dreadfully busy and to him Estella was just a stubborn old lady with mobility issues, a patchwork memory and a dodgy heart. If he'd given her the time, she would have explained how her weak heart was the legacy of rheumatic fever. Maybe he would have liked to hear about the days when this building was a sanatorium. Did he even know why the crumbling old hospital had balconies and sunny terraces which made the most of the views across the estuary, or was it an anachronism to him? A Victorian inconvenience better off flattened and developed? Did he yearn for a modern steel and glass hospital instead? Estella had no idea. She'd hardly had time to grasp his name, but levelling the past and concreting over it seemed all the fashion these days. There were enough folk hoping to do the same thing to Pencallyn House when she finally did the convenient thing and died.

Well, not yet. Estella wasn't ready, and she wasn't letting them bundle her into a home on the grounds she was too weak or too gaga to look after herself. She had a story to tell, and until the right person arrived to hear it Estella Kellow was going nowhere.

"And how are we coping?" The doctor had asked, smiling at her across the desk.

Estella had made a point of looking around the room.

"We? There's only one of me here, young man."

The doctor had smothered a sigh. He was probably sick and tired of cantankerous old biddies. Maybe he was dreaming of a more exciting role. Field medic maybe? Or a swanky Harley Street practice with Botox and celebrities? It certainly couldn't be any fun spending all day asking old folk what year it was and who the prime minister was. Estella had been seriously tempted to answer that one with 'Winston Churchill' just to see the look on his face, but managed to resist. Her future at Pencallyn was precarious enough without giving them an excuse to trundle her into an old folks' home.

"How are things at home? Your GP says you've refused carers. You live alone, don't you?" The doctor squinted at the paperwork on his desk.

How much fun it would be to say she cohabited with her toy boy lover! Evie would have made a remark like this if she was ninety-five and being talked down to by some young whippersnapper. Evie had never let anyone talk down to her, and the day Cook had called her 'vaccy vermin' was one the household never forgot. They'd all learned a few choice expletives.

"Miss Kellow? Did you hear me?"

Jolted, Estella swam back to the present as she and Alex had once swum through the waves of Pencallyn Cove, white limbs ghostly in the underwater world and silver streams of bubbles chasing their path as they broke through the surface, gasping and laughing. She couldn't sink now.

"Yes, I live alone. And I'm absolutely fine. I don't need carers."

"You're managing, but we have to put a plan in place. You've been diagnosed with early stage dementia, Miss Kellow. You do understand what this means?"

"Of course I do," Estella snapped. "I also know I'm not so far gone I can't be in my home. I have a daily help from the village, and I wear the Care Line thing you insist upon."

She tugged it out from beneath her sweater and brandished it at him. What a dreadfully clumsy thing it was too, always bashing against her breastbone and catching onto things. No wonder it spent more time on the kitchen dresser than it did around her neck – not that Estella was telling him this. Tell the grown ups what they wanted to hear, that was the best way.

Wait a moment. Wasn't she a grown up? How did that happen?

"I'm glad to see that, Miss Kellow, but your GP's assessment suggests things are becoming more of a struggle lately. The stairs, for example; how do you find those?"

Estella fixed him with a beady look. "Young man, I am ninety-five years old. Do you expect me to be an Olympic athlete?"

He flushed. "No of course not, but we need to think about adapting the house. Maybe Occupational Health could come and make some things a little easier? Maybe a stair lift? Some handrails? A downstairs shower?"

The dear boy hadn't a clue about Pencallyn House if he thought a stair lift would be suitable, Estella thought, feeling amused. The oak stairs with their heavily carved newel boards, gracious return beneath the cupola and wide banisters would not suit a stair lift – although it could be awfully good fun to whizz up on one. Almost as much fun as sliding down the banisters had been all those years ago. And as for a downstairs shower? The water pressure gasped and wheezed when she ran the kitchen tap; a shower would most likely finish it off for good. No, Estella would wash from the sink as she had done ever since accepting she could no longer clamber in and out of the bath.

Pencallyn House, like her, would remain exactly as it was.

"I sleep downstairs," she said, crossing her fingers under the table. It was half-true. She slept a great deal in the daytime, slumped in the armchair by the range if it was winter and out on the terrace in the sunny months, and seldom made it up to her bedroom.

"That's good," the doctor said and proceeded to talk about care packages and meals on wheels, none of which interested Estella in the slightest – as she'd already made clear to the social worker who'd called in to Pencallyn a few days before. Having her very own social worker did tickle Estella. Poor Evie could certainly have done with one of those in

1939, but that was a different time, of course. It was a far harsher one in so many ways, and in others far more forgiving. At least back then you knew who your enemy was.

Even if sometimes he was beneath the same roof …

She shivered. Eyes like glass and a smile colder than the winter wind when it blew across the river. Sometimes Estella thought she saw him in the shadows. He knew the truth, but like so many others he had taken it to his grave. Omaha Beach, or so they said, and Estella had been glad. He hadn't deserved a hero's return.

She hoped his end had been bloody. She hoped he had suffered. And if that was wrong of her, she didn't care. A man like that deserved the worst.

Her appointment done, Estella had been making her slow way out of the consulting room, her stick tapping on the linoleum, when the young doctor cleared his throat nervously.

"Miss Kellow?"

Estella had turned around. When she saw the look on his face, she knew exactly what he wanted to ask, and it was nothing to do with memorising random addresses or recalling prime ministers. Estella recognised his expression of excitement because she had seen it a thousand times before.

And her answer was always the same.

"Yes, I wrote *Mysterious Garden*," she said wearily. "And no, I cannot tell you what the secret is or whether the faces are real. Only you can decide those things."

He was disappointed, she could tell, but people always were and Estella was used to this. Her work had found its way into the national canon, and for a while the name of Estella Kellow had been as famous for her children's book as that of Enid Blyton, and as intrinsically linked to Cornwall as Daphne du Maurier. Yet unlike these other authors Estella had written only one book. Like a speck of grit in an oyster, the pain in her soul had created one piece. Once her heartache had been written and painted and purged, she had nothing left to give. Estella hadn't known that her old governess, dear Miss Toms, had taken her paintings and her notebooks to London to secure a publisher until the deed was done and the contracts ready to be signed.

"You need money to live on," Tommy had insisted. Her thin face was etched with lines and her forehead criss-crossed with worry. "There is nothing left. Nothing! Do you understand, Estella? You father has borrowed against the lot." She pushed the paperwork across the kitchen table. "It's not a fortune, but it's take this offer or sell Pencallyn House. It's your choice, my dear."

Estella's head had snapped up like elastic. Selling Pencallyn House was unthinkable. If Pencallyn was sold, where would she go? She belonged there.

Her dear one slept nearby …

She'd picked up a pen and signed the contract and the money duly arrived. Not a fortune, Tommy said, but enough to pay the bills and put food on the table. The war years had taught Estella all she needed to know about growing food, and Tommy was a genius at make do and mend. Pencallyn's woods had enough timber to keep the fires going for years, and she could have learned to shoot pheasants if the worst had come to the worst. She knew they would survive.

As it turned out they more than survived, and Estella knew it was all due to canny Miss Toms. Estella owed Tommy everything. Not just for returning when Estella had needed her most but also because she'd generated an income which had supported Pencallyn ever since. The royalties had dwindled in later years as the book fell out of fashion, but sometimes Estella's name sparked a childhood memory and the adult she was speaking to slipped back into the child they used to be, wide-eyed and filled with wonder. They longed to know what the secret was at the heart of the mysterious garden, but Estella Kellow was as enigmatic as her paintings and didn't say. She never gave interviews or wrote another book because her stories had died a long time ago.

If indeed they *were* stories …

As she waited for her cab at the hospital, the warm sun on her cheeks, Estella listened to the calling gulls. Their plaintive cry would always signify empty beaches and broken hearts. She could stand on Bury Barrow until the world ended, eyes shielded against the light as she scanned the horizon, but those boys would never return. They were all lost. *He* was lost.

But something was stirring. Estella could feel it. This was why she had to make sure she could remain at Pencallyn. It was why she hadn't admitted that the teeth gnawing her heart grew more ferocious every day or confessed that it was harder and harder to draw breath with each pull of her lungs. She unfolded her right hand and peered at the silver whisper of a scar which bisected it. Still there after so many years, the faint scar meant more to Estella than anything else she possessed. It was everything.

She pressed her palm to her lips and closed her eyes. The time was coming. There were changes. Something had shifted. Her dear ones would come back for her, and when they did Estella had to be exactly where they had left her. Otherwise she might lose them again.

And Estella Kellow wouldn't survive that a second time.

CHAPTER 3

Nell
The Present

I can't shake the sensation I'm prying into affairs which are none of my business, but I can't turn back now. This unexpected find is a final link with my father and not one I expected, or dared hope, I would find. Of course I'm hoping it could be a last message he's left for me. Maybe a letter written before he fell sick. A missive written secretly while I was counting out pills or changing sheets – an outpouring in which he tells me he loves me and that I am enough, and that all my mistakes, my failed marriage and my lack of a secure career don't really matter at all because he is proud of me.

I'm not sure what I'd expected at the end of my father's illness. Maybe a deathbed scene when he told me important things; I'd imagined he would hold my hand in his and whisper that I was a good daughter and he was proud of me. Maybe I thought he'd give me his blessing, although this is a vague notion I'd picked up when Nanna Summers took me to church. Yes, a blessing might be good; something to wear like armour in the empty months and years ahead.

One moment my father was watching afternoon television, the next a morphine driver was whirring and he was unconscious. Nurses rushed about, shooing me out the way and doing things with tubes and needles that made my knees turn to water. I'm no medic and every day I feel the sting of failure for not being of more use. I was adrift in a sea with no means to navigate; no charts, no GPS, not even the light of the kindly stars. I sat and held my father's hand but there was no time to say goodbye and when he slipped away it was without ceremony. There were a few rasping breaths, the final rise and fall of his frail rib cage and that was it – he was somewhere else. My father had left me.

I tumbled into the void. Andy called to offer his support, knowing how I would feel, and Lou did too – but what could they say to soothe the loss? Where was my father? How could he be here one minute and gone the next? Why wasn't he here for me? I was his child. I wasn't meant to be abandoned. What was I going to do without him? How could he be gone?

Now, finding this envelope fills me with hope and terror. What if it's a message? What if it isn't? What if it's something banal like an over sixties bus pass or more old paperwork? I'm not certain I can handle the disappointment.

What do I want it to be? A letter to me? And if so, what would I like him to say? My father was a private man, and I would give anything for the smallest insight into him. What did he think of the way his life had played out? Was he content? Did he ever stop missing my mum? Was he proud of me and what I've achieved, or did he feel disappointed I hadn't provided the grandchildren he was hoping for? Did he understand why Andy and I parted, or did he secretly blame me for not being good enough? Not trying harder?

It's mad, I know. I'm thirty-two, an independent woman in my own right with a relatively successful career. None of this parental approval stuff should matter – except it does. It really does. Since he left, I am rudderless and going around and around in circles. The words for my books are knotted up in my mind like fishing wire pulled from the canal, the plots and ideas lumps of weed caught up at random intervals and, like the sluggish waters of the Grand Union, nothing flows.

I slide my hand into the envelope. Small pieces of paper swim about under my touch like tickled trout. There's a something heavier weighing down the far end and tightly wedged in the corner of the envelope. A chain, I think. Perhaps a necklace? I want to be slow, to savour this moment of discovery but am too excited to draw out the revelation any longer. With a sharp tug the contents come free. Yellowed paper and faded photographs slip into the daylight, and a delicate silver crucifix on a fine chain pools into the palm of my hand. Apart from these there is nothing else. Nothing.

There's no letter. No last words of wisdom. No final reassurance of love. Although I know it's futile, I shake the envelope in case something may have been lodged within, but there's only emptiness. There's nothing left here specifically for me. It was just my imagination gathering speed.

The crucifix swings on its chain. I'm puzzled. My father wasn't religious, so why keep this? Who gave it to him? What does it mean? I fasten it around my neck. The crucifix slips beneath my tee shirt and nestles against my breastbone. Its presence is comforting, and I feel protected.

I shove newspapers out of the way and lean against the sofa while I examine the hidden photos. Are they clues to my father's birth family? I'd had no idea Dad had possessed anything related to his birth mother and, as far as I know, he never attempted to trace his biological parents. All I know is what Nanna Summers told me: my father had been orphaned as a tiny baby when his mother was knocked down in Bristol. She had been carrying him across the road outside the children's hospital when she was hit by a car, and although he survived she died almost immediately. Unusually for wartime she'd had no identification on her. Nobody had reported a young mother missing and nobody came forward to claim the child, so eventually my father was placed in an orphanage. These events took place in early 1945 when Britain was still at war, and it was presumed that an anonymous young woman with a mixed-race baby must be on the run from an angry family or husband. Perhaps she was even on the way to abandon her baby at the hospital. There must have been many such incidents like this happening. Nanna told me how, according to witnesses of the accident, this girl's last words were 'son' and 'fail', which is absolutely heartbreaking. How she must have suffered!

Or perhaps she didn't love him enough to fight for him. In those days plenty of mothers did keep children born out of wedlock. Or was she on her way to the hospital, trying to get help for her baby? Maybe he was sick and she wasn't planning on leaving him at all. Of course, Nanna couldn't have answered these questions, and contemplating them now overwhelms me with sadness.

My father must have pondered these things many times. The seam of his hurt would have run far deeper than mine. Was his hoarding an attempt to build a past? As with so much about Dad, I'll never know the answer now, just as I had no idea he'd kept these few mementos. Had he been planning to trace his birth family once Nanna Summers had passed away? He never would have dreamed she would live to such a ripe old age, so that in the end he only outlived her by a matter of months, by when he was too sick to begin a search.

I feel a tingle of excitement because it's not just my father's history I am contemplating. This is my story too, and being a writer I love stories. There's such excitement when the spark of an idea first catches light, followed by the wildfire in the imagination when it starts to burn as thoughts lick the dried tinder of possibility. The heat of the narrative consumes me, and I type until my fingers ache and my eyes are sore. Hours will pass in what feels like moments, and I step away from the screen blinking and disorientated. I need to know what happens next. I *have* to know the ending once the twisty turny excitement has taken hold of me. I can't not know. I have to be in the world of the story. I cannot stop until I reach the conclusion.

This obsessive desire to know more is exactly what I feel as I sit on the floor of my father's sitting room, surrounded by his boxes and papers and endless stuff, and hold in my hands the closest thing he had to a past. Our story is right here in these faded images, hidden behind the long-gone faces and sunny days captured for ever in the click of a lens. Something of my father is here. Something of my family. Maybe there are more of us? I long for this; it's a lonely thing to be the last one.

I have three images to study. The first is a simple postcard of a pretty seaside village. I see a horseshoe cove and a small harbour like the crook of an arm which nurses fishing boats and rocks them gently on the tide. Whitewashed cottages are stuck to the valley sides like postage stamps, a cat suns itself on a wall and lobster pots pepper the road. The words 'Pencallyn Cove' swirl across the top right-hand corner in bright scarlet, and the dress of the unwitting people captured in the scene, dragonflies in seaside amber, is in the style of the 1930s. The reverse side is blank, and the postcard is nothing remarkable, but it's the first piece of a jigsaw. My father's story could have its origins here. Or maybe my grandmother holidayed in Pencallyn Cove. Did she meet my grandfather here and have a holiday romance? There are countless possibilities for a starting place and all good stories need one of these. My father had a guidebook to Cornwall too. Was he planning a visit?

I turn my attention to the second image. This is a photograph, yellowed by the years and soft at the corners from handling. It's a simple shot in sepia, faded and creased from where it has been folded to fit in a pocket, and it shows a pretty dark-haired girl outside a farmhouse. She's in the yard with her head tipped back as she laughs at something somebody has said. Everything about the shot is full of life, from the tilt of her chin to the way her hair lifts in the wind to the black spaniel jumping up at her. I scrutinise her, desperate to see a resemblance between us, but the girl's face is cloaked by shadow and I can't really tell. How strange to think somebody so alive and young is old now and most likely long dead. How much better not to know our happiest moments are fleeting and that life can alter in a heartbeat.

Or, as Andy and I discovered, in the lack of a heartbeat …

I feel the old familiar folding inwards of my stomach and I breathe in and out to push the panic away. There are some things best not thought about, things you can never change no matter how much you wish you could: small tragedies which derail your life and smash you into pieces and which go unnoticed by the world. You glue yourself together eventually but, like a mended vase, the repair is never quite as good as new and the cracks only show if you look closely enough.

'Look at the final picture,' I tell myself sharply. Focus on this photo of a handsome young black man in military uniform. Jaunty hat. Smart. Proud expression in his eyes. 1940s style dress. He looks like he's stepped out of the movie *Pearl Harbor* – an American GI maybe. What was it they said? 'Overpaid, oversexed, and over here!' No wonder the British girls were smitten if this lad is anything to judge by. He's the sort of man any girl would look at twice and then a third time to make certain her eyes weren't deceiving her …

Rather like my father.

"Oh my God," I whisper. "It's impossible!"

But it isn't impossible, and the more closely I study this photograph the more possible I realise it is; the two men are mirror images. The pure line of the jaw, the high cheekbones, the full lips ready to smile at any moment, even the twinkle in the eye – this is like looking at a youthful picture of Samuel Summers.

This is like looking at my daddy yet not my daddy. Oh, my goodness. Surely not?

I trace the unknown GI's face with my forefinger.

"Hello, Grandpa," I say.

CHAPTER 4

Estella
The Present

Estella requested a detour on her way home from the hospital.

"Would you kindly stop somewhere before Pencallyn House?" she asked.

"All right, Miss Kellow, but we can't be long. I've the school runs from three. The shops, is it? I can pull in by the Spar and nip out for you, if you like? Save your legs?"

Save me falling over and carking it, more like, thought Estella darkly.

"That's a kind offer, but it isn't the shop I need. Could you stop at the church for ten minutes?"

"The church?"

The taxi driver couldn't have sounded more surprised if she'd requested they swing by Ann Summers on a trolley dash for sex toys, Estella thought with a wry smile. And he would sound even more shocked if he thought an old dear like her knew about such things! Young people always thought they had the monopoly on youth and sex. She hadn't been any different. Estella wanted to tell him she hadn't always looked like this, bird-frail and with snow-white hair, but what would be the point? The real version of herself was as long gone as endlessly sunny childhood summers, the stomach-dropping wail of sirens and the scores of brave young men who never saw twenty. Estella was blessed to be old. She must always remember she was one of the lucky ones.

"Yes, St Brecca's," she said. "You may keep the meter running."

"I won't do that, Mrs Kellow."

"*Miss* Kellow," Estella corrected sharply. She'd never been married. Had never worn a white dress and foaming veil or looked into smiling brown eyes as a ring was slipped onto her left hand. Oh, but how badly she'd wanted that to happen. What she wouldn't have given to have been a wife? She would have traded her money and success and fleeting fame in an instant. The house and the land too. She would have given up everything for him and gladly too. Without him, what was the point of any of it?

But she didn't speak of any of this. Estella never had. Her secrets were sealed deep into her heart. Journalists had longed to speak to her about her life. What was the inspiration for *Mysterious Garden*? Whose are the faces in the trees? Is there really a sundial? What is the answer to the riddle of the labyrinth? Estella had never spoken to any of them, which had only made them more curious. They wanted another du Maurier or Christie; Estella wanted to be left in peace. Besides, she didn't have any answers, for *Mysterious Garden* had been an organic process. In those dark days after everything happened, she'd painted like a creature possessed and often late into the night with only the light of a paraffin lamp to guide her. Faces and images loomed from the shadows to dance with those in her imagination or mate with the horror in her nightmares. In the daytime she would take her easel and her paints and wander deep into the garden to set up by the pond, or opposite the gunnera, or even in the heart of it, where all the paths led to, the sundial glen. The garden was impassable now, and Estella was glad because these were places where only the chosen were permitted to roam. The ghosts of the past could slip easily through tangles of brambles and ropes of stealthy ivy. Once the paintings were completed, she had never touched a brush again. Paint and pain were too closely akin. Estella would have painted herself out too, if Tommy hadn't been there to keep a close eye on her.

Today some might call her art and writing therapy. Estella thought of it as a penance. She had failed him. Evie had failed her. The garden, once her delight and playground, had become unbearable and it had been easier to let Nature reclaim her realm. It hadn't taken long for the manicured gardens, deep koi pools and grottos to be consumed. The rhododendrons grew woody and tall, camellias bloomed unseen in the cool green depths, and only scampering woodland creatures could find the sundial. The mysterious garden became Estella's creation in every way. She wished her father could have watched its slow destruction. How it would have pained him.

And what perfect retribution this would have been.

Estella had let the famous Pencallyn garden vanish. Her antipathy towards it had faded long ago, but she'd no desire to return to a place filled with memories. She had thought it better to allow the trees at the lower end of it to grow high and obscure the view down through the valley to the cove; that way she could pretend the warships were still anchored there, crewed by merry boys so full of life. They had danced in the schoolhouse, shared cigarettes, stolen kisses, given out gum and whistled from their jeeps. The empty bay was another painful reminder they would never return.

The taxi crept along the sunken lane which petered out at the ancient church of St Brecca. Who Brecca had been was as long forgotten as the faces of those who slumbered beneath grassy tussocks, their worn headstones as crumbly as fudge and their names erased by the winds and rain of centuries. It was here Estella had been christened nearly a century before and where her parents were laid to rest alongside the generations of Kellows who had come before them. Legend had it this spot had once been a pagan site and a powerful one too, as it was on the St Michael ley line, the same invisible energy path which allegedly cut its way through Pencallyn's garden to bisect another line at the point where the sundial observed the heavens. Whether fact or truth, though, it was hard to tell. In Cornwall, myth and mystery were hand in hand with the everyday; the tapestry of saints and sinners was stitched with the threads of old lore and magic.

As she pushed open the lychgate and made her slow way along the path, hemmed neatly by headstones and rippling grasses, Estella accepted that it wouldn't be too long before she joined them. How strange that this notion no longer filled her with fear but had become a comfort. Those dear faces she hadn't seen for so long were drawing closer with every passing hour; she saw them in her dreams and often in her waking moments too, and she had missed them dreadfully. She wouldn't have to wait much longer to see them again.

Estella had always loved the churchyard. The quiet here belonged to a different time, one when the world turned more slowly and when the air didn't thrum with engines and haste. During the bleak time after the war when she was all alone, wrecked on the sharp rocks of loss and betrayal, Estella had spent hours here, wandering amongst the ancient tombstones as she wandered through grief's labyrinth. There had been a certain peace in knowing the chasm of pain would eventually be filled by time, and grief's sting soothed by the balm of turning seasons. Birdsong tumbled from unseen beaks, always the same notes so unchanging and timeless no matter who heard them or when.

With old age Estella had come to accept life was as tremulous as the birdsong. She realised humanity was little more than thistledown blown in the breeze no matter how much we might try to convince ourselves otherwise. Perhaps it was the curse of youth that you felt invincible. You strove to change the unchangeable and railed against that which was as immovable as the Cornish granite cliffs, dashing yourself onto the rocks again and again until you were broken and despairing. With old age came acceptance and peace. Loss remained – but Estella understood more now, and fought less to change what was inevitable.

She was a contradiction, Estella thought. At peace and restless. Lost and yet at home. Old and yet young. She missed the voices that would never speak again, and yet she heard them every day. She missed his touch, yet felt it every day. She couldn't find him, yet she saw him everywhere. Was it her failing mind dropping her through the cracks in the floorboards, or was she only now beginning to understand the reality of existence?

In the churchyard, Estella shook her head and leaned heavily on her walking stick. Such thoughts were overwhelming, but they were nothing new. Her imagination had always had a fanciful slant – quite lucratively as it had turned out – but it was exhausting to always think this way. How much easier must it be to see the world in black and white. Would her life have been happier if she'd viewed the world another way?

"I am what I am," she said out loud as she continued her slow progress. She was an old lady and she must remember this. She was not a scabby-kneed schoolgirl or a willowy seventeen-year-old with a head full of dreams and a heart full of love. The rolling hills and cool woods surrounding the churchyard may not have changed a great deal, but Estella Kellow certainly had, and so had the world around her. The tractor grumbling from across the valley might till the same rich soil as Pencallyn Farm's plough horses had once turned over in glistening folds, but those ways were as lost in time as the girl she had once been. Everything changed and moved on. You just didn't always notice.

Estella's slow journey ended at the farthest part of the churchyard. This was a seldom-visited spot where headstones were sucked into the earth. In some places just a gentle swelling of soil hinted at what lay beneath. Here, barely inside the perimeter of consecrated land, wildflowers grew in abundance and drowsy bees droned in the sunshine. The grass was rarely mown, and nothing marked the place Estella sought except the twisting of her heart and the old prickle of tears. How was it possible she still wept after so long? A tear ran down Estella's cheek and fell onto the grass where it would soak into the earth with the countless others. It was a blessing of some sort and Estella hoped he knew he was loved and missed a lifetime on. Her heart ached for him still.

She placed her hand on her chest. There was a pain there, but this was a new fire which ignited every day and with a growing intensity. What would consume her first? The fire in her heart, or the furnace burning away her memories? A clock was ticking, and the countdown was in progress. She needed to tell her tale soon and before it was lost – but who would listen? There was nobody left to understand the importance of her story. There was nobody who cared. To most people, Estella's fragmenting memories and closely guarded secrets were little more than history. She was a faded footnote in a familiar chapter about ration books, evacuees and dogfights high up in the cloudless blue sky.

"You still matter," she whispered. "You matter to me, my darling; I think of you every day. I love you and I'm so sorry I didn't take better care of you."

There was no answer, but Estella knew her words had been heard. She dearly wanted to stay longer and say more but the toot of a horn signified she had to leave. Estella Kellow knew that the next time she returned to St

Brecca's it would not be under the power of her own legs.

"I'll see you soon, my darling," she whispered. "Just a little longer. It won't be long. I promise."

CHAPTER 5

Estella
The Present

The cab bumped down Pencallyn's drive, slowing to walking pace as the ruts grew deeper. The grassy ridge in the middle rose as high as the wheels, and Estella could tell from the driver's tight grip on the wheel, he feared it only a matter of time before the car was grounded. When the cab bounced out of yet another rut, the exhaust pipe clonking so loudly Estella jumped, the driver stopped.

"How much further, Miss Kellow?"

Estella considered his question. If walking she would have known in a heartbeat: from the house it was a hundred and fifteen paces to the bend in the drive which was there for the sole purpose of showcasing the house in all its glory. Years ago, the gravel on this drive had been neatly raked, and the lawns, manicured to softest green velvet, had rolled down to the formal gardens. It had been an undulating mini-Eden sprinkled with ornamental beds, silent groves, lily ponds and follies, beautiful features linked by hidden paths like beads strung on a necklace. When had it become so wild? As with the stealthy creeping up of old age, Estella hadn't noticed.

But they hadn't got to that last bend yet. "Maybe a quarter of a mile?" she offered.

"How about we reverse and I try the bottom way in? There is one, isn't there? The old road they built in the war goes from the beach to the top?"

Time shredded. The layers were peeling away. Estella saw black servicemen toiling in the rain and wind, swinging picks and lifting stones as they worked to lay a new road for top secret ends. How angry her father had been! Bad enough that part of his precious garden had been ripped apart by order of the War Office, but even worse that black Americans were on his land and billeted in the village. His rage had swirled through the house for days, and Anthony Eden had received a strongly worded letter. Poor Violet had sported a bruise and claimed a hatbox had fallen on her head, but Estella had known better …

"Miss Kellow? The lower gate?"

The memory faded like the bruises had on Violet's white skin. As magenta to purple to yellow to nothing, so the past ebbed away. Estella blinked and she was back in the taxi.

"I'm afraid the gate hasn't been opened for a long time," she said. "It's chained and locked."

The chains would be rusted by now. It had been such a long time since she'd looped it through the gate and snapped the padlock shut, so long ago that her hair had still reached her waist in thick black curls. Nobody came into the grounds that way any more. Pencallyn's garden wasn't a place anyone ventured into easily. Even the village children stayed away, unsettled by stories of witches and the ghostly marching of booted feet. It was all nonsense, but it had brought Estella some very welcome solitude.

The driver sighed. "I don't think I can risk it, Miss Kellow. The underneath of my car's going to be a right mess if I carry on. How did the other driver manage when they picked you up?"

"Kelly took me to my appointment," Estella said.

Kelly Jones, a young woman from the village, was Estella's unofficial home help. This was a rather misleading job description, as most of the 'helping' took the form of Kelly drinking tea and moaning about her husband while working her way through Estella's biscuit tin. When she wasn't complaining or tea-drinking, Kelly did do Estella's shopping and washing, cooked her lunch and flicked a duster around the place.

"That makes sense. Darren Jones has a Ford Ranger not a Ford Focus. Look, how about I drive you back to the village and ask Kelly to pop you up the drive?" suggested the driver.

"Absolutely not. Kelly's children need her," said Estella firmly. At least she thought they did. Kyle and Ryan were eight and ten, weren't they? Or maybe they were older? It was hard to remember when her recollection was so blurred. Small people running about in the long grass of the lawn came to mind, but these images were overlaid with others of gangling Amazons in hoodies and baggy jeans, who carried shopping bags and scuffed trainered feet on the parquet.

"I shall walk the rest of the way. It isn't far," she said.

Before the driver could argue, Estella pushed two ten-pound notes into his hand, shoved the door fully open and hauled herself from the back seat. Determination rather than dexterity won the day as she managed to clamber out without any assistance. If the young doctor of earlier on had seen these moves, he certainly wouldn't be questioning her ability to live alone, Estella thought triumphantly. Mobility issues? Pah! She'd show him. Estella Kellow wasn't done yet!

Feeling determined, Estella made her slow way along the drive. She heard the taxi reverse but unlike Lot's wife she didn't look back. What a scary Bible story that was! As a child it had terrified Estella. Imagine looking over your shoulder for one tiny peek and turning into a pillar of salt! What a cruel punishment for curiosity. Evie had scoffed at this tale and said it was all bollocks, which had earned her a black mark from Reverend Keveth, but Evie had been defiant. It *was* all bollocks, she'd said. And if God was so great, why had he made Nazis? Tommy had said Evie was too sharp for her own good, which Estella hadn't really understood although she did now. Gods, old and new, needed respect, and it was safer not to doubt. A questioning mind could lead you into danger.

After twenty minutes Estella rounded the final bend in the drive, taking care not to stumble on the ruts, and there it was – Pencallyn. The house stood proudly at the head of the gardens, facing south and drowsing in the sunshine. A row of magnificent 60-foot leylandii obscured the sea view these days, but observed from this distance and through failing eyes the house was still stately and proud, a white galleon sailing in a sea of endless green. From such a vantage point one couldn't see the crumbling paint which fell off in chunks like icing on a Christmas cake. Neither was it apparent the window frames were rotten, that unchecked creeper slithered across the façade and rogue slates were sliding from the roof. To Estella, Pencallyn House looked just as proud today as in its glory days as a gentleman's residence with a specimen garden famous across the county.

"It was deceptive then, too," Estella said out loud. Who could have guessed what had really gone on behind those elegant walls? Things were never what they seemed. She surveyed the house through narrowed eyes. She'd guarded it for as long as she could, but the pain in her chest and the mist in her mind were warnings she couldn't do so for ever. The vultures were already circling.

Well, they could circle a little longer. Estella Kellow wasn't done yet. Her story had to be told.

CHAPTER 6

Estella
The Present

The walk along the drive had been tiring and Estella was already weary from wandering through the churchyard. With each tap of her stick she felt more exhausted. With relief, she let herself into the back of the house.

Estella seldom used the front door, partly because nobody important visited Pencallyn House these days and partly because the steps up needed repairing and there was no sense risking a tumble. Besides, she inhabited the back part of the house now, and it was far more welcoming. As a girl Estella had loved spending time in the kitchen, listening to Cook's gossip or sneaking in with Evie to steal a slice of cake. Evie's big blue eyes had almost fallen out of her head and rolled across the flagstones when she'd arrived at Pencallyn and spotted the amount of food on offer. Estella would never forget the way she'd eaten, cramming food in with her fingers and at high speed, her eyes darting back and forth as though checking nobody was about to snatch her meal away.

"She gobbles like a starving dog," had been Cook's observation, and Estella had understood the comparison instantly. If she'd stepped any closer, the new addition to the household would have surely snarled.

There were so many memories here. Sometimes they merged with the present, and Estella would find herself chatting to people long gone. She would turn from filling the kettle only to discover they'd vanished, leaving her abandoned and overflowing with sadness. How many times could you lose somebody? It was yet another curse of this creeping forgetfulness that the losses were forever fresh. Old age could be so cruel.

Late afternoon sunshine slid into the kitchen with Estella. A soft breeze stirred the notes scattered about the place or taped onto available surfaces in spots Kelly thought Estella likely to come across on her daily travels through the house. They were a liturgy of the mundane and, Estella reflected, a sharp reminder of how far she'd come from her reading of Chaucer and Dickens. 'Check gas off! Lock back door! Take today's pills!

Turn off light!' ordered the notes. But the writing was bubbly, with jolly circles dotting each 'i' and smiley faces and hearts added in as though they could soften the blow of losing her mind. What would happen when the fog stopped her from being able to read? Might she take the gas? Lock up the pills? Wander away out the back door and over the hills and far away?

The kitchen smelled of the lemon wipes Kelly favoured for cleaning. Not for her, carbolic soap and good old-fashioned elbow grease. Estella placed her bag on the table and contemplated filling the kettle to brew a pot of tea but the thought of lifting it was too much. The old kitchen table, scored with criss-cross scars from long-blunted blades, was piled with post. Estella was choosing to ignore the lot. There was nothing here that required urgent attention. Bills were paid from her bank account, and her royalties and pensions were dealt with by the firm of solicitors who'd handled the Kellow family affairs for generations. All this would be enquiries from estate agents or leaflets advertising nursing homes, all glossy and staged to look like high-end hotels rather than the Reaper's waiting room. There would also be a letter or two addressed to the author of *Mysterious Garden* brimming with questions about the story and ending with the hopeful wish this devoted fan would be one gifted with the truth. Didn't they know truth was subjective? Who was to say their own interpretation was any less valid than hers, anyway?

At least the burden of the estate was dealt with now. Whether or not the recipient of her bequest would be pleased, Estella couldn't say. Her time was running out; it was the pain in her heart rather than forgetfulness that would undo her and she was relieved about that, because she was struggling. The dust fell faster than she could whisk it away, and climbing the stairs could take all morning. Heating ready meals in the microwave was an effort too, and Estella found it easier to live on toast and cereal. No wonder she was growing thin. But go into an old folks' home, however plush?

Never.

Still, the reality was she needed more help than Kelly could offer. Maybe she ought to put an advert in *The Lady* for live-in help. Estella had hired a housekeeper few years ago but the woman had only lasted a few weeks, finding Pencallyn House too isolated and insisting she couldn't bear the man who lived at the far side of the woods.

"It's the way he looks at me," she'd told Estella before she left. "His eyes are just so ..."

She paused while Estella waited, unnerved.

"So cold," she'd finished helplessly. "He looks straight through me and he won't even say hello. It creeps me out, Miss Kellow. I know he's a neighbour and harmless, but I don't like him being around."

It was impossible for Estella to say anything without frightening her housekeeper or sounding insane. Besides, the woman was right; the man's eyes were cold. But he wasn't a neighbour and he certainly hadn't been harmless. Far from it. She may not have seen him herself, at least not in over half a century, but the fact that he couldn't rest frightened Estella. Just like the swirling images in her paintings her fears regarding him were deep and dark. It was better to pretend he wasn't here at all. Some people didn't deserve to rest in peace.

The housekeeper duly departed and Estella carried on without her. She'd draped dust sheets over the heavy old furniture in the dining room and morning room, locked the gun cabinet, sold the grand piano which she had never played very well, closed the blinds in the library and said a silent farewell to the beloved books whose print she struggled to read. Then Estella ventured upstairs and made sure all the beds were stripped, the wardrobes strung with mothballs and the linen folded away before closing all the doors and leaving this part of Pencallyn to slumber. When it would awaken she could not tell, but Estella's heart understood and accepted this wouldn't be in her lifetime.

It was too late now to consider hiring another housekeeper. The house was too far gone and so was she. When she couldn't manage the stairs, Estella had become resigned to sleeping in her armchair. It was positioned by the range and since she only slept for a few hours at a time what did it really matter where she rested? Estella could carry on like this. She had Kelly helping; and Josh Richardson, the son of the people who had bought Pencallyn Farm next door, often lent a hand with the more physical tasks.

Josh chopped wood and chatted to Estella over a pot of tea. It was a break, he said with a shy smile. A few hours of respite from project managing his father's renovation of the farm. Having met Martin Richardson on several occasions, and having been the child of an overbearing parent herself, Estella understood this need for an escape. Gardening was Josh's passion and he had been delighted to find himself living next door to the once renowned Pencallyn. Estella saw the light of love in his eyes when he talked about designs and specimen trees and rare plants. It was the same fire she had seen in her father's, except she perceived that Josh's love was true, fostered by his delight in nature and beauty rather than the covetous desire to possess rarities other collectors lusted after.

Estella had first met Josh when he called at Pencallyn to apologise for his father. Martin Richardson had visited on the pretext of being neighbourly but in reality to discover how far from death she was. He hadn't said as much, of course, but Estella realised what he really wanted to know when he enquired after her health and asked solicitously how she managed in such a big house. He'd made a few remarks about buying the garden, and when she didn't respond he demanded she cut down the row of trees which blocked his sea view, as well. At this point Estella had enormous fun pretending she couldn't hear him ('Bees? What bees? I don't keep bees, dear!') before falling asleep mid-sentence, which everyone knew was a hazard of being old. Ignored, Martin Richardson had stomped off in a bad humour and Estella had chuckled about the episode for days. It was petty, but she felt as though she had won a small victory for the millions of other women bullied by men like him.

Josh was mortified by his father's behaviour and had introduced himself the next morning, arriving at Pencallyn armed with cake and a huge apology. Estella sensed sadness in him and she'd gleaned enough of his past to understand that Cornwall was a place Josh had sought for healing. The deep kindness in his soul and the gentleness in his manner caused a torrent of memories to swamp her. He was so much like …

No. She couldn't think of him.

If Josh noticed the tears in Estella's eyes and the quaver in her voice, he was sensitive enough to pretend he hadn't, asking gently if she could tell him a little about the history of the garden and the plants. She recovered herself and thoroughly enjoyed their chat. Josh's love for nature shone in his beautiful green eyes, and as they drank tea and ate cake he confided that his dearest dream was to be a garden historian and designer.

"I can't imagine my father will be pleased when I announce my new career plan," he'd told Estella with an eye roll. "Dad thinks I need to 'man up' and get back to the City. Wasting my education pulling up weeds is not quite what he had in mind. Gardening is what he pays people to do. He's utterly horrified I might join their ranks."

Having met Martin Richardson, Estella could well imagine his reaction. She placed her cup back in the saucer and fixed Josh with a stern look.

"And what do *you* think?"

Josh ran a hand through his dark auburn hair.

"Me?"

"Yes. It is, after all, your career and your life."

He studied the crumbs on his plate as though reading runes.

"What I think is that no matter what I do, I'll never please him."

"You shouldn't need to. You're not here to please anyone. You're here to live the best life you can and do what makes you happy. When you are old like me, and your father's long gone, what will you look back on? A life half-lived because you tried to meet someone else's expectations? Or a life that's been full and happy? Trust me, you don't want to have regrets. It's the things you *don't* do that haunt you, not what you did."

Estella had made mistakes, but she'd also known more happiness than she could have ever imagined. If she could live her life again, she wouldn't change a second of it.

"I think you know the answers to those questions," Josh said.

"Yes, and so do you because the answers are in your heart. It's the best guide we ever have. So, what does your heart tell you?"

Josh's answer was a smile of such utter beauty Estella was rendered speechless. The foxfire hair, emerald eyes and sweet curling mouth came alive and they were a devastatingly attractive combination. Estella might be ninety-five but she could still appreciate a handsome man. Josh Richardson was like Pencallyn's hidden garden; beneath the weeds of cares and the briars of sadness there was something so special that once glimpsed you could never, ever forget it. You would never want to let it go. He was sensitive and true and he felt things deeply. A man like this loved once and for ever.

Josh Richardson was a rare treasure.

"My heart tells me I want to restore gardens," he told her. "It's what I've always wanted – but being a horticultural historian didn't fit in with Dad's grand plan."

Estella regarded him thoughtfully.

"Your father had a plan?"

"Maybe 'plan' is the wrong word. Expectations? Hopes? A glittering career in the City followed by eventually taking over the family business. That's what my father wanted. It's what he still wants. I've tried, Miss Kellow, but it really isn't for me. I couldn't do it. Trying nearly finished me."

Josh fell quiet when Kelly arrived, full of Darren's latest antics and making lots of clatter with cups and plates. She was taken aback to find an attractive man in the kitchen, and several times Estella spotted her checking her reflection in the microwave window. Estella steered the conversation away from personal matters and back to Pencallyn's garden, and saw her visitor's face light up like the Calmouth Christmas lights.

"I was thrilled when I realised Dad's latest project was next door to Pencallyn," he admitted. "I've read about the great Cornish gardens – Heligan, Trebah, Glendurgan – so to be this close to a hidden gem is incredible. I was almost glad when I heard how difficult he'd been, because then I had an excuse to come over and meet you."

Estella laughed. "You could have come over anyway. As for the garden, it's certainly hidden but I'm not sure quite how much of a gem it is these days. I'm afraid it's terribly wild."

"But it's all there, presumably? Underneath?"

"I believe so," Estella said. It must be, in the same way that beneath the wrinkles and grey hair she was still the same girl who'd slipped through the garden and made wishes at the sundial.

"It's the *Mysterious Garden*, isn't it?"

"Yes. Yes, it is."

Estella braced herself for the usual barrage of questions, but they didn't come. Interesting, she thought. This was a young man who understood the importance of privacy and of keeping one's own counsel.

"I'd love to have seen it in its heyday," was all he said. "It must have been wonderful."

In Josh's voice Estella recognised a longing for the landscape of the past. He was right; the garden *had* been wonderful, and sometimes she still saw it as it had once been. Her mind, it seemed, would not allow the weeds to flourish.

"Help yourself if you want to explore and have a look," she offered. "It's dreadfully overgrown but I'm sure you'll recognise some plants and trees. The garden was my father's passion, and his father's before, but you already know the history of the garden. There isn't much I can tell you."

"I doubt that, but I'd love to have a look. Thank you!" The wonderful smile was bestowed on her again, like a ray of fitful sunshine brightening a winter landscape. Warmed by his pleasure, Estella smiled back. It was a small thing to do, to allow this young man access to her garden, but instinct told her that seeing it would be a balm to his aching heart. Painting the garden had soothed hers all those years ago. It could be a healing place.

This meeting had been a few months ago, at the start of the spring when the world was slowly returning to life and Pencallyn's garden was painted with bright splashes of daffodils and camellias. Since then Josh had slipped into the habit of popping by to chat whenever he had a free moment. Estella inferred his father was a demanding taskmaster, but Josh still found time to clear a couple of the ornamental areas, unable to contain his delight when he discovered surviving specimen plants and intricate bed designs from the nineteen twenties. He chatted to Kelly as they drank tea, chopped and stacked firewood and even planted up a small vegetable garden. He'd quickly become woven into the fabric of the place and it was hard now for Estella to imagine Pencallyn without his calm presence.

Estella knew she would miss Josh when his father's house renovations were complete. She enjoyed joining him in the kitchen for a cup of tea and listening to his tales of the building site. Kelly loved hearing what Darren was up to, and when Josh was present Pencallyn rang with laughter. It felt as though he belonged here, and she could see he loved what he did and how good he was at it too. Already he was sketching new designs which reflected the history of Pencallyn. He was researching the history of the garden in a respectful way which never pried or sought to uncover too much of Estella's own history. That was hers alone.

Estella rose. She needed to remind herself of that history, and what better way to do this than an excursion upstairs? It was always slow progress to make the ascent, but finally Estella reached her old room. It wasn't the master suite – that would never feel rightfully hers – nor had she moved into Violet's pretty boudoir. Even all this time on, that room made her shudder. She still couldn't bear to go near it. Instead, Estella had remained in her childhood bedroom. It was at the front of the house and on the second floor, a south-facing room bathed in light all day long and with a wonderful view over the gardens, even if no longer all the way down to the sea.

As she stepped into the room, pale beams of light streaming over the worn floorboards, it seemed to Estella that two girls sat in the window seat with their dark heads close together as they pored over a book. Against the glare it was impossible to distinguish who was who, and Estella smiled. What fun these two had had!

"Read it again, Evie! Do it like Tommy this time!" ordered the girl on the left.

"All Gaul is divided into three parts, one of which the Belgae inhabit, the Aquitani another, those who in their own language are called the Celts," said the second in a clipped accent which delivered the words like rapid gunfire.

"Evie! You sound just like her!"

"That's nothing, Stell! What about this? Who am I?" The second girl slipped from her seat and waddled up and down the room as she repeated the same lines in a broad Cornish burr. Everything about her was utterly transformed and she was no longer a slender schoolgirl but an overweight woman with bunions.

"Cook! You're Cook! Oh, you're so clever! You should be an actress! You could be anyone you wanted!"

"Yes. I think I could be," the girl called Evie said.

The sun slipped behind a cloud. When Estella looked again the girls had vanished and she sighed. They did this all the time. They never stayed long enough to answer her questions. Who did Evie choose to be in the end? Where did she go? Like so many things from those days it was a mystery Estella would never solve. She missed the girls and their youthful energy. Why had she dragged herself all the way upstairs? What had she wanted?

The girls. The garden. The past. These images began a chain reaction in her mind. Estella propped her walking stick against the bed before bending down. Her tongue protruding a little, and puffing from exertion, she stretched out her hands until they met leather, warm to the touch and a little flaky from age. It was still there, and what was more she had remembered where it was. She must make sure she wrote this down on a Post It in case a few more holes were nibbled in her Swiss cheese memory.

One tug and Estella had in her hands the thing she'd been searching for – a small leather suitcase with a brass lock and age-yellowed label. It opened with a click and then as the lid fell back, still held in place by frayed black tape, she nearly wept to see her old and most precious belongings. Old friends and memory keepers, unlike their owner, they looked the same as they always had. Time had truly been locked away.

It was a treasure trove. Old photos and curling notebooks. An old Box Brownie camera, leather strap cracked and case battered from many trips through the garden, and an old red coat once much worn and discarded after the last fateful outing yet never parted with. At the bottom of it all, tucked away from prying eyes, was what she was seeking – a faded blue shawl still soft and warm to the touch. As though in a dream, Estella lifted it to her nose but no scent clung to the fabric except for the musty taint of the years. She let it fall from her grasp, withdrawing her hand as though stung. Now Estella remembered why she seldom opened her own personal Pandora's Box.

Some things were too painful even after all these years.

"You're a fool," she said to herself but there was no real anger in her voice, only sadness, because her treasures still possessed magic. If she spent some time with them, perhaps they might help keep the present and the past apart. Estella needed a bridge over the quicksand. She couldn't let herself be sucked under. If she sank now she would never see the surface again.

CHAPTER 7

Nell
The Present

"Nell! At last! I'm bursting to hear everything!" Lou ushers me into her kitchen. "Wine? We've a bottle of Pinot on the go – haven't we, Ant?"

"You know we have; you're already a third of the way down it!"

Antonio's at the hob, searing scallops. My stomach rumbles. I never cook these days. It seems too much of an effort just for one, so I live on toast.

"It's been a tough day," Lou laughs. Once cold white wine is sloshed out to her satisfaction and a dish of glistening olives placed between us, she raises her glass.

"To uncovering family mysteries!"

We chink glasses. The wine is crisp and dry, exploding across my tongue in a ballet of flavours and a far cry from the cheap stuff we used to glug as teenagers, hiding out in Dad's potting shed.

"Don't keep me in suspense a second longer," says Lou. "I want to know everything!"

"There's not much more to tell. There's a simple crucifix and the three pictures I told you about."

"Let's see them."

"Aren't you tired of examining evidence?"

"Trust me, this is far less mundane than the usual list of who did what wrong in a marriage. Seriously, why bother to get married at all if you can't be arsed to work at it?"

I don't say anything and Lou flushes. "I didn't mean you and Andy. That's totally different."

"Is it?"

I'm not always so sure. Andy wanted to work at our marriage. Forget what had happened, he said. Let's try again. Move on. The bottom line was I didn't want to forget. I *couldn't.*

"Of course," says Lou firmly. "That came out wrong. I've had a crap day and a demanding client, that's all. Will you take my mind off it and show me what you found? Before I put my foot in it again?"

"And before supper," adds Antonio. "My scallop linguine can't wait for anything."

"See what I have to live with?" Lou grumbles, and I laugh.

"Yep. Must be hell having dinner cooked for you!"

"He's bad for my waistline," Lou sighs. "I must eat less."

Ant winds his arms around her waist.

"All the more for us, Nell!"

Lou leans back against his chest and he kisses the top of her sleek blonde head. I smile, feeling rather like an indulgent spinster aunt. These two are so touchy feely. Andy and I were never like them, that's for sure. Sometimes we held hands if we were out and about but, if I'm truly honest with myself, I'm not sure we were ever passionate about one another. We got together at school and plodded on after that. Our relationship felt like coming home and changing into a comfy pair of slippers after a long day at work, and I never expected passion or fireworks. I'd always assumed writers made that stuff up but when I'm with my best friends I suspect I've been mistaken. I do miss Andy and what we had, but Lou and Antonio make me believe there is something more, something Andy and I could both have missed if we'd stayed together. Perhaps the loss of our baby simply showed we were never really meant to be?

"It's all right for Nell; she never puts on an ounce," Lou moans. "She could eat all day and stay skinny."

"And it's all right for you because you grew tall and got boobs," I counter. We've said these things to one another so often we've worn grooves in the words. "Who didn't need a Wonderbra and could get served in pubs? Not me."

"You're both gorgeous!" Ant says diplomatically. "I'm off for a quick shower. Feel free to talk about me while I'm gone!"

"We've far better things to talk about," Lou grins. "So, let's see what you've found, Nell."

I haul my bag onto the counter. A red spotty satchel with tattered corners and frayed handles, it's the last present my father gave me and I treasure it.

"So, here are the pictures. This crucifix was in the envelope too."

I fan the photos out onto the counter then pull down my sweater to fish out the small cross. The metal feels warm from the heat of my skin. It's been comforting to wear the necklace. Perhaps it once belonged to my grandmother?

Lou examines the pictures, turning them around and moving them back and forth as though seeking a different perspective. I had studied them most of the way in the train back to London, squinting at the faded faces as though my gaze alone could bring them back to life. It worked in a manner of speaking, because my imagination, boulder-blocked for weeks, started to erode the obstacles in its path. With each jolt of the carriage, ideas for a new novel had started to flow. Pulling the tray forward to create a makeshift table, I started to make notes. By the time the train reached London a host of characters were chatting away and a synopsis was taking shape.

"Thanks, Dad," I whispered as the train snaked its slow way into the station and I closed my notebook. "I think you wanted me to find the envelope. It's helping me to write again and I hope you know that."

As always, Paddington teemed with life. The press of bodies and muffled announcements, combined with the growl of engines powering into life, was overwhelming. I threaded through the commuters and headed into the warm fug of a coffee shop. Once settled with an Americano and a celebratory muffin, I called my literary agent to pitch my idea. Hannah had asked me to get in touch as soon as I had something to give her, so I didn't see the point of hanging around, especially as my bank account was looking so poorly.

My idea was for a historical romance set in Cornwall, my own special blend of *Poldark* and *Call the Midwife*, but with a dash of American GI glamour, and centred on a young woman determined to keep her family together – a little like my unknown grandmother, perhaps? As I described my plot, I felt a wave of enthusiasm build, surfing me effortlessly through the conversation and carrying my agent with it. By the end of the call she'd requested the full synopsis and several chapters.

"Well done, Nell," she said warmly. "Send it over and I'll pitch it to a couple of editors who I know are looking for this kind of book. I'm sure we can do something with it."

This was the most productive I'd been for months. Now all I had to do was write the book …

"These are fascinating," Lou says now as she looks at the pictures. "This handsome GI is the absolute image of your dad. He has to be your grandfather."

"I think so too, but I've no idea how I'll begin to find out. There must have been so many lads like him stationed here during the war."

"How about the uniform? Would it be a clue to his rank? Could he have been an officer?"

"It's unlikely. I've had a quick google and there weren't many black officers in the US Forces in those days. The American army ran along Jim Crow lines and segregation was a part of everyday life."

Lou's brows draw together. "How horrible. OK, so we think a young black American GI had a love affair with a British woman resulting in your dad. That makes sense, doesn't it? What a shame there's no birth certificate or anything else for Sam."

"There's nothing like that at all."

"It's fine. We have a location to explore, and this picture has to be a clue." She holds up the photograph of the girl by the well. "Could she be your grandmother? She's slim and dark-haired like you too."

"That's true, but I get my hair from Dad and my mum was slight. It could be a coincidence."

She shakes her head. "There's no such thing as coincidence. People leave clues even when they don't think they have. It's been the downfall of many a cheating spouse and the success of a good brief! My guess is that this picture's a link to Sam's birth family."

After dinner, a seafood linguine as delicious as anything you'd find in Italy, I stack the dishwasher, Lou brews coffee and Antonio heads into his office. Lou carries a cafetière and mugs through to the sitting room. Outside, night has fallen over London, casting blue and violet shadows across the dark lawn while lights warm the windows of other houses and flats, rooms filled with people living their own lives and holding their own secrets close. It's simply overwhelming how many thoughts and dreams and fears are out there, how many worlds of the mind and the imagination coexist. When Lou draws the curtains and shuts the world out, I'm relieved – thinking like this can overwhelm me. Panic is never far away. Clawing my way back from it was hard enough with Andy and Dad beside me. Now, I don't think I have the strength to fight it alone.

"Let's start with Pencallyn," Lou suggests, typing the words into her Mac. "Maybe we can find some clues there."

Once my friend has a goal in mind there's no stopping her. Before long we've studied maps of the area, examined images of the village itself, and discovered that Pencallyn Cove is one of the most desirable holiday locations in south-west Cornwall. There are no less than two celebrity chefs in nearby Calmouth, a glossy spa hotel is based in an ivy-smothered manor house, and Rightmove boasts a wealth of eye-wateringly expensive ocean-facing properties. Further googling also reveals this area played a huge role in the preparations for the Normandy landings in 1944.

"There's a living history project in the area," Lou reads. "And Calmouth University's history department has published a lot about that time. They could be a good starting place. There's an entire research department dedicated to the Second World War."

Lou is a speed reader extraordinaire and she blasts through pages of text, picking out snippets which may be of use.

"Pencallyn Cove was really important to the D-Day operation," she continues, scrolling through the text so rapidly it becomes a blur. "Eisenhower visited in 1944 and lots of high-ranking American officers were billeted in the area. The local manor house was requisitioned for tank practice and lots of GIs had billets in the surrounding villages. There's loads of information here that might help you."

"So, it's possible Pencallyn is where this young guy based in the war," I say slowly. How would he have felt, this young American boy, to find himself in Cornwall? Was it a huge change from home? Was he lonely? Homesick? Afraid of what lay ahead? Or was it all a great adventure? Was the love he found here worth every hardship?

"I think it's highly likely he was stationed at the Pencallyn camp," Lou agrees. "Let's see what more we can find on this website."

An image of a house fills the screen. An elegant white structure with a large veranda and big windows which gaze across a lawn, it draws the eye with the ease and inevitability of a supermodel. Although the picture is in black and white the surrounding foliage appears lush and tropical. I lean closer, puzzled. It feels as though I am recalling fragments of a long-forgotten dream.

"What's this place?"

Lou squints at the screen. "Pencallyn House, apparently. It's where some US officers were billeted. It says here it was home to the local MP and had a famous specimen garden. A children's book was written there too, in the forties according to this. It's called *Mysterious Garden.* Have you heard of it?"

Of course! No wonder the house is familiar. The white façade, cloaked in greenery, is an image I've seen before in an old book Nanna Summers owned. I can't remember a great deal about it except there was something about it which both frightened and compelled me in the most delicious way.

"I read it as a child."

"Any good?"

I consider the question. "It was … intriguing. It gave me bad dreams, and I think that's why Nanna stopped reading it to me. It's quite old-fashioned. I can't imagine children read it now."

"Not if my nieces and nephews are anything to go by. It's all Minecraft and YouTubers for them. When did we get so old, Nell?"

"At least you know what a YouTuber is," I sigh.

Lou clicks the mouse and the picture changes to another view of Pencallyn House. This time the house is glimpsed from the beach, coyly peeking out at the world from thick trees like Princess Diana from beneath her eyelashes.

"It's unlikely your grandfather had anything to do with a place like this if he wasn't an officer. What a stunning house!"

I make us more coffee and we continue the search. By the time we've worked our way through stories of wartime Cornwall, memoirs of GI brides and countless heartbreaking tales of war babies, now pensioners, who spent years attempting to trace their long-lost American fathers, my head's spinning.

"Tracing someone without a name or birth certificate is going to be really tricky," I say. All the websites we've visited require these details; without them needles and haystacks spring to mind. My vague idea of travelling down to Cornwall, booking into a B and B and asking around for details seems naïve.

"It won't be easy but there are ways. Going there is a start. You can use it as a writing retreat. You can write it off to tax that way! I've just booked you into a B and B at the local pub for a week. You can make a start on your search and begin your book. Genius, huh?"

"I can't afford it, Lou, and I don't want you to pay for me."

"Tough. It's already done on the plastic. No protests. This is on me and Ant. Pay us back when you get your massive advance and find you're related to a billionaire American oil tycoon!"

I laugh. "Thanks, Lou. That's really generous and I *will* pay you back – that isn't up for discussion. But what if the man in the picture is nothing to do with me? I've no proof he's my grandfather."

"Are you kidding? You and he have the same cheekbones and the same smile. Of course he's your grandfather!"

It's difficult for me to see any resemblance. Maybe it's there but it's hard to say for certain. I could just be wishing so much for a link with my father that I'm projecting onto the image similarities which aren't there. It hurts when there is nobody left who truly belongs to you. No grandparents on either side, no parents, no siblings, no child of your own …

Stop, Nell. Don't go there. Not now.

"There might be a way you can find out more, if you're up for it," Lou says.

"Really?"

"Really. Look."

Her fingers fly over the keyboard and moments later a website flashes up. With grey and sage accents, soft-focus pictures of smiling people of all ages, and a sepia map of the world serving as wallpaper, I immediately recognise it. I've seen adverts for this company on billboards and in magazines and on the television too. They are everywhere lately.

"Heritage.com. Aren't they the DNA testing people?"

"They're the family tree people," Lou corrects. "Their DNA kit was the number one Christmas present last year. Tracing your ancestors is huge business."

"Heritage.com," I read out loud. "Dig up your Family Roots today with a Heritage DNA Test! Discover the secrets of your DNA and trace the origins of your family. Find relatives you have never met. Reunite your genes!"

"This could be a way of finding out who you're related to and if they have any links to anyone who may have served in the US military during the war. It's dead simple to do. All you do is register for a kit, send away a saliva sample and the results are back in a few weeks or even faster if you pay for an express package." Lou's eyes are wide with excitement. "Can you imagine, Nell? You might have a whole other family waiting for you! American family!"

She's right. I could. It's a thought both exciting and terrifying, and now it's in my head I'll never be able to put it aside. It will be whispering to me at odd moments until I cave in and order a test.

There's no choice. I have to know. I *have* to.

I turn to my best friend.

"How soon can we get one of those kits delivered?" I say.

CHAPTER 8

Estella
The Present

Estella was washing up the breakfast things. It was a task she undertook every morning, but – and in the strange way time seemed to operate lately – it seemed to be taking longer each day. As every year of her life passed there seemed to be fewer things she could manage. Simple jobs once taken for granted had become Herculean challenges that her tired old body couldn't handle. It was impossible for Estella to hang out laundry by herself; carrying a basket of washing and pegs while leaning on a stick was difficult enough, but attempting to peg wet garments onto the line had resulted in a nasty tumble. The same was true of carrying in firewood to stack by the range or changing the bed linen; over she would go, and each time it was harder to haul herself up. Knowing her bones were china-fragile, Estella had admitted defeat on those tasks but it was beyond frustrating. Her younger self would never have believed it possible that one day she would long to put out the rubbish or bend over to clean lavatories. It was another of life's bitter ironies.

Still, the washing up had yet to beat her. At least Estella could prop herself up against the sink and swish a cloth around in warm soapy water. Kelly worried she would slip on the water sloshed onto the floor, but Estella was weary of such scaremongering. At least she felt a little useful this way. She could also stack plates on the drainer and then dry them – although Kelly said this was a pointless exercise because they dried themselves if you left them on the drainer long enough. Estella often wondered what Joan Tullis, Pencallyn's cook formidable and housekeeper, would have made of such a slapdash attitude. Cook would have taken young Kelly to task in an instant.

"Drying's waste of time, Miss Kellow," Kelly would always say, totally at a loss as to why anyone would want to spend a second on such a pointless task. "There are better things to do!"

Maybe there were for Kelly, who had a family and two jobs to keep her

busy, as well as her husband, Darren, who sounded as though he were an extra child with all the demands he made. Yes, Estella could imagine the idea of cutting corners to glean an extra five minutes reading *Closer* magazine would be heaven for Kelly. If only she could gift the younger woman some of the acres of empty time that weighed her down, Estella thought sadly. There were many long hours when she longed for the past, or simply sat in her chair wishing for strength that would never return. It was a strange thing, time. Once it had wings and, as the old adage went, flew. Sweet stolen hours and enchanted evenings had passed in the beat of a heart, and the sundial's shadow had whirled across the metal plate, a shadowy reminder time was rapidly running out for the brave boys who piloted Spitfires and boarded landing barges. Now, time wore concrete boots and each weary second trudged by like an hour.

Today, and as she washed up, Estella looked out of the window. The kitchen faced the old stable yard and through the grimy glass it sometimes seemed the dear old horses were still peering over half-doors and pulling at their hay. Then she would blink and see the loosebox doors listing drunkenly on rusting hinges and the once neat cobbles stitched with weeds. It was all long gone, and Estella realised with a pang she hadn't ridden since contracting rheumatic fever. That was over eighty years ago. What a thought!

Josh Richardson appeared around the corner of the old coach house, his hands crumbed with earth and loosely holding a bunch of newly picked onions. He'd been busy harvesting the small vegetable patch he'd created, and Estella's kitchen table was already piled with tomatoes, runner beans and courgettes. Wondering what on earth she was going to do with all this food when she had no appetite, Estella mimed tea-drinking and Josh gave her a thumbs up.

"Oh lovely! Time for a brew!" Kelly, recently returned from Calmouth and halfway through unpacking Estella's groceries, caught their exchange. "Good idea, Miss K. Have a sit down for a moment. I'll make it."

"I'm washing up," Estella protested but she was already being gently propelled out of the way and towards her chair. She would have argued but after her walk the previous day her legs were weak and the pain in her chest a little more insistent. A sit down was very welcome.

"The washing up can wait," Kelly said, and for once Estella didn't argue. She sank into her chair while Kelly rattled about with mugs. Fingers of sunshine caressed Estella's cheeks as the soft shush of the kettle lulled her into a doze. She dreamed of two girls as alike as sisters running through the garden and calling to one another as they leapt the ribbons of light streaming through tall trees to criss-cross the pine-strewn earth.

"Tread on it and you die!" warned one girl but the other laughed scornfully.

"That's all bollocks, Stella! You make stuff up! Look!"

She flicked out a coltish leg and touched a golden band with her toe, filled with daring for a split second before whipping the limb back as though stung.

"Still alive!"

"For now," muttered her friend darkly. "For now."

Estella woke with a start. The girls were gone, lost in time and hidden by the years. The sun had slipped behind a cloud and the kitchen was pooled in gloom. A mug of cold tea was on the table beside her. So, she'd been asleep a while. It happened quite often, Estella was always tired these days, and she was used to jolting back into consciousness after a doze. The rise and fall of voices carried her like the tide and Estella tuned in to the conversation. There was comfort in sitting quietly yet held safe by company; it could be lonely at Pencallyn with only the stillness and the memories for company. The nights often felt longer than the days – time working its strange magic once again.

Josh and Kelly were at the kitchen table. Kelly was slicing runner beans, Josh working his way through the biscuit tin as they chatted easily. After a few confused moments when their words made no sense, the syllables falling like soft rain onto mossy earth, she realised they were discussing the renovations at Pencallyn Farm.

"It's going be something else when it's all finished," Kelly said longingly. "Is it true the marble bath came all the way from Italy?"

Josh cleared his throat awkwardly. "To be honest that's not really my department. The interior designers oversee that kind of thing. I just organise who arrives and when."

"Interior Designers. Get you. It's Trago Mills for us peasants." Envy stained Kelly's voice, and chop, chop, chop went the knife. "What about the kitchen? Darren says it's going to be good enough for a restaurant."

"Mum likes to cook. You know how it is."

"Not really. A microwave going *ping* is cooking as far as my mum's concerned. We were lucky not to grow up with scurvy, the crap we all lived on."

"I'd have killed for a microwaved TV dinner. Micro Chips were the height of excitement to me," Josh said kindly. He was so good at putting people at their ease, Estella thought, and Kelly, clearly intimidated by the level of wealth on display at the farm, was comfortable with Josh. Since he had been visiting Pencallyn, he had come to know all about Kelly's life, Darren's love of the pub and how Kelly had once dreamed of being a ballet dancer. Josh listened with interest, gently drew the speaker out of herself and, although she constantly attempted to interrogate him about his personal life, he never once lost patience but steered her away gently but firmly. In a past life, Estella thought, Josh Richardson would have been a priest, although he was far too handsome to be wasted that way in this one!

She was tickled by her train of thought. She might be old but she was still able to appreciate certain things from a purely aesthetic point of view. Every old person was a collection of Russian dolls, each previous incarnation of self encased within the next, until somewhere near the centre, between the unhappy twenty-something and the carefree schoolgirl, was the seventeen-year-old Estella Kellow who would have certainly noticed Josh Richardson. Once upon a time, a very, very long time ago, her fingers would have itched to sketch the pure lines of his face, and she often found herself wondering what colours from her palette would best work for his hair. It was the deep, rich red of the beech woods, shot through with glowing damsons and russets, unusual shades which picked out the flecks of gold in his striking green eyes and drew the gaze like a magnet. Ochre and burgundy and burnt sienna. Oh, but he would have been a wonderful addition to the dreamlike images in *Mysterious Garden!*

"Is your mum a good cook?" Kelly scraped chopped beans into a bowl. Soon enough they would be boiled into a pulpy mush for Estella's lunch.

"My mum used to work in catering," said Josh. "It's how she met my father."

Estella could imagine the rest. It made sense because she'd often wondered how Sarah Richardson, a slender redhead with the big eyes and tremulous countenance of a roe deer, had ever married a boar like Martin. A pretty girl, fresh out of finishing school and doing catering for shoots and parties, thrown into the path of a powerful older man, then. It was her father and Violet all over again, and the path her own life would have taken if the war hadn't come along and changed everything.

She shuddered.

Kelly continued to grill Josh about the renovations. Even with the scant details he revealed it was obvious no expense was being spared. By the time the project was completed the farmhouse would bear little resemblance to the simple dwelling Estella remembered. She hadn't visited it for many years but the place had once been close to her heart. Crumbling walls furred with moss, cowslips and daisies running riot in grassy banks, empty rooms with sunlight streaming in through broken windows and outside in the weed-strewn yard, the blinded eye of an ancient well …

"Evie! Get back! You'll fall in!"

A girl stood on tiptoes, peering into the depths. She loved the imprisoned sky which shivered in the watery depths, and relished the dark drop. Her pulse raced when the handle spun around and around as the bucket plummeted into the depths, and she would press her stomach into the lip and pivot for a few glorious seconds as she teetered between earth and water. Then a hand would clutch her bony shoulder and yank her backwards, away from the delicious brink.

"It's dangerous!"

"I know, Stella! That's what makes it fun!"

But Estella hadn't visited Pencallyn Farm for a very long time, and now her heart fluttered with panic because it was changing for ever. If she didn't return soon, the place she knew would exist only in her memory. The skeleton of old floors and beams and cob walls would be hidden for ever beneath glass and steel and wood. Estella had seen more than enough expensive developments around Pencallyn and Calmouth to be under any illusions of what the farm would become, yet when she heard Josh explaining how the well was going to become a part of the new kitchen she felt a torrent of panic surge through her.

Everything was being erased. Everything. All that had once been theirs was being rubbed out. If she was to see the place for one last time, before her past vanished for ever, the time was now. It wasn't such a long way to walk; there had once been a time when her feet had floated over the winding footpath which stitched Pencallyn House to the farm, and Estella felt sure she could still make it. She would wait until Kelly had departed and set off once the coast was clear. Estella wouldn't attempt to fight her way through the woods, but if she made her way to the lane somebody might pass by and offer a lift.

There. A plan was made and, a woman on a mission, Estella didn't have a moment to waste. She needed to get her strength up.

"I think it's time for lunch," she announced.

* * *

Miss Toms had taught Estella poetry, and nearly a century later stanzas still echoed through her head. As she made her cautious way along the rutted drive, the penultimate lines of Robert Burns' *To a Mouse* scampered across her memory like rodent feet:

The best laid schemes o' mice an' men
Gang aft agley.

If she tripped and broke her hip right now, things would certainly go agley, and if she lost focus for a second, allowing the mist to occlude her reasons for having ventured this far, the social workers would descend like buzzards. Estella would become another old dear who got confused and went wandering. You heard stories like that all the time. The old soldier who did a runner from his care home to attend D-Day reunions in Normandy or the elderly woman who walked all the way in the snow to her childhood home and refused to budge once the new owners had let her in. Or – and to Estella this was worse – those poor souls who wandered out of the front door one day and ended up being taken to hospital with no idea where they were headed or why. Had they, like her, started their journey with a clear purpose in mind only to make a wrong turn and step into the marsh of forgetfulness? How many such missions ended in confusion when the memory decided it was time to curl up and sleep?

She must not be among their number.

Estella had waited until Kelly left before fetching her jacket and stick. It was another glorious late summer day and, as she had tapped her slow way along the drive, she enjoyed the sunshine that was drizzled across the world like honey. Birds sang and bees droned in the long grass which flanked the drive. Tired from her exertions, Estella was just gathering her strength by the gate when one of the trucks from the local builders' merchant came trundling along the lane. She flagged him down and when she learned the driver was making a delivery to Pencallyn Farm this felt like a nod from Fate. The driver would have delivered her right to the farmhouse door if Estella hadn't insisted she wanted to walk up the path. It felt only right that she approached the old dwelling on foot.

The farmhouse stood at the edge of her own land. In front of it was a small yard and cottage garden. To the side were fields that undulated to the west. If you climbed higher through these and out through the wood, you would arrive at Bury Barrow, an iron age fort where still-sharp arrowheads and old bits of pottery clawed their way out of the soil. From here you could see across the ruffled sea to the Calmouth headland. It seemed to Estella only moments ago she'd stood up there and watched planes dance a deadly ballet. Was one of the boys up there her brother? she'd wondered. And what about the Germans in their aeroplanes? Did they feel any fear or guilt at all? This question had been answered on another brilliantly sunny day, and Estella could still hear the terror in the foreign voice calling out. It was one memory she wished would sink for ever into the quicksand.

So. The farmhouse. She had to focus on that, because this would be her last visit and the final time she'd see the place that had been their haven. It was the place where she had known, and had lost, love. Estella dragged her aching legs forward. She would make it to the farmhouse today, and she would remember why this mattered to her.

In those long-gone days the house had been little more than a shell. The tumbledown walls were scarcely distinguishable from the woods, so heavily blanketed were they with ivy and moss and creepers. A small, squat building with half the roof missing, windows open to the elements and wooden sills splintering, it had been a favourite spot for children to make camps and for young lovers to hide away. As secluded from the world as any desert island, there had been an air of peace as though the world events beyond the crumbling walls had been paused …

"Evie! Evie! Take some pictures!"

"Only if you take one of me!"

"Down, Poppet – you're in the way! Smile, Stella!"

Those girls had so loved it here. The farm had been one of their places, woven into the games they'd played. Estella glanced at the knotted old fingers gripping the handle of her walking stick. Had she really run along this path and climbed the walls? Impossible, surely?

As she shuffled forwards it seemed to Estella that although there were builders everywhere, busy worker ants in yellow hard hats trundling barrows and unloading trucks, the place was unusually quiet. She couldn't hear a thing. The usual torrent of birdsong was absent, and the soft wind had died away. The tall grasses were poised and watchful and the path a winding rope, tightening noose-like around the old building. The scene was blurred by something more than the new walls and bright glass. If pressed to explain what it was she felt, Estella would have said the atmosphere was bruised, as though the pain of some long-ago injury was only now being felt.

The old stone building had expanded outwards to embrace the courtyard, wrapping itself around what had once been roofed by the sky. Soon it would seal the well away with steel and glass and huge oak beams. Although it was a warm afternoon, Estella shivered. The water which ran beneath the land, following the ancient path from the hill fort to the well and through Pencallyn to the sea, was held, scared, and the idea of shutting it away frightened her. Cornwall was a magical place and today the old well seemed to be calling to her. She hobbled towards the newly constructed part of the house, oblivious to the uneven ground and the machinery around her.

"Watch where you're going, my girl! Don't trip up!"

Estella whipped around.

"Tommy? Is that you?"

But there was nobody there and Estella tutted, irritated with herself. This was not the time to slip into her memories. She had to focus on the sunshine, the brightness of high-vis vests and the sheer effort of putting one foot in front of another. She needed to see the well before it was gone for ever. This felt important. Vital.

"I'm here! Can you hear me? I promised not to leave you!"

This time Estella couldn't ignore the past, not when it was pulling her close, arms holding her as tightly as a lover while these words were whispered into her ear. Abruptly, the bubble of silence burst and the whole place thrummed with sound. Diggers, hammers and the whir of cement mixers joined in a chorus of sound, drowning the dearly missed voice and drilling into her thoughts. Panic consumed her.

"I'm still here! I never left, either! Where are you?" Estella cried. "My love? Where are you? I'm here!"

Despair was a millstone crushing everything; hope, faith, promises – all were dust beneath its weight. Grief slurried in her belly and Estella sank to her knees, her face buried in her hands. Time and memory swirled. A marsh of loss was sucking her under. Oh! When had her mind stopped being her ally, turning from a sharp-witted defender and friend to a bully and a memory thief? Why was this happening now?

"Miss Kellow? Can you hear me? Are you ill?"

Estella looked up at a beautiful red-haired woman. Who on earth was this?

"Where's Tommy?" she cried. "Where's Tommy gone?"

The woman glanced over her shoulder at a young man, handsome enough but with coarse features blurring in the fashion Estella always associated with drink. He was familiar. Did she know him? Was he one of the soldiers? An American? It was hard to tell, there were so many of them in Pencallyn these days.

"Darren, could you fetch Tommy?" the woman said.

The young man shook his head. "There's no one called Tommy on site, Mrs Richardson. I don't know who she means."

Estella stared about her, wildly. Her hands shook and when she glanced down at them and saw liver-spotted claws rather than her own smooth white skin, she cried out in terror. What was happening? Where was she? Where was Tommy? And where was Evie?

"Evie? Where are you?" she cried.

"My missus says the old girl gets confused. She shouldn't be outside," Estella heard the man called Darren say. What old girl? Who was he talking about?

"Miss Kellow? Please let me help you. What can I do?"

The woman placed a hand on her shoulder but Estella shrank away, terrified. Who was this person? What was she doing at their farm? She raised her hands to her face, crying out at the sensation of the loose skin beneath her touch. What had happened to her? Why was she so old? Why was she here? Who were these people?

"Evie!" she called. "Where are you?"

"Miss Kellow? Can you hear me? Who is Evie? What's wrong with you?"

Everything! Estella wanted to scream, but terror parched her mouth and the words couldn't come. And then, by the time her heart rate steadied and her voice returned, she couldn't remember what it was that had distressed her. She was offered a plastic seat and somebody took her stick. Without knowing why, she opened her right hand and studied the silver echo of a long-healed scar. Estella couldn't remember why it should be, but seeing this old injury always soothed her. It was her talisman.

It meant something important.

"Fetch Josh," she heard somebody say. Estella had no idea who this Josh might be but his name calmed her. He must be somebody she knew.

Perhaps Josh could find Evie for her? Evie would get Estella home to Pencallyn. She would look out for Estella.

She'd *promised!*

"Oh Evie," Estella whispered. "Where did you go?"

But there was no answer. There never was. The thick mist swirled around her, and tired after a lifetime of searching, Estella Kellow stepped into the sinking sand of her yesterdays.

CHAPTER 9

Nell
The Present

I leave the city on a colourless day. As my train snakes its way out of town beneath skies the colour of dishwater I settle into my seat and watch the terraces of London peel away either side of the tracks. I think about the multitudes of people living within the smoke-blackened walls, all with their own thoughts and hopes and closely guarded secrets, and my search feels overwhelming. If my grandparents had vanished and there's nobody left to search for me, one swab of my cheek cells isn't going to tell me anything. There are billions of people on this planet. Whatever makes me think I'll find one who belongs to me? I'm a tiny needle in a haystack of lives and loves and family ties.

As the train gathers pace, breaking into the land of semi-detached houses and emerald glimpses of parks jewelled with brightly hued swings and slides, my increasing despair matches the increasing velocity. It's a spiral of panic I know of old and if I allow myself to swirl into it there's no saying where those feelings will take me; I only know it will be nowhere good.

The train clatters over a viaduct, high above the streets and rooftops of Hanwell, and I open my laptop to pull up the notes for my new novel. With five hours to fill between London and Calmouth I'm determined to make the time work for me and to avoid the siren song of despair. The loss of my father has unravelled me in so many ways, but his passing, unlike that other smallest yet biggest loss, is a part of the natural passage of things. I could, and I would, get through it. This time, writing is going to help me. I can already hear new characters speaking. Perhaps my narrative begins on a train from London to Cornwall? My heroine is a teacher accompanying children as they were evacuated? This is a start, and what do I know better than how a city girl feels as she travels into the unknown?

Tap, tap, tap go my fingers in time with the rattle and clack of the carriage. Writing has always my best escape, and as the train wends its way westwards words knit themselves together with the magic no author can fully explain. When I pause, my hands stiff and achy, I see to my delight that the railway line is hugging the Devonshire shoreline, threading its way past rich red cliffs and smart white villas, while sunlight turns the water to diamonds. Small boats laze in the calm waters of an estuary and further out to sea a wake laces the path of a speedboat as it pulls a matchstick skier through the blue. Enchanted by the childlike wonder of spotting the sea, I save my work and close my laptop in order to enjoy the unfolding seascape. My heart is already lighter and the closer the train draws to Cornwall the more certain I become that visiting Pencallyn Cove is the right thing to do. If nothing else, I'm writing once again, and have a few weeks to do so in a beautiful part of the world. After the long months of nursing Dad, and the dragging grief of the dark time before, I need a holiday.

I change trains at Truro and the final part of my journey involves taking a single railcar which rattles through deep green countryside like a runaway roller skate. I press my face to the window, squinting beyond the ghost of my reflection as she floats alongside, and drink in the views. The railway track hems an estuary where herons paddle along the ribbon of half-tide and willows peer narcissus into the shallows as though trying to admire their blonde tresses through the drowned sky. A sculling swan is the sole vessel crossing the water, and I crane my neck to follow his leisurely progress but the train veers into the woods and the creek is lost from sight, veiled by trees and before long just a watery memory.

Is this the Calmouth Estuary, I wonder, as I stare at my own pale face, white against the dark green of the foliage outside the train. Is this where boats had once been hidden, huddled tightly against the banks and tucked up beneath the camouflage of reeds and willow? I've spent a lot of time researching the area and in my imagination this stretch of water boils with surreptitious activity. I discover a landscape the young GI in my father's picture might have known, and finding it so peaceful comes as a surprise.

And so I arrive at Calmouth. Here, I take a taxi to Pencallyn Cove, and my journey west is almost at an end. Will the village still look the same as it did in the postcard? I've studied the image so many times I won't need directions when I arrive; I can see it all in my mind's eye: the sickle of beach, doughty white houses clinging to steeply wooded hills, and lobster pots and nets heaped on the quay. The pub has kept its name, The Pilchards, and the closer I get the more excited I feel to be in a place which may have been home to my grandparents.

The driver is chatting nonstop on his phone, so I study the unravelling views as the cab crawls through the town and meanders into the countryside. The late summer landscape basks in rich sunshine and, although it's not peak season, the narrow roads teem with tourists holding ice creams or carrying buckets and spades down to the beach. The lanes beyond feel so quiet after London it's as though I'm journeying back to 1944. High-banked lanes foam with cow parsley and the verges are splattered with egg-yolk-yellow buttercups. Whitewashed cottages huddle beside the road, window boxes spilling nasturtiums and geraniums, and ripe cornfields ripple like the sea.

The lanes grow wider as we approach Pencallyn, altered to accommodate the tanks and jeeps of an army on the move, and narrow again when the road plunges downhill towards the coast. The American army camp had been situated at the top of the hill and the humps of ivy-clad Nissen huts lurk in fields and farmyards, a slumbering reminder of what was taking place in this peaceful spot seventy years ago. According to my research a road once ran through the grounds of Pencallyn House to transport vehicles to the shore. Everywhere I gaze, the past slips over the present and with every mile I feel more and more excited.

The driver ends his call, the drive downhill demanding his full attention. As the road hairpins sharply to the right, Pencallyn Cove lies before me like a model village. As the cab slows, the lane narrows and suddenly I'm in the middle of my postcard. The road ends outside the pub, and the driver executes an elaborate three-point turn, muttering when tourists get in the way of his manoeuvre. When I open the car door, the air smells of salt and seaweed – scents which whisk me back to holidays where the sun always shone and nothing tasted better than warm orange squash, sipped from sharp-edged plastic beakers, and heat-curled ham sandwiches.

I glance around me with pleasure. This small street has barely changed, and I recognise it from the postcard. Although there are now cars parked in any available gaps, and the tourists sitting on the harbour wall are wearing shorts and wetsuits rather than flowery dresses and slacks, the view is familiar; if my grandparents appeared, they would still know Pencallyn Cove. Even the old schoolhouse looks the same, although it has morphed into luxury holiday lets complete with sage paint, floral curtains and smart Range Rovers parked outside.

I pay the driver and stand with my suitcase at my feet, absorbing the village. I listen to the soundtrack of shrieks from the beach, the growl of a speedboat engine and the call of keening gulls. Heat presses down on the crown of my head. I feel very far away from everything I know. Nobody here knows me. Nobody cares that Sam Summers is gone. And nobody knows about my baby.

This adventure is new and untouched. It is all mine.

I pick up my case and step into the pub. It's dark and low-beamed, lit with fairy lights and candles, and crammed with horse brasses. Deep window seats frame sea views and as I look out, I spot the headland which shelters Pencallyn Cove from the Calmouth Estuary. I won't get any work done with views like this to distract me!

My room is tucked under the eaves. A small window overlooks the pretty beer garden and there's a little desk beneath which makes it the perfect spot for writing. Feeling happy, I unpack and freshen up before wandering downstairs.

"Everything all right with the room, maid?"

The landlord, a tall bearded man who wouldn't look out of place on the Poldark set, is standing behind the bar and polishing glasses. Several drinkers work their way through pints of real ale while a holidaying family enjoy a late lunch. In the afternoon quiet, all eyes swivel to me.

"It's lovely, thanks," I say.

"Would you like a cold drink after your journey?" asks the landlady. She wipes her hands on a bar towel and picks up a half-pint glass. "On the house. It's hellish hot today."

It's glorious outside and the last thing I want to do is stay in the dark pub, but I'm here on a mission. Village pubs are usually a fount of information. These customers at the bar look like locals. They might be able to help me with some background.

"I'd love an orange juice, thanks," I say, hopping up onto a bar stool.

The landlord's eyes swoop down and size me up.

"So, where are you from?"

I suppress the impulse to ask him the same question. The eighteenth century, maybe?

"London," I say wearily as I anticipate the usual 'but where are you really from?'

"Ah. I thought you were a Cornish lass with your colouring," he replies, an answer I wasn't expecting since my idea of what a Cornish woman looks like is based on Demelza, all red curls and snow-white skin – in other words, nothing like me.

"Do I?"

"Oh yes. Cornish folk are often Spanish-looking, after the Armada, see. Lots of Spanish lads were washed up here when their ships were dashed onto the rocks. Those who survived married into the Cornish families."

His wife slides my drink across the bar and chuckles.

"What nonsense you talk, Toby. Any Spaniard washing up here would have had his throat cut in a jiffy."

"Quite right too, bleddy emmets," jokes a drinker at the bar. At least I think he's joking.

The landlady smiles at me.

"Don't look so worried, love. Most people in the village aren't Cornish born and bred. Take my husband for example. Toby might look like an old sea dog but he's from Kent."

The landlord looks mutinous. "I'm a Pengelly, though, Jen. Proper Cornish, us Pengellys. Through and through. That's my roots."

This leads nicely to my subject matter.

"I'm here looking for my roots, actually. I think my grandfather might have been stationed here in the war, if he was in the US army."

"That's very likely. Pencallyn had an American army camp, and lots of soldiers were stationed here back then," Jen says.

"If you look around the pub, we've lots of pictures of those days." Toby gestures at the walls which are covered in framed black and white photographs of warships and young men driving jeeps.

"There's all kinds of stuff left over from those days," he continues. "Half the concrete apron's still covering the beach and a chunk of the embarkation pier's survived. Pillboxes too and tank traps."

One of the regulars looks up from his pint. "My old man used to talk about what it was like in those days. When I was growing up, we used to find all sorts on the beach. My mate, Jimmy Jago, blew two fingers off when he dug up an old grenade!"

"A German plane crashed in the woods below Bury Beacon," recalls another. "Messerschmitt, I think it was. My dad went and collected a piece. He kept it for years."

"Ah yes, Dead German Woods. We used to dare each other to play there as kids," Jen recalls.

"I used to make camps in the old huts where the army camp was before they cleared it for the estate." This comment is from a customer wearing an unseasonal woolly hat. "We thought the pillboxes made great hideouts."

This is fascinating but nothing new. I open my bag and pull out the plastic folder containing my precious pictures.

"I'm hoping to find out some more about him," I say as I hold up the picture of the young soldier. "I think he could be my grandfather."

Jen rummages under the bar for her glasses and, settling them on her nose, sighs.

"Oh! Look how young he is. And so handsome. Did he make it through the war?"

"I don't know. My dad passed away a little while ago and I found some photographs with his things. He was adopted, so I've not got much to go on."

"I'm sorry, love, that must be tough," Jen says. "Hmm. I think there's something in the chin, maybe? And you have his smile, I think."

"You really think so?"

"Yes. Yes, I do. What was his name?"

"I don't know," I say.

"Without a name it won't be easy," Toby points out. "It was such a long time ago. There's nobody left who'd remember those times."

I bite my lip. What was I hoping for? That somebody, somebody very old of course, would look at the photo and say they knew him? Come on,

Nell, I scold myself. Did you think you'd find the answer straight away?

"What about the old girl up at the house?"

This suggestion comes from the drinker in the hat. With his plaid shirt and jeans, his weathered skin and faded eyes speak of years spent scanning the horizon. His slow accent is rich and warm as honey. He looks like a local born and bred. Is he somebody who may be able to help?

Toby the landlord crosses his arms over his rotund belly.

"Do you mean Miss Kellow, Davey? She must be in her nineties."

"Aye, ninety-five, I'd say. She's old enough to remember those times, and she's lived here all her life. The Kellows had officers billeted with them, and the army camp was on their land as was then."

I'm doing rapid sums in my head. Anyone who remembers the war properly, as an adult rather than as a child, would be in their nineties. It's possible; look at Nanna, living into her hundreds. People do live longer these days, don't they?

"She's very muddled nowadays," Jen Pengelly says doubtfully. She pulls a pint, and the head foams into the drip tray as her attention strays from the task. "I heard she's started wandering. Darren Jones said she managed to get herself all the way to Pencallyn Farm the other day. She was in a terrible state and they nearly called an ambulance."

"I heard she's mad," says one drinker.

"My nan told me she'd had her heart broken years ago and wears her wedding dress everywhere."

"She's loaded."

"She's a lesbian, I heard."

A discussion breaks out at this point and I learn Estella Kellow was a spy in the war, is mad, a millionaire, penniless, gay, a jilted bride and many more far-fetched stories. The truth lurks in there somewhere, and I hold onto the knowledge that she lived here at the same time as the young man in my photograph. This is a fact.

That she may have known him is hope.

"She's the oldest person in the area. My old man told me Churchill stayed with her family in the war," Davey confides. Eyes the colour of stonewashed denim twinkle at me from beneath the hat. "That has to be worth a pint."

I laugh at his cheek. "Depends whether it's true!"

"Of course, it isn't!" hollers another customer. "It wasn't Churchill, you harris! It was the American one. General what's his name!"

"Eisenhower!" bellows somebody.

"Eisenhower?" I echo. "Seriously? He visited Pencallyn?"

Davey winks. "It could have been him. Or not. Or maybe they both visited. There were Americans based there, anyway. Officers, I think. My auntie, Joan Tullis, was the cook back then. There were some right goings-on, according to her."

The writer in me is intrigued.

"Like what?"

Davey grins. "I'll tell you for a pint!"

"You will not," scolds Jen. "You leave my guest in peace!" To me she adds, "Estella Kellow rarely leaves the house. Her home help says the place is in a right state. I can't imagine she'll be able to stay there much longer, poor old soul."

"The developers can't wait for her to die," sighs Toby. "I saw that Martin Richardson driving past there only yesterday. He's got his eye on the place, you mark my words."

I've no idea who Martin Richardson is, but the faces pulled at the mention of his name tell me all I need to know.

"Do you know Miss Kellow?" I ask Jen.

"No. We used to sometimes see her in the graveyard. We feared her as kids. She's reclusive and a bit odd. We would dare each other to go in her garden and were proper scared if we saw her! We'd run then, let me tell you. She wrote a kids' book years ago and people still come here because of it, don't they, love?"

"They do. It's a cult thing. They all come wanting to see Pencallyn's famous gardens and get right teasy when we tell them the place isn't open for visitors."

The penny drops.

"Oh! You must mean *Mysterious Garden*! Estella Kellow's the author?"

"That's right. The book's meant to be based on the garden at Pencallyn House. It was famous once but I can't imagine much is left now."

Jen tuts. "Just think, something so special left for nature to reclaim. It seems a crying shame. They say the garden was on a par with those of Trebah and Glendurgan. It's all very overgrown now and the bottom gates haven't been opened for years."

"It would have been nice for trade to have the garden open, and a famous author too," says her husband wistfully. "Fowey's been dining out on Daphne du Maurier for years. When's it our turn?"

"Could I visit Miss Kellow?" I ask, feeling excited.

Jen and Toby exchange a look.

"She's really reclusive. We could always ask Kelly Jones what she thinks. She's Miss Kellow's home help. I'll introduce you," Jen offers.

"Thanks," I say. An introduction would be very welcome, although I'm not sure I can wait until the weekend – I'll pop!

The door swings open and two walkers enter, hot and bothered beneath heavy rucksacks, and keen to have pints of cold cider. While Toby serves them, Jen examines my pictures again.

"There's something about this one," she says, her forefinger hovering over the picture of the laughing girl outside the farmhouse. "I feel like I know this place. Hey, Davey. Have a look at this, will you? And yes, I'll put a half in for you this time."

He chuckles. "I knew I'd wear you down in the end, Jenny."

"You've had a lifetime to practise. Look at this place. It seems familiar. Didn't we play there as kids? Have a den?"

She passes the picture over and they study the image, his woolly hat and her grey head meeting over the bar. An image flashes into my mind of a little girl with pigtails and a scabby-kneed boy with a tooth missing, shrieking and laughing as they explore a ruin, long-ago playmates and partners in crime.

Then Davey whistles. "Well, I never. We used to play there as nippers."

"It's was a strange place. I didn't like it," Jen recalls.

"You know where this is?" I ask.

"It's Pencallyn Farm," Davey replies. "There's the old well, Jen. Remember? The farm used to belong to the big house back in the day, but it fell into disrepair after the First World War and I think the land was sold after the second one. That place has changed hands more times than I've had pints."

"That's a lot," Jen teases.

"It's being done up by incomers. Good luck to 'em. They're welcome to it," Davey says. "They've messed with the well and things they don't understand. No good will come of it."

"Locals don't like the place much," Jen explains. "We think it's unlucky."

"It *is* unlucky. The Richardsons should have stayed away," says Davey.

"Because they're incomers?" I say.

"No, because it's no place for them. It's no place for anyone. It's a sad place and restless. It's haunted."

I can't quite believe what I'm hearing. Do they really believe this, or are they spinning a tale for a gullible tourist?

"You probably think we're being superstitious, but there's magic in the earth here and the old ways hold true," Jen says softly. "People mess with the old ones at their peril. This county demands respect."

I glance at the girl in the photograph. Head thrown back and laughing, she looks as though she's having the time of her life. The house, bathed in sun, appears welcoming. It doesn't seem sad or unhappy to me.

"Do you recognise her?" I ask.

Davey shakes his head. "No, maid."

"Long before my time," Jen says.

"Can you take me to the farm?" I say to Davey. "I'll buy you a drink."

But Davey knocks back his pint.

"Not today, maid. Not today."

And beneath his words I hear a resounding 'not ever' and I have the distinct impression the subject's closed.

I scoop up my folder and push it back into my bag, half-puzzled and half-amused. I'm not in London now, that's for sure. I glance at my watch. It's the afternoon but there are hours of daylight left for me to explore the area. I have so many new ideas I hardly know where to start.

I figure Pencallyn Farm will be as good a place as any.

CHAPTER 10

Nell
The Present

Exploring Pencallyn village doesn't take long. After walking along the beach, I sit on the quayside and devour an ice cream. Sailing boats dance across the sea and all is calm, but in 1944 this scene would have been very different. The pictures in the pub showed a black and white world where warships wallowed in the bay and the cliffs were tangled up in barbed wire. Young soldiers would have seen this exact view as they departed for Normandy, and for many it was the last voyage they would take. Were they afraid as they sailed away under cover of darkness, or was there a sense of resolution and purpose? Was my grandfather with them? My mind picks over these questions as the gulls are sorting through heaps of seaweed abandoned by the retreating tide. Like them, if I persist for long enough there's bound to be a morsel hidden amongst the detritus.

I finish my ice cream and begin the long climb out of the village. There's a gateway which cuts off a wide road which vanishes into an overgrown garden. Once upon a time this entrance must have thronged with trucks and tanks and jeeps and all the paraphernalia of war. Boys in boots would have marched through on their way down from the army camp at the top of the hill to the landing barges in the cove, maybe my own grandfather among them?

Ivy grasps the gates with tenacious emerald fingers. Brambles claw and scratch me when I try to peer through the metalwork. At my feet weeds have prised the surface open, and writhing briars knit a shield to repel intruders. The light within the dense foliage is otherworldly and disorientating. I frown because I've seen this scene before, but where? Proud gates, choking undergrowth, a woodland path trickled with moonlight …

It's an image which makes a connection. Of course! This must be the lower gate to Pencallyn House, the locked entrance which landlady Jen mentioned. No wonder this place feels so familiar. It would for countless readers across the globe, because this is the inspiration for *Mysterious Garden*. How strange to know those long-forgotten childhood images really do exist, even if cloaked in thick shrubbery and the jungle of tame specimen plants turned wild. As I peer through the gate, it seems to me faces swim out of the deep pools of shade, distinct from the rustling leaves for just a pulse beat before turning away and slipping back into the land of the imagination.

The breeze shifts, the bushes shiver, the faces recede and I'm all alone again, a small figure with her hands curled around flaking ironwork who stares, like so many others must have done, into the mysterious garden. I feel the strongest compulsion to explore. In the book paths twist and turn through the garden, looping around a deep pool where golden fish circle lazily in the still depths, and wind between the trees until they lead the reader to the sundial at the heart of a labyrinth. I used to sit on Nanna Summer's lap tracing these paths with my finger. We loved to make up our own adventures, and no matter how we threaded our way through the book, or which page we turned, the story always led us back to a little girl called Nell who was loved very, very much.

The knot in my throat is as tangled as ivy in the garden. Nanna Summers was old and so tired at the end, and I'd forgotten the woman she used to be, the woman who had looked after me while my father was working, soothed away my tears, read me stories and pushed me on my swing. I miss her. How excited she would have been to know this place was real!

I know I need to keep moving forwards before I'm sucked into the grief spiral. There's nothing like physical exertion to distract a girl from melancholy and the steady climb uphill. I catch my breath and study the map on my iPhone, expanding the image with my thumb and forefinger. I have at least another mile and a half to walk before arriving at Pencallyn Farm. If I could cut through the garden it would be less than half a mile. For a moment I toy with the notion of clambering over the wall and making my way through bushes and over tangled roots as I follow faint traces of old paths. Like aerial images of old field boundaries and iron age settlements, those footpaths are sleeping beneath the surface. I'm sure I could find them if I looked carefully enough. Or maybe there's a secret part of the garden where the past seventy years are just a dream and where the topiary's still dagger sharp and the flowerbeds laid out in mathematical perfection?

I laugh at my own imagination. What a crazy idea! The garden's long gone. Even if it wasn't, trespassing won't endear me to the enigmatic Miss Kellow. I continue on my way and eventually reach another entrance with ivy woven around the elaborate metalwork. These gates are wide open but list drunkenly on rotten hinges, and the drive beyond is a stegosaurus spine of grass flanked by deep ruts and pimpled with stones. It stretches away for a good quarter of a mile before veering sharply to the left and vanishing, leaving me wondering what lies in wait around the corner and lurking in the buddleia and elder. The past? The mysterious garden? Estella Kellow herself?

I press on towards Pencallyn Farm. Another locked gateway, the twin of the lower one, sits at the farthest boundary and it's here that the lane forks, one branch truncated at the weed-choked gate while the other continues eastwards. I remember this part of the road from my earlier journey to the village because I'd been struck by how wide it was, made this way to accommodate the US army as they moved their military equipment through Cornwall. Everywhere I turn it feels as though history is rising up to meet me. Instinct whispers I'm close to my father's past. His roots, and mine, are here – as tightly packed into the earth as the twisting roots of the gnarled trees.

I follow the road, stepping aside when the odd car passes, before skirting the boundary of the farm and arriving at the entrance. In contrast to its neglected neighbour, Pencallyn Farm is a hive of activity. The house is approached by a proper tarmacked road – no ruts here, and no weeds threatening to smother the grounds. The building itself appears a work in progress. Half of it is clean and fresh, a blend of honeyed stone, thick blond beams and sparkling glass, while the other half remains partially ruined. Squinting against the sunlight, I see jagged walls and missing rooftops which leave old rooms open to the sky. Birds fly in and out of empty windows, and ivy crawls up the walls, as though seeking the sky above.

I hear the rumbling of a cement mixer and the clank of tools. Somewhere a power-saw wails and, as I draw closer, voices call to one another across a busy building site. I pull the plastic wallet from my bag so I can compare the photograph to the structure before me, but everything feels jumbled up. The fenced-off area to my left must be the well, so the girl in the photo would now be sitting inside the skeleton of an extension. Would she even recognise this place?

Could this be where my father was born? Or where his mother had lived? Perhaps she was the farmer's daughter who fell in love with a handsome young GI? It's a romantic idea and so, as if it's a plot from my novel, I'm halfway to believing it already. With my excitement rising like a helium balloon, I throw caution to the wind and make my way onto the building site.

CHAPTER 11

Nell
The Present

"Hey! You! This isn't a right of way!"

There's a man marching towards me and his red face is a perfect match for the sweater draped over his blue and white striped shirted shoulders.

"I'm sick of people traipsing across my land! What part of 'Private Property' don't you understand? Eh? Can't you bloody read? It says 'Keep Out! Private Property!' "

He brandishes his hand in the direction of the entrance and I'm appalled to spot a huge sign attached to the gate which declares this message – although not quite so angrily. Swept up in my mission, I hadn't noticed it.

"I'm really sorry," I begin but this man hasn't finished. Not by a long shot.

"What do I have to do to get it through to you? There's no footpath here so clear off before I call the police. Do you hear me?"

I certainly do. My ears are ringing and when he launches into another rant about rights of way and lawsuits and gypsies they ring even more.

"This is my land!" he snarls. "Mine! I'm sick of trespassing and people where they've no business to be!"

I'm trying hard not to quake. "I'm so sorry. I was just looking for a well!"

"That bloody well! I've a good mind to have the damn thing filled in. When will you lot get it into your thick skulls there's no right of way to it? It's on my land. My land!"

His face is so close to mine that our eyeballs are practically touching. Blood races to my face and my heart beats so fast I feel faint.

"What's going on?"

A younger man hurries across the site, a worried expression on his face. At a quick glance I wouldn't think he's more than forty, and his clothes are clean, with none of the dust or paint splatters to suggest he's working manually. The foreman? Or maybe an architect?

"It's another one looking for the bloody well," barks the older man. "If it's not the well they want then it's the old bat's bloody garden. I'm sick of it. I've a good mind to call the police."

"Let's not be hasty. There's no harm done," says the new arrival. Turning to me, he spreads his hands apologetically. "I'm afraid this is private land. There's no right of way to the old well."

There's a calm strength to this man's voice and it eases my panic. Dressed in faded jeans and green tee shirt, and with a hard hat rammed onto hair the same rich colour as autumn leaves, his physical presence draws the attention easily. A tribal-style tattoo dances on his left bicep, swelling under tanned skin, and transposes him from present to past, into a Celtic warrior. If I wrote this man into a novel, he'd be a highlander or a druid prince because he brings to mind thoughts of wide spaces, vast skies and free landscapes. His eyes, widely set above deeply valleyed cheekbones, are the same hue as soft moorland moss. As they sweep over me, gold and green and deep, I feel self-conscious because with my hair pinned in a loose bun and coming down over my face, and sporting a tee shirt patched with sweat from my walk, I probably look exactly like the kind of girl who sneaks into places where she has no right to be.

"I'm so sorry," I say. "I didn't mean to upset anyone, I promise. I only wanted to see the well."

The angry man slams a fist into his palm. "I'm sick to death of the bloody well. I've a good mind to have the damn thing filled in."

"Calm down, Dad," says the warrior. "She's not doing any harm."

"Not doing any harm? She's on private property!"

"I'm sorry," I say desperately.

The warrior smiles at me, and it's a smile of such genuine warmth that something unexpected roils deep within me.

"Please don't worry," he says kindly. "I'm sure you didn't mean to upset anyone."

"They never do, bloody hippies. Peace and love and bloody right to roam," grumbles the angry man.

"Dad, how many times have I asked you to let me deal with anyone who comes looking for the well? Calm down. No one's doing any harm."

"You're too soft, Josh. I'll remind you of that when one of them steals something."

"One of *them*?" I echo in disbelief. "What do you mean by that?"

The ground feels like liquid beneath my feet and it's like all the blood has migrated to my extremities. *One of them.* How many times had my father heard that expression? And his father? And his father? And back and back and back?

Maybe I'm closer to uncovering my roots than I'd realised?

Warrior Josh looks mortified. A flush mottles his strong cheekbones

"I'm so sorry," he says helplessly. "I don't think he meant …"

"Jesus Christ, Josh! Of course, I didn't. I meant trespassers and hippies! Not … anyone else," backtracks the older man, shoving his hands into his pockets of his beige cords and looking mutinous. To me, he adds grudgingly, "Everyone comes looking for the well, you see, and it's a bloody menace. There's no right of way through the property but that doesn't stop people trying it on."

"They've come here for years, that's why." Josh is exasperated. Pulling off the hard hat, he rakes a despairing hand through his titian mane. "It's a tradition."

"Time it stopped then," snaps the father.

What a charmer.

"Some people think the well has magical powers, Dad. They like to come and tie bits of cloth in the blackthorn bushes and make wishes. It's all harmless enough," sighs the son, and I have the impression they've discussed this topic many times before.

"It's not harmless when they're on private property. Anyway, it's a load of old nonsense. I'll soon put paid to all that when the well's capped and it features in our new kitchen. The security will be in place by then, too. Then let them try."

"I'm not sure that's such a good idea," Josh begins, but his father isn't listening; he's far too busy complaining about how the specialist well clearing company charges extortionate fees and how slow the local builders are. It's fascinating seeing other families communicate, and hearing this exchange makes me appreciate my gentle father more than ever. Dad always listened to me and took the feelings of others into account. He would never have dreamed of hollering at someone this way or ordering me about like this long-suffering Josh.

I miss Dad so much.

"It's not too late to rethink the kitchen. Maybe we should leave the well outside and have a small path to it so people can still visit?" Josh suggests hopefully.

"So all and sundry can wander onto our property? Absolutely not. The well isn't listed, and removing all access is the best way. I'm at the end of my patience with the bloody cover too. They think they're so clever just because we never see who lifts it off. I'll find out who's responsible, though, then they'll be sorry."

"It's village kids having a laugh, Dad," says Josh wearily. "Maybe we can set cameras up? But that's another discussion and none of this is down to – " He looks at me and smiles. "Oh, I'm sorry. I don't know your name."

"Eleanor Summers," I tell him. "Everyone calls me Nell. I'm not from the village, though, I'm from Bristol and I promise that I've had nothing to do with your problems with the well."

"Nice to meet you, Nell, although the circumstances aren't ideal! I'm Josh Richardson and this is my father, Martin. Dad owns Pencallyn Farm," Josh explains while Martin glowers at us both.

"I'm sorry to have trespassed, Mr Richardson," I say again. "I didn't mean to cause any trouble."

"None of the problems here are your fault, Nell," said Josh. "You made an innocent mistake and it's hardly fair to blame you for any trouble here. Isn't that right, Dad?"

Martin Richardson's eyes slide away.

"I suppose not. I just saw her and I thought …"

His voice tails off and an awkward silence descends. We all know exactly what he thought when he saw me. Stereotyping is alive and kicking in this farmyard.

"Anyway, I apologise for losing my temper," he says. "Still, you are trespassing on private land. There's a sign on the gate."

"I'm so sorry. I didn't see it. I was so excited about seeing the well because I think my grandparents may have lived here once. During the war. I found this picture and I think it's here."

I hold out the photo. I may as well see my mission through before I get thrown off the property or arrested.

"It's definitely this farmhouse and the well. It's changed a bit, though," says Josh once he's examined the image.

"It bloody well should have done, the amount of money I've poured into the place," grumbles his father. He looks at the picture more closely. "Hey! That's the dog!"

"What dog?" I ask.

"The one I've seen here. A black spaniel. Bloody menace!"

"Dad, of course it isn't," says Josh, exasperated. "That picture's over half a century old. It can't possibly be the same dog."

"Hmm," says Martin. He knows he's wrong, but the expression on his face suggests he's disconcerted and he changes the subject swiftly. "So, who's the girl? Your grandmother?"

Josh glances from me to the picture.

"I can see a resemblance. She's a very pretty girl."

I feel a little glow of pride for this unknown young woman. When I feel Josh's green eyes sweep over me, something else I can't quite pinpoint ripples across my skin.

"The thing is, I've no idea who she is. My father died recently and I found a few old pictures when I was clearing his belongings. There was one of a young GI, a postcard of the village and this photo. Dad was adopted, so I thought finding the well might be a link to something I could trace to find out more about his birth family. I can see now it was a stupid idea."

I feel deflated. My idea of coming here and finding out about my past was naïve and little more than a dream. I was always going to find a dead end, because the laughing girl was here a lifetime ago. She's no more present now than at the moment in time when the camera shutter clicked.

"This is a good starting point," Josh Richardson tells me. "And I'm really sorry to hear about your father. That must have been tough."

I slide the picture back into my bag.

"Yes. It was. Look, thanks for your time. I'll leave you in peace now."

"Don't go, Nell," he says quickly. "The least we can do is show you around and offer you a cold drink. We don't want it said in the village that the Richardsons don't know how to conduct themselves, do we, Dad? Not when we need the parish council on side if we're to get any more planning through."

I'm impressed. Josh Richardson may be calm and measured, but he's sharp, too, and he certainly knows his father. Cornered, Martin Richardson nods his head.

"Yes, yes, show her around if you must. I've got to get on. I need to see that bloody woman again about her trees. They're ruining our views. And I saw her bloody dog was here again."

"She doesn't have a dog, Dad," says Josh wearily.

"Well, somebody does. Get it sorted, Josh, and manage the damn project. It's what I'm paying you for."

"I'm so sorry about him," Josh sighs once his father's stomped off to the far end of the site. "Dad had no right to say what he did to you. All the messing with the well must have really unnerved him. It's only been going on for a few days but he's really wobbled – as you saw."

"I can understand why he might have thought it was me. Please don't feel bad. I ought to have contacted you first and asked to see the well rather than just turning up."

"I'm glad you did – turn up, I mean," Josh says. He looks away quickly, suddenly fascinated by the inside of his hard hat. "You're here now, and the least I can do is show you the well. You may be disappointed, though, because it doesn't look like much. Watch your footing. It's a bit uneven."

He places his hand on my elbow and guides me over the rutted earth. Without the presence of Martin Richardson, my knots of anxiety unravel. It may be my imagination but I hear birdsong now, and even the sky seems bluer. There's an energy here and something is calling to me. I can't explain this at all, and it makes no sense, but I know it.

There *is* a link here. But what to?

The well is, as Josh has already warned me, not much to look at. There's nothing to suggest it's a holy spot or anything other than an average well in an average farmyard. There's a low wall around it, no more than three feet high, and the top is sealed by a crude wooden cover. The past slips over the present and I see the scene as it was – the sunshine, the dog and the laughing girl – before they fade away and I'm standing in a building site once more.

"The plan is to extend the kitchen," Josh explains, pointing at the far wall of the old building. "This section of the yard will become a big dining area and the well's going to be the star feature. It should look stunning."

"Can I look into it?" I have a sudden longing to peer into the dark drop.

"I'm afraid not. The cover's been nailed down in case our vandals come by to pull it off again."

"Do you think they will?"

"No, not with this many nails. They'll lose interest in winding Dad up when it gets tricky."

Taking the well lid off seems a strange thing to do to me. It makes no sense at all.

"Wouldn't it be easier to pinch tools or move things? Taking the lid off the well is an effort. What point could it make?"

"I can't think what else it could be," Josh doesn't sound certain. He shrugs. "Hey, this is a small place and the locals can get funny about incomers rocking up and changing things. Maybe it's their way of saying the well still belongs to them? To be honest, I wish Dad would leave the well alone, but he's a man who won't be told."

"I can imagine," I say.

He turns his hard hat over and over in his hands and a small frown creases the place between his eyebrows.

"Dad's determined this development will be a big success. He wants to show everyone around here that he calls the shots. That's how he runs things and he's not going to back down, I promise you. He's a property developer. Have you come across Richardson's?"

Everyone has heard of Richardson's; their new build housing developments are mushrooming on brownfield sites everywhere, and some of my old school friends have purchased small semis under shared ownership schemes. The thin walls and small gardens of their homes are a world apart from Cornish farmhouses remodelled with glass and steel, and boasting feature wells in large kitchens.

"So you work for him?"

I'm being nosey but I can't help it. Josh Richardson is so different to his father; although I've known him less than a quarter of an hour, he strikes me as old-fashioned and kind and true. A chivalrous knight who prizes truth and honour above money and status, not somebody I would have classed as a ruthless property developer.

Oh dear. Now who's stereotyping?

"It's a long story and I won't bore you with it. The short version is I'm project managing here while he winds things up in London. The problem is, he's set his sights on the place next door. Dad wants the big house, the sea views, the land – the whole deal. This project is really to make sure he has access to the entire area if, or when, it happens."

"Your father wants to buy Pencallyn House?"

"You know it?"

"Yes! Of course! *Mysterious Garden!"*

He beams at me. "You know the book!"

"I read it as a child but I don't really remember the story," I admit. "I remember pictures of gardens, though, and a sundial. They're based on the house, aren't they?"

"That's right. Pencallyn House has an incredible garden, although it's all but lost now. I'd love to restore it. That would be like waking Sleeping Beauty." He flushes. "I can't believe I just said that out loud! You must have magic powers, Nell. The restoration of Pencallyn garden's a cherished dream of mine because I love gardening and garden history. It's a Holy Grail of horticultural archaeology."

"It's good to have dreams," I say. "And yours sounds like a great one."

"I'm not sure my father would agree. Not high-powered enough for him, I'm afraid, but it's something to dream about. Estella Kellow's been kind enough to let me explore the grounds when I have a spare moment. It's all there waiting to be awoken, and I hope to God my father never gets his hands on the place. He'd bulldoze the lot for car parking and executive estates."

"You know Estella Kellow?" I'm excited by this stroke of luck. "I was wondering if she might be able to help me with my research?"

"I do, yes. Dad was a bit *forceful* when he went to Estella with an offer he thought she couldn't refuse. I had to scoot over and make amends." He flashes me a wry grin. "That probably surprises you?"

"Doesn't sound like your father to me," I deadpan, and Josh chuckles.

"I think you have the measure of him. Anyway, I got chatting with Estella and she's absolutely fascinating. The things she must have seen in her lifetime, hey? So now I help her out a bit with some gardening and a few chores." He places his finger on his lips and winks. "Top secret, of course! In return she lets me loose in her grounds and tells me what she remembers about the garden."

"Would she remember anything about when the Americans were here in the forties?"

"I expect so, but she can get muddled at times," he warns. "I could ask her if she'd like to talk about it."

"Would you? Thanks! I'd really appreciate it."

We smile at each other. The yard is shadowed by the late afternoon sun. The well casts a long shadow across the ground and I shiver. It feels melancholy.

"Cold?" Josh asks.

I rub my arms, unable to find the right words.

"No."

His eyes are trained on my face. "Uneasy? This place exudes something I can't quite put my finger on. Not unpleasant exactly but it's watchful, isn't it? And sad."

He's right. It is.

"My mum doesn't like it here," Josh confides, "which is a terrible shame because she loves Cornwall. She doesn't like being here on her own. She says it makes her uneasy."

"What does your father say?"

"He says she's being ridiculous. Dad can't feel the atmosphere. He's not the sensitive kind. He thinks she feels gloomy because of the overgrown trees next door, so his solution is to bully Estella into felling them to let in more light and a sea view."

"And will she?"

"I'll let you answer that question once you've met Estella but Dad may have met his match this time!" Josh's mobile trills and he pulls a face. "And right on cue, here he is. Excuse me a moment, Nell."

While Josh steps away to take the call, I study the well. It looks so ordinary, the kind of simple structure seen in farmyards across the country, and yet there's something watchful about it. Perhaps echoes of the pagan past still tremble in the air even if the original purpose is long forgotten? I brush my fingers against the rough bricks and despite the sunshine they're cool to the touch. My hand recoils. I'm not superstitious at all but something deep inside of me is shouting out in alarm. Unsettled, I step away and wait for Josh.

"I'd better go and row with the other galley slaves," he says, once he's ended the call. "It's been nice to meet you, Nell."

"It's been nice to meet you too," I reply. As he shakes my hand, I feel a fizz of something unexpected and I see from the surprise in his eyes that he feels it too. I pull away sharply because this is something I haven't asked for. A complication I do not need.

"I'll let you know about Estella," he says, as we regard each other rather awkwardly. "You're staying in the village, right?"

"I'm at The Pilchards for a week."

"Well, don't believe a word Toby says, don't let Davey fleece you for drinks and avoid the pub quiz at all costs! I'll catch you soon."

I feel Josh's gaze follow me back to the gate but I don't turn around. I daren't. I'm not quite sure what to do with the way being near this man, a total stranger, is making me feel.

I need space to think. To rationalise. To recover.

My return walk is downhill and far less eventful. Whether it's exhaustion after a long journey, or the heat or the tension of my encounter with Martin

Richardson, I'm not sure, but by the time I arrive at the pub my head is pounding. I can't face the bar or food but instead let myself into my room where I turn the key in the lock, draw the curtains and crumple onto my bed.

When I wake, it's pitch black. I'm roused by my own cries of fright and my heart is galloping. Fragments of a dream float before my vision, but I can't piece them together fast enough and they fade before I can make any sense of them. There was the darkness of water, a floating moon and a long, dark drop.

The well. I was dreaming about the well.

I click the bedside lamp on and scoop up my satchel, pulling out the pictures and studying them again while my headache flutters at my temples. If the GI was my grandfather, who was the girl? Why did my father have her picture? What *is* the link between them?

I sit with my knees hugged tightly against my chest. My hand curls around the crucifix and its solid weight calms me. I am safe with it. Protected. Loved.

As slowly as an invalid, I walk to the window and look out, expecting to see a full moon, but it's a dark night and indigo clouds have rolled in, obscuring the stars and cloaking the village in darkness. All I can make out is the thick line of trees which encircle the mysterious garden and shield its elderly guardian. Somewhere within that garden I know I will find the answer to my questions, and tomorrow I will walk to Pencallyn House.

Something tells me Estella Kellow holds the key to the mystery.

CHAPTER 12

Estella
The Present

Estella was sitting in the garden enjoying the sensation of the sunshine warming her skin when Martin Richardson arrived. She sighed, irritated at having her peace and quiet interrupted. He really was a ghastly individual, given to hollering as though she was both deaf and stupid; having to make small talk with him seemed a terrible waste of a beautiful summer morning. Estella didn't claim to have psychic powers but she suspected she wouldn't see another August. For a moment she considered pretending to be asleep but men like Martin seldom gave up and she would only be putting off the inevitable. Best get it over with.

"Good morning, Miss Kellow," Martin Richardson barked. His face was sweating with the exertion of walking the long way around from the farm, and he fanned himself with his tweed cap. "It's a warm one again."

"It certainly is," Estella replied, shading her eyes as she attempted to judge what kind of mood he was in. Would he be all sweetness and light, with another ten thousand added to his offer for Pencallyn House, before unleashing veiled threats and impatience when she turned him down? Men like Martin were so predictable; they were charm personified until thwarted. Her father had been cast from the same mould – and so had another, the one with eyes that had glittered like sunbeams bouncing from ice.

"I hope you don't mind me wandering out here to find you? Kelly said you were on the terrace," Martin Richardson boomed, sitting down without being invited. "Phew! Isn't it a bit much for you, this heat?"

"I enjoy it," Estella said mildly. "When you're my age you feel the cold more."

"It must be chilly in that house without proper central heating. I don't know how you survive. The winters down here are so damp and miserable. Wouldn't you be better off in the warm?"

Estella knew from Josh that his parents spent the colder months at their villa in Spain. Not for them bowls catching leaks and asthmatic heaters bravely wheezing out dusty gusts of lukewarm air.

"Don't you fret about that, my dear. We Cornish are a tough bunch and it'll take more than a bit of mizzle and sea fog to carry me off," she said, crossing her fingers under the table because nothing would be more annoying than to be proven wrong. Obviously dying of pneumonia wouldn't be much fun, but even worse than death would be knowing Martin Richardson was drinking sangria and saying he'd warned the silly old girl she needed to live somewhere warm. If for no better reason than annoying him, Estella was determined to stay alive for as long as possible.

"Glad to hear it," Martin Richardson said, although he looked as though he felt the polar opposite. "Just showing neighbourly concern."

Estella smiled. They both knew this was nonsense but it was the standard opening move in their game of social chess. He'd no doubt make an attack in a moment which she would counter and eventually he would depart, checkmated and belligerent.

"So, to what do I owe the pleasure of this visit?" she asked.

"Your trees need cutting down, Miss Kellow."

"They do? Who has told you that? I thought they were perfectly healthy."

"I'm sure they are but they are obscuring my view and cutting out the light, as I've mentioned before. They need to be felled." Martin crossed an ankle over his knee and gave her a determined look. "I'll pay. I have a great team of tree surgeons at my disposal. The best."

"How lovely," said Estella. She paused, enjoying knowing he was having to wait for her answer. Making a man like this wait for her was a small revenge on her father but she was enjoying her moment. How Reginald Kellow had made poor Violet weep, and how many times had Estella sat quietly in the schoolroom because his work was important and couldn't be disturbed? Evie said he was a bully, just like her own pa.

"So, shall I send my team round? Get it all taken care of for you?"

The demand plucked Estella from the past and for a second it was disorientating to find herself sitting at a table opposite Martin Richardson.

"Get what taken care of?"

Irritation flared in his eyes but he pushed it away hastily. Estella reluctantly admired his composure. She knew Martin longed to throttle her.

"The trees, Miss Kellow," he hollered. "The ones obscuring my sea view. I'll have my team take care of it, shall I? They're very good. The best!"

Ah, yes. The trees. The same towering trees which blotted out her own sea view. Estella rather liked them this way. Her brother had died somewhere above that stretch of water, his gallant little Spitfire tumbling down in a plume of smoke and flames. It lay on the seabed and Alex's bones were pearl white now, only known to the sea creatures who visited his resting place. No, she would keep her trees as they were.

"I'm quite sure your men are excellent, Mr Richardson, but as any local tree surgeon will tell you, all trees here have preservation orders. What's more, we're in a conservation area so felling them requires special permission."

Checkmate. Estella sat back in her seat and waited for his response. Was it going to fury or would he have another tactic up his Barbour-shirted sleeve?

Martin nodded. He didn't seem at all perturbed.

"Yes, I'm aware of the restrictions. That's why I've a proposition for you, and one I think could be mutually beneficial."

Estella didn't say a word. What on earth did he think she could possibly need at her age?

"I thought I could buy the land that divides our two properties. Maybe two acres?" He leaned forward eagerly. "It's a no-brainer. The land's wild, and I'll pay you good money for it too. How does thirty thousand sound? That way the legalities of felling trees are my problem, not yours, and trust me, it will be fine. I know people on the council who can make things happen."

Estella didn't doubt this for a moment. Men like Martin Richardson always knew the right palms to grease. Her father would have liked him immensely, and this was another reason why she would never do business with him.

"It's generous offer but I'll have to decline," she said.

"Isn't the money enough? Name your price. What do you want?"

What did she want? Where to start? Estella thought about telling him how she longed for faces she could no longer recall and how much she wanted to stop tripping over the cracks in her mind but he wouldn't understand.

"When you're my age you'll understand the things you really want can't be bought."

"Such as? Tell me what you want. I'll sort it."

She smiled and shook her head.

"You'll know one day. Thank you for your offer, Mr Richardson, but I don't wish to sell any of my land or chop down my trees. I'm more than happy with things as they stand."

Martin looked as though he was about to argue but Kelly joined them, bearing a tea tray, and began to set out cups and saucers on the wicker table.

"May I offer you some refreshments?" Estella asked politely as Kelly poured her a cup. She knew he would sooner drink hemlock, but it was fun to watch him forced to be civil when she knew he wanted to strangle her.

Martin Richardson rose to his feet, scowling.

"No, thank you. I just want those bloody trees topped. I'll write to the council. We'll see what they have to say about it."

"Do so by all means," said Estella mildly. "That's enough, thank you, Kelly dear. Have we any biscuits?"

"And you can keep that bloody dog of yours off my land too," Martin Richardson added, ramming his cap onto his grey head. "I'm sick of the bloody thing."

Estella looked up sharply. "Dog?"

"Your black spaniel. It's always there. If I see it again, I'll call the warden. Or shoot the damn thing."

"Miss Kellow hasn't got a dog," Estella heard Kelly say, but her voice sounded all echoey and distorted, as though it was coming from a long way away. "You don't have a dog, do you, Miss Kellow? Miss Kellow?"

A huge crevasse had opened in Estella's mind but this time there was no warning. One moment her feet were on firm soil, the next she was plummeting downwards.

"I'll be going, but you haven't heard the last of this," Martin snarled. But Estella, looking around frantically, barely registered his presence.

"Poppet!" she called. "Poppet! Where are you? Where did you go? Come back!"

"Miss Kellow? Estella?

The distant voice came from a place she didn't recognise. Blinking, Estella looked up at a sweet-faced young woman who was crouching beside her. Had she seen the spaniel?

"I can't find Poppet," Estella whispered. "I think he's killed her."

"Estella, you're scaring me," said the girl. "Who's Poppet?"

"My dog!" Estella's voice rose. "He's killed her! I know he has!"

"You killed her dog?" The young woman was asking a man, her voice ringing with shock. He was red-faced and old, and Estella didn't recognise him either, and when he spoke there was no languid drawl in his voice. She was relieved. At least this wasn't Hamilton.

"I've done nothing of the kind," the man cried. "She's muddled. I'm sorry I mentioned the damn thing."

"So am I," said the young woman. "Look how upset she is."

Estella blotted her eyes with her sleeve.

"He didn't kill my dog. I think Hamilton did."

A face, proud and aloof, flickered through her mind. Then he was gone and she was glad, as glad now as she'd been when she'd learned he'd perished on the Normandy beaches.

"Who's Hamilton?" asked the girl gently. As she placed her hand on Estella's arm, her name swam through the years, and like one inhaling oxygen after too long under water, Estella gulped the present deep into her lungs. Kelly. This was Kelly, Kelly her helper, and the belligerent man wasn't Hamilton Mason but the new neighbour, Martin somebody or other.

"Nobody you need to worry about, dear, he's long gone," she said. "Oh! I do feel shaky. May I have some water?"

"Come inside and I'll fetch you some," said Kelly, helping her up. "It's cooler in there too. I don't think the heat helps you."

"I'll talk to you later about the trees," called the man, but Estella scarcely heard him. She was still mourning the brave little dog who'd vanished over seventy-five years ago.

The kitchen was cool, and seated at the table and sipping iced water, Estella felt better. Time had stopped spinning, and the loss of Poppet had retreated into the shadows where it would always be a sad memory but one which lacked the bite of immediacy.

Kelly slipped into the seat opposite. "How are you feeling? You've stopped shaking, thank God. What a fright you gave me."

"I think the heat came over me," Estella fibbed.

"More likely it was Martin Richardson, upsetting you by throwing his weight around," said Kelly. "What an arse, 'scuse my language! You should hear some of the stories Darren tells about him. I swear Josh must be adopted."

Estella laughed. "But Sarah Richardson's a lovely lady. She was very kind to me the other day. Josh must take after her."

"I feel sorry for her being married to Martin," said Kelly. "Josh must be mad working for his dad. Why would he put up with that?"

Estella knew exactly why Josh worked for Martin. He'd told her in confidence and she understood. Bullying fathers cast long shadows.

"I'm sure he has his reasons," was all she said.

Kelly twiddled one of her gold hoop earrings. "Down the village, we all feel sorry for Sarah and Josh, and not just because of Martin either. It can't be much fun living at the farm. It's a weird place."

"Is it?" Estella was surprised. She'd always loved the old farmhouse. Evie had made up all kinds of games there. During the war they'd enjoyed the run of the place, playing with Violet's Box Brownie camera, and later on attempting to smoke the Camel cigarettes the Americans gave out so freely.

Kelly nodded. "Darren says it has a really creepy atmosphere."

"It used to be such a peaceful place. It belonged to my family in the thirties and I played there as a girl," Estella recalled. "My father sold it after the war. He sold a lot of land then, because he'd run out of money."

"None of the boys like working there after dusk. You wouldn't catch me there after dark either– unless Josh was about. That would be a different story! He's lush, isn't he?"

"I think I'm far too old to be the judge of that!"

Kelly grinned. "You're never too old to appreciate God's creation, Miss Kellow! But don't tell Darren I said so. He gets well jel."

Jealousy was the emotion Estella feared the most. Jealousy was dark and dangerous. Its invisible tentacles wrapped themselves around your soul, their grip tightening until hope and joy and love were strangled. Evie had been the jealous kind. And Hamilton …

While Kelly set about her tasks in the kitchen Estella thought about Pencallyn Farm. Perhaps Kelly was right about the place having a strange atmosphere? A memory flickered like the bright fin of koi carp in the deep garden pools her father used to prize, but it dived back into the depths as soon as she grasped for it, leaving Estella with scattered images of livid scarlet scratches on white skin, screams in the night and a missing dog.

Whose memories were these? Hers? Evie's? Frustrated, Estella shook her head as though trying to shake them loose, but to no avail; the fragments didn't settle into any form that made meaning and the fog was swirling in once again. How long would it be before they were obscured for ever? The thought made her stomach churn, for who was Estella Kellow if she didn't remember the past? What about the sleeper in the churchyard? Who would check they were all right and whisper words of love? Estella gripped the edge of the table tightly. Nobody would know about the special place. She had to tell somebody the truth, but who? Who would have the time to listen and follow her down blind alleys, or wait for her when she fell through the trapdoors in her mind?

Who would want to hear about two little girls and the promise they had made a lifetime ago?

Estella supposed the literary world might be interested. The truth behind *Mysterious Garden* would spark interest in the book and shift a few more copies, but she had never written it in order to spill her secrets to the world. Estella longed to tell her tale to somebody who wanted to hear it and who might understand. There wasn't long left and this was her confession – it *had* to be heard.

She needed absolution and she would need it soon.

Leaning heavily on her walking stick, Estella made her slow progress from the kitchen table to the sink where today's washing up was waiting. It was better for her to be occupied than to be mired in regrets for things she couldn't change. Hot water, the chink of china and mindless repetition were a balm to her at times like this, and so she filled the sink and squirted in thick green washing-up liquid until bubbles foamed over the top of the plastic bowl. She was slowly drying a plate when she heard voices and, looking up out of the open window, Estella spotted Kelly talking to a young woman in the yard. Their heads were close together as they chatted, Kelly's bright blonde one with its inch of dark roots a contrast to the glossy head of ebony hair beside it.

Dark ebony hair with the sheen of a magpie's wing …

Impossible!

The plate slipped from her fingers and shattered on the floor but Estella barely noticed. Even the fire in her chest didn't matter. She was seventeen again and Evie was home! She was back at last!

"Evie!" she cried. "Oh Evie! You came back after all! I'm coming! I'm coming! Wait for me!"

But in her haste to reach the kitchen door, Estella failed to notice the floor was slick with soapy water. Her walking stick shot out from beneath her and, unbalanced, she tumbled onto the hard floor with such force her breath was punched from her body and her hip smashed into the flagstones, shattering like eggshell.

Then all the lights went out.

CHAPTER 13

Nell
The Present

I sit on the hard seat, my hands wrapped around a cup of scalding coffee, watching the tide of medical staff ebb and flow. Every few moments a buzzer sounds and I jump, even though I've been listening to this sound for over an hour. Surely a doctor will come along in a minute and give us some news?

I gnaw the skin at the side of my thumbnail. Hospitals make me nervous. One whiff of the antiseptic smell bungees me back to a time I'd rather forget. Cold gel on my tummy. A sharp breath. Above me the eyes of the sonographer and my husband meeting in a sad gaze of understanding …

I push the memory down, squeezing the cup so tightly coffee slops onto my bare legs. Burning liquid on skin is a welcome distraction, and I busy myself mopping the spill with a tissue retrieved from the depths of Kelly's giant handbag.

"I always carry loads. You have to be prepared for all kinds of accidents when you've got kids," she tells me. "I carry wet wipes. Plasters. Calpol sachets. I've even got a crochet hook in case our Kyle wedges something up his nose. He's a bugger for that."

"I promise that's not in my repertoire. Just third degree burns and scaring the wits out of old ladies," I say.

"You didn't scare the wits out of her, Nell! She slipped on the wet floor. I've lost count of the times I've told her not to wash up. Estella sploshes water everywhere because she can't see so well. It was an accident waiting to happen."

But I'm not convinced. Although the paramedics said Estella Kellow's walking stick had slipped on the tiles I think Miss Kellow had mistaken me for somebody else, and in her haste to greet her she'd lost her balance. So I unwittingly made an old lady's confusion a hundred times worse, and now she's in hospital with a broken hip. This is all my fault.

I bite back tears. What if she dies? Old people break their hips and die all the time, don't they? If only I'd waited for Josh to introduce us. If only I hadn't been in such a hurry to meet her. If only. If only. If only. The two bleakest words in the English language.

The day had begun with such promise. I'd been full of excitement as I'd walked along the drive to Pencallyn House and buoyed by the chance, no matter how slim, that somebody might remember my grandparents. The cloudless blue sky and warm sunshine filled me with optimism, and it felt wonderful to shake off the residue of my unsettling dreams with a brisk walk. My stomach was stuffed full of Jen's cooked breakfast, fresh air filled my lungs and I felt certain I was just a conversation away from finding more out about my family. Even Pencallyn's neglected garden seemed romantically pastoral on such a bright morning, and when I rounded the final curve in the drive the reveal of the impressive house made me gasp.

A young woman was pegging out washing in the garden. Her name was Kelly and she was Miss Kellow's home help, she said, once I'd given her an explanation for my visit. I played the author card because it had seemed like a good link and Kelly was certain Estella would love chatting to a fellow writer.

"She loves books," Kelly confided as we crossed a courtyard flanked by neat raised vegetable beds. "She's very well read and I haven't a clue what she's on about half the time. There's hardly time to go to the loo at my place, never mind read a book! You'll be a breath of fresh air for her and I'm sure there's lots she can tell you about the war too. Estella can get a bit muddled, though, so don't be surprised if she doesn't make sense."

"If she can tell me anything at all I'll be really grateful," I replied. "And I'm a big fan of *Mysterious Garden*."

Kelly screwed up her freckled nose.

"Don't mention that, whatever you do. She's dead funny about it and never talks about the book. Like I say, she can be quite odd and what she says doesn't always make sense, poor old soul. I'd stick to talking about the war, if I were you."

"You're sure it's OK to see her? Josh Richardson said he'd introduce me, but it was such a glorious day for a walk and I so wanted to meet her. The truth is I can't wait."

Kelly gave me a sideways look. "So, you've met Josh, have you? And what did you think of him?"

"I thought he was nice," I replied primly, sounding like a Jane Austen heroine. 'Nice' was such a bland adjective. It certainly didn't do Josh Richardson justice. Compelling? Beautiful? Haunting? Sexy? All the above?

"*Nice*? Sex on a stick more like!" Kelly cackled. "Yes, Josh is very *nice*. He does a lot to help Estella out, and he's easy on the eye too! Anyway, come on in and meet Estella. I'll put the kettle on and —".

Her words were interrupted by a shout of 'Evie! Oh Evie!' and some words they couldn't catch, then a loud crash and a wail of distress.

"Oh shit," Kelly said. "She's fallen over."

We sprinted across the yard and Kelly yanked the back door open. Inside, an elderly lady was sprawled on the kitchen floor and groaning. Her leg was twisted at an angle which made me feel quite ill.

"Estella!" Kelly flew across the room.

"Evie," gasped Estella Kellow. Her face was a rictus of pain. "Evie. Where are you? Where did you go?"

Kelly dropped to her knees amongst broken crockery and pools of water. She brushed wisps of white hair from the old lady's face.

"Estella? It's me, Kelly. Estella, can you hear me?"

Eyes, the same soft blue as rain-washed skies, opened slowly and settled on me. She looked furious.

"You're not Evie! Where's Evie? What have you done with her? Where did she go?"

"Who's Evie? Can I fetch her?" I asked helplessly.

"God only knows who she is," said Kelly. "Must be somebody from years ago. Estella's always on about her. Jesus. I think her hip's broken. We need to call an ambulance. Do you have a phone on you?"

I passed her my iPhone and Kelly called the emergency services, warning them access to the house was difficult for anything other than a four by four and suggesting the air ambulance was scrambled. When it arrived, Estella became terribly agitated by the sound of the helicopter, calling for Evie while the paramedics attended to her. Lines were soon in, painkillers administered and Estella was lifted onto a stretcher, all the time calling for the mysterious Evie.

"Help me get him out, Evie!" she shouted. "We can't leave him. He's a boy. For God's sake, Evie! Help me!"

"Which one of you is Evie?" asked a paramedic, looking up from his patient. "If Evie comes with her, she might be less distressed. Old folk can be frightened at the thought of going in the air ambulance, especially if they've never flown."

Estella was still shouting to the invisible Evie and imploring her to help. She was decades away, but to me she seemed angry rather than afraid and I doubted she even knew the air ambulance was present. The more closely I listened, the more it seemed she was pleading for someone's life while the mysterious Evie refused to help.

Kelly shook her head. "I don't know who Evie is. Miss Kellow's in the early stages of dementia and she can get confused."

The paramedic straightened up. "Poor old soul. Well, she's had enough pain relief and we're good to go. One of you'd better come with her."

Kelly grabbed a bag from the kitchen table and pulled out a bunch of keys which she thrust at me. "Sorry to land this on you, Nell, but would you be able to drive my truck to Calmouth General and meet me there? And lock the house? It's the big brass key in the back door. Shove it under the plant pot."

"Of course," I said. I felt terrible because I was sure my arrival had upset Estella Kellow. Whoever the mysterious Evie was, the old lady had been convinced I was her and this confusion was the catalyst for her fall. How I wished I hadn't been in such a hurry to meet her.

Once Estella and Kelly departed in a whir of blades and ripple of grass, the air ambulance circling high above the house before veering to the left and in the direction of the town, I was alone in the kitchen. The old house felt still and shadowy and as though it was swallowing me whole. Trying to shake off this notion, I found a dustpan and brush beneath the sink and busied myself sweeping up the broken plates before locking up and hiding the key.

Kelly's Ford Ranger was parked at the far end of the yard beside what must have once been stables. I clambered in and rested my head on the steering wheel for a moment. The interior was littered with old McDonald's boxes, snapped crayons and empty boxes of fruit juice. A vomit-yellow teddy bear swung from the rear-view mirror. When I started the engine, 'Let It Go' belted out at full volume.

Let it go. Seriously? Was this a message from the universe? Should I let my search go? It hadn't got off to a great start. Maybe it was better to leave the past firmly in the past. If Dad had wanted me to uncover our family history, wouldn't he have said something to that effect? Look what I'd achieved today by meddling in things that maybe should be left in the past. I bit back tears because it was too late now. I didn't think I could turn back even if I wanted to.

By the time I arrived at the hospital and managed to park, Kelly was busy working her way through a pile of *OK!* magazines in A and E. I found a seat next to her and returned the car keys. Then we waited. The doctors suspected a broken hip and Estella was in X Ray. It was going to be a long day. I wouldn't have any skin left on my fingers by nightfall.

"Hey look at this!" Kelly says now, shoving her latest celebrity magazine under my nose. "You look a bit like her. Ever thought about being a lookalike?"

"Meghan Markle? In my dreams! And no, I can't say it's crossed my mind."

"I'd do it like a shot if I looked like anyone decent," Kelly says. "Daz thinks I look a bit like Baby Spice but nobody wants her any more, do they?"

With Kelly's blonde hair pulled into a high ponytail, baggy tracksuit bottoms and bright white trainers I guess there is a passing resemblance, but she isn't expecting an answer.

"I feel awful about this," I say for the hundredth time. "If I hadn't turned up and given Estella a shock, she'd be fine."

Kelly gives me a stern look over the top of *OK!*

"Honestly, it was only a matter of time before something like this happened. Social Services have been worried about Estella for ages. They think she ought to be in a home or have full time carers. This isn't your fault, Nell."

But Kelly hadn't seen the way Estella Kellow had looked at me when she had opened her eyes. She genuinely thought I was somebody else and she recognised me. Do I look like my grandmother? Does this mean Estella Kellow knew her?

"She thought she knew me and she got really agitated."

"Estella thinks all kinds of things these days and I wouldn't read anything into it. It's a shame, poor old soul. She gets so upset when she can't remember stuff."

I pluck the photograph of the young GI from my bag. "I was going to ask her if she'd ever seen him."

"If she had, I bet she'd remember! Is he your granddad?"

"His picture was with my dad's stuff, so maybe."

"Did your dad look like him?"

"I think so, but it might be wishful thinking."

She looks at me and then back at the picture.

"He's your granddad, all right. You have his smile and his looks!"

I'm thrilled to have my hopes spoken out loud. "Thank you. I'm really hoping he is."

"I hope our Kyle takes after me. Daz had to have his ears pinned when he was fifteen. 'FA Cup' we called him at school. Anyway, no problems with anyone taking after your hot grandpa. Do you think Estella knew him?"

"No, that's too much of a long shot. I'm hoping she might have seen him about the village or heard rumours about a girl who was involved with a black GI. A servant or a land girl who fell pregnant? It would have been a big deal back then."

Kelly looks thoughtful. "Trust me, it would still be a big deal for some folk. Estella would definitely tell you so. I think her father had a lot to say about it."

I already know that Reginald Kellow was notorious for writing to Anthony Eden requesting that no black Americans were stationed in his constituency. He sounded just the kind of bigot who'd throw a servant out for being involved with a black American soldier. Perhaps Evie was a maid at Pencallyn House and this is what happened?

"Does Estella ever talk about her father?"

"No, but there wasn't much love lost from what little I know. I think he came to a sticky end. Didn't he drown himself in the fishpond when he lost all the money? It was something grisly. With a father like that no wonder Estella never got married. That's probably how she's made it into her nineties. Running after men wears women out. My Darren's blooming hard work. Worse than kids, men, aren't they?"

And Kelly is off on a rant about Darren's faults. It's a scarily long list, and I may be here some time. She's right in the middle of a detailed description of the state he leaves the toilet in when a woman with a stethoscope slung around her neck joins us.

"Hello, I'm Doctor Norris. Are you with Estella Kellow?"

"I'm her home help," Kelly says, switching seamlessly from Darren's toilet woes into professional mode.

"Is there a next of kin? Or any family?"

"Not that I know of," Kelly replies.

"How about a social worker?"

"Not yet but I guess there will be now."

Doctor Norris nods. "She's broken her hip and she won't be able to go home, so I imagine Social Services will have to intervene."

"Oh God. Estella will freak. She's never left Pencallyn," Kelly says.

"Can we see her?" I ask. It feels important to be at this old lady's bedside. Nobody should be in hospital without somebody beside them. I never left Dad alone when he was so ill there, but I saw plenty of old people who never had a single visitor and it broke my heart to realise how lonely they were.

"I don't see why not," says the doctor. "She may be rather sleepy. She's had a lot of pain relief."

She ushers us into a side room where an air mattress purrs and sighs. A million memories race back; my father'd had one of these at home and, later on, in the hospice too. When at the end we'd switched it off the unaccustomed silence was shocking.

Estella Kellow lies on this mattress, gazing up at the ceiling in a regal style reminiscent of the princess and the pea. Her white hair is swept back and her fine-boned face is as pale as the pillow. When her eyes dart to us they are bright. The clouds of earlier have cleared.

"Oh Kelly, what an utter menace! I seem to have broken my damn hip. You were right – I should have left you to do the washing up. I must have slipped on the wet floor."

"You did," Kelly says, sitting at her bedside. "I was pegging out washing and I heard a dreadful crash."

"I don't remember falling. I thought I saw …" Estella Kellow frowns. "Well, never mind what I thought I saw. I was wrong. The next thing I know, I'm in this place. How did that happen?"

"I had to call the air ambulance. You came here by helicopter!"

"Goodness!" says Estella. "And I missed it? How terribly irritating. I've always wanted to fly. My brother was in the RAF, you know."

"There'll be no flying for a while for you, Miss Kellow," says Dr Norris as she checks a drip. "You've broken your hip, remember?"

Estella throws her an exasperated look. "I know that. I wasn't about to jump into a Spitfire. How long am I going to be in here? How long before I'm able to go home?"

The bed wheezes. The doctor doesn't reply.

"When can I go home?" Estella says again. "It's not a trick question. Anyone care to tell me?"

"It might be a while, Miss K. You'll need to have the hip set and get walking again. Take it easy for a bit, yeah?" Kelly says gently.

"I can't take it easy! And I can't stay in here! I'll never get out again! They'll put me in an old people's home and make me sell Pencallyn to pay for it! Oh, Martin Richardson must be clapping his hands with glee. I need to go home! I have to go home! Please, Kelly! Tell them I need to go home."

"Can I have a word?" Dr Norris says quietly, and Kelly nods.

"Sure. I need to call Darren and let him know what's going on. He'll have to cook tea, and the kids will probably end up in here with food poisoning. Shall I book them in with you?"

Once they've left the room, I step forward and Estella studies me. Her faded eyes are narrowed.

"And who might you be?"

"I'm Nell. Nell Summers."

"And why are you here, Nell Summers?"

I step forward. This could be the only moment I have to ask my questions.

"I'm hoping you'll be able to help find out more about my family. I came to your house today because I wanted to ask you something. Do you remember seeing me there? In the courtyard?"

Estella Kellow blinks.

"Oh. It was you I saw earlier, wasn't it? Before I fell?"

"Yes. I'm sorry if I frightened you. I feel like this is all my fault."

She laughs. "I wasn't frightened, my dear. I was ecstatic! Excited! Thrilled! As for my fall being your fault? Utter nonsense. I slipped on the floor. Everyone kept telling me I would one day, and I should have listened to them."

I decide to take a chance. "Did you think I was Evie?"

Estella Kellow's white brows rise.

"You reminded me of her at a distance, but how could you be Evie? She would be nearly as old as me now. I get confused sometimes, my dear.

Time shuffles itself when you're as old as me."

"Do I look like her?"

She tilts her head. "A little, maybe? Evie never came back, you know. Her room was empty and all her things were gone. She never even left a note. Why would she do that to me? When we were blood sisters? She promised she would never let me down. She broke her vow. Why? Why did she leave when I needed her?"

A sad tear rolls down her cheek and splashes onto the pillow. The loss of Evie, whoever she was, is as painful today as the day it happened. Estella wipes her eyes with the back of her hand.

"I'm so sorry to upset you," I say quietly. "I didn't mean to. I only came to Pencallyn to talk to you."

"It isn't about the book, is it? I don't talk about that."

"No; what I want to talk about has nothing to do with *Mysterious Garden* but it can wait until you feel better."

Eyes as sharp as paper cuts meet mine.

"I think we both know nothing can wait now. I won't get better, Nell Summers. I know what happens when old ladies break their hips. Whatever you need to say, best you say it now."

I hesitate. The hospital bed sighs air and whirs to itself, a constant backing track to our exchange.

"Don't be shy, girl. 'Had we world enough and time, this coyness, lady, were no crime'. I take it you've read Andrew Marvell?"

"Years ago."

"Well then, heed his advice," she says. "Time goes faster than any of us realise."

I swallow. My father had said something similar: 'It goes so quickly, Nell, so quickly. Treasure every moment. Every happy time.'

No. I need to focus on the present.

"Miss Kellow, I wanted to ask what you remember about Pencallyn in the war years."

"That's a huge question," she says. "Everything and nothing, mostly. To paraphrase Dickens, it was the best and worst of times. Mostly the worst, but it had its moments too. Oh yes, it really did. Maybe it was the danger, or perhaps it was because I was so young, but I think we all felt more alive then. I certainly did."

I retrieve the photo from my bag and offer it to her.

"Did you ever see this man during the war?"

Estella Kellow stares at the picture.

"Where did you find this?"

"It was with some belongings of my father's. Did you know him?" I daren't let myself hope that she does.

One gnarled hand reaches out and takes the photograph. The picture trembles in her grasp.

"Oh! How is this possible? It's been over seventy years since I saw this face. I thought he only existed in my memory. I never dreamed I'd see him again. Not in this life, anyway."

My heart is thudding. "You think you know who he is?"

"I don't *think* – I *know*! This is Jacob Miller."

"You knew him?"

"Yes. I knew Jay. How did your father get this photograph?"

"It was with his things. I think this young soldier is my grandfather."

But Estella Kellow dismisses my hopes in an instant.

"Impossible. Jay was nineteen. He didn't have children."

"Nineteen's old enough to have a child. Could he have had a British sweetheart, maybe? A secret romance?"

"No! Absolutely not."

"But if it was a secret love affair? Or a baby no one knew about? Not even him?"

"*I* would have known," says Estella Kellow firmly. Her chin juts out at a determined angle and her tone says she will not be corrected. Not wanting to offend her, I change my line of enquiry.

"Were you friends with him?"

She stares into the distance. Is she looking into the past? I can only see the window, blanked out by a blind, but does she see faces? Long-lost friends?

"I knew him for a while when he was stationed here. Jacob Miller was an army combat medic, and sometimes he would attend dances in case fights broke out. How those American boys liked to fight over the girls! I wrote to Jay's family after the war but they never replied. I imagine they were too ashamed."

"Ashamed? Why?" I glance at the photograph she is still clutching. "He looks like a young man to be proud of."

"Jay Miller was accused of deserting the US military." Estella closes her eyes as though the words pain her. "It was dreadful, and they must have been so hurt and utterly let down. They'd been so proud of him, you see. Jay was going to be a doctor and he had been at university before he enlisted. It was no small thing for somebody from his background to get into medical school back then, but he was such a clever and brave young man. He was going to change the world, he said, one small step at a time."

"And he deserted?"

"So they said," Estella replies quietly. She opens her eyes and now they are full of anger. "The military police insisted that Jay Miller had done a flit from his billet before the troops left for Normandy. None of us ever saw him again and that was the end of it. My dear, you must think I'm very foolish crying about this after all these years, but when you're old the past feels closer than the present. It might have been a long time ago but some things never leave you. For years if I was outside and a low plane flew over, I'd run for cover and wait for the ground to tremble and the heat of the flames. The war changed everything, you see. It changed people and it certainly changed me."

"Sometimes things happen that turn us inside out," I say quietly. "We do our best to pull ourselves back the right way again but we're never quite the same."

"How true. You may be pieced back together but the cracks remain for ever."

I think about the fissures which have split me. The heartbeat that stopped. The dreams which vanished like smoke in the sunshine. The words of comfort I couldn't listen to. Oh yes, those cracks remain. Andy stood on one side of them and I was on the other. When I looked again, the Grand Canyon divided us. No wonder we couldn't cross it.

"How are we doing, Estella? How's the pain?"

A nurse enters the room, towing a trolley filled with all kinds of medical equipment. "Sorry to interrupt, but we need to do some obs, and Miss Kellow has to rest now."

"I'll leave you in peace, Miss Kellow," I say. "Thank you for talking to me."

"Come back tomorrow, Nell," she whispers. "And would you do something for me?"

"Of course I will. Anything."

"Go back to the house and fetch the book by my bedside. Promise me you'll do that for me and come back? There's more I need to tell you, and a story you might like to hear. You do remember what I said about time running out?"

"I do and I'll come back. I'll find your book and I'll come back tomorrow. I promise."

"Don't break your promise, Evie. If you do, terrible things will happen," she warns. "Remember the sundial. Remember what you promised me."

The memory mists have drifted back. Estella Kellow has slipped back into the past and is lost to me. I leave the room, turning over and over in my mind all the things she has told me, trying to fit them together like a jigsaw, if one with pieces missing and no picture to guide me. Is the enigmatic Evie my grandmother? Did she abandon my father because of the shame of Jay Miller's desertion? Is Estella still protecting her? Or am I deflecting my grief with a wild goose chase?

I don't have the answers to these questions, but I feel certain Estella Kellow's story and mine are linked. When I slide my hand into my bag to pull out the pictures and study them once more, I realise Jay Miller's is missing. Estella had it in her hand while we were talking and she must have slipped it under the covers. Caught up in her story, I haven't noticed until now.

Interesting. I wonder what it means that Estella Kellow, having found him once again after all these years, doesn't want to let Jacob Miller out of her sight for a second time?

CHAPTER 14

Estella
The Present

When she was certain the girl with Jay Miller's smile was gone, Estella slid her hand beneath the scratchy sheet. If this was another trick of her age-nibbled mind the pain of a fractured hip would be nothing in comparison to the spearing disappointment. Her tired old heart hadn't felt like this since she was seventeen.

Estella held her breath. Only when her fingertips brushed smooth paper did she exhale.

It was real. This wasn't a cruel trick of old age. There really had been a visit from a girl named Nell and there really was a picture of Jacob Miller tucked beneath the covers.

"Hello, Jay," she said quietly. "I've missed you."

Who was this girl, this Nell Summers? Estella's mind shuttled back and forth as she attempted to weave a narrative. When she had first seen Nell, Estella's immediate thought was that Evie had returned. Seventeen in her heart, Estella had been consumed with excitement and in such haste to greet her friend she'd forgotten she was old and frail.

'More haste less speed,' Tommy would have said, and she would be right.

"If you could see me now, Tommy," Estella sighed. "How you'd shake your head and ask why I never listen!"

Tommy would have blamed Evie for this accident. She'd never taken to the new arrival. Evie Jenkins had been Violet Kellow's pet project, or rather Evie had been a pet project until Violet had grown bored and found something more exciting to occupy her butterfly brain. Then Miss Toms had been landed with Evie.

"She's Little Miss Heathcliff," Tommy had once remarked. "And we all know how *that* story ended."

Had her old governess been right? Was Evie the dark force that had driven them all apart? But she had vanished and, without her there to explain herself, Estella didn't want to be judge and jury. Besides, Estella had loved Evie dearly and felt nothing but joy when she believed she'd glimpsed her earlier on. For a few blissful seconds Estella truly thought Evie had come home to Pencallyn. At last!

Except this wasn't Evie. It was Nell who had visited, and Estella hadn't imagined her. Nell had been at Pencallyn. This much she remembered because her mind was obedient now, returning when called rather than tearing away. Her dear little spaniel had been a terror for that. How many times had Estella trailed through the gardens calling for Poppet? And how many times had an irate farmer or the butcher's boy brought the naughty little dog back in disgrace?

No. Stop. She wasn't thinking about Poppet, or Evie, or any event which had occurred decades before. Estella yanked the leash on her mind and it came to heel. The fog was swirling in more frequently and it was thicker too. Sometimes it stayed for days at a time and when she stumbled back into the present, swathes of time were missing. Time's sands were trickling fast and would soon run out. Estella couldn't afford to waste a moment being confused; her day in the sunshine was almost at an end, the shadows were lengthening and soon it would be night. There was so much to do. So much to be said. So much she needed to uncover.

Estella ran her fingers over the photograph. Although she saw Jay every day in her memory, she'd often wondered whether the passing years had blurred the reality, gilding him with a beauty that hadn't really existed. How wonderful to know he had been just as glorious as she recalled! If anything, her memory had underplayed his perfection, for even with old eyes and a head woolly with pain, Estella could see beyond all doubt Jay Miller had been every bit as handsome as she remembered. The picture didn't show how tall he had been, and being in black and white it didn't convey the true beauty of his eyes. They had been sherry-warm and flecked with amber, and were always lit from within with his good humour and kindness. But this headshot did showcase his strong jaw, infectious smile and the smooth skin of his throat and if it failed to connote the warmth of that flesh to the touch and the delicious scent of his skin, her memory was more than willing to supply the details. As Estella studied the boy in the photograph, she marvelled at how he had remained unchanged while she was not the girl he used to know. He wouldn't recognise her now; of that she was certain.

"Where did you go, Jay?" she whispered. "What happened to you?"

It was wrong of her to have secreted Nell's photo away but Estella had needed to keep Jay's face close. This image was her bridge between the past and the present; whenever the sea fret started to swirl, she would look at it and hold fast to his smile. Jay Miller was the answer, but what were the questions? Oh! Where had they gone?

She would start with the girl called Nell. Somehow, this Nell had acquired Jay's picture and along with it the peculiar notion he was her grandfather, something utterly impossible and a theory Estella would have dismissed outright except for one undeniable fact – Nell had Jay's heart-stopping smile. Half shy and half hopeful, it lit her blue eyes like sunshine through Caribbean waters and danced dimples in her cheeks just as his had done. Like Jay Miller, Nell Summers also possessed a warmth which drew you in and made you feel valued. These similarities were striking but as for her being his granddaughter? That was simply impossible. Jay Miller had been nineteen when he was stationed at Pencallyn and scarcely older when he vanished. There had never been a child in whom Jay lived on, so Nell Summers, whoever she might be, was mistaken.

Was she a distant relative? If so, she could be all that remained of him. Estella pressed the photograph against her heart and although the circumstances couldn't have been worse, with her hip fractured and the mists growing thicker by the hour, she hadn't felt so filled with optimism for a long time. Nell was the person she'd been waiting for all these years, the person who would hear her story and find the answers. Fate had sent Nell to Pencallyn, and just in the nick of time.

Estella Kellow wasn't a fool. She knew what it meant when people her age fractured their hips. She also understood what it meant to undergo surgery at ninety-five. She was elderly and her heart had always been weak, and the likelihood was she would never recover from an operation. She might be old but her hearing was still sound, and when the doctors thought she was asleep Estella was busy listening to their discussions. The lessons of her childhood illness had prepared her well when it came to discovering things doctors would rather patients weren't party to.

"Will we pin the hip?" one of the younger medics had asked

"It's not advisable at this stage." This measured reply came from an older man, her consultant, Estella presumed. "The injury's vascular and the chance of infection's very high if we operate. We'll keep her on strong IV antibiotics and painkillers until she stabilises and re-evaluate the possibility of surgery at that point, if it comes."

Footsteps shuffled away. Estella remained motionless as she assimilated what she had heard. The consultant's meaning was clear; she was going to die. Not of a broken hip necessarily but from some other complication along the line. Her heart maybe? Or perhaps an infection from the internal bleeding? Maybe pneumonia? Didn't old people always get that when they broke their bones? Estella supposed the cause didn't really matter if the result was the same. She shouldn't be surprised, not at her age, but even so you never really thought it would happen, did you? Not even when you were in your nineties. Not to you. How did she feel about dying?

Estella chewed on the idea as she and Evie had once chewed sticks of gum the GIs handed out.

"Got any gum, chum?" The children would ask and they were never disappointed. How generous the Americans had been with their candy, cigarettes and plentiful food. Estella didn't think anything had ever tasted as delicious as tinned peaches and evaporated milk eaten in a secret haven beneath the shy moon. Soft lips on hers, the sweetness of syrupy kisses and the thrill of that first trembling touch. Lying in strong arms, racing hearts in tandem as perspiration cooled on bare skin, Estella had known even then this was a moment she would remember on her deathbed.

And now that time was drawing closer.

"Jay," she whispered. "Are you waiting?"

But there was no reply, only the whir of the air mattress and the beep of the machines. So, it wasn't her time yet. Estella was surprised how glad this made her feel. Was anyone ever ready to leave? Even at ninety-five years old the instinct to live was strong and she felt the tug of resistance. How much harder it must have been for those brave boys with their whole lives ahead of them! What courage it must have taken to board those boats and slip away over the horizon to a place where unknown horrors lay in wait. How did they feel as the ships rose and fell on the roiling sea? Were they resigned? Bitter? Proud? Afraid? Jay Miller had told Estella a soldier felt all these things, but most of all he knew he was doing what he had to do. What it was right to do.

"But you're so far away from home. This isn't your war," she'd said.

"This is everyone's war," was Jay's firm reply. "That's why it matters. I don't want to see what's happening to the Jews happen to my family or to my country – and trust me, the Nazis want to do the same to everyone. Standing up to them is the most important thing anyone can do. It doesn't matter where I'm from, because I'm fighting for more than a place. I'm fighting for what's right."

Were these the words of a man about to desert his post and run away from his duty? Estella had known they weren't, had known Jay Miller never left Pencallyn willingly, but who would have believed her? She was just a girl and, more importantly she was the daughter of Reginald Kellow; nobody would have dared upset her father by listening to what she had to say, let alone acting upon it. The disappearance of one young African-American soldier was of no real concern, and Jay Miller had been swiftly dismissed as a coward and a deserter. The injustice still bit deep.

Now time was running out and there was so much Estella still needed to do. She had to tell her story in case Evie returned. She had to clear Jay's name. And she had to warn her beneficiary of the power contained in promises made at the sundial. Oh yes, that was very important, because you took the old powers lightly at your peril.

Nell Summers would help her, Estella decided. Nell was linked to Jay somehow, and Estella wanted to know more. Fate had sent Nell; there was no other explanation for her arrival. When she returned to the hospital, Estella was determined to fight the pain and the mist in order to plunder the treasure chest of memory. It was time she set the past free, because the faces from the lost years, both loved and feared, were growing closer every day. They wanted their stories told.

Estella tucked the picture beneath her pillow and closed her eyes. Soon it would be time to unlock the rusty gates, push the weeds aside and reveal the secrets of the mysterious garden for the first and the very last time.

[illegible]

CHAPTER 15

Nell
The Present

Kelly drives us back to Pencallyn House. For most of the journey she's on speakerphone to Darren, who's arranged an after work drinking session and isn't impressed with having to come straight home to feed his children. By the time she ends the call my ears are ringing.

"Men!" Kelly says with an eye roll. "As if today hasn't been bad enough, now he decides to throw a wobbler. If I could go back in time I wouldn't say 'yes' when he asked me to the Year 11 disco."

I smile, because Andy and I had got together at a school disco too. If things had worked out differently would I be moaning about him and our kids as well? My throat tightens with loss. Sometimes I really miss the life we nearly had.

"And I know I just work mornings," she continues, grinding the gears merrily as the truck lumbers up a steep Cornish hill, "but what does he expect me to do? Leave Estella and sod off because I only get paid until half twelve? Knob. Tosser."

"Won't Social Services pay you for the extra time?"

"They'd charge me for the helicopter ride, most likely! Anyway, I don't work for Social Services. Estella and me, we have a private arrangement. My mum used to work up at the house too, back along, and my nan did too. There's always been Penders working at the house."

"Your gran might have known the boy in my photo?"

"More than likely. Dolly Pender was a right one for the boys, by all accounts."

Kelly swings the car off the Calmouth road and onto the widened lane to Pencallyn Cove. It's evening and the sun has that maple syrup richness which turns the fields of shorn wheat into a golden buzz cut. It's full of the bounty of life and I hate to think of Estella Kellow shut away in hospital. Glorious evenings like these are summer's last breaths; the parallels are impossible to miss. At least she has Jay Miller's picture to keep her company and, if I never discover anything more, the expression of delight on Estella Kellow's face when she saw him after so long has made every moment of my trip worthwhile.

The return journey takes us past the gates of Pencallyn Farm, pulled closed tonight and sporting a huge Private Property Keep Out! sign. Martin Richardson has upped the ante since I wandered up his drive. I must have really upset him.

"We ought to let Josh Richardson know what's happened," I say, prompted by the memory of my visit.

"He'll know," Kelly promises.

"Will he? How?"

"You're not from round here, are you? Nothing happens in Pencallyn that the bush telegraph misses. Josh's old man's probably already poised to buy Estella's house. At the very least he'll be onto all the estate agents to keep him posted. What a vulture."

Having met Martin Richardson, I'm inclined to agree.

Kelly sighs, turning the truck onto Pencallyn's drive where it bounces along like Tigger. "Maybe it's for the best if somebody like him takes the place off her hands? I can't see Estella coming back."

"Not even once they've set her hip? She could live on the ground floor, couldn't she? And have more help?"

"They can't set her hip. They think it's too risky."

"So how will they mend it?"

"They can't."

"But that means …"

My voice tails off. We both know what it means.

"Yeah. Maybe. But she's tough, Nell. She's been through worse than this. Can you imagine what it's like to lose everyone?"

Oddly, yes. I wake up in the night with a pounding heart because I can imagine exactly this.

"She's always on about this Evie too," Kelly says. "She must really miss her, whoever she was."

"Wasn't Evie her sister?"

"No. Estella Kellow had a brother who died years ago. There's no Evie Kellow. Never was. Estella's always having conversations with people who aren't there and it's been getting worse. Half the time she's talking rubbish. She's started wandering off lately too, so it was only a matter of time before something like this happened." Kelly glances at me and her sweet face is troubled. "Oh, bloody hell. This is all my fault. I should have said something to Social Services but it felt like a betrayal, you know?"

"Yes, I do. I felt exactly like that when I knew my dad wasn't coping. He had cancer, and eventually caring for him at home became too much. I couldn't give him the care he needed. When I called the hospice, I knew I was doing the right thing – but in my heart?" I feel all over again the knife blade in my guts when I'd dialled the number. "I think betrayal was exactly what it felt like."

"I can't win either way," Kelly says bleakly.

"No," I tell her. "You couldn't."

We fall silent as the truck judders along the driveway. Is it my imagination or does the garden seem a more overgrown? Were the shrubs pushing this close to the drive when I left? I don't remember them clawing the paintwork with such tenacity. It's as though the garden is furious we haven't brought Estella home.

Kelly parks the truck and retrieves the door key. I follow her into the kitchen and the house feels wary, as though it's watching us.

"I've never been here without Estella. It feels weird," Kelly says.

She switches on the lights and we venture upstairs. Kelly's mission is to collect a toothbrush, wash things and several night dresses while mine is to find the book Estella requested.

The first floor is still and silent. Murky half-light makes me feel as though I'm stepping into another age, one belonging to dark mahogany furniture and watchful portraits, and where I have no right to be. The stairs creak and with each step the sensation of climbing into another era grows stronger. The wallpaper on the landing, an old-fashioned print of flowers and blue birds, is yellowed and peeling away in damp curls. Plaster has crumbled down from the ceiling and the floorboards beneath my feet are spongy from water which must have been dripping in for decades. The landing handrail is loose, and the spindles of the balcony feel soft to the touch. Pencallyn House is poised to crumble into dust.

"Is it safe?" I ask.

"It's rotten as a pear," Kelly admits. "I don't really come up here, to be honest. I do my jobs, give the bathroom a quick once over when I have a moment, and put the washing away, but otherwise I'm downstairs. Estella sleeps in the kitchen in her chair – although she likes to pretend otherwise."

"That's really sad." My chest tightens at the thought of the old lady snatching a few hours' rest in her armchair, defeated by stairs she raced up and down as a child. It's the small tragedies which hurt the most and the little defeats that cause hope to crumble.

Filled with melancholy, I make my cautious way along the landing to the farthest room, which Kelly says belongs to Estella. I give the door a gentle push and step inside. The room is bathed in golden light and it's as though I've moved from night to day. Estella's bedroom seems separate from the rest of the house; it's warm and welcoming. Two single beds, complete with iron frames and tarnished brass bed knobs, stand either side of a bedside table topped with a lonely fringed lamp. Beneath this is a clock, long stopped, and a small book.

Curious, I retrieve what turns out to be a slim volume of poems, turning it in my hands and loving how the sunlight makes the embossed title glitter. It's a copy of Shakespeare's Sonnets, the spine cracked and the pages yellowed with age. It's well-thumbed and with several corners turned down as makeshift markers. Intrigued, I flip the cover open.

Jacob Miller
English Prize 1935
With congratulations and best wishes,
Miss Kathryn Gray

Impossible!

For a second I can't quite believe what I'm seeing. Estella Kellow's sent me to fetch a book of poems which belonged to the young man in the photograph. Why does she have this? What does it mean? As I flick through, my heart beats faster with each page because I could be holding something that once belonged to my own grandfather. To touch a treasured item of his feels overwhelming. Jay Miller owned this book and, judging from the worn edges of the pages, he read it often, too – maybe to my grandmother?

I trace the dedication with my forefinger, moved by this unexpected link to the handsome young man in the photograph. Now I know a little more about him, in addition to him being brave and principled, yet suffering the the shame of being a deserter. Gifted in his studies of English and with a love of poetry, he was more than a soldier – he was clever and talented and sensitive too. An exceptional man for his time. Is this where my own love of writing and literature comes from? Have I inherited these qualities from Jay Miller? Was there once someone else with my father's easy laugh? My habit of nibbling the skin around my nails? My love of stories? Dad's kindness? To be a part of something greater than myself is overwhelming; this is what it means to belong and to have family history. My mother's family passed away a long time ago; I never knew them, just as I never knew her, but their history is fully recorded and clear. There are no gaps. No cousins or relatives in the wings. I know as much as I need to know about them. My father, though, must have always wondered about his origins and would have had so many questions.

To find a possible link to Dad's past, and to him, means more than I can say.

"Did you find it?" Kelly stands in the doorway. Her arms are piled high with a clothing mountain, and she is balancing a flowery wash bag on the summit.

I hold the book up. "I did."

"Shakespeare? Yuk. They dragged us through 'Romeo and Juliet' at school. So boring. Still, I like the bit when they see each other through the fish tank, and Leonardo di Caprio was dead fit back then. Trust Estella to want you to bring Shakespeare to the hospital. I told you she was brainy."

"It's not hers, or not originally anyway." I lift the cover and show her the dedication. "It was Jay Miller's book."

"The guy from the picture? I wonder why she had it?"

I'm wondering the same thing and I have all kinds of wild ideas catching fire in my already vivid imagination.

"Do you think she and he …"

What am I hoping for? That Estella Kellow had a fling with Jay Miller? They had a baby she gave away? The hypothesis sounds unlikely enough when voiced in my head; spoken aloud it would sound insane. Besides, I already know my grandmother was killed outside the children's hospital when she was on her way to leave him there. 'Son fail,' she had gasped, 'son fail'. Estella Kellow and this old house, however fascinating and compelling both may be, are nothing but red herrings.

I need to find out more about Evie. Something tells me she's vital to solving this mystery.

"Do I think what? That they were shagging?" Kelly grins. "I'd have thought it highly unlikely, but Estella wasn't always an old spinster. I bet she got up to all sorts in the war!"

"Did she have a baby and give it away?"

"I wouldn't have thought so. Nothing goes on here the village gossip-mongers don't know about and I bet it wasn't any different then. I've never heard anything about her, especially not a fling with a black American. Bloody hell, that would have been a massive scandal especially with a racist father like hers."

"How about a secret relationship?"

Kelly looks doubtful. "Unlikely. Secrets like that would have been hard to keep with servants about. My great-granny would have known, seeing as she worked at the house, and she never breathed a word. More likely this boy was involved with her friend Evie – the one Estella's always looking for."

As a theory it's as good as any others I've come up with. Plausible too. Maybe Evie ran away with her child? This would make sense. I'll have to see what I can find out when I visit Estella tomorrow.

"Can I hang onto this?" I ask Kelly as we make our way back to the kitchen. I can't explain why but I need to have this small book with me for a little longer.

She laughs. "It's not as if I'm about to read it! Besides, it's you Estella asked to fetch it. You'll visit her tomorrow so you might as well keep it till then. Hey! Maybe you could drop off her night things too? It will save me a trip into Calmouth and hopefully stop Darren from moaning."

I'm more than happy to do this and I'm very keen to see Estella Kellow again. Although nibbled by forgetfulness, Estella's intelligence is agile and her splintered memory littered with fragments of the past. Pieced together, these could answer so many of my questions.

Once Pencallyn House is locked up, the building assuming a resentful air as it is left to spend the night alone for the first time in decades, Kelly drives us into the village. She lives on the estate at the top and I offer to hop out and walk the rest. Twilight is falling but I'm more than happy to be outside. We swap phone numbers and I take the bag of Estella's belongings with me.

The village is busy for a weeknight. The early evening air is still warm, and visitors are eating supper outside in the gardens of the holiday cottages. The pub's beer garden is full of drinkers chatting beneath patio heaters. Music and laughter drift on the breeze and it feels as though I've been transported back to the forties. Couples could be dancing cheek to cheek, handsome young Americans smoking Camels in the shadows or making out with village girls while across the darkening water danger gathers, straining to leap closer like a snarling dog on a chain.

"Hey there, Nell."

I start, snatched back across the years by Josh Richardson, who is smiling down at me.

"Sorry, I didn't mean to make you jump. I'm on my way home after a walk," he says.

I return his smile instinctively. It's hard not to.

"That's OK. I was miles away."

"Anywhere good?"

"Here, about seventy years ago. I was imagining how it must have been when the war was on."

Josh contemplates the horizon.

"It's incredible to think this was a military stronghold and about all that prevented an invasion. It must have been a frightening time, knowing an enemy was across the water and growing stronger every day."

"Hey! That's exactly what I was thinking. If my grandfather was stationed here in the war he could have walked down here too and looked out to sea."

Josh indicates a large holiday let, all sage paint and flower baskets.

"That used to be the village school. I think the Americans held dances there. I'm sure he would have come down for those. It must have been party time. Carpe diem and all that."

"Being a black American, would he have been allowed to attend dances? The US army was big on segregation, wasn't it?"

"The American army might have been, but the Cornish weren't. From what little I know about that time the locals were up in arms about that kind of thing, although I can imagine not everyone was quite so approving. I gather Estella's father was pretty unpleasant."

"Some things don't change," I say, and he flushes.

"I'm so sorry about Dad," he says.

"It wasn't your fault."

"Even so, it was unforgivable. I did have a word with him. He says he wasn't thinking and it came out wrong."

We both know this isn't true. Martin Richardson was thinking, and very hard too, but this isn't Josh's fault.

"It must have been really hard for my grandparents back then," is all I say. "I do understand why my father might have been given up for adoption. It couldn't have been easy for my grandmother, especially if the young man wasn't on the scene to support her."

I think about what Estella told me regarding Jay Miller deserting the army. There would be a treble stigma to survive, surely: being an unmarried mother, having a mixed-race baby and being the partner of a coward. This word stings and I can't believe the young man in the picture was a deserter. Why would he run away? And where would a young man like him have gone? He would have found it hard to go unnoticed in 1945.

"After talking to you I did a bit of googling about the 'Friendly Invasion', which is what they called the arrival of the American forces in the UK," Josh says. "It's made me really think, because that past is all around us here. Half the time I don't notice it. There's the remains of tank traps on the beach and the concrete apron for loading the D-Day ships. Even up at the farm we've got an old Nissen hut, and I found a rusted-out US jeep in one of the sheds. I've chatted a little to Estella about the war and she's fascinating."

"Do you know she's in hospital?" I ask nervously.

"I saw the air ambulance come over. Kelly's husband, Darren, works for us and he said Estella had taken a bad tumble."

"It's more than a tumble. Miss Kellow's broken her hip. She looks terrible." I can't look at him. This is all my fault.

"You've seen her?"

"It's my fault she fell," I blurt. The words I spill will forever colour his opinion of me, like paint seeping outwards onto wet paper, but I must tell him the truth. "I was so excited by the idea she might be able to help that I went to see her this morning. She mistook me for someone else and slipped on her way to meet me. She thought I was someone called Evie."

"Estella's often talking to Evie," Josh says. "She misses her terribly. If Estella thought Evie had returned, she would have been over the moon."

"She was so excited she slipped on her way to the door. If I'd waited for you to introduce me, she would never have fallen." I gulp my misery down. "I'm so sorry. It's my fault she fell."

I wait for the shutters to come down in his clear green-eyed gaze, but he lays a hand on my shoulder instead. It's a tiny gesture but vast in terms of reassurance and compassion.

"That's not true. Estella Kellow's in her nineties, Nell, and she's been diagnosed with early stage dementia. She can be very confused at times and she's really frail. If anything, it's incredible this hasn't happened before – especially when she wanders off. You're not to blame, I promise."

"But she fell in the kitchen because she saw me."

"I imagine her walking stick slipped on the wet tiles," Josh corrects. His hand increases its pressure on my shoulder, keeping me grounded on the earth when everything within me is poised to spin away in panic. "I've lost count of the times I've told her not to wash up, because she gets water everywhere. She could have slipped trying to fill the kettle or poking the biscuit tin down from the dresser with her walking stick. Besides, the same thing might have happened if you'd been walking across the yard with me. We've all told her to be careful, but Estella's a very determined person and she won't listen to a soul. Trust me, this accident isn't down to you."

It's odd, but I do trust him. "Thank you," I say.

"You don't need to thank me. It's the truth." The hand falls away as he steps back. "Anyway, I'd better be getting home. Dad's gone to London and Mum hates being alone at the farm when it's dark."

"I remember you mentioned she was nervous there."

"Nervous doesn't come close. She's terrified, which isn't like her at all." He sighs and runs a hand through his hair. "It doesn't bode well for a happy retirement in her dream home, but I do understand what she means. Anyway, I'll visit Estella tomorrow – if I can fight my way past Dad in his haste to snatch the place from under her nose."

I sense he's only half-joking.

"I have her night things to take with me," I say. "And a book of poetry she wanted me to find. Turns out it belongs to the young man in my picture. He was called Jay Miller. I've no idea how, but apparently Estella knew him and she wants to tell me more."

Josh's eyebrows take a trip into his thick auburn hair.

"Sounds as though you've been busy. I'd love to know more, but Mum will be seriously freaking out and I need to get back. Look, say no if you'd rather, but how about I pick you up tomorrow and drive you to the hospital? I want to see Estella too and it will save you a bus ride – *if* there's a bus, that is. They come about once a month here."

"You don't need to do that."

"I know I don't need to but I'd like to. Besides, I'm nosey! I want to hear all about your family quest and what Estella has to say. We don't get out much here. You can fill me in as we drive and I'll show you a few places your GI might have known. It might help you picture how the place was for your grandparents."

The invitation hangs in the air, glittering with the promise of friendship, but I hesitate. Do I want Josh Richardson's friendship?

Or am I afraid he may want more?

I study him. Josh's face is an open book and genuine kindness is written there. Nothing more. There are no strings.

"Are you sure?" I ask.

He grins. "Oh yes! Dad's away, so I can play truant for day and have a break from the site without getting caught. Look, I don't think hospital visiting hours are until after one, so we've time to have a bit of a mystery tour first. Maybe get some lunch? If you like?"

Lunch and a mystery tour with a good-looking guy? If I tell Lou about this, she'll be picking a hat by teatime!

"That sounds great, thanks," I say.

We plan to meet and I return to the pub feeling strangely excited. It must be the thought of seeing places which could have been known to my grandparents. Yes, that's why I have a little fizz of excitement deep down inside, and absolutely nothing whatsoever to do with the notion of spending time with Josh Richardson.

[illegible]

CHAPTER 16

Nell
The present

I wake, nudged from slumber by elbows of sunlight poking through the curtains. Despite the previous day's drama, I've slept heavily, lulled by the constant suck and sigh of waves, and soothed by deep darkness and an even deeper silence. Salt-heavy air, a busy day and a stomach full of rich pub food closed my eyes almost as soon as I climbed into bed, and when I glance at my watch, I'm shocked to discover it's ten o'clock. Not wanting to waste a moment, I shower quickly and dress.

It's another beautiful day. Although it's not yet eleven, beachgoers have already staked their claims with windbreaks, and excited shrieks fill the air as swimmers brave the cold water. I snap some pictures for Lou before walking along the sea wall, marvelling at the concrete scars of the D-Day preparations which remain even after all this time. Children balance on the wave-nibbled fragments and jump from the far end into the water. The juxtaposition of innocence and the mechanics of war is striking.

Did Jay Miller help to build this pier or the concrete apron? The limited research I've managed to do so far suggests these were jobs which fell mainly to the black GIs, along with road building and digging latrines. What was the Shakespeare-loving Jay Miller's experience of life at Pencallyn Cove? Was it a welcoming place? Were people kind to him? Or were they suspicious? Nervous of new arrivals who didn't look like them? Recalling the hopeful face of the young man in the photograph, my heart twists to think this might have been the case.

Like the tide has eroded these old defences, so time has blurred the ugliness of the past. I wonder what else has faded with the years? The story of this young man has all but been erased, save in the patchy memories of an elderly lady. Who was Jay Miller? What kind of young man was he? Did he go to the dances at the schoolhouse and drink in the pub on his evenings away from the camp? Or was he a quiet soul who preferred reading poetry to dancing? So many questions. I wonder whether Estella Kellow will be able to help me answer them?

I shield my eyes against the glitter of the water and watch a small yacht skim the horizon before it vanishes from view. Just like that little vessel, the story I'm seeking feels out of sight. Will it slip away with Estella Kellow, or will she find the strength to tell me a little more?

"Nell! Hi! Hope I'm not late?"

A gleaming black Land Rover Defender draws up alongside the wall and Josh Richardson waves at me. He's wearing a white shirt open at the neck to reveal tanned skin the colour of warm honey, his autumnal hair is tucked behind his ears, and dark wraparound shades cover his emerald eyes. I see myself reflected in the lenses, a small figure with her hair caught up in a messy bun and wearing a simple sprigged cotton dress. Suddenly I feel shy.

"Hop in," Josh says through the open window. "Today's magical mystery tour starts here."

He leans across and opens the passenger door. It's more than a hop to get in, practically a hill climb for my short legs, so Josh reaches for my hand and hauls me inside.

"That is not a hop," I say once I'm settled and hopefully not showing the world my knickers.

He pulls a face. "Dad insisted on buying the Defender with the full lift kit even though he needs a Stannah to get into the thing with his dodgy hip."

"I guess it's good for off-roading?" I offer. I really hope Josh doesn't want to expand the conversation because this is about as far as I go. Not a lot of off-roading goes on in Finchley.

"You won't see this thing near a field. It's Dad's utter baby," Josh laughs, pulling a mock-horrified face. He executes a three-point turn, expertly avoiding holidaymakers, and drives slowly out of the village. "If I get a speck of dirt on the Landy he'll disown me – although he's already on the brink of doing that. This car is owned purely for the purposes of posing as a country gent, but I thought if you needed to collect anything else for Estella it might be handy for getting down her drive. Not much else will make it."

I glance down at the carrier bag Kelly packed. "I think I have everything. Any news on how she is?"

"Nothing at all, which has to be good. I told you, she's tougher than she looks. Ready?"

I click my seat belt into place. "Ready."

The Land Rover's height gives me a good vantage point, and I'm able to peer over hedges and observe the village from a new perspective. The old part, with its narrow streets and whitewashed cottages, is spread out at the foot of the hill like a pretty picnic blanket. Higher up is the ex-council estate where Kelly lives. The houses here all have incredible sea views but, unlike those in Pencallyn Cove, they are not held safely in the embrace of the valley but face out to sea and must be pummelled by gales in the winter. Josh turns left at the top and takes a route past a cluster of new build houses and a grocery store.

"Are we going to the shop?" I ask.

He grins. "I've taken girls on some crap dates but a trip the local Spar would be a new low! Not that this is a date, but you get my drift. As great as the local grocery shop is, I think there are more inspiring destinations to show you."

Josh's fair colouring means he blushes easily and now he is puce. I take pity on him. Of course this isn't a date. I never thought it was – well maybe for a split second when he made his joke – and how did this make me feel? Excited? Nervous? Pleased? Scared? A blend of all four?

He clears his throat. "Anyway, I thought we'd stop here because it's where the American army was based in the forties. It's all long gone and the area's known as Pencallyn Heights now. It's a small housing estate, but in your grandparents' time it would have looked very different. There would have been roadblocks and check points and tents and Nissen huts – all kinds of military activity."

"It's hard to imagine," I say, glancing at the cluster of bland houses.

"It's pretty ordinary, isn't it? Strange to think of all the history just below the surface. I guess the wider roads and the levelled land made it a good choice for a sixties housing development. I think Estella sold the land off back then. Still, if you imagine it without the buildings we see, and picture an army base with huts and tents and even a Donut Dugout, you can visualise how it would have looked in your grandfather's time. But it's savage up here when the wind blows in the winter, so that must have been a shock for some of those boys."

I try to picture the scene. How would Jay Miller have felt when he arrived? Did he like the sea breeze and the open water? Or was he a city boy, more used to the shadows of skyscrapers than those cast by racing clouds in the open sky? Did he miss the warmth of the southern sun, or was he used to the bite of wind and the cold kiss of rain?

"From here it's not far as the crow flies to Estella's house or the farm. It wouldn't have taken a fit young man long to walk to either," Josh observes.

"Or a fit young woman," I parry.

"Fair point! I'm right though, aren't I? If you cut across the garden and pick a path through the woods the distance isn't more than a mile."

He's right. If Evie was my grandmother, which seems likely, she could easily have met up with a GI boyfriend in secret. There must be hundreds of places where young lovers could be alone.

"Everything's closer together than you think," I say slowly, "but the roads seem to take for ever."

"By sea's the best way to travel. Calmouth's across the river from the headland, ten minutes at the most in a boat. And see that hill?" Josh leans out of the window and points to a distant field "It's Bury Barrow, the site of an old hill fort. If you believe in ley lines and that kind of thing, there's meant to be one running from there through the church to our well and on into Estella's garden."

"Do you believe in them?"

One hand stokes his chin, clean shaven today rather than dusted with auburn stubble. Is this for my benefit?

"There's something about the well that makes me think maybe I do. How about you?" he asks.

"There must be something in it with stone circles and wells and churches built on energy points," I reply.

Josh looks thoughtful. "Well, no matter what we believe, Bury Barrow has incredible views across this whole area, and out to sea too, which makes it a perfect strategic site in any century. There are the remains of pillboxes up there and there would have been anti-aircraft guns to fire at the Luftwaffe when they came over on bombing raids. The skies must have lit up with gunfire and searchlights, which seems unbelievable now because it's such a peaceful spot. I walk up there when I want to clear my head and get away. Listening to skylarks and watching swifts is better than any therapy."

Head clearing. Therapy. I feel the tug of a chord of mutual sympathy. Josh Richardson also knows what it is to fight demons. I follow his gaze across the hill, green rippling grass meeting clear blue sky, wondering why Josh Richardson needs peace to clear his head. I understand the need for it, and I recognise the shadows in his eyes because I see them in my own …

I yank my mind away from melancholy thought to focus on what he's telling me. The recent past is too painful. Far better to think about the war and dogfights above the sea than the loss of a life which only drew breath in my dreams.

"Calmouth was an important dockyard, and the deep river was the perfect spot for concealing ships in the estuary and practising military operations," Josh explains. "If we have time before we go to the hospital, I'll swing by the docks so you can see them for yourself. It's still pretty industrial around there, and it took a heavy hit of bombing in the war."

"So, this area really was in the thick of it? With bombing too?" I know all about the London Blitz – who doesn't? – but I've never really thought about the reality of the war in a quiet place like this.

"It really was," Josh says. "I'll point out some other things on our way to the hospital. Let's head to the church so you can see where Estella's family are buried."

He turns the Defender down a narrow lane. Long grasses tickle the car's flanks, and dried ruts test the suspension. I fill him in on what Estella's told me about Jay Miller, and Josh listens intently. There's something about his quiet manner than invites confidences, and if I stay in the car for too long I'm afraid of what else I might divulge. I dig my nails into my palms. It's best to focus on the story I'm following rather than my own.

It's far easier to tell other people's stories.

"So I think it's possible Estella's friend Evie could be my grandmother," I finish. "She was here at the right time. I know my grandmother died in 1945, which could explain why Evie never came back here. I think Estella was looking after some of her things, including the poetry book, and that's why she was so excited to see me. I'm a link to her two dearest friends. Maybe she was their go-between?"

"It's certainly one theory," Josh says carefully. "Or … how about this? Jay Miller ran away with Evie? They could have been together somewhere waiting for the baby except something went wrong and they were separated?"

"Possibly, although Estella did seem adamant Jay wouldn't have done such a thing. She seems to have known him really well."

"Maybe she covered for them? Women cover for each other all the time, don't they? Like you go to the loo in pairs!"

"Only when we're about fifteen!"

"Estella and Evie wouldn't have been much older than that. Do you remember what you and your best friend were like at that age? I bet you told each other everything."

I smile wistfully. When we were fifteen Lou and I finished each other's sentences, had all kinds of secret plans to travel the world in a camper van, and when we weren't together we were glued to each other on the phone. I would have done anything for her. Would I have lied? Covered for her? Helped her to have a baby in secret? Waited faithfully for her to return until I was old? Made promises that lasted a lifetime? Of course I would. Teenage female friendship is intense and no other relationship ever compares. I would have done anything for Lou and I'm willing to bet Estella would have done anything for Evie.

I need to find out what this was.

"Come and look at the church." Josh sprints around to open the passenger door for me and his warm hand takes mine as I leap down from the car. Skin against skin and strong male fingers on mine come as a shock and, unused to physical contact, I'm jolted.

"Ok?" he asks.

"It's a long way down," I say quickly, sliding my hand away.

"I'll bring the parachute next time, shall I?"

He's expecting a next time?

"Anyway," he continues, "come and look at St Brecca's. It's a beautiful church."

Josh strides along the lane and his long denim-clad legs make easy work of the distance between the car and the entrance to the churchyard. I hoist my bag onto my shoulder and jog after him. A small gate leads into an overgrown graveyard where wildflowers, nodding grasses and rampant ivy hold dominion over crumbling tombstones. At the far end of the graveyard a small church faces the sea bravely. It must have observed the marching of the waves for generations and watched the water for many invading armies.

Pencallyn Cove is a fishing community and I count many weathered headstones commemorating men lost at sea, some during the same disaster. I brush lichen away and try to read the inscriptions, but most names are rendered smudges by the years. Some headstones bear testament to children lost at a young age and I can hardly bear to look at these. It doesn't matter how many centuries have passed; the death of a child still feels like a fist in the stomach. I straighten up from the grave of four-year-old Bess Tremar and brush my fingers over the stone in a soothing gesture before I walk away. Is this comfort for Bess or for myself? It's hard to say.

"The Kellows have their memorials inside. Come and have a look," Josh calls from the porch. Sunlight catches his hair, turning it to flame and brightening his white shirt, outlining the firm lines of the strong body beneath. Celtic warrior turned angel, I think, and laugh at myself. He's handsome and kind, and has a tortured edge too, all in all perfect inspiration for a new novel. Hero material. No wonder I keep staring. It's research, that's all.

"All OK?" he asks when I catch him up.

"Yes. I'm fine."

"When a woman says that it usually means the exact opposite."

"No, I really am fine. Oh, it's daft really. I was looking at some of the tombstones and thinking how young the children were. I know it's in the past, but it feels really sad."

"That's not daft at all. Any life cut short is a tragedy. I suppose this was a hard place to live. It might look pretty but most of the cottages in the village would have been squalid. I don't think it was so great in Estella's youth either. No vaccines. No NHS. Unless you were rich, if you got sick you took your chances. There was no medicine to save you then."

Medicine can't save everyone today either, but I don't say this out loud but I simply follow him into the church.

It's dark and cool inside. Old windows let in slivers of stained-glass light which illuminate the stone columns and arches and pour rainbows over the flagstones. The dark pews are polished, and flowers are placed on the windowsills of the thick framework of stone which pins the ancient roof into place. Petals curl beneath drooping blooms, drifting now and again onto the floor like floral tears, while dust dances in shafts of light. Josh and I pass memorial stones and monuments until we reach the small chapel where the Kellows' memorials lie.

"There's a lot of them," says Josh, craning his neck. "The family has lived here for a quite a while. No wonder Dad's upset a few locals by annoying Estella."

Accolades smother the wall. Brass or bronze or etched into marble, the material matters far less than the praise and tributes which stretch from the eighteen hundreds and end abruptly with the death of Reginald Henry Kellow, MP for Calmouth and Pendray. Amelia May Kellow's is next to him, and I do some swift maths.

"Goodness, she was only twenty-six. Was she Estella's mother?"

"Must have been. I think she died having Estella, but don't quote me. She's never said much about her family. Like this poor soul here, her stepmother Violet. Blink and you'll miss it."

Josh is right; it would be easy to overlook the tiny square of Cornish slate at the bottom of the wall. She'd died young too. Seems that marriage to Estella's father was a dangerous occupation.

"Was it childbirth for her too?"

"I think she died in a bombing raid," Josh replies. "I'm sure Estella said something along those lines when Kelly's kids were doing a project on wartime Calmouth. She lost her brother in the Battle of Britain too. It must have been awful."

"It's very small memorial."

"From what I know of things the Kellows ran out of money towards the end of the war. After her father died Estella sold a lot of land to pay off his debts." Josh glances at his watch. "We'd better make tracks if we're going to see a few more things and grab a bite to eat."

As we drive away from St Brecca's I feel as though the ghosts of the past are watching us leave. Turning in my seat, I shiver at the thought of unseen eyes following the car's slow passage along the lane. Some shades are willing me forward with my quest, but others warn me not to meddle, and to step away. It's nonsense, a product of my busy mind, and the church is as deserted as it was when we arrived. The only shadows falling are those cast by the trees which overhang the ancient lane. There's nothing sinister here. I have nothing to fear from finding out more. Absolutely nothing.

All the same, I'm glad of the little silver crucifix around my neck and can't help touching it for reassurance.

[illegible]

CHAPTER 17

Nell
The Present

A sunny journey to Calmouth, filled with easy conversation and detours to abandoned airfields and old Nissen huts, chases away any strange thoughts about the church and unseen watchers in the shadows. A lunch of crab rolls eaten on the sunny steps of the Marine Museum forces me to focus on fending off greedy seagulls, and by the time Josh parks at the hospital the odd feelings I had St Brecca's feel as though they belong to something I once read in a novel. I'm intrigued by what I've learned about Estella's family history, and a little inspired, too, for my own novel, but I'm not unnerved any more. Talk of ley lines and untimely deaths has triggered my imagination. It was nothing more sinister.

It's visiting time and the hospital is busy. Josh and I make our way to the medical assessment unit, where Estella is tucked away in a side room. A sliver of afternoon sunshine slips through the lowered blind and strokes her pale face. Estella is surrounded by beeping machines and tethered by the lugubrious fall of fluids from a drip anchored to the back of a hand already purpled with bruises. Beneath tissue paper skin the calligraphy of veins and arteries tell a tale of a life still ready be lived, and when her bright eyes snap open it's clear she's nowhere near ready to give up.

"Nell! Did you find my book?"

"I did!" I say, opening my satchel. "It's right here."

I perch on the corner of the bed and pass The Sonnets to Estella. She holds it against her heart.

"Thank you, my dear. Thank you."

"How are you feeling, Estella?" Josh asks, dropping a kiss onto her cheek. "You gave us all a right scare.

"I gave myself a scare too," she says. "Oh dear, what a silly old fool I am to cause all this trouble. You and Kelly were right; I shouldn't have been slopping water all over the floor."

"Are you up to visitors or would you like us to leave you to rest? Nell and I can always come back later." Josh says.

"You came together?" Estella's lips twitch. "I see."

She really doesn't.

"We met at the farm. I was looking for a well. Josh helped me out when it became clear I shouldn't be there," I explain.

"Martin Richardson didn't take kindly to trespassers, eh? Told you to get off his land?"

"In fairness to him, I was on his land."

Estella snorts. "The well belongs to nobody. He's waiting for me to hurry up and die so he can have Pencallyn now, no doubt. He must be praying I cark it."

"I'm not sure he's that mercenary," Josh says awkwardly, and Estella laughs.

"Aren't you? Well, never mind him – his chance will come, and sooner rather than later."

"Don't say that. Everyone knows how strong you are. Especially my father. He's still moaning about the trees."

"I'm ninety-five, love. I've broken my hip and they don't want to risk setting it because they think my heart's too weak and the operation will finish me off."

Josh is shocked. "They said that?"

"Oh, not directly. They give me a lot of old flannel and talk to me as though I'm a child but I'm not as deaf as they think I am, and you'd be surprised how much I hear when they think I'm asleep. When *anyone* thinks I'm asleep. You learn a lot that way, you know."

"But they need to at least try – " Josh begins, but she cuts him off.

"I'm old and I'm tired. Don't let's waste precious time arguing. I'm not in pain and the mist isn't falling. I want to remember everything while there's still time. There are things I have to tell you, Nell."

"Are they to do with why you kept my picture?"

Estella Kellow sighs. A small figure propped up against the pillows and with her white hair loose over her shoulders, she's the oddest mixture of the very old and the very young. The book is clutched tightly against her heart, but one hand drops away to slide beneath the covers, and surfaces with the photograph.

"I'm so sorry, my dear. I only wanted to look at it."

"But why? And why did you keep this book for so long? What was my grandfather to you?"

"The man you *think* is your grandfather," she corrects sharply. "It's not possible."

"But what if he had a secret relationship? What if your friend Evie was seeing him secretly? Could she have had his baby? Is that why she left? Or maybe they eloped?"

Estella looks amused.

"What an imagination you have, my dear. I'll tell you what I know, but it won't be nearly as exciting. Fetch a chair, Josh. You're making me nervous hovering around like this."

Once Josh has left in search of seats, Estella presses the photograph into my hand: "I'm sorry I took it."

"Keep it, please, I can see what it means to you. Besides, I've scanned it into my computer. I also have this one I wanted to show you." Reaching into my satchel, I pull out the picture of the laughing girl and realise I've started the wrong way around; even with the wrinkles, lines and the deep hollows beneath her eyes now it's apparent I'm looking at the same person. The firm set of the chin, widow's peak of thick hair and small tilted nose haven't changed in over seventy years.

Estella leans closer. "Good Lord! Where did you find this?"

"It was at my father's house. I found it with the one of Jay Miller. It's you, isn't it?"

"Oh yes, that's me. Wasn't I something?"

I laugh. "Yes, you were very pretty."

"And very young. I must have been fourteen at the most." One trembling finger traces the figure in the picture. "It's as well we don't know what life holds in store when we're that age."

When I was fourteen I was busy worrying about having thick curly hair and being short, problems which today hardly seem worth gracing with that adjective but which felt insurmountable back then. If somebody had told me that less than two decades later I would have buried my father, lost my baby and be divorced, I would have had a meltdown. Estella's right; it's best we don't know the future.

"I had no idea the best and worst times of my life were just ahead of me. Isn't it funny to think the war was going on too? I look so happy, as though I haven't a care in the world."

"This picture was taken during the war?"

"I think it must have been taken in '42," Estella says slowly as she takes the picture and peers closer. "My little dog, Poppet, is there. We spent a lot of time at the old farm; it was one of our favourite places. My father took the camera away soon after that picture was taken."

"You father took your camera? Why?"

"He said we could be accused of spying for the Germans by taking pictures, and he did have a point. It was a dangerous time and the troops were making the preparations for D-Day. Not that we knew that then, of course, but there were lots of Americans and it was all rather thrilling."

"Was that how you knew Jay Miller? Was he billeted here with the American forces? Were you friends?"

She looks beyond me to somewhere far, far away. "Yes. Jay Miller and I were friends."

The scrape of chair legs on the floor summons me back from a sunny farmyard, where two girls are snapping pictures, back to a hospital room.

"Sit down, Josh," Estella says. "And you too, Nell. Make yourselves as comfortable as you can. There's a story I want to tell you – if you have time to hear it?"

"We've got plenty of time," Josh tells her, sitting down at my side.

"I haven't," Estella warns. "So let's make a start."

She leans against the pillows and closes her eyes. Words drift down from her lips.

"Once upon a time," Estella Kellow begins, "there were two little girls …"

CHAPTER 18

Estella
1939

The last days of summer were always beautiful in Cornwall. Estella loved this time of year most of all. It was rich and glorious but a little melancholy too, an emotion which resonated in the mists and plump blackberries and tint of wood smoke in the air. Where better than this window to watch the garden billow russet and gold? How many Kellows had stood at this spot to gaze over the vast garden they had planted?

She really ought to sketch the scene. So often images flashed through her mind like the flicker of a trout in the river, a glittering silver flash of brilliance gone for ever unless you grasped it at once, hooking it out and capturing it not with rod and line but with pencil and paper. Too often Estella's thoughts darted away before they surfaced, leaving her with a sense of loss she couldn't quite explain, and as though she'd been on the brink of something wonderful only to let it slide through her fingers. Her notebooks were full of such jottings and sketches, and sometimes she thumbed through them with the vague idea they could be cajoled into a poem or a story. Miss Toms told her great writers like the Brontës and Keats had kept notebooks of ideas to draw upon later and Estella, always a diligent pupil, had taken her governess at her word. She might only be twelve, and her early notebooks did not contain anything more significant than what pudding Cook had made that day or what the weather was like, but her later work was going to be far more interesting. One day scholars would pore over her scribblings and debate what Estella Kellow meant by this image or that piece of alliteration.

She gazed out of the window, trying to decide how best to paint the orange wash thrown over the fields by the sinking sun. This was the time of year when the land was at its most replete and beautiful, rich with nature's spoils and turning to golds and coppers which spread autumn's burnished hues across the county like honey over toast. Yes. She could use that.

Estella scribbled the image down, feeling pleased with it. She underlined the sentence twice before lowering the book and resting it on her lap. There were so many stories waiting to be told, but surely to be an author she needed to do a little more than rest in bed and be fussed over? She'd certainly had lots of time to think about stories while she'd lain in bed, watching the sun crawl across the sky and the stars light up the night. When her fever had been high, she'd had bright dreams and strange visions to rival anything Coleridge could create but whenever she'd requested a pen and her notebook, Violet said she needed rest and so the visions had slipped away. Too weak to argue, Estella wondered how many great works of literature had been lost. She supposed one day critics would debate this too.

"It's your all fault for putting ideas into her head, Miss Toms," Violet Kellow had said disapprovingly to Tommy. "It's not good for her to get agitated. Writing books, indeed! The child needs to rest."

Miss Toms had caught Estella's eye. Putting ideas into Estella's head was *exactly* what the Right Honourable Reginald Kellow paid a governess to do, but Tommy was far too well-mannered to point this out to his young wife. Instead, she laid a cool hand on Estella's forehead.

"I don't think she has a temperature, Mrs Kellow. It wouldn't hurt Estella to have something to do as a distraction."

"Goody!" said Violet. "In that case I'll pop back up with some copies of *Tatler* and *Vogue*. We can read them together, darling, instead of all the dreary stuff Tommy makes you look at. Won't that be fun? I'll do your hair too if you like. Maybe we can set it?"

"Lovely," Estella agreed meekly, although inside she was sighing. Try as she might, she couldn't get excited about fashion magazines. She couldn't imagine for the life of her what Papa and Violet found to talk about, and had once overheard Cook saying something to this effect.

"She's a flighty piece, that one. She'll bring nothing but trouble," Cook had declared. "Mr Kellow should have known better at his age. Still, we all know he didn't marry her for conversation."

Tommy, who was making tea, bristled at this comment and flushed when Estella asked her later what Cook had meant.

"You really shouldn't listen at doors," she scolded.

"I wasn't," Estella protested. "I wanted some cake. What did Cook mean?"

But Tommy changed the subject and Estella had been forced to resort to asking her brother. She'd cornered him in the boot room when he'd returned from walking the dogs on the beach and Alex had laughed for ages, in that condescending big brother way of his, before ruffling her hair. Irritated, Estella ducked her head away.

"I'm not a child."

"You're twelve."

"Almost thirteen, actually. Anyway, you're only fifteen."

"Almost sixteen, actually," countered Alex, with a grin. "Which means I know a jolly sight more about the world than you do, silly little goose. Poor old Tommy. No wonder she was red-faced! Cook was talking about things Tommy wouldn't have a clue about."

"Tommy knows about everything!" Estella flared, indignant on Tommy's behalf.

Alex, still fiddling with the boot jack, smirked.

"Trust me, she really doesn't! Cook meant *sex*, and I don't think our Tommy's an expert there, do you?"

Estella stared at him. Alex was four years older than her but sometimes it felt like four hundred.

"What do you mean, sex?"

"Oh Lord, sis! You don't seriously need me to explain, do you? Please tell me you know where babies come from? You don't still think it's the stork?"

Estella flushed.

"Of course I don't! I've seen Hercules serve mares."

"Well, then. It's the same for people except they make a right old song and dance about the whole deal. Much easier to be a horse, I should think. Old Hercules doesn't have to buy the mares dinner, does he? Or take them shopping. Let's be honest, Violet's nice, but she's hardly Pa's intellectual and social equal."

Estella had never wondered why her father married Violet, but she'd often wondered why Violet had married *him*. She'd been thrilled when Papa had brought Violet home because there had been parties and music and picnics and all kinds of fun. So what if sometimes Violet treated her like a doll to dress up and put down again on a whim? She was fun and kind-hearted, and she made Pencallyn feel alive, unlike Reginald Kellow who was stern, bad-tempered and luckily in London most of the time. He was much older and he seemed to disapprove of all the things she liked most. Pretty Violet loved to dance to the gramophone in the drawing room and throw parties for her glamorous friends, and she was always singing. When Papa first brought her home, he'd seemed enchanted and he'd smiled a lot more. Pencallyn had felt as though it was heaving a huge sigh of relief too, and Estella had loved being petted and whizzed about in Violet's little Jaguar. She was like a happy butterfly flitting about the place, or at least she had been until Reginald started to snap at her and seem irritated by everything she did. The singing stopped when he was at home and the butterfly's wings drooped a little more with each passing day.

"He married her because she's pretty and rich," Alex explained. "That's what Cook really meant. Our old man didn't marry our stepmother for her conversational skills. He's like January in 'The Merchant's Tale', and that's all I'm going to say. If you want to know any more go and translate some Chaucer with good old Tommy. And when you've done that, ask her what Henry the Eighth did to Anne Boleyn once he was tired of her. Violet should be careful."

Estella knew all about Henry VIII, but she couldn't imagine her stern father would chop somebody's head off. Anyway, it wasn't as though Papa needed a son when he already had Alexander to inherit Pencallyn. Irritated by her brother, she'd called the dogs and stomped through the garden to gather her thoughts. Whichever Kellow had designed the formal gardens must have known what it felt like to be cross and confused, because they'd planted its labyrinth out of box hedging, creating the perfect place to calm down in solitude. Whenever Estella was at odds with the world, she would walk around it for a while and she nearly always felt better. Now it was there, at the sundial, that she went to reflect on what her brother had said. The new knowledge made her feel all prickly and strange inside, as though she'd had a glimpse of a place she wasn't quite ready to visit.

When she was calmer, Estella went straight to the library where she spent the rest of the day ploughing through Middle English. Once she'd finished, her mind boggling with new knowledge regarding what it was possible to do while in a pear tree, she thought she understood a little more about why her father had married Violet. In return, Violet had a beautiful home in Cornwall, a smart town house and a step up society's ladder. Jane Austen would have applauded the match, but it made Estella shiver. A romantic to the marrow, she would only marry for love when she grew up. Love and nothing else.

In any case, Tommy with her functional brown crop, sensible tweeds and unmade-up face wasn't pretty or as exciting as Violet, but she had been to Oxford and was the most intelligent person Estella knew. Tommy was far brighter than Papa, although Estella wouldn't have dreamed of saying this to a soul. Apart from embarrassing Tommy, it would have put her father in dreadfully bad mood, and Estella always did everything she could to avoid this happening. They all did. Nobody wanted to be on the sharp end of Reginald Kellow's temper. Estella had often thought if there was a bright side to being poorly it was knowing that Papa wouldn't want to spend time in a sickroom. She could easily avoid him by being ill.

"I could certainly write a book about him," she said to Poppet, her faithful black spaniel. Poppet, who had been on the receiving end of many kicks when she made the mistake of getting under Reginald Kellow's feet, thumped her tail in agreement, although the expression in her eyes said it wouldn't be a wise move. Estella had to agree. One day in the future, when Papa was long gone and she was very old herself, perhaps about forty, she would eviscerate him in fiction, which would serve him jolly well right.

Unfortunately, since she'd been ill with the rheumatic fever, Estella felt too tired to even write a few sentences and would often fall asleep with her pen clutched in her hand. When she awoke any ideas had departed, slipping into the shadows falling across the bedroom and leaving her bereft. This kind of behaviour was not going to help her become a great writer and it was all very annoying.

She sighed and shifted underneath her blanket, tucking it carefully around her legs as instructed. Tommy had left the window open, filling the bedroom with salt-sharp air, but on the strict proviso that Estella remained wrapped up and didn't allow herself to catch a chill. Estella thought it highly unlikely anyone wearing a flannelette vest, thick pyjamas and woolly socks could possibly catch a cold, and even more unlikely if they had a heavy counterpane draped over them too, but she hadn't argued. After weeks of being confined to bed it was a wonderful freedom to be allowed to sit in the window and feel the breeze. It felt a little like before she was ill, when she had roamed through the garden, swum in the cove and galloped her pony across stubble fields. That Estella, the one with strong legs and flesh on her bones and who didn't feel weak and tired, seemed like a character from a book now. Had she ever really been that girl? And would she ever become her again or would she spend the rest of her life under the watchful eye of doctors? How would she ever write books if she stayed like this?

Such thoughts made Estella feel quite desperate and her throat went all tight and funny, like it did when Papa shouted at her. She stroked the silky dome of Poppet's head.

"I'm going to get better," she said firmly and Poppet's plumy tail thumped the rug in agreement. "We'll soon be out in the woods or swimming in the river, just you wait. Silly old rheumatic fever isn't going to stop us."

Feeling resolute, Estella picked up her latest notebook. Maybe she could attempt a sketch? The tantalising triangle of sea at the bottom of the garden was so bright it made you think longingly of the shade beneath the chestnut tree at the far end of the lawn, thick canopy outlined in gold and boughs pimpled with spiky emerald cases. Soon these would tumble to the ground, bursting open to reveal conkers as shiny as the coat of her old pony and as smooth beneath her fingertips as his coat after a good going over with the dandy brush. Maybe if she begged, Tommy would let her go outside to collect a few conkers? She was stronger now, Dr Pengarland had said as much this morning. In fact, he'd been astounded by how improved she was.

"You're a medical miracle, young lady!" he'd declared after sounding her chest, examining her throat and taking her temperature. He'd made Estella take several turns around the bedroom, which had made her legs feel a little bit wobbly, before listening again to her chest and taking her pulse one final time.

"Well and truly on the mend," had been his diagnosis. "Rest, sea air and no strenuous exercise are still the order of the day, mind. That and a big spoonful of cod liver oil."

"I'm a medical miracle," Estella said to Poppet.

She really was. When Estella had succumbed to the fever nobody had thought she would survive. At times she'd wanted to close her eyes and drift away, but she'd had the strangest dream about her long-dead Mama telling her to be strong and to fight because she had a long life to live. There were also faces she'd never seen before, and one especially made her heart sing. This belonged to a young man and although he was a stranger Estella recognised him and understood he was waiting for her somewhere. He was her soulmate and made for her in every way. This special knowledge was exciting and thrilling and enough to make her fight the dangerous drowsiness.

"Wait for me," he'd whispered, and although his voice was like no voice she'd ever heard, Estella knew it as well as she knew her own. She knew him.

She had always known him.

"I'll wait," she'd whispered and although the only sound she could make was a hoarse gasp, Estella knew he'd heard because he'd smiled before slipping away. After this there were cold cloths and gentle hands before everything concertinaed into emptiness. They said that this was when she'd nearly died. Maybe the man she'd seen was an angel? He certainly had the face of one, or at least Estella thought he had, for only fragments of the dream remained. Sometimes when she was in that drowsy hinterland between sleep and wakefulness, Estella caught the fading flash of a smile and the turn of a head, but he was always out of reach, as though waiting for the time when she was ready to catch him up.

She might be twelve but Estella understood this man was her destiny. He was her other half, part of her soul, and he had sent her back so they could be together one day. How she knew this Estella couldn't say; it was simply a deep and innate conviction that brought with it the greatest sense of peace. He was her person and one day she would be with him. There would be no more tiptoeing around her father or cowering when the tempests of his temper raged through Pencallyn; only the wonderful sense of peace and wholeness that had infused her dream.

Estella had attempted to write something of this down in her notebook. It was a dream yet more than a dream, as insubstantial as the mist that scarfed the River Cal in the morning, yet also the most real and solid certainty. It made no sense and it made total sense. She struggled to remember what he looked like but his image was as elusive as the certainty she'd felt towards him was tangible. In the end Estella had given up, realising for the first time some things couldn't be expressed in words.

There was nobody to tell, or who could explain what had happened, so she hugged the knowledge close to her heart and trusted that one day something important was going to happen. Although she'd heard the grownups talking about her when they thought she was asleep, and knew they were worried about damage to her heart, she would live to be a very old lady. Of this, Estella was certain. A long and exciting life awaited.

While she'd been unwell spring had bounced into summer; the world had turned without her and the Germans had annexed Austria, which Tommy explained was a very bad thing indeed. Before she had fallen ill, Estella listened to the grownups at dinner as they discussed the growing ambitions of Herr Hitler. Although the general talk was filled with confidence that peace could be maintained, and Papa was certainly adamant that Mr Chamberlain was the very man to ensure this, a sense of foreboding slipped over Estella as though some future self had stolen into the room to whisper warnings over her shoulder. The Nazis should not be appeased. It was time to think carefully where one's loyalties lay.

Something dreadful was coming …

"Churchill's nothing but a warmonger," Papa had said scathingly during one dinner party. "He's been bleating on about German military power for years. The man's paranoid with all his talk about nations submitting to some German plan of domination. It's nonsense, I tell you. Utter nonsense!"

He'd slammed his hand down on the dining table as he'd made this announcement, making plates jump and cutlery shiver. Violet's glass toppled over and the pallor of her face had matched the linen.

"Is Mr Churchill right?" Estella had asked Tommy, once she had been excused from the table and the men, armed with cigars and brandy, had departed for the library.

"He's right that the Germans appear to be upping the ante with their military. They certainly seem to be on the offensive," Tommy replied grimly. She might be coy when it came to talking about sex, but she didn't hold back when it came to politics and she didn't seek to shield Estella from what was taking place in Europe either.

"Papa says nobody wants another war," Estella parroted. Reginald Kellow had fought in the last one. Sometimes at night she heard him shouting. Cook said when he came home his hands hadn't stopped shaking for months, but at least he had come home. All three of Estella's uncles were buried in French soil and the Pencallyn estate had nearly been without an heir.

"Of course nobody wants a war," Tommy agreed. "But I'm afraid the German chancellor is an ambitious and dangerous man. Maybe I'm wrong. I certainly hope so."

Estella hoped Tommy was wrong too, but she could see events in

Europe were gathering momentum. Just as the season was at the tipping point, the sun slanting his rays a little longer across the lawn to say winter was on its way, so subtle changes were also taking place in Europe. What would the close of 1939 bring? If there wasn't going to be a war, then why had they been told to fit blackout blinds and turn the cellar into an air raid shelter? Papa said it was all a waste of time, but to Estella these preparations were a premonition of what might come. She'd also read in the papers that children from the cities were to be evacuated into the countryside just in case.

"Just in case of what?" she asked Poppet, but the little dog stared up at her sadly, as though all the ills of the world rested on her silky head. Estella sighed. War was coming. She could feel it in the chill of the air and see it in the shadows lengthening across the lawn. Something was waiting over the horizon, something dark and inescapable.

Estella realised life at Pencallyn was poised on the brink of something irreversible. Danger was creeping closer and there was nothing anyone could do to stop it. With a small cry of fear, Estella slammed the window shut.

CHAPTER 19

Estella
1939

Evie Jenkins arrived on an ordinary Wednesday evening. The weather was sunny, there was still a fidgety peace between England and Germany, and Estella's life was rolling along on the well-oiled wheels of routine. There were never any signs that the points on the tracks were about to switch or that the signal was broken. There were no clues that life at Pencallyn was about to change for ever.

Whenever she looked back on that day, Estella was always amazed it had started as such a mundane one. She'd eaten breakfast with Violet, spent the morning working on algebra and the afternoon reading *Pride and Prejudice.* Then she'd had a walk in the garden with Poppet before trying to learn her French vocabulary. There had been no painting or writing, no sense of something important building on the horizon, and nothing of any note at all except spotted dick and custard for pudding – and, since Alex was staying away with a school friend, the possibility of seconds.

Every life contains turning points, places where destiny pirouettes and pivots, and moments that change the course of events for ever. The day Evie Jenkins came to Pencallyn was an interlude such as this. Later on, it would seem impossible to Estella that she hadn't sensed its significance.

Estella was eating supper in the kitchen, something she often did when her father was away, and Violet was out and about, 'gadding',as Mrs Tullis, Pencallyn's formidable cook, like to put it. Estella preferred taking her meals this way, not least because it was far more relaxing not to be seated at the vast dining table with her father scrutinising her table manners while Violet pushed her food around the plate before declaring herself stuffed after a few mouthfuls. What kitchen suppers lacked in etiquette they more than made up for in exciting gossip too. The housemaid, plump and giggly, was called Dolly Pender, was wonderfully indiscreet, and if Tommy forgot to shush her then Estella was able to learn huge amounts about the goings-on in Pencallyn village. None of the grownups ever told her anything, and

Estella was used to using her wits to work things out. You had to operate this way at Pencallyn if you wanted to navigate the unpredictability of her father's temper. Not upsetting Reginald Kellow was the one rule that underpinned the entire household.

"The Mistress has really gone and done it now!" Dolly announced, bursting into the room. "There's going to be hell up!"

"What's she up to this time? Not decided to have another house party, I hope? There won't be nearly enough time to get ready," grumbled Cook. She wiped her hands on her apron and placed them on her well cushioned hips in the perfect picture of indignation. "That one thinks I can magic a five-course meal out of thin air. Well! I'm not doing it and I shall tell her so."

"It's worse than that," breathed Dolly. Her eyes were bright with excitement and delicious shock. "The Master will be proper upset when he finds out what she's done – and without asking him first too!"

Estella abandoned her pudding to focus on listening in. Any appetite had vanished the instant Dolly mentioned her father being upset. Reginald Kellow was given to explosive rages which came out of nowhere and knocked you off your feet with the same ferocity as the storms which swept up the English Channel. There was no moderation either, and the smallest misdemeanour could result in the most severe punishment. Alex had once been strapped so hard after taking a pie from the kitchen he hadn't been able to go hunting all Christmas holiday, and when Violet dared suggest Reginald was being harsh his fury escalated so greatly she hadn't come out of her room for three days. Anything that upset the equilibrium of Reginald Kellow's existence, or which he perceived undermined his authority within the household, never ended well. Estella's heart was already fluttering at the mere thought of an upset. Why couldn't Violet tiptoe around him and keep the peace like the rest of them did? Why did her stepmother insist on doing things which made him so angry?

Tommy's spoon clattered into her empty bowl.

"Don't keep us in suspense. What's she been up to?"

"The Mistress has brought an evacuee back home with her!" Dolly announced. "She's picked one up from Calmouth Station and brought it back to Pencallyn House. Did you ever hear the like?"

Estella's eyes opened wide. Whatever she'd been expecting Violet to have been up to, it certainly wasn't this. Random guests arriving unannounced, endless bags of shopping, new clothes from Paris and once a brand-new Jaguar – these things were far more her stepmother's style.

"My goodness," said Cook, astonished. "My sister saw some arriving yesterday. Filthy they were, she said. Little guttersnipes as likely to stab you as soon as look at you. What do we want the likes of them here for? They'll be robbing and thieving before you know it."

"They're children, Mrs Tullis," Tommy said.

"They may well be children, Miss Toms, but why do we have to have them here?" Cook's face was growing redder by the minute and she waved a spoon in time with her words. "It's not as if we're at war!"

"Yet," Tommy replied grimly. "You've surely seen the papers? I'd say war's looking more likely by the day. You'd not begrudge innocent children a safe place to stay if London comes under attack?"

Estella had sneaked a look at Papa's paper that morning and been shocked to see pictures of children alighting from trains at St Austell and Bodmin. Small, lost, and labelled like human parcels, they had been lined up by volunteers from the Red Cross while they waited for prospective families to offer them a billet. Brothers and sisters held hands tightly as though the grip of their fingers would keep them from drifting apart like flotsam carried on the tide. This was frightening enough, but what had really made terror tighten its grip on Estella's heart was to notice how each child was carrying a square box over their shoulder. Those boxes contained gas masks and Estella understood what it meant when children were evacuated from London and issued with these. Papa could protest as much as he liked about the Germans wanting peace, but it was clear to her that Mr Churchill was right; war was coming.

Cook was looking mutinous. "Moving children like this is a waste of time and money. You'll see. It will all come to nothing."

Tommy didn't bother to reply. 'Don't argue with stupid people, they will drag you down to their level and beat you with experience' was her favourite quotation. Mark Twain, Estella recalled. Maybe he had met Cook?

"War or not, we're getting an evacuee," Dolly said. "Lord! What's the Mistress thinking?"

"That we need to play our part, I'd imagine." Tommy pushed her bowl aside. "Somebody has to take these children in, and I imagine Mrs Kellow quite rightly believes that a Member of Parliament's household ought to set an example to the rest of the population."

Cook snorted. "More likely one of her friends was having one so she joined in too. The mistress doesn't think beyond what ribbons are going on her hat or how her hair looks."

Estella giggled and Tommy shot her a sharp look.

"Enough, Mrs Tullis," she said shortly. "Remember your place."

Cook's mouth set in a grim line. "Oh, I remember it all right, and it's to run the kitchen. Not to look after little urchins. That will be your job, I shouldn't wonder."

"I suppose some could be useful and work in the fields," suggested Dolly. "My auntie said they'd have a couple to stay on her farm."

Tommy frowned. "These are children, Dolly, not farm hands. They'll need to go to school."

"So you'll be teaching our one, will you?" Cook parried. "Ah well, like you say, it's good we set an example and do our bit. The child'll no doubt know a lot of Latin and Greek and not give you a moment's trouble."

Tommy opened her mouth to reply but the scrunch of shoes on gravel distracted her and they all looked at the window. Dolly was the first there, her nose pressed against the glass.

"There's the child! Oh! It looks filthy. It'll have nits too, I shouldn't wonder. Whatever next? Look sharp! Here comes Mrs Kellow!"

Estella leaned forward in fascination as everyone's attention was trained on the kitchen door. She was wildly curious to be meeting a real live evacuee, and excited at the idea of a new arrival. This could be somebody to play with. A friend even – although she hoped Dolly's prediction about nits wasn't true. When Poppet had caught fleas in the spring, they'd had to douse her in paraffin and the poor dog had stunk for days.

"Everyone, this is Evie Jenkins! She's an evacuee from London and she's come to stay with us for a while."

Violet Kellow bowled into the kitchen, a manicured hand resting on the shoulder of a skinny child.

"I know this is a surprise," she continued, propelling the new arrival forwards. "It's a surprise for me too, but I was out for lunch with Stephanie Harrington and she was telling me about all the work she does with the Women's Voluntary Services organisation. Steph does all sorts of marvellous gala fundraisers and charity work. Super lunches too up at Harrington Hall for shoots and hunt suppers. Anyway, Steph mentioned how she was involved with billeting evacuated children so I had to offer to help. The next thing I know, I'm at the town hall and I spot Evie here all alone and with nowhere to go. I couldn't leave her, could I?"

Estella smiled at Evie, who was staring at the floor and looking utterly miserable. Poor thing. How awful it must be to leave behind everything you knew. She must be so scared.

"Of course not," she said when nobody else replied and Violet threw her a grateful look.

"I thought she looks a bit like you, Estella! They could be sisters, I said to Stephanie. What a rum thing! We'll take her in!"

Evie raised her chin and Estella glimpsed an expression of such scorn it felt as though she'd stepped into the icehouse. Whatever was Violet talking about? The two girls were nothing alike! Estella, dressed in a white cotton dress and with her hair braided, was clean and fresh while the new arrival looked more like a heap of grubby rags able to walk by itself.

"I can't see it myself, Mrs Kellow," said Cook doubtfully. "But I'm sure you're right. She's filthy and needs a good wash and a delouse, if you want my opinion."

"We don't," snarled Evie and the rage in her low voice made Estella quail.

Cook pressed a hand against her chest. "I never heard such lip!"

"Please don't be rude to Mrs Tullis, dear," said Violet.

Evie glowered at Cook from under her matted fringe. The eyes in her dirty face were bright blue against the grime. They were a very similar shade to her own, Estella thought. How funny!

"She said I've got lice. I never said she was fat even though she is. I ain't the rude one," Evie said.

Estella smothered a giggle; Evie's logic was undeniable. Cook was hugely fat, probably because she sampled everything she made, and she was always free with personal remarks. Estella felt a spark of admiration for the new arrival. Although she must be scared, Evie was refusing to show it. To Estella this felt rather like watching her own shadow side being unleashed; a sensation both exhilarating and frightening.

"Are you sure about this one, Mrs Kellow?" Cook huffed, and Violet sighed.

"This must be so hard for Evie. She's tired, far from home, and everything is new. I'm sure she didn't mean to be rude, Mrs Tullis."

Estella and Evie's eyes met and Estella knew the girl meant every word.

"Hmm," said Cook, unconvinced.

Violet changed tack.

"Do you think you could put the kettle on and maybe find a slice of your delicious plum cake? Evie will have never tasted anything like it," she said warmly, laying a red-nailed hand on Cook's arm and treating her to a radiant smile. When Violet turned that smile on you it felt as though you were basking in sunshine. People would do anything for her then. Cook melted straight away.

"Oh, go on then. I'll see what I can do," she said grudgingly.

"Come and sit down," Violet said to Evie. "Dolly will take your things up."

"Where to?" asked Dolly.

"The nursery," said Violet. To Estella she added, "I thought you girls could share a room while Evie settles in. You'll be able to chat and have midnight feasts." She clapped her hands. "What fun it will be!"

Estella wasn't so certain. She couldn't imagine chatting to Evie all night any more than she could imagine drifting off to sleep with her brooding presence across the room. There was a jagged energy about the girl which made her feel jittery and excitable and not at all like her usual self.

Evie's fists were clenched. She looked every bit as miserable as Estella imagined you would if you had left your family and been pitched into a strange household. She tried to think what might make Evie feel better. Pets usually worked.

"This is my dog, Poppet," she said, hauling the spaniel out from beneath the table. "You can stroke her if you like."

Evie's top lip curled. "I hate dogs. Pa's always betting on them."

"On spaniels?" Estella said and Evie flashed her a look of pity.

"Greyhounds, of course. I ain't never heard of racing spaniels. Have you?"

Mortified by her own stupidity, Estella felt heat flood her cheeks. She studied the grain of the table, whirls and spirals circling endlessly like her attempts to make conversation had swirled into the void of Evie's contempt. She felt dim, and it wasn't a nice sensation.

"I've never seen a dog race," said Violet cheerily. "Plenty of horses racing at Ascot but never doggies. Anyway, never mind that, Evie. Come and have a seat. You must be pooped."

Still wearing her gas mask across her chest, Evie inched herself onto a chair. Violet chose the seat beside her, still smiling brightly although the strain was starting to show as small lines appeared around her eyes like delicate cracks on a porcelain vase. Soon she would vanish on the pretext of having a bath or making a call and that would be the last they saw of her for a few hours. Her good work was done for the day, and Evie would be left for Tommy to take charge of while Violet Kellow sought out another distraction and mixed a cocktail. Estella had seen it all before with puppies, hence Poppet, and tennis lessons and endless parties.

"How old are you, Evie?" Tommy asked.

"I think I'm eleven."

"You *think* you're eleven? Don't you know when you were born?"

"Not really," said Evie. "Pa left me with my gran. He never said when I was born. June, I think. Or maybe July. In the summer, anyhow."

Estella felt dreadful. Poor Evie not having a birthday.

"So, all your friends in your class at school are aged eleven?" Tommy asked, gently.

"When I go to school, they are."

"If you're taught here by me it might be a little harder to play truant, so be warned," said Tommy.

Evie looked mutinous. "I hate school."

"You'll like Tommy's lessons," Estella said, leaning forward eagerly. "We do all kinds of things like French and geography. And we draw, and write stories."

Evie didn't look impressed.

"English? Music?" Estella was trying hard but getting nowhere. "Algebra? Latin?"

"I hate it all," said Evie.

"Oh, leave her alone, you two swots!" laughed Violet. "We're not all brain boxes! I was a terrible dunce when I was at school. Just as well I married your father, Estella, because I was utterly hopeless at most things. I thought I would be an actress like Maureen O' Hara, but it turns out I was useless at acting too."

Evie sat up. Her eyes were bright with interest.

"I saw Maureen O' Hara in *Jamaica Inn* when it was on at the flicks. She was wonderful!"

"Did you?" Estella was impressed. Her father wouldn't allow her to go to the cinema.

Evie nodded. "They sometimes let kids in for free if there's an empty showing. My gran likes to go too – although she sleeps through most of it. Gran sleeps a lot. She ain't well."

Evie's face twisted and the words sounded as though they were caught in her throat. She swallowed hard and stared down at the table, shrinking into herself. Estella imagined she was thinking of her grandmother who was so far away and waiting for the bombs which might or might not fall in a war which most people said was coming as surely as autumn was hard on the heels on the summer.

"So, Evie's eleven and Estella's twelve! How perfect," said Violet, not noticing Evie's grim expression. "I'm sure you two will soon be the best of friends."

Estella was glad Violet was so certain. She had the distinct impression Evie thought she was rather pitiful. The new arrival's eyes were glued to the table-top and she showed no inclination to reply.

"You can take your gas mask off, if you like," Violet suggested.

"Waste of time having one anyway," Cook chipped in as she returned bearing a cake. "There's not going to be a war."

Evie stared at her. "Don't talk bollocks. Of course, there's going to be a war. Why do you think they gave us the gas masks? For a laugh?"

Dolly giggled before she caught Cook's outraged expression.

"Oh dear, I think we'll need to do a little work on language before my husband comes home," Violet said to Tommy, with a giggle. Tommy didn't laugh.

Estella tried again.

"Where about in London are you from, Evie?"

"Bethnal Green. My gran's still there but she wanted me to come here."

"I expect she wanted you to be safe in case the worst occurs," Tommy said kindly. "And you're certainly safer here. Why don't you put your gas mask on the table, dear, and let go of your bag?"

Slowly, Evie did as she was asked. Although she still radiated truculence, without her props to hide behind she looked very small and very young. Her nose was running too, and as she wiped it on her sleeve Estella noticed the girl's knuckles were grazed.

"Oh! You've cut yourself! Are you hurt?"

Evie's eyes flashed. "No, I ain't! But Harry Smith is. He called me a bastard, but I got him back because I blacked his bloody eye. He cried like a baby."

"Language!" said Tommy automatically but the new arrival curled her lip scornfully at the admonishment. Estella was impressed. Imagine being the kind of girl who blacked a boy's eye when he called you a name! That would shut Alex up. Her brother was always saying girls were sissies and telling Estella to push off and play with her dolls when she wanted to explore the garden with him or go sailing.

"Poor Evie had a little altercation on the journey," Violet explained quickly. "One of the boys was most unpleasant to her. She was jolly upset, but it's all sorted now."

"Sorted with her fists," tutted Cook.

"Violence isn't how we sort things at Pencallyn House," said Tommy sternly. "It would be a good thing if you understood that right away, Evie. There are other ways to sort our differences besides using fists. You're in a gentleman's household now."

Evie stared back at Tommy with mingled incomprehension and insolence, but fortunately at this point Dolly placed the cake on the table and poured their tea. Lecture forgotten, Evie fell onto the food as though she hadn't eaten in a decade, stuffing as much in as she possibly could and chewing with her mouth open. She ate with gusto, her head down and her elbows out like a duck, and Estella watched in fascination. Once the cake was finished, Evie wiped her mouth with the back of her hand before gulping back her tea and belching. Violet winced and stood up.

"I'll leave you to settle in, Evie. Maybe pop her in the tub before bedtime, Miss Toms? She's a little ripe."

It was true. Evie smelt unwashed and her hair was stirring with a life of its own. This made Estella's skin itch and she had to sit on her hands so as not to scratch.

"Looks like you've got your work cut out, Miss Toms," Cook observed once Violet had departed.

"It would seem that way," Tommy agreed. She ran a hand through her short brown crop then stood up and clapped her hands. "Right, Evie. Bath time. I'll need to borrow you, Dolly, to lend a hand and find some clean clothes. Estella should have a spare nightdress Evie can use for tonight, and there are clean towels in the nursery linen cupboard. Mrs Tullis, could you ask Bert for some paraffin? We'll need to treat Evie's hair too."

Evie looked up in alarm. "I ain't having no bath."

Tommy crossed her arms. "You certainly ain't having no bath. You are having a bath and it's not up for discussion. Ready when you are, young lady."

Poor Evie was frogmarched up to the bathroom and the ensuing shrieks and yells could probably be heard down at Pencallyn Cove. They were certainly loud enough for Violet to claim her head was pounding and for Estella to be unable to concentrate on her book as they sat in the drawing room. It sounded as though Tommy and Dolly were trying to drown Evie Jenkins rather than wash her.

"Dear Lord! What will they think in the village?" Violet exclaimed, rising from her chair and walking to the open French windows. Dusk was falling and a fat harvest moon floated above the small V of sea like a pendant nestled above the neckline of a low-cut evening dress. Violet stepped out onto the terrace, cocktail glass held loosely in one hand and cigarette in the other, and gazed out over the darkening garden while blowing lazy smoke rings.

"I do hope she won't be a problem, darling. Perhaps it was a bad idea to have her here?"

"Maybe she hasn't had a bath before?" Estella offered.

Violet swirled her drink. "Oh dear. What a dreadful thought. Perhaps she would be better off with her own sort down in the village? Should I send her back?"

Estella thought about Evie. The wary blue eyes. The grazed fighter's knuckles. The feisty spirit. Estella felt as though she had gazed into a mirror and seen her own reflection peer back, distorted and alien. Evie couldn't go back. She was the most exciting thing that had ever happened!

"Well, she can't go back, anyhow. There's probably going to be a war," Estella said firmly.

Two plumes of smoke huffed through Violet's nostrils and drifted into the dusk. "What a dreadful bore that will be if it happens. You're right, darling, of course you are. Evie must stay. Will you take care of her for me? Take her under your wing a bit?"

"Of course," Estella said, although she wasn't certain Evie would appreciate this.

"Thank you, darling. Oh dear, I'm rather worried Daddy won't be happy she's here. He might be angry with me. It seemed such a good idea at the time. I do hope he isn't cross."

Reginald Kellow was never happy except when gloating over his precious garden. Estella fully expected him to be annoyed by Evie's arrival.

"Of course, it's a good idea," she fibbed. "Daddy will want to set an example. Tell him how everyone will be so impressed he's doing his bit for the evacuees. He'll be pleased about that, I should think. His constituents will have to follow suit and they'll think he's marvellous."

Violet smiled shakily. "You are clever, darling. That is exactly what we'll say. By the time Daddy's home Evie will be so well settled he'll hardly notice she's here."

Estella wasn't quite so sure this would be the case. Evie Jenkins struck her as the sort of person it was impossible to ignore, especially while having a bath.

Eventually her screams stopped and Pencallyn was peaceful again. Estella was returning to her book when the drawing room door opened and Tommy marched in, propelling Evie into the room in the style of somebody showing off a piece of art.

Evie Jenkins was a new creation. Dressed in a white nightgown, her long dark hair tied back from her suspicious face with a ribbon, and minus the layer of grime, she looked like a different girl altogether. One who certainly smelt of paraffin, and who still had grazed knuckles, but also a girl with big blue eyes, bone china skin and a perfect rosebud mouth.

"What do you think?" Tommy said.

Estella stared. Violet hadn't been wrong. Now Evie was clean the resemblance was unmistakable.

"I think she looks like me," she whispered, and Evie smiled.

"We could be sisters, couldn't we?" she said.

And as these words fell from Evie's lips, goose bumps shivered across Estella's arms. She was sure that somewhere the stars had shifted into a new and fateful alignment.

CHAPTER 20

Estella
1939

Evie's first few days at Pencallyn were uneventful, or at least they would have appeared so to any adult. She said little and although Estella tried to engage her in conversation her replies were monosyllabic. She yawned a great deal too, claiming it was too quiet to sleep at night. When she heard owls, she jumped, and when night fell the thick countryside darkness frightened her. On Evie's first night Tommy left a lamp on in the nursery but even so Evie sat bolt upright in bed, hugging her knees to her chest and staring wide-eyed into the shadows. Estella had eventually fallen asleep, but when she woke the next morning the new arrival was in the same position and had dark purple smudges beneath her eyes.

"It smells funny here," Evie whispered. "It smells of dead stuff."

Estella rubbed her eyes. She could smell salt and earth and the decomposing vegetation of the specimen garden, a deep leaf litter that spoke of years of mulching and bedding down and the rich rotting remains of creatures and plants that expensive roots dined upon. Decay was part of the garden.

"It's the earth you can smell," she said kindly. "The gardeners are digging before the sun gets high."

She hopped out of bed and pulled up the blackout. Sunshine streamed in, and the sea in the dip of the valley was turned to gold with the promise of another glorious day. Peering down from the nursery window, Estella spotted the straining rumps of several under-gardeners as they toiled away preparing the formal beds. Others were raking the gravel paths and trimming the lawn's edges to mathematical precision. Not a blade of grass would be out of place when Reginald Kellow arrived back at Pencallyn that evening.

"Come and look," Estella said, beckoning Evie over. "See? They have to get the soil right and dig in fertiliser. Papa must have ordered some more plants."

Evie looked at her blankly. "Why?"

"Why? Because that's what you do."

"But why? Why do you need more plants? Are you going to eat them?"

Estella laughed. "No! Of course not! We eat the vegetables from the kitchen garden. We don't eat the plants."

"So, what are the plants for?"

Estella was thrown. The garden was such a part of her life she rarely questioned its purpose. Pencallyn was famed for its fine collection of exotic plants and trees, and experts would often visit to examine certain plants or write pieces for journals about it. But what was it for? It wasn't for anything but pleasure, surely? It just was. How on earth did she explain this?

"This is a special garden," she said eventually. "It was planted a hundred and fifty years ago by my great-grandfather, and it contains plants and trees from all around the world. There's aloe vera and Japanese acers and something called *Trachycarpus fortunei* which comes from China." Estella felt proud to remember this. "Our tree is over one hundred years old, and the tallest in the country!"

"But what's the garden *for*?"

Evie was a girl who demanded answers, and Estella thought hard.

"It's a bit like a plant museum, I suppose. My father says we have to look after it for the next generation because it belongs to them."

"It ain't yours?"

"Well, it is but I think he means it will still be here in years and years when we've all died which makes it our legacy."

"Legacy." Evie rolled the word on her tongue. "Is that something posh?"

Estella supposed it was compared to Evie Jenkins' legacy of flea-infested clothes and boots with holes in them.

"It means we hand the garden on to future generations. My father's very proud of it and I think he loves the garden more than anything. It's quite famous too. I'll show you around later, if you like? We even have our own labyrinth."

"What's one of them?"

"It's a sort of maze. Like in Theseus and the Minotaur. Or at Hampton Court." There was no flicker of recognition from Evie, so Estella changed tack. "Anyway, there's a sundial at the middle and it's a very magical place. I'll take you there later."

"If you must," Evie said, and Estella felt ridiculously disappointed she wasn't more enthusiastic. The sundial was her most special spot in the world.

"The garden goes down to the sea," she added, in case this was an incentive. "There's a path through the woods that takes you to the beach. Have you ever been to the beach, Evie?"

Evie thought for a moment. "I've been to one on the River Thames. It was muddy and it stank. There was dead fish and I found a boot."

"It's different in Cornwall," Estella replied tactfully. She hoped so anyway. The Thames was grey and sullen-looking, and from Evie's description, its beaches were disgusting, whereas the beaches in Cornwall were sweeping expanses of clear water and shining silver sand.

"I dunno if it is or isn't," said Evie with a scowl. "I ain't seen those."

Estella felt rather rebuffed, but reminded herself that coming to Pencallyn must be a huge shock for Evie Jenkins. How much the girl's life had changed! She was clean for a start, and she was dressed in a pretty sprigged cotton dress rather than her grubby knitted tights, skirt and patched jumper, all of them now burned because they had been crawling with fleas. The brown boots had been spirited away too, and she wore new shiny leather shoes; and now she had ribbons in hair which, washed and deloused, was as thick and as glossy as a raven's wing.

There were a few incidents that would stick in Estella's mind from Evie's first day. The new arrival had never seen a boiled egg before and was absolutely disgusted by the taste of whole milk, which she promptly spat out all over the table. She wanted to spoon sugar onto everything and swore like a trooper when the sugar pot was removed by Dolly. She had a ravenous appetite, but her table manners were non-existent; she mostly ate with her fingers and a teaspoon, head down and almost in the plate as she scooped up food and wiped her mouth on the back of her hand. Estella watched in shocked fascination but Alex, unimpressed to arrive home and find a female evacuee at Pencallyn, was disgusted.

"Do you have to eat like that?" he asked, screwing up his nose in distaste.

Evie looked up. Clods of porridge plopped down from her chin and splattered onto the table.

"Like what?"

"Like this!" He mimed her eating, complete with snorting sounds. "You're like an animal in the trough! Guzzle! Guzzle! Oink! Oink!"

Evie's cheeks were stained red. Her spoon paused halfway to her mouth and trembled in her grasp.

"Say that again," she said. Her voice was low and dangerous.

"Don't be so mean, Ally!" Estella protested.

"I'm not being mean, sis. I'm pointing out a fact. This girl's manners are revolting. She eats like a pig. We may as well throw swill at her."

"Maybe nobody has ever shown her how to eat properly?"

Estella felt indignant on Evie's behalf. Alex could be so smug sometimes, and he was always a hundred times worse when he'd been staying with one of his stuck-up friends.

"Perhaps she ought to learn?" Alex said. "It's putting me off my breakfast. Hey! What are you doing? Get down from there, you utter lunatic!"

Evie had leapt from her seat and scrambled across the kitchen table as she lunged for Alex. Plates and toast went flying, and seconds later her foe was wearing a bowl on his head and sporting a porridge beard. He looked utterly ridiculous and Estella started to laugh.

"You little cow!" Alex hissed. He slammed the bowl down on the table. "You're lucky you're not a chap or I'd call you out."

Evie held her small fists in a fighter's stance.

"Come on then, you bugger! I ain't scared of you!"

Alex was utterly stunned. This wasn't how girls behaved. Seeing he was wrong-footed, Evie crawled back across the table and turned her attention back to her food.

"Blimey," said Dolly. "What a temper, young lady!"

"That's not a lady," Alex spat as he mopped porridge from his shirt. "That's a savage."

"Don't dish it out if you can't take it," said Evie. "Just because I'm a girl doesn't mean I can't stick up for myself. You have to where I come from."

"And where's that exactly? The gutter?" Alex pushed back his chair. "Maybe you should go back? It's where guttersnipes like you belong."

For a dreadful moment Estella thought Evie would hurl herself at Alex again, but he turned on his heel and slammed the kitchen door so hard the plates on the dresser rattled.

"Would you fetch us a cloth please, Dolly, so we can clear this up?" Estella said quickly.

Dolly hastened to the sink and fished out a dish cloth.

"Don't make a habit of behaving like that," she warned Evie as she wiped the table clean. "The Master will send you packing if you do."

"Good," said Evie. "I want to go back to me gran. She needs me. I do everything for her."

Her bottom lip trembled. Estella's heart went out to Evie. It couldn't be much fun being miles from home, worried about your loved ones and stuck with strangers. Violet had meant well, but Evie was a fish out of water at Pencallyn. Alex had been unkind to make her feel even more awkward.

"I'm sorry about my brother," Estella said. "I'm sure he didn't mean it."

"Of course he bloody did," Evie replied. Estella saw her eyes fill with scorn at this attempt to make an excuse but, feeling bad, she tried again.

"He's an idiot and always ten times worse when he's been staying with his stupid friends. Alex knows a gentleman shouldn't make a guest feel uncomfortable."

"Will they send me home because of what I done?" Evie asked hopefully.

"I'd send you packing in a heartbeat," Dolly told her staunchly as she rinsed the cloth under the tap. "Mrs Kellow won't, though. She's a soft touch, bless her."

Evie turned her big blue eyes on Estella.

"If you tell your pa what I done then he might send me home."

If her father knew about Evie's outburst, Estella thought he'd pick her up by the scruff of her neck and throw her out himself. Then he'd give Alex a thrashing and probably Violet too for inviting Evie into their house. Estella's heart began to beat faster and her hands felt all tingly with terror. She couldn't let this happen, and neither could Alex. Like Estella, he'd grown up learning how to tread lightly around their volatile parent.

"Lord, don't go upsetting the Master whatever you do!" Dolly said, horrified. "He doesn't want to be bothered with squabbling children. He's a busy man and he has very important work to do."

"It'll blow over," Estella promised. "Alex will feel an idiot and he'll say sorry. He started it anyway."

Evie looked disappointed. As they returned their attention to their boiled eggs, Estella realised she didn't want Evie Jenkins to leave. Life was far more interesting with her around. Estella couldn't imagine ever being brave enough to pour porridge on her brother's head. She was filled with admiration for a girl who could.

"Evie, you were …" Estella paused. A bubble of emotion was pushing itself up inside her and she wasn't certain she could articulate it. "You were magnificent!"

But Evie looked puzzled.

"I was just me," she said.

As Estella had suspected, nothing more was said about the porridge incident. Alex avoided the girls, and breakfast the next day was eaten in the nursery and supervised by Tommy. As she ate, Estella felt Evie's sharp eyes absorbing her every move; each lift of her spoon was copied and the delicate way she dabbed the corners of her mouth was imitated too.

After breakfast Tommy took the girls to the beach so Evie could encounter the sea for the first time. This was a real treat for Estella, who hadn't been allowed to walk so far since she'd been ill, and she was thrilled to feel the cool damp sand beneath her toes after so long. The sun was warm, and while Poppet raced up and down the beach chasing seagulls Estella peeled off her stockings to paddle.

"Come on, Evie!" she called. "It's not too cold, I promise!"

But Evie hung back, fearful of the wide expanse of water. No amount of encouragement could tempt her near it, and she huddled on a tartan blanket with her knees hugged against her chest. She flatly refused to take her shoes off, and nothing could entice her anywhere near the water. Estella realised this was a new experience too far for the wary Londoner, and she must be patient with Evie. She would soon learn to have fun in Cornwall. How could she not?

Cook had packed a picnic basket filled with bottles of lemonade, fruit cake, scotch eggs and hunks of cheese to eat with slabs of freshly baked bread and yellow butter. To Estella's surprise Evie screwed her nose up in disgust when Tommy passed her a slice of the loaf.

"I ain't eating no dirty bread!"

"Dirty?" Estella repeated. "It isn't dirty!" She took a mouthful of her own slice and chewed for a moment before swallowing. "It's delicious."

Evie's face was tight with suspicion. "Why's it a funny colour?"

Tommy laughed. "It's brown, you mean? That's because it's wholemeal – it isn't dirt, I promise. You must be used to white sliced bread. Try it, Evie. It's very nice."

Evie shook her head and no amount of cajoling would persuade her to eat the 'dirty' bread any more than she could be tempted to hunt for shells or paddle. She showed little inclination to do anything, except watch Estella intently. It was rather unnerving to be the focus of such scrutiny.

"It's a shame you won't paddle, Evie, because I'm not sure how much longer we'll be able to come down to the beach," Tommy remarked as she packed their belongings away.

Evie gave a one shouldered shrug to connote her lack of concern, but Estella was alarmed.

"Why not, Tommy? It isn't winter for ages."

"It's not the weather that will stop us coming to the beach." Miss Toms pointed to the quay wall where rolls of barbed wire were stacked alongside lobster pots and tangled fishing nets. "If war comes then the coastline will be defended in case there's an invasion. It'll be out of bounds to us and I suspect there will be mines and guns and barbed wire here before very long. We'll have to keep away."

Estella's heart sank. It was a beautiful sunny day. Children were climbing over the rocks with shrimping nets, several swimmers were bobbing up and down in stripy costumes and holidaymakers were perched on the sea wall and eating ices. Everything looked so normal and safe. Would the Germans really attack them here? Could there really be an invasion?

"Is there really going to be a war?" she asked. The question was meant for Tommy, but it was Evie who answered.

"Of course, there is," she said. "I'm here, aren't I?"

Tommy sighed. "I think lots of things are being put into place in case of war. The schools are late going back too this year because so many men have joined up and all the children are needed to help with bringing the harvest in. I'm afraid it's simply a matter of time."

Estella swallowed. The perfect summer's day seemed to dim as though already a memory; an image of blue sky and sunshine and a carefree life pasted into a scrap book to remind them all how life had been. Nostalgia for a time yet to be lost pierced her heart.

Tommy's words had created a sombre mood and as they walked back up hill to Pencallyn none of the trio had a great deal to say. The sun slipped between billowing grey clouds and by the time they were inside fat raindrops were splashing down.

For something to do Estella showed Evie the library and her favourite books. As the rain lashed down, they tucked themselves in a window seat with a copy of *Jane Eyre* but Evie wasn't interested in the story. To engage her, Estella attempted to share her own stories and drawings, but Evie said little. It was rather disheartening. So much for having a new friend and comrade in arms. Estella already had a brother to ignore her; she didn't need Evie to join in too.

"It's going to rain for ages," she said finally. "Why don't you choose a book and read for a bit? There's nothing else to do when it's like this."

Evie slipped from the window seat and wandered to the shelf where Estella had found *Jane Eyre.* She picked a book just as Estella had done, checking spines closely and running her finger along the shelf before making her choice and settling down once more.

"*Villette*," said Estella, impressed. "I haven't read that one yet."

Evie didn't reply but bent her head over the book and studied it intently. She glanced at Estella, watching how she flipped pages and traced text with her finger, before doing the same. It was a convincing display of dedicated reading except for one small detail – the book was upside down.

Oh! Evie couldn't read!

Now Estella understood how Evie Jenkins operated. Her sharp blue eyes watched everything and missed nothing. Being watchful was their new arrival's strategy for survival, and although Evie might say little her quick brain was shuttling back and forth as she observed relationships between people, evaluated Pencallyn's rules and decided how best to work within them. She had to navigate uncharted territory without the social skills needed to survive – no wonder Alex's cruel comments had provoked such a reaction. As sharp as a blade and a born survivor, Evie could black a boy's eye and curse like a navvy when the mood took her. She was at home in the East End, but in the world of Pencallyn she was hopelessly out of her depth. She might get away with acting a part, as she had at breakfast time today, but there were some things she couldn't hide.

"Let me help," Estella said.

She leant forward and turned the book the right way up. Evie flushed.

"I can't read."

"And I can't fight," said Estella. "Or swear. Or be brave like you."

Evie shook her head. "I ain't brave and the other stuff's easy."

"Not for me. I've been really ill, and nobody lets me do much at all. I'm scared most of the time too. And you *are* brave. Really brave. I'd love to be more like you."

They stared at each other. As their eyes locked the intensity in Evie's gaze was so powerful that Estella was lost for words. She felt as though she was being consumed.

"I'd love to be like you," Evie said slowly. "A proper lady with manners and what can read and all that. I dunno how to eat like you, or speak proper, but I can pretend I know stuff until I really do."

"You really can," Estella agreed. "Look at how you chose the book just now. If it hadn't been upside down, I would have never guessed. Evie, if there is a war, like you and Tommy say there will be, you could be living here a while. This is going to be your home until it's over, so you can have lessons with me. Tommy will help you learn to read. Why don't we try to teach each other the things we don't know?" She placed her book spine up on the window seat and held out her hand as though making a deal. "What do you say, Evie? Shall we help each other? Can we be friends?"

Evie held out her hand. It was small but the grip was strong. It was the hand of a survivor.

"I think we can," she said.

As they shook hands Estella caught sight of their reflections in the windowpane, a blurred pair of forms with two sets of wide blue eyes, two small heart-shaped faces and two dark heads bent close together.

How funny. They could almost be sisters …

CHAPTER 21

Estella
1939

As Estella had predicted, Reginald Kellow was not thrilled to discover that Violet had taken in an evacuee without seeking his permission, but he could hardly protest when his constituents were going to be asked to provide billets for at least one child, any more than he could continue to deny that war with Germany was inevitable. Everyone was issued with gas masks and identification cards, and it was clear that tensions were escalating. When blackout practice took place at Pencallyn House and an air raid shelter was fashioned in the wine cellar, Estella knew even her father expected war. The family would gather in the drawing room to listen to the wireless, and Reginald Kellow would rant about the Germans' audacity and Herr Hitler's 'absolute nerve'.

"We licked them last time and we'll lick them again," he'd growl, pacing up and down the drawing room. "Yes, we damn well will!"

Although war seemed closer than ever, this was a glorious time for Estella. Evie had resided at Pencallyn House for a short time, but it was already impossible to imagine life without her. Since Evie's confession in the library, the girls had become firm friends, sharing secrets and making up games together, and the long lonely hours of bed rest and wandering alone through the garden seemed as though they belonged to another life. Now Estella had a partner in crime, someone to join in with her elaborate games and who she could tell her stories to. Estella wanted to be a writer and an artist, but Evie's dearest dream was to become an actress. She idolised Vivian Leigh and Maureen O' Hara, had memorised huge chunks of dialogue from their films, and was a born mimic. After just a few days at Pencallyn Evie's own speech was already changing, the double negatives and cursing drifting away, and she could imitate a gesture to become another person. In the twitch of an eyebrow, or the flick of a hand, she was Tommy. A waddling flat-footed gait made her Cook, and soon Violet's nervous patting of hair was in her repertoire. She was brilliant and had

Estella in stitches.

"I can be anyone I like," Evie declared, and this wasn't a boast but a fact. She was a consummate actress, a chameleon, and a sharp observer. She studied Estella carefully, shifting her own posture, draping her hair over her shoulders and widening her blue eyes. "See? I can be you if I like! I bet some people couldn't even tell!"

It was true, and although Evie was a little taller they were similar enough to able to fool the butcher's boy when he delivered to the house, and as long as Evie didn't speak and they kept a little distance, they could do the same with Bert the gardener too. But when they tried to trick Cook, she wasn't fooled for a minute and ticked the girls off for playing silly games.

"It's not nice to deceive people," she'd said, a disappointed note in her voice. "I'm surprised at you, Miss Estella."

Estella had felt bad, but Evie laughed.

"We're going to have such fun with this!"

And Estella *was* having fun. More fun than she had had for a long time. Evie was fearless, and being with her made Estella feel braver than she'd ever been. Soon her illness was forgotten as she ran through the garden, slid down banisters and filched pies from the pantry. When Alex made up with Evie, it felt as though life at Pencallyn couldn't get any better.

Evie and Estella had been in the schoolroom when Alex had sought them out. He stood in the doorway and seemed far too big for the little room with its small chairs and desks. Her brother was almost a man, Estella realised with surprise.

"May I have a word, Evie?" he said.

Evie put aside the exercise book into which she was painstakingly copying the alphabet. She'd been obsessed with this activity ever since her confession she couldn't read, and had spent hours in the schoolroom working on her letters. Her determination was exhausting to watch, and although Estella begged her to come outside and play in the garden, she flatly refused to be distracted from her task.

"Come to call me more names?" she had asked. There was a hint of challenge in her voice.

Alex cleared his throat. "Look, I'm sorry for what I said to you. It was unforgivably rude. Thanks for not ratting on me."

"I ain't no grass. Anyway, you could have told your old man on me."

"I don't think I could," Alex said slowly. "Anyway, I had it coming after what I said to you."

Evie shrugged her skinny shoulders. "You was right. I don't eat nicely like you."

"Maybe not quite like me, but it still wasn't a gentlemanly way to speak to a lady."

"I ain't no lady!" Evie said. "But I ain't a pig, neither."

Alex ran a hand through his hair. "I'm really sorry I said that. It wasn't fair."

"No, it wasn't. I ain't never had no one show me what all them knives and spoons and forks are for. I'd never seen so many in all my life!"

"No, I can quite imagine you haven't," said Alex. He dug his hands in his pockets. "Look, if you like I can show you what to do with a proper dinner service. It really isn't hard. I think you'll pick it up jolly fast."

And so Estella's brother found himself giving Evie Jenkins lessons in table manners. As with the handwriting, she was intent on learning, and within a few days she was wielding cutlery with ease. Watching her sit up poker-straight, lay a napkin on her lap and select the correct knife and fork for the appropriate course, Estella thought nobody could ever guess that until a few days ago the girl had only eaten with her fingers or a spoon.

The ripening days of early September 1939 hung heavy over Cornwall. The air shimmered above the sea like a mirage, not a whisper of wind stirred the trees and Pencallyn's gardeners were run ragged watering plants and snipping blooms in the cutting garden. On the first Sunday of the month, another hot and sunny day, Reginald Kellow was in London and Violet was sleeping in after an evening out dancing. Tommy was visiting her father in Truro, and with no adult to chivvy them to St Brecca's, a day of glorious freedom stretched ahead for the children. Alex had walked down to the beach for a swim, leaving Evie and Estella to their own devices. They played in the labyrinth for a while, watching the sundial's shadow slice the hour, before becoming too hot and plunging into the cool gloom of the woods. The shade was bliss after the heat, and the girls lay on their backs in the ferns, staring up at the patches of blue sky puncturing the green canopy and drowsing in the shade. A woodpigeon's call trembled in the air before all was still. It felt as though time was holding its breath.

"There are people hiding in the leaves," Estella said dreamily. "Can you see them?"

It was a trick of the light, of course, but if she narrowed her eyes Estella could make out faces peering through the trees and floating in the ferns. If you squinted a little you could even catch figures turning away as they melted into the undergrowth and faded back into the foliage. Estella had always seen them and, in her imagination, they were shades of the past. A lady in a cloak, a boy in green tights, a hooded man – she had been watching them for years and making up their stories. Sometimes she tried to paint them too, but they were every bit as elusive on her brush as they were in the heart of the garden. She'd tried to paint herself in, and Alex, but the resulting ghostly images made her uneasy, so she had tucked them away in her folder of abandoned work where they waited for resurrection. Once she'd painted the face of the handsome young man from her long-ago dream but her clumsy brushwork didn't do his beauty justice and she had given up in a fit of frustration. One day she would see him for real. One day he would find her.

Evie sat bolt upright. "Where are they?"

"Everywhere. Squint a bit, like this." She screwed up her eyes. "You'll see them."

Evie scrunched up her face. "I can't see nothing."

"Anything," Estella corrected. "You can't see *anything*."

"I can't see anything," Evie said sulkily. "You're making it up!" But she looked around anyway, a worried scowl drawing her dark brows together.

"Am I?" Estella said softly. "Maybe. But maybe not. This part of the garden is very, very old. They say it's on a magical ley line which comes all the way from France and goes all the way to Stonehenge. It goes through this garden, under the sundial, up through the farm where there's a well, and to the church. All were pagan sites. In the olden days the pagans knew this spot was powerful. It still is."

"Bollocks," scoffed Evie, but Estella knew she was disconcerted.

Estella lay right back and stretched her arms above her head. The dank floor was cold against her skin and the earth held the primal scent of decay. Damp seeped into her thin cotton dress. She felt part of the garden, and maybe she was because she was a Kellow? Her ancestors had made this place. Like God, they had made their very own Eden.

"It's true," she said. Tommy had told her all about the ancient Cornish legends of Arthur and druids and Merlin. Cornwall was full of myths and legends, watchful standing stones and secretive wells and odd saints that weren't found anywhere else. Estella had also heard the gardeners and the maids whispering about the garden – they found parts of it eerie. Sometimes little bits of ribbon were found tied into the box hedge by the sundial, fluttering offerings to long-forgotten deities from unseen visitors who still honoured them. These thoughts made Estella shiver; she was intrigued and inspired. A lonely child, her imagination had created a game called Mysterious Garden, a game filled with magic and legend and enigmatic creatures, and now she was ready to share it with Evie. How wonderful to have a companion to join in! What worlds they could create!

"You're making it all up," Evie said. She rubbed arms pimpled with goose bumps. "I don't like it in here. It's odd."

"That's because this garden is powerful and mysterious," Estella told her solemnly. "You can feel it, Eves. Maybe that was why my great-grandfather brought all the foreign trees and plants here? The garden told him to? It commanded him to serve it?"

"Don't talk rubbish!"

"Once upon a time," Estella began softly, "there were two girls. They looked the same in some ways but in others they couldn't have been less alike. Only the garden could tell them apart. Only the garden decided which one was allowed to leave. One would have to stay with all the others it had already kept. The ancient sundial had a Latin message written on it, *Silens loquor,* because it was watching them. The old gods were watching them and waiting to claim them."

Evie jumped to her feet. Her face was white.

"I'm going back."

"It's just a game!" Estella giggled, but Evie was running away through the trees, tripping on roots and stumbling on the path. No amount of calling from Estella could bring her back. How silly she was, Estella thought as hauled herself up from her bed of ferns. It was only a story. She supposed if you were from the city, and not used to the silent depths of the woods and the crack of twigs from unseen passing of secretive creatures, a story could seem real. Or maybe there really were faces and she wasn't making it up at all? Perhaps it was true?

Estella shivered then, and hurried after Evie, not wanting to be left alone with the watching trees. Was it her imagination, but were they pressing closer and closer?

"I'm sorry, Evie!" she called, sprinting up the path. "I was playing."

But there was no answer. Evie could run fast, and Estella was still weak from her illness. By the time she reached the neat formal gardens, Evie was at the terrace where Violet was waving and shouting. Even from a distance it was clear she was upset. Her usually styled hair was loose over her shoulders, her mouth invisible without its habitual slick of scarlet lipstick and she wasn't wearing shoes.

Goodness! Her stepmother looked as though she'd raced out of the house halfway through dressing. Alarmed, Estella tore across the lawn.

"What's happened. Is something wrong?" she panted.

Violet's lip trembled.

"Oh girls, it's terrible news. You will both have to be brave and try your best not to be frightened."

But Violet's ill-disguised fear was contagious, and Evie's hand stole out to grasp Estella's.

Violet's own hands were clasped against her chest.

"I've just heard Mr Chamberlain speaking on the wireless and I'm afraid it's terribly, terribly serious – Herr Hitler has refused to withdraw his troops from Poland."

Estella knew the Germans had invaded Poland, Papa was incandescent about it, but Poland was very far away. Why did this matter so much? Why was Violet so distressed?

"I don't understand," Estella said.

But Evie did. In many ways she seemed to understand so much more.

"It means war," she said softly. "See, Stella? Didn't I tell you that was going to happen? There's going to be a war with Germany after all."

[illegible]

CHAPTER 22

Estella
1939–1940

At first the war felt unreal because nothing really changed at Pencallyn. There were some obvious differences, such as buckets of earth kept by the back door in case an incendiary bomb set light to the house, air raid practice in the cellar, and Estella and Evie being allocated weeding duties as part of their war effort because the younger gardeners had all enlisted, but otherwise life continued in its own gentle rhythm. In some ways Estella thought it was better because Reginald Kellow was away in London for most of the time, which meant the entire household exhaled with relief. There was also Evie to play with, and although she was way behind Estella in terms of her schoolwork, they shared lessons and the days seemed to fly.

But little by little the reality of being at war began to catch up with Cornwall. It was impossible to ignore the warships in Calmouth Bay or the silver barrage balloons tethered on Bury Barrow. Swarms of doughty British planes flew over the hills from the airfields where fighter pilots were being trained, and Alex would watch them with longing in his eyes.

"As soon as I'm eighteen I'm going to join the RAF," he vowed. "Then watch those Germans run for cover! I can't wait to do my bit."

"I haven't seen any German planes. Maybe they won't come?" Estella said hopefully.

"Oh, they'll come all right," Alex told her. "And when they do, we'll be ready for them. But don't panic, sis. The searchlights will spot 'em and barrage balloons will stop planes from coming in low. Besides, the Jerries won't bother with Pencallyn Cove. They'll be more interested in cities like London."

Evie gnawed the end of her plait. "My gran's in London."

"She'll be fine, I'm sure," Alex said quickly. "I heard on the wireless they've built air raid shelters in each street and it sounds like quite a lark when everyone goes inside. You mustn't worry."

Estella couldn't imagine how Evie could not worry.

"I can write to your gran and find out how she is."

"Don't be daft. My gran can't read nor write neither."

"Maybe somebody could read a letter to her?" Alex suggested. "At least that way she'll know you're safe too."

Evie liked this idea, so she and Estella spent a rainy afternoon composing a letter which told Evie's gran all about life at Pencallyn. They included a little bit about their favourite game, Mysterious Garden, which they played most days with its complex set of rules and characters, and they wrote her some lengthy descriptions of food. Although rationing was a part of life now, Pencallyn's kitchen garden was plentiful and there was no shortage of game from the estate. Violet Kellow was a cracking shot and most days came home with a pheasant or a rabbit for the pot. She applied for a couple of land girls to take the place of the lads who'd joined up, and they quickly settled into the groom's quarters above the stables and filled the kitchen with colourful gossip. Although Estella and Evie didn't think there was anything in the letter which might prove dangerous if it fell into enemy hands, Alex checked it just in case. Loose lips and all that, he said.

There were other changes. The beach, once Estella's playground, was out of bounds, lassoed with spiteful coils of barbed wire and guarded with anti-aircraft guns mounted on pillboxes. Piano wire was suspended at the top of the beach to trip the unwary invader and dragons' teeth tank traps snarled up from the sand, ready to snap at unwelcome German vehicles. The sea was no longer a place for swimming and fishing but had become the first line of defence, England's moat as it had been for centuries. When Tommy walked the girls down through the woods and into the village, Estella wanted to weep because the shore looked so angry and hostile, and the very thought of invaders arriving in the depths of the blacked-out night was terrifying. The only thing more frightening than the absolute darkness was the treacherous moonlight which could guide the enemy all the way to Pencallyn's front door.

The beach wasn't the only place forbidden to the locals. The south coast of Cornwall was home to many hidden creeks where willows trailed golden tresses in the drowned sky and kingfishers ruled untrodden banks. By the end of 1939 these were no longer a secluded haven for small boats or picnicking by the ancient churches that slumbered beside mudflats. Instead, the flat expanses of water were claimed by the RAF and it was Spitfires that practised low-flying manoeuvres rather than waterfowl. The overgrown shallows became secret places to moor all kinds of craft. Guarded by guns mounted on the crests of the hills and loomed over by the barrage balloons which tugged at their tethers like naughty ponies, Calmouth and Pencallyn's creeks were the preserve of the Home Guard and out of bounds to anyone else. At first the Cornish had protested, and some had continued to steal out at night to fish, but when two boys were blown up by a mine in the entrance to Calmouth harbour, it became clear that danger wasn't the sole preserve of the Germans and the locals, although still grumbling, stopped fishing.

The end of the year was bitterly cold, as though Hitler had even enlisted the weather. Although Pencallyn had a well-stocked woodshed it seemed a waste of fuel to light all the fires, so during her husband's absences Violet decided all meals were to be taken in the kitchen. With the big range constantly in use, it was the warmest room in the house, and before long became the centre of daily life. When the temperatures plummeted in November, Evie and Estella had lessons at the kitchen table so they didn't freeze. Cook made soup and baked bread – which Evie ate with gusto these days rather than complaining about the colour – and in the evenings the household gathered to listen to the news on the wireless. There was a party atmosphere at times. Land girl Beth taught the girls to knit, and when Violet lugged the gramophone in they all learned how to foxtrot, and a new type of lively American dancing called Swing. Evie, a natural mimic, picked this up in a heartbeat.

"I give up! When you're older you'll have to be a dancer!" Violet panted after an hour of being the tireless Evie's partner.

"When I'm older I shall dance in all the movies," Evie replied, spinning around and holding out her hands to Estella. She tossed her glossy dark hair back from her flushed face and added, "I'll be a famous actress! You'll see!"

"Too big for her boots, that one," was Cook's observation, but Estella thought Evie was marvellous. How must it feel to have such confidence? To know you were brilliant? And Evie *was* brilliant. Whatever she put her mind to she was able to achieve. Her speech was changing, the cockney accent smoothed by listening closely to Estella, the days of bad table manners were long past, and she was already reading fluently.

"I'll soon catch you up," Evie promised Estella, and Estella didn't doubt her for a moment.

There was one area, however, where Estella knew she would always outstrip her friend, and this was making up stories. Evie was a born mimic but she wasn't imaginative. She loved watching Estella paint and clamoured for her stories. The girls would lie awake at night in the thick darkness of the blackout as Estella wove fantastical tales and mysteries and, the heart of it all, the magical sundial. Mysterious Garden shifted into a tale of pagan religion, old enigmas and magical slips in time; the more Estella spun her web of imagination the deeper in Evie was drawn. They drew maps, made up their own language and painted pictures of the characters from their garden games. When the darkness pressed against her eyelids and the Germans seemed to be creeping through the woods and across the lawn, Estella truly believed her imaginary creations could keep her safe. Maybe if she tried hard enough, she could believe them into being?

The handsome prince from her long-ago dream would rescue her one day. Estella knew this with all her heart, but she hadn't shared him with Evie. His warm smile, gentle voice and noble beauty were all hers, and she held them close to her heart. There was something special about him and Estella wanted him safe with her.

Safe. That was an odd choice of word. Was this what she meant? Maybe it was more that Estella wanted to keep something for herself. She loved sharing everything with her new best friend, but sometimes the intensity of Evie's attention was almost too much to bear and Estella had to retreat into a story of her own and a world which belonged to her alone.

When winter fell the sparkling garden was extra magical, and as long as you went nowhere near the beach or the river it was easy to forget about the war. Pencallyn was its own world, and tucked in the embrace of the woods and garden there were no signs of the defences and barrage balloons. There was much disgruntled talk of a phoney war since there had been so little fighting and many people felt that evacuation measures had been far too hasty. Some children returned home to the cities, but to Estella's relief Evie's gran did not want her to go back. Alex was still talking about joining the RAF and hoping the action wouldn't be over before he had a chance to do his bit. Tommy's mouth was a tight line of disapproval at such comments, but Reginald Kellow clapped him on the back and said he was proud to hear such fighting talk. Estella had never seen her brother look so happy, but she quietly hoped Hitler would give up before Ally flew a Spitfire.

The closer it came to Christmas, the busier Violet Kellow became, and she spent a lot of time driving to Truro for dinner parties and dancing. When her husband was away she was free to spend her time any way she liked, and Estella thought it was nice to see her stepmother so happy. She would sing about the house, giggle with the land girls and spend hours setting her hair and fixing her makeup before tearing away in her little Jag, gravel flying beneath the wheels as she made the most of her MP husband's petrol ration.

"She's got a fancy man," Evie remarked one chilly December afternoon as Violet tore down the drive.

Estella looked up from her sketch book. "Who has?"

"Violet, silly. She's got a fancy man."

"That's a horrible thing to say!"

"Not if it's true. Why do you think she's so happy? And why else would she be buying silk underwear when your father's always away?"

"Don't make stuff up, Evie." Estella was angry. She'd been having a nice afternoon. Her chilblains had stopped throbbing, her hands were thawing out enough to sketch, and Tommy was visiting her father which meant there was an entire afternoon free. Now Evie had ruined everything with her horrible remarks.

"I don't make stuff up. That's what you do. I watch and I listen. I've heard Cook and Dolly gossiping, and I see what Violet wears and when she wears it. She always dresses up when she goes to Truro and she never comes back the same evening."

"She goes out for dinner, that's why, and she stays with friends!" Estella cried.

Evie threw her a pitying look. "If you say so. Come on." She snatched Estella's sketch book. "I said, come on! Stop scribbling!"

Estella was angry and turned her back on Evie. "I'm drawing."

"You're always drawing, and I'm bored! Come on! I'll prove I'm not lying!"

Evie grabbed Estella's hand, yanked her up from her cosy seat by the range and towed her upstairs. When they paused outside Violet's bedroom, Estella realised what Evie had in mind.

"We can't go in there!"

"It's fine. Violet's not coming back tonight and your old man's in London."

"We're not allowed in their room!"

"They won't know if they're not here, will they?"

"We'll know," Estella protested, and Evie laughed.

"I won't tell if you won't! Come on! Don't be such a chicken."

"I'm not a chicken!"

"So, prove it! Don't you want to see if I'm telling the truth about the silk underwear? Or prove I'm wrong? Besides, I want to try on the furs and her red lipstick. I'll look just like Vivian Leigh; you know I will!"

Evie's eyes were bright with excitement. She loved going through other people's belongings. Estella had often suspected her of rifling through her own clothes, because she sometimes found items just slightly askew. She imagined the younger girl trying her ribbons and hats, peering in the mirror and slanting her features until the speckled glass blurred her into Estella and her role was perfected.

Now Evie wanted to become Violet.

Or ruin her.

Estella felt dizzy. Was Evie telling the truth, or was this her idea of a joke? She had a cruel streak at times too, but her pluck and sheer energy made up for it. Ever since the reading confession, Estella also knew Evie was fiercely loyal to her. She frowned, feeling torn. If Violet did have a fancy man shouldn't Estella's loyalty be to her father?

Before she had a chance to decide Evie turned the handle, but the door remained shut. She turned the handle in disbelief.

"Bugger! She never usually locks the door. She must be worried we're onto her."

"You've been in her room before?"

"Of course, I have. Nobody keeps secrets from me. Silly old Violet. Fancy thinking she'd get away with it. There are loads of women like her where I come from. Gran says my ma was the same before she pushed off. Violet might be posh but she's still a tart!"

Estella's mouth was dry with dread. "What are you going to do?"

"I'm not going to do anything. It's just another secret. It might be useful, who knows?"

"Useful?" Estella echoed.

Evie smiled. It was a strange smile and seemed too tight for her face, as though it would rip her skin from ear to ear.

"It's good to know everyone's secrets. That's what keeps you safe."

"I don't have any secrets," Estella said. Except for the man in her long-ago dream, but surely an imaginary person didn't count as a secret?

Evie looked at her with eyes as blue and as cold as the bright winter sky.

"Good," she said. "Best friends should never have secrets. Let's promise we never will. No secrets between us. Ever. Promise, Stella?"

Estella was trembling, which was ridiculous. Evie was being dramatic, as always, and probably acting out a role from a film.

"I promise," she said, and they linked the little fingers of their right hands.

But deep in the folds of her woollen skirt, and for a reason she couldn't wholly explain, Estella Kellow kept the fingers of her left hand firmly crossed.

CHAPTER 23

Nell
The Present

I lean forwards as Estella speaks, drinking in every word and desperate not to miss a detail when her voice grows weaker. The hospital room has receded, and I'm transported to Pencallyn as two young girls run wild in the chaos of a household plunged into war and secrets become as tangled as the briars in the garden. I see it all so clearly: the vast garden which two girls make their own magical kingdom, the warships basking in the bay like seeping sea monsters, the barrage balloons sailing from the hilltops and the beautiful old house in all its true glory – no longer crumbling away beneath the dust and the years but magnificent and proud as it stands guard over the garden and gazes at the long-lost sea view. The rooms aren't filled with shrouded furniture but peopled with the faces of the past; watchful Evie with her knowing gaze, Estella whose heart is worn on her sleeve, red-faced Cook, sharp-eyed Tommy and the bored young wife, Violet, beating her wings in curtailed flight like a butterfly trapped against glass. So many secrets and tensions ribbon the narrative, pulling tightly like a corset, and, when Estella pauses, I'm holding my breath in the expectation of more revelations.

"What happened? Did she tell? *Was* Violet having an affair?" Josh asks. He's leaning forward too, barely seated on the edge of his plastic chair, and Estella smiles at his impatience.

"I never knew whether Evie really discovered anything. She loved secrets, I imagine it was her way of having a hold over someone, but she told lies too – not that she would have ever seen them as lies. She was acting out another role, trying a new version of the truth on for size, the way you might try a new hat or pair of shoes. She could become anyone and anything she chose, and she would have been a phenomenal actress. But once Evie was determined to do something it was impossible to change her mind."

"Did she become an actress?" I ask. As Estella has been speaking, Evie

Jenkins has leapt from the story. She's a vibrant, fiercely clever and larger than life character although not one I'm warming to even though I strongly suspect she's my grandmother.

Estella stares into space. "I don't know what happened to her."

Josh rubs his chin. "Well, she sounds intriguing. If she could teach herself to read and write so quickly and was able to adapt her language and behaviour to fit in, she must have been a really bright child."

"Oh yes! She was, she really was!" Estella's lined face glows with admiration, and for a shimmer in time she's twelve again, proudly watching her protégée form letters. "It didn't take long before you would have been hard pushed to know which one of us hadn't been born and raised at Pencallyn. 'Little Miss Heathcliff' was what Tommy called Evie. Not that Evie gave a hoot. Once she'd read the book she cared even less. Heathcliff was right up her street!"

"Heathcliff was a psycho," I say before I can help myself. Everything I am learning about Evie Jenkins alarms me. I really don't want to share that kind of genetic code, even though from what I know of her she couldn't be more different to my lovely, gentle and kind dad. "Sorry, Estella. I love *Wuthering Heights,* but I've never understood the fascination with Heathcliff. Dog-hanging and digging up graves isn't romantic! If I wrote a hero like him, I wouldn't sell many books."

"Ah," Estella says, "but you're assuming *Wuthering Heights* is a romance when maybe it's quite the opposite. It's a story about obsession, first and foremost, and our hero is the outsider who comes from nowhere and takes what he wants for himself. Heathcliff ends up with everything that had once belonged to the Earnshaws. He's the cuckoo in the nest. An interloper who destroys everything."

"Which is why Miss Toms didn't like Evie." Josh leans back in his chair and nods. "She thought Evie was too close to you when it wasn't her rightful place."

Estella closes her eyes. For a moment I think she's fallen asleep, but when she opens them again I realise she's been pondering his remark.

"Yes, I would imagine so, but Evie loved me. We really were as good as sisters, and when she went missing I was so shocked – I'd never thought she would abandon me."

"Evie went missing?" I pounce on this information. If Evie Jenkins went missing was it because she was pregnant with Jay Miller's baby and on the run? I know my paternal grandmother died outside the hospital, so was this where Evie's brief time on earth was ended? She wasn't missing at all but was killed before she could return to Pencallyn House?

I want to ask Estella some more about this, but the doctors arrive and Josh and I take a break in the hospital canteen. He fetches coffee while I settle in a seat by a window which overlooks the River Cal. Blue water teems with pleasure boats today but all I can see are grey warships while the air shudders with the blast of a mine triggered by two naughty boys out for an afternoon's forbidden fishing. Today's peaceful scene overlays the machinery and violence of war, yet Josh was right; look a little deeper and the pillboxes and concrete scars are still here.

"Coffee and carrot cake." Josh deposits the spoils of his trip onto the low table and lowers his lean frame onto the split plastic sofa opposite me. "Dig in."

I don't need asking twice. Moist cake and plump raisins soon party on my taste buds.

"I bet people would have killed for this in the hard days of rationing," he remarks.

"Especially Evie with her love of sugar," I agree.

"Do you think she could be your grandmother?"

I pull a face. "I hope not. She sounds horrible!"

"I think she was a little city kid thrown into a strange situation. She must have been out of her depth and homesick."

"That's true."

"It sounds as though she was very intelligent. The governess spotted that straight away."

"You're on Team Evie?" I say, and he laughs.

"Maybe I like to stick up for the underdog. Anyway, whoever she was she must have been special to Estella because she's always talking about her. When her mind wanders, it's often Evie she's talking to."

I frown. Something about Evie doesn't feel right. The time scales fit, but there's nothing solid which links her to Jay Miller. Estella hasn't even mentioned him yet.

"I'm not sure," I say.

"Fair enough. If Evie's a red herring, what about Estella's stepmother, Violet? Could she have had an affair with Jay Miller? It sounds as though she was looking elsewhere for affection, and from what I know of Reginald Kellow I can't say I'd blame her."

"It's a good theory unless this whole thing is a wild goose chase? You said Estella gets muddled."

"She isn't muddled today. She's recalling everything in amazing detail. It's as though she has to say these things before it's too late and she's taking her time to get it right. There's a lot of detail for sure, but if I know Estella there'll be a good reason for that. It's her style. *Mysterious Garden* is just the same."

"Josh! You're right! That's *exactly* it. The book has all kinds of blind avenues and faces that don't fit until you find the answer." My heart lurches. "But there's no answer. Everyone agrees on that."

"They might, but what would Estella say? She's the only one who can answer these questions." He drains his coffee. "Time's something she doesn't have much of, so we should get back. Another hour with her should be fine. The nurses don't seem to mind."

I'm in agreement, so we make our way back to Estella's room. Every moment must be cherished. When she sees us, Estella smiles.

"So you came back. I hoped you would."

"Can you talk for a little longer?" I ask. "I don't want to tire you out."

Estella snorts. "I'm ninety-five and I'm always tired. Just sit down, dear, and stop fussing. Let's get on with this before I start to forget things. Today is a good day and I want to make the most of it."

Josh catches my eye and smiles.

"So now the war was happening for real." Estella's eyes close as she begins to speak, drifting away from us with her memories shuffling like playing cards. "It's funny how something so awful can become a way of life. For us it was almost a game. We had such fun swapping place names in case the enemy arrived, and I loved helping the land girls drive the Land Rover. Although we sometimes saw planes fly overhead, they never really seemed to have much to do with Evie and me. We were hungry sometimes, with rationing, but there was usually enough to eat, and we were luckier than most because we lived in the countryside. We played spies with Violet's camera, and took it in turns to be the Germans, but my father stopped that game in case we got into real trouble! The garden was our world and our games seemed far more real than the war beyond the gates. We used to leave little messages to each other in the sundial and make up treasure hunts. Oh, we used to love doing that! Funny how we stopped as we grew up. I haven't thought of it for decades. I wonder if any are still in there? We used to put them in an old tobacco tin."

"The sundial was in your book! I thought it was made up."

Estella opens her eyes and raises an eyebrow.

"Maybe it is? Maybe it isn't? You decide. Anyway, Evie wrote to her granny a few times but she never heard back. I think she eventually stopped hoping for a reply, and London probably seemed like another life. She never showed any inclination to mix with her old friends billeted in the village, and in the end she stopped talking about Bethnal Green. It felt as though she'd always lived at Pencallyn.

"We used to listen to the wireless in the kitchen with Cook and Dolly, but the events of the war felt like a story. Apart from blackouts, an overgrown garden and having to stay away from the beach, little changed in that first year. Even Dunkirk seemed like a boys' adventure to us because we didn't really understand what was happening. We saw the fishing boats and pleasure boats leave, but Tommy kept us away when they returned with the injured men and Cook switched off the wireless when we came into the kitchen. My brother and some village lads went over in his little clinker boat, and afterwards Ally would shout in his sleep and wake us all up. That made my father furious because it wasn't manly in his eyes."

"Dunkirk was carnage," Josh says, and Estella bows her head.

"Yes, so I learned later, but at the time it was just another thing that happened, like enemy planes flying over and rationing and the air raid practice in the cellar. That was always fun and we thought of it as an excuse to stay up late. Alex never spoke to me about Dunkirk, but I know what he saw changed him. He joined the RAF not long afterwards. He said he had to do his bit." Her voice quavers. "Dear Ally. He was eighteen, just a boy, and we lost him during the Battle of Britain. My father wished it had been me who'd died. He couldn't understand why a mere girl survived rheumatic fever and Alex was taken instead. Poor dear Alex. One of the few." She passes a hand over her eyes. "Oh, dear. How can it still hurt so much after such a long time?"

"I think loss always hurts," I whisper. A fuzzy screen. My little astronaut. The tiniest, saddest shake of a head. My throat aches with sadness. Loss is loss.

"Sometimes I think I see him, you know," Estella continues. "In the garden or about the place – but it's my mind playing tricks. My memory shows me things that can't exist and takes me back in time until I'm lost, and it's becoming harder to find my way back. And when I do? Then I lose my dear ones all over again."

I hold her trembling hand. Bird bones. Rose petal skin. Age spots and blue veins. One day my own hand will look like this.

If I'm lucky.

"I have wrecking balls that undo me," I tell her. "It can be a few bars of music. A hospital corridor. Dad's aftershave. Or seeing somebody with the same walk."

"I know those," Estella agrees. "They hang inside my mind and swing at will, and I'm frightened they'll take my memories with them. Then it will all be gone."

"What happened after you lost Alex?" Josh asks her.

"My father began to spend more time in London. He was involved with the War Office. The house felt lighter without him in it, and Violet spent all her time in Truro socialising. When I was fifteen and my formal education at an end, Tommy joined the WVS and our lessons stopped. Evie and I ran wild. It was a happy time in many ways."

"Even with a war on?" I say.

Estella nods. "We were free and that was exciting for us. It was only when we were issued with leaflets instructing us what to do in the event of an invasion that I think I finally realised England could go the same way as France. We were told to burn any maps, puncture the tyres of our bicycles and make sure we didn't give the invaders any food. Poles were planted in fields to prevent German gliders landing. Pillboxes and observation posts were cemented on the tops of hills, with anti-aircraft guns and searchlights. Trucks rattled along the lanes and more barbed wire was strung along the beach while barrage balloons glittered in the sunshine. The enemy was just a cat's whisker away and growing ever closer, and as the Cornish had once watched the Armada sail by, so we watched the Luftwaffe swoop over the Channel. My father said he would shoot us all if we heard the bells ringing to warn of an invasion and I had no doubt he meant it. He'd already had our horses shot. Even my old pony, and I cried about that, I can tell you."

My eyes flicker to Josh's. He looks horrified.

"Why on earth would he do that?"

"So that the invading Nazis couldn't eat them or use them, I suppose, and because they were mouths to feed we could ill afford. I tried not to think what happened to the meat, but I have my suspicions. So, to answer your question, Nell, it wasn't always a happy time. It's not trustworthy, memory. It's selective and serves up only what it fancies."

She's right. And often memory offers you what you least wish to recall …

"When the bombing started, we watched Calmouth burn," Estella continues. "The night sky turned orange with flames, and by day the surviving houses stood like broken teeth in an old man's mouth. The village cowered when the German planes flew over, and Pencallyn House shrank into the garden as though trying to hide while we gathered in the cellar and prayed for a cloudy night. We soon discovered the Germans would dump any leftover bombs before their flight back and I grew to hate the sound of those returning planes. Evie could tell just by the sound of the engines what planes were overhead. She loved to watch them swarm and dogfight high up in the sky, but I would shrink away from the noise. I'd pull out my sketch book and draw the garden or write more stories about the games we played there. Evie was riveted by the deadly dancing in the blue, and I think she would have loved to be a boy and gone to fight. That life would have suited her.

"Evie loved danger. She was fearless, always the first to instigate a dare or to try something dangerous. Climbing trees, scaling the garden wall, clambering onto the roof; there was nothing she wouldn't attempt. I was in awe of her pluck and did my best to keep up, but always felt as though I was in her shadow. Later, I understood how she was in awe of me, too. She was brave and resourceful, a born rebel who loved nothing more than pushing the boundaries and getting one over the adults in our life. Evie possessed all the qualities I felt I lacked and she made my life, until then so quiet and sheltered, hugely exciting. In return I shared with her the magic of Pencallyn and my stories, and spent time helping her with her reading. We were a team. Mirror images. Sisters in all but blood. I loved her and I thought she loved me. But if she hadn't? What if she let me down because she had never loved me at all?"

Estella pauses. In her eyes I see lifelong sadness and endless questions.

"In that case," she says thoughtfully, "It might have been a very different story indeed …"

CHAPTER 24

Estella
May 1941

It was a hazy May afternoon, the kind of day that in the past meant sea bathing and picnics on the beach, shrimp paste sandwiches, lemonade and doorsteps of fruit cake wrapped in crackly brown paper. Alex would plunge into the cold water with a dive, sinewy white limbs slicing through green waves before bobbing like a cork half a mile away in the cove and waving with one hand as he dared Estella to join him. She seldom did, shrieking when the cold water tickled her toes and barely wading further than her knees before retreating to the prickly tartan blanket and a book. Straw hats and sunburned noses, scratchy swimming costumes and knees scraped from slipping on barnacle-crusted rocks, simple days – but when Estella looked back, they seemed a distillation of pure happiness.

Maybe this was how it felt to lose your innocence? Those long-ago days felt like one of Evie's beloved movies, a stage set of a perfect English summer's day when there was nothing more pressing to think about than a game of cricket on the sand or squabbling over who lugged the picnic basket home. But Alex was gone now and those days would never come again. The beach was out of bounds, any picnic would be a sad, rationed affair, and Estella didn't think she could ever look at the sea again without picturing her brother's brave little Spitfire spiralling into the waves.

It was hard not to think of Alex when there were so many planes dancing in the sky. Often as Evie and Estella played Mysterious Garden, the old games of dinosaurs and explorers and pandas, no longer so compelling now they were older, planes would drone overhead and the girls would dive for cover beneath the big tree ferns or shelter in the bells of the gunnera. The garden was more overgrown than at any time Estella could remember, the neglected bamboo as thick as a man's wrist while bindweed and briars choked the paths as though doing their bit to thwart invading Germans. The garden was the girls' domain, and the games they played were still their world. They made maps and left notes in the sundial and sometimes they didn't come home until long after the blackout. Cook grumbled and left supper out, but otherwise nobody noticed. Nobody cared.

Today it was hot and even the green depths seemed to droop. The air was thick and, longing for a breeze, the girls set off to climb Bury Beacon. Estella had her sketch book and Evie was reading *Macbeth* and doing her best to memorise it, an alarming activity for Estella who was constantly forced to listen to speeches about blood and witches. Still determined to be an actress, Evie was scathing when it came to a horror of blood and protests about nightmares. Nothing seemed to frighten her.

Bury Barrow had the best views across the bay, stretching past Pencallyn Cove towards Calmouth. On a clear day like this it was possible to see even as far as the Helford, and the air shimmered with heat. When the sun shone, skylarks sang and the air carried the scent of mown grass as the land girls cut hay, it was possible to believe the war was a bad dream – possible as long as you ignored the barrage balloons and pillboxes and the black cloud of smoke out on the horizon which spoke of battles over the sea. Estella closed her eyes and leaned back against the grass. Now, how could she capture this tranquillity in her prose?

Two planes tore through the high cloud, hurtling from nowhere and ripping up the peace. Estella's eyes snapped open. A Spitfire was chasing a Messerschmitt just a few hundred feet above them and so close she could see the pilot. Engines screaming and guns firing, the planes flew low above the crest of the hill, and the earth beneath Estella's back shook. Her heart was ready to burst but before she could run for cover Evie had hurled herself on top, shielding Estella's body with her own as her wiry arms pinned them close to the ground. Gunfire rattled and seconds later the pilots circled away, followed by another salvo as the dogfight continued further inland.

"Bloody hell," Evie panted, rolling onto the grass. "That was close."

Estella's fists were bunched as she tried to contain her terror at Death sneaking up and tapping them on the shoulder in a deadly game of grandmother's footsteps. Not the newsreels of the Blitz, Mr Churchill's rousing speeches on the wireless, or even the loss of Alex had made the war as real as the past few seconds.

"That was so brave, Evie," she gasped.

"What was?"

"What you just did. You could have been hit instead of me."

"You're all I have in the world, Stella," Evie replied. Then, as though it was obvious, "You're my family. My blood sister. What would I be without you?"

Back at the end of 1940, Evie's grandmother had been killed when a night-time bombing raid obliterated her entire street.

"She's an orphan now," the WVS lady had told Violet. "There's no mother, and her father's long dead. I have no idea where she'll go."

"She'll stay with us, of course," had been Violet's reply. "Good Lord, I wouldn't throw the poor child out. Of course not. We're Evie's family."

Estella wondered whether Violet would have been quite so swift to say this if she'd known how often Evie slunk into her room and rummaged through her belongings or claimed to know why Violet stayed away in town. Evie never breathed a word, but nothing missed her sharp blue eyes and Estella suspected she was keeping this knowledge close in case she needed it. Poor afraid and suspicious Evie! So quick to fear the worst. When Violet had repeated her generous words, Evie's first response had been to wonder why.

"Why? Because you *are* family," Estella said.

"I'm a cuckoo in the nest. You heard Tommy."

"Sucks to Tommy. She's not in charge here anyway; Papa and Violet are. And if Violet says you're a member of our family, then that's exactly what you are. We're sisters, you and me."

"But we're not, are we? Not really. Blood's what makes you family.

"No, it isn't. Family is more than blood, Evie. If it helps, we can be blood too."

Interest flickered across Evie's face. "How?"

Estella thought fast. "We'll swear to be loyal unto death, and we'll make our promise where the ancient ley lines cross at the sundial. It's the most powerful spot for miles around, and magical too. We'll make a small cut in our palms and hold our hands tightly together, so our blood mingles. That's when we become blood sisters."

Evie's eyes were big blue circles. "Proper blood sisters?"

"Proper blood sisters," Estella replied solemnly. "But I must warn you, Evie, this is a serious thing to do and if either of us ever breaks our promise something very, very bad will happen. 'Though silent, I speak', remember? The sundial sees everything."

Evie frowned. "How bad?"

"I don't know, but it would be very bad," Estella replied. She wasn't sure where these ideas came from – a mixture of local folk lore and her own imagination mostly – but there was something watchful and otherworldly about the hidden spot at the heart of the garden where the noon rays beat down upon the blank face of the sundial.

Estella and Evie were up at first light the next day. The ground was thick with frost and as they ran across the lawn their footprints were vivid green against the white. Once they were deep within the garden, through the labyrinth and in the clearing where the tree ferns and hydrangeas didn't dare encroach, Estella had pulled out Alex's old Swiss Army knife and carefully traced a thin scarlet line across her own palm. It was fascinating to watch the blood bubble up from the flesh and, as they clasped hands, she thrilled to think her own blood would flow in Evie's veins. The garden was still, not even a rook cawed, and Estella had the strangest feeling this ceremony had taken place here many, many times before.

Though silent, I speak.

She shivered. What had begun as a silly idea to reassure her best friend now felt deadly serious.

"We're blood sisters now and if we ever break our loyalty we're cursed. We'll die or worse," Estella said.

"What could be worse than dying? There ain't nothing worse than dying," Evie scoffed.

Their palms were still touching. Estella could feel Evie trembling – she was scared by a story Estella had made up! Estella heard the siren call of the writer's power. It was addictive and she wanted more.

"I don't know but I think it would be very, very bad whatever it was," she said carefully. "This is a druid site and it's ancient. I think even the druids stole it. We've used the old magic to make our vow."

"Don't be soft. There ain't such a thing as magic," scoffed Evie, but there was no conviction in her voice.

"Don't say 'ain't', Evie! And anyway, of course there's such a thing as magic. This place is ancient, and way, way before Jesus people came here to ask the old gods to grant them favours. You don't think the sundial's here by accident, do you? Look at all the cloths tied on the trees, if you don't believe me. Those are offerings to the old gods."

Evie glanced over her shoulder and shivered when she spotted the scraps of fabric knotted to the ancient trees. Who left them there she had no idea, but they always appeared. Maybe it was Cook? Or the housemaids? They were superstitious enough, with all their talk about magpies and not walking beneath ladders. "Don't talk daft! That's nonsense!" she said.

"Is it? Break your promise and see if you don't believe me. Everyone knows my family are so unlucky. Maybe one of them broke a promise made here and now we're cursed. Why do you think my brother died?"

"Because the Jerries killed him, that's why! Not some silly old sundial. You make stuff up! This is just one of your stories." Evie sounded scornful, but Estella heard a note of fear and snatched it.

"Is it? You can believe that if you like, but do you really want to take the risk of being wrong? And the sundial is a symbol placed where the ley lines cross. They go all the way from here to France and beyond. This is Cornwall, where the old magic is strong and it never, ever forgets a promise. Promise we will be blood sisters until we die. Promise we'll always be true to each other. To never let each other down. To watch out for and protect each other. And promise on the sundial and the magic garden, we will never, ever allow anyone or anything to come between us."

Evie moistened her lips with the red tip of her tongue. "I promise on the sundial and the magic garden I will never ever let anyone come between us. I will watch out for you. I will protect you."

And so Estella and Evie had become blood sisters. The promise they had made didn't seem onerous in the slightest, since neither girl could imagine a time when they wouldn't be friends or would dream of letting the other down.

But today, as she lay shaking in the long grass of Bury Barrow, Estella wasn't sure whether her new sister truly meant some of the things she said and did. Was Evie fiercely loyal or simply pragmatic? Did she truly love Estella, or did Evie feel their friendship was a means of guaranteeing her own survival? Evie's short life had been so utterly removed from Estella's, it was often hard to understand what drove her. Still, there was one thing Estella couldn't deny now; Evie Jenkins was prepared to lay down her life for her.

Surely it was better to have a girl like this on your side?

Evie leapt to her feet but Estella's legs felt like boiled string. The planes were buzzing bees in the distance as they performed a deadly tango. They swooped low and then began to race towards the coast.

"They're coming back!" Estella cried. "Run!"

But Evie clutched her arm.

"Oh my God, Stell! The German plane's hit! Look out! He's going to come down!"

Sure enough, orange flames plumed from the Messerschmitt as the plane twirled and pirouetted on its rapid descent. There was something mesmerising about watching it plunge from its element, dropping like a stone rather than soaring high above; what Estella was witnessing didn't feel real. Unlike Evie, who was whooping and cheering, all Estella could think about was the young man in the cockpit, probably a boy like Alex who was hurtling towards his end far away from home. Engines screamed and then there was the sound of splintering trees, followed by an almighty bang. The Spitfire circled the woods and waggled its wings at the girls before swooping over Pencallyn Cove and back out to sea.

Evie's eyes shone with excitement.

"That stinking Jerry's got what he deserves!"

But in Estella's imagination Alex was in the cockpit, desperately trying to pull up the nose of his plane as it hurtled towards the ground. Was the pilot still alive and frantically trying to free himself? Or was he badly injured and unable to move? He would know his plane could burst into flames at any moment. Alex had told her about chaps he knew who'd suffered horrific burns and said his biggest fear was being burned alive.

Enemy or not, Estella couldn't stand back and let this happen.

"Come on," she said.

"Come on?"

"We've got to help him. His plane could catch fire."

Her legs pounded faster and faster as she jolted down the hill, each thud of her feet in time with her heart. Evie was hard on her heels. As Estella climbed the stile, Evie yanked her back. Bony fingers bit into Estella's arm through the thin cotton of her dress.

"He's a rotten, stinking German. Let him burn and die."

The venom in her voice made Estella freeze. "We can't do that!"

"Yes, we bloody well can. The Germans killed your brother and my gran," Evie hissed as her fingers tightened their grasp. "We're at war, remember? One less German is a good thing."

"You don't mean that," Estella said.

"Don't I?" snarled Evie.

A wood pigeon called, its hesitant song filled with the promise of summer days and at odds with the horror lurking within the trees. Normality was balanced on a precipice, and Estella knew if she so much as glanced at the drop below, the drop where Evie waited in the shadows and where you could leave a man to die alone, she would never, ever see the world in the same way again. She would never be the same again because she would be changed for ever. *She* would become the sort of person who could let another die.

Estella couldn't be that person.

She ripped her arm from Evie's grasp, wincing as the other girl's nails sank into her flesh. Hurling herself over the stile, Estella plunged into the shade of the copse. She was running so fast her chest hurt, and she thought she would be sick. Knowing the woods far better than Evie, Estella remained ahead of her friend. She ran deeper and deeper into the trees. The leafy canopy above was torn, the boughs broken, and the dark branches had turned to spillikins. Estella hurtled onwards, following the trail of devastation, until at last she saw the Messerschmitt tangled in a knot of ash and sycamore, like a silver moth caught in a butterfly net. Ignoring Evie's frantic calling, she pressed forward and her skin prickled when she caught sight of the black crosses on the wings which so regularly heralded destruction.

The air was tainted with fuel but there were no flames. The fuselage was twisted as the aeroplane had buckled on impact. Metal shards speared the soft earth, pinning bluebells and wild garlic beneath jagged edges and scoring deep brown scratches into the green like the stripes on chocolate limes. The cockpit was shattered and when Estella drew closer, she could see two men strapped into their seats, the one at the back with his head twisted at such a peculiar angle she nearly vomited. The second German was groaning and tugging at his harness. When he turned his head and saw Estella, his mouth twisted in pain and he reached out a hand. "*Bitte, helfen Sie mir*," he whispered. "*Bitte*!"

He couldn't have been more than twenty. In his eyes Estella saw undiluted terror. A deadly shard of glass was lodged in his neck and bright red blood soaked the slate grey of his uniform. Estella had seen her father shoot deer, and knew this boy didn't have long before his life bled out. Could she staunch the flow? Should she send Evie to fetch the Home Guard for help, or would they also say there was a war on and the bastard had got what he deserved?

Oh God! What should she do?

"*Helfen mir*," the boy whispered, blood trickling from his mouth. "*Bitte*!"

This young man was her enemy. His people had killed Alex and countless others. Their planes razed cities to the ground and forced people to huddle together in shelters while bombs shook the ground around them. Estella understood this intellectually, but as she watched this young man plead for help all such logic fled. He was hurt, frightened and, like her brother, far from home and caught up in something that hadn't played out as he had imagined. He was a fellow human being and he needed help. Nothing else mattered.

"I'm coming," she called, grabbing hold of the wing and wincing at the heat of the metal against her palms. "*Ich werde dir helfen*! I'm coming!"

But she was too late. The young man uttered a blood-frothed gurgle and his eyes grew wide, fixed on something far away only he could see.

"No! No!" Estella cried, frantically trying to haul herself onto the wing so she could crawl to him. Her legs thrashed in thin air as she sought to grasp the slippery metal. "No! Alex! I'm coming! Alex!"

"Estella! Stop it! It's not Alex in there!"

Hands were on her waist, tugging and pulling so hard her palms slipped and she began to slide backwards. No matter how she kicked or tried to clamber up, the hands continued to pull her back. Finally, slick with sweat, her palms lost purchase and she tumbled onto the earth. Then she was pinned down by wiry limbs and Evie's eyeballs were inches from her own.

"Alex!" Estella wept. "I have to get him out!"

"He's not Alex!" Evie yelled. "He's just some bloody Jerry! Jesus Christ, are you mental? The plane could catch fire. We need to get away."

"No!" sobbed Estella. "We can't leave him!"

"We bloody well can. He's a Jerry and he's sodding well dead! For God's sake, Estella, come on! What's wrong with you?"

Estella dashed tears away with the back of her hand.

"What's wrong with *me*? You were going to leave him there to die. Why?"

"Because it's what he deserves. It's what all of them deserve. Anyone!"

"Anyone?" Estella asked, confused.

"Yes, anyone who hurts *us*. Germans. British. Anyone. That's our promise, remember? The Germans killed Alex and that hurt you. So all the

Germans are our enemies. We never let each other down. We watch out for each other. We protect each other. Anyone who wrongs us will pay. And that's a promise. Remember?"

Estella was lost for words. Their blood promise was a game – a silly game which, in a world where boys bled to death in shattered aeroplanes, seemed childish and from another time. Yet for Evie it was deadly serious. It was a blood oath. It was everything.

Suddenly Estella understood exactly what it was Tommy had realised; Evie Jenkins remembered everything. She held grudges and she forgot nothing.

You upset a girl like her at your peril.

CHAPTER 25

Nell
The Present

"You must think me foolish getting upset over something which happened so long ago," Estella says. "My brother's been dead nearly eighty years but sometimes it feels as though I've just heard the news."

Josh pulls a tissue from the box.

"Not at all," he says while Estella takes it and blows her nose. "The whole episode sounds awful, doesn't it, Nell?"

I nod and my mind fills with images of crashed planes and wounded Nazis and arguing girls in summer frocks.

"I dreamed about that German boy for years. Sometimes I still do," Estella sighs. "He was so young. What did he really know about the Nazis and their ideologies? He was doing what he thought he had to do. I couldn't save him, you know. I really couldn't."

The knotted hand clutching the tissue trembles.

"Of course you couldn't save him. Not with injuries like those," Josh tells her. "But you tried, Estella. Not many people would have done what you did. Most people would have left him because he was the enemy."

"Like Evie," I add. I'm not warming to Evie at all – bad news, since it seems more and more likely she's my grandmother.

But Estella shakes her head. "Don't judge her too harshly. Why, later on that day villagers flocked to the crash site to take bits of the Messerschmitt away as souvenirs. Evie's piece took pride of place on the mantelpiece in our room, but I could barely stand to see it. It made me think of that young lad. In the end I made her put it out of sight. Goodness knows where it went."

Josh grimaces. "That's macabre."

"They were different times, dear. There was a war on, and we were losing at that point. The Americans hadn't joined us yet, and most of Europe was under threat from Hitler. Everyone in the village was thrilled some of their enemies had got what they deserved. The Home Guard called us heroes for reporting the crash."

"But Evie would have left a young man to bleed to death," I say. "That's more than being pleased your enemy's beaten."

Estella nods. "Evie was never one to forgive a slight or let a grudge go. Once we'd made the blood promise, she was fanatical about things. I quickly came to regret that game. I often think that was the point when things began to go wrong."

She's shredding the tissue. Kleenex flakes drift onto the covers.

"Oh Evie," Estella says sadly. "What did you do? Was it because of me? Or was it Hamilton's fault? Evie? Where are you?" Her voice begins to rise. "Where did you go? What did he do? Evie! Evie! I'm coming!"

She tries to swing her legs out of bed and the drip topples with a crash. The cannula is plucked out of her hand and blood beads her thin skin. Josh jumps to his feet, trying to soothe her and stem the flow of blood. My ears fill with a swirl of sound and my heart pounds. Panic. It feels like panic.

I need to get some air

Hospitals. Blood. Machines. The sounds of trolleys. The firm tones of the nurses as they set up the equipment. It's whirling and plunging until I'm falling down the mine shaft of my own memory in unison with Estella Kellow. Time blurs. Logic flees. All that remains are horror and loss.

Leaving the hospital as two when we had been three …

"Evie!" shouts Estella. "Where's Jay? What has Hamilton done to him? Tell me!"

"She's agitated," one of the nurses explains. "Don't worry, it's not unusual when elderly patients get muddled. We're going to give her more pain relief and something to make her sleepy."

I remember this so well. First the needle's cold kiss. Then blissful oblivion. I craved it for months. Sometimes I still do.

The nurse hooks up a bag of fluids to the drip stand while her colleague reinserts the needle. "She'll be asleep for a while. Don't worry. She's in safe hands."

I stand up, but the floor lurches beneath my feet. Only Josh's grasp on my elbow stops me pitching forward.

"You need some fresh air," he says, and I nod.

"Please," I say. My heart is thudding in my ears and I try to steady my breathing. I thought the panic attacks had passed. They can't come back. Not now.

Josh rests his hand in the small of my back as we walk outside. I sit on a bench with my head between my knees while he fetches a paper cup of water from the cooler. I sip and the rushing sound fades. Cold water soothes my tongue.

"Was it seeing blood? Or the grim tales of plane crashes?" he asks.

"No, it wasn't that." I raise my head and, thank God, the world has stopped spinning. "It was something else."

This is the point where most people press for an explanation. 'What?' they'll ask, eyes wide as they lean forward in hope of some exciting titbit. Or they'll say that I don't have to tell them anything but if I ever need a listening ear … I wait for Josh to choose one of these options, but he merely drinks his water. Silence falls between us.

Something shifts in me. Something that has never happened before. Suddenly I want to speak about what happened. I don't want to lock my sadness away. I want someone to know about my baby, and why losing her changed everything.

And I want Josh Richardson to be that person. I can talk to him.

The bench is placed to look over the river. The windows of the houses across the Cal glitter in the afternoon sunshine and the water sparkles. There is still beauty and life, and I dredge my soul for the right words. I need to find the language to do my baby justice.

"Eighteen months ago, I was in hospital," I begin, and it's as though I'm looking down on the scene, listening to a dark-haired girl tell a tall flame-haired near-stranger the closest secrets of her heart. Why I want to tell Josh Richardson these things I have no idea, but something deep inside of me says he needs to know my deepest self and be cogent of the savage pain which has fired me into who I am. I don't want to hide my true self from him. Nothing's happened between us, maybe nothing ever will, but there could be more. He could be more. Estella has shown me that I don't want to lock my heart away until I'm in my nineties.

I search for the right words.

"My husband and I were expecting a baby. Our first. We'd wanted a child for so long, and when it finally happened we were so excited. I didn't allow myself to hope until I was four months into the pregnancy, which was when Andy and I thought things were past the dangerous stage. We'd had our first scan and everything looked good. It goes to show really, doesn't it? You never quite know. Nothing's really safe."

"Nell, you don't have to explain anything to me. Not if it's painful —" Josh begins but I shake my head. His quiet way inspires a conviction that you can tell him anything and he'll understand. I want him to know this thing about me, this huge and life-changing thing which divides me for ever into two people: pre-miscarriage Nell and post-miscarriage Nell. It's made me what I am – a mother without her child.

"I don't have to, but I *want* to. If I don't speak about it then it will be lost. That's worse."

He stares across the estuary. "If we don't let people in, we all take our secrets with us. Our history dies with us."

I don't want my most precious person to be forgotten. Andy seldom mentioned her afterwards and, since we barely speak these days, who does remember her? His way of grieving was to move on, not mention it. I think it was lack of words that finished us in the end. No wonder we didn't make it if we never spoke. It was Dad who carried me through. Dad held me and let me cry until I could hardly breathe, but even he has left me now so who else can I turn to? Although Lou tries to understand, it's my pain which hurts her rather than my baby's loss. Who else knows or cares there was once another member of the Summers family? One I'd named and loved and woven dreams for? Spoken to in the darkness and carried with me for nearly one hundred and forty days? Someone I loved more than I had thought it possible to love anyone?

Nobody.

"I don't want my baby forgotten," I say. "She was here. She was real and we loved her desperately. We planned for her and we talked about her and to her. Her future was exciting, and we had so much to look forward to. I know you shouldn't let your dreams carry you away, but I couldn't help it."

I close my eyes and movie plays through my imagination. It's a film I haven't dared to watch for so long and it spools quickly – a lifetime speeding past in swift clips. First steps. Skipping out of school and into my arms. Cooking supper in a kitchen decorated with bright splashy paintings. Andy running down the street chasing a wobbling two-wheeler. Secondary school and homework I'd help with. Prom dresses. Packing the car for university. A frothy white dress and flowers. But this film was never really made. The only real shot is a grainy image tucked away in my bedside table and which I look at only when I feel brave enough.

Josh is quiet but I feel his unspoken sympathy and it carries me forward.

"Then I had my twenty-week scan and there was no heartbeat. She wasn't there any more. She'd left me."

I see the fuzzy screen and the sonographer sweeping the ultrasound wand over my belly, back and forth as though what she sought was hiding.

"My baby'd died and I hadn't noticed. What sort of a mother doesn't know something like that?"

"I'm so sorry, Nell," Josh says. "I can't begin to imagine how it must feel."

"Nobody can." I close my eyes and relive a silent car journey home, the inane babble of the car radio punctuated by my sobs. Andy so lost but not sure what to say. He was also adrift on the sea of unacknowledged grief, but in a separate vessel which sailed further and further from mine with each day. Then there were the practicalities to attend to and which nobody ever talks about; the appointment at the hospital, the waiting room filled with women puffed up like peonies and where I sat until my name was called. The operation was nothing compared to the ache of loss and the sense of being struck dumb. How do you mourn a person who never drew breath? There's no space for it. People are sympathetic but say things which feel like a knife to the heart. 'You can try again' and 'Plenty of women go on to have healthy babies after a miscarriage'. They didn't understand at all. I didn't want to try again. I didn't want another baby.

I wanted *her*.

Andy tried to help, but it wasn't him who had failed to keep our little passenger safe, and although he denied it I knew he felt I'd let him down too. He was sad and disappointed, but how could he know the depths into which I plummeted? I fell so fast and so deep there wasn't a ladder long enough to help me climb out and even if there had been, my fall damaged me beyond all recognition. I wasn't the same person. When we split up I was sad, but I knew it was the right decision because our loss had driven us apart. It had highlighted the lack of common ground, and proven familiarity had been the only glue which had kept us together. But when the landscape changed neither of us had a map or the will to navigate the new territory together. In a strange way we were relieved to part.

"They were never able to tell me why my baby died," I say. "It was one of those unexplained things, according to the consultant, and the chances of a heathy pregnancy in the future were excellent. They wanted me to feel better about that."

"Yes. It probably didn't feel like much of a comfort."

"Not to me, but Andy saw it as a green light. He was desperate to try again."

"That felt like replacing her."

It isn't a question and my head snaps up because he gets it.

"Exactly! I couldn't think straight, and I certainly couldn't put myself through that heartache so soon. It felt like a betrayal on Andy's part too. All that mattered was being a father; the child was immaterial. I know now it wasn't true, but it felt that way at the time. Poor Andy. I hated him for a quite a while."

"Christ, Nell. What an awful thing for both of you to go through. I do see how pressing on might have been his way of coping, though, and I think it's quite a male response. All our conditioning says 'chin up, soldier on' and all that crap."

"I do see that now," I agree. My paper coffee cup is crushed. I've been crumpling it as I speak. Like me, it will never return to its previous form.

"I'm sorry, Nell. That must have been tough."

"Yes it was, but everything had changed and there was no way of going back. Losing our baby just exposed the things that weren't right between us. I might have known why he hated lamb chops and what football team Andy supported but we never talked about the important things. We never shared our fears or our hopes and dreams. Maybe we'd never truly connected?"

"Do you think any couples do?"

"I really hope so. Dad always said he'd met his soulmate in my mum."

"I don't think my parents are soulmates," Josh says, "and I've often wondered what the point is of being in a relationship if you can't tell your partner everything. Or be their best friend. I want my wife to be the person I can't wait to see when I wake up in the morning, the one I'm always talking to and the first person I think of when I have good news to share. I want us to be best friends, confidants, lovers – everything."

"You're a romantic," I say.

He colours and stares down at the ground. "Guilty as charged. It's probably why I'm single."

Josh's single status certainly isn't on account of his beautiful body, Pencallyn Cove-hued eyes and heart-stopping smile, I think to myself. Then I look away sharply because this sudden twist of attraction feels a little inappropriate after telling him about my baby and my marriage break-up.

I clear my throat. "Anyway, to answer your earlier question, I don't want my story to die with me even though I'm the last."

"You don't know you're the last," Josh says softly.

"I suppose there could be more of my family out there?"

His eyes meet mine and something in their amber-flecked depths makes my pulse quicken.

"That wasn't quite what I meant. I'm glad you told me about your baby, though, Nell. Glad you felt you could, I mean."

"Not as glad as I am that I could tell you," I say. Sharing my secret sadness makes me feel lighter. It's still there, it will always be there, but it isn't in between us now. It's with us and acknowledged.

Josh takes my hand and our fingers knit together as though they've done so a thousand times before. His touch is comforting. It feels right.

We sit in companionable silence, watching the ever-changing view of the estuary. It's hard not to picture the place as it was during Estella's childhood, and I imagine the dark hulls of battle ships gliding towards to the horizon, the sweep of searchlights across the night sky and the deadly shadows thrown across the valley when enemy planes are flying overhead.

"I need you to know something about me, Nell. It's not something I tell many people – not because I'm ashamed but they don't always understand – but I know you won't judge me," Josh says eventually.

"You don't have to tell me things because of what I shared. It's not an exchange. That isn't how it works."

His fingers tighten. "I know but, like you said, it feels important not to have any secrets. I'm not sure what's happening between us, Nell, but I want to tell you my version of the story before the local gossips get to you."

"It's far too late for that," I tease.

He rolls his eyes. "I'm afraid the truth will be very dull in comparison with anything the rumour machine comes up with. Then again, you're an author. You could imagine something far more exciting."

I'm an author who hasn't written a word in days. My novel has been totally overpowered by Estella's tale of war and orphans and bombing raids.

"Please don't disillusion me. You're a playboy with a harem of women, aren't you? The type who puts Hugh Hefner to shame?"

"The only women I hang out with are Estella and Kelly, if you don't count my mum," Josh laughs. The breeze blows an auburn curl into his eyes and he shakes his head, partly to dislodge it and partly to dislodge the image I've given him. "Sadly, nothing so exciting, although my father might prefer I lived life of hedonism if it meant I was still making money in the City. He doesn't find it easy having a disappointment for a son."

"You're not —"

"But to him I am, Nell. It's complex thing, this parent–child stuff. You understand that better than anyone. To my father I was going to be the son who lived the life he'd always wanted. Public school, Oxford, a job in the City, the family firm one day – he'd planned it all. I had the right contacts, the accent, the Harrow education – in short, every advantage he could give me and then more. I can't blame Dad for feeling as though I've thrown it all back in his face by not wanting any of it."

"You can't live your life for your father," I say helplessly, more grateful than ever for my own wonderful dad who'd wanted nothing more than for me to be happy.

"I know that, at least intellectually anyway, but it certainly didn't feel that way. I did exactly what he wanted even though I hated school, was miserable at Oxford and bloody useless in the City. As I've said before, I wanted to work in horticulture – it's my passion – and I've always loved being outside. Mum has amazing green fingers and she taught me all I know, but this was never real work in Dad's eyes. It certainly isn't a career for the son and heir of Martin Richardson."

I can see how this might be an issue. Martin's bullying ways have echoes of Estella's father – something I imagine bonds her and Josh.

"So I took a job in the city – one of Dad's pals had a word, which is how these things work – and off I went to put in all the hours under the sun making money and trying to make him proud," he continues, his eyes still fixed far across the water. "For a while I did OK. I even convinced myself it was all fine, but I couldn't keep going. A couple of trades went belly up because I wasn't on the ball enough to cope with the pace. The pressure was unbearable. I began to drink and, I'm ashamed to say it, I took whatever I could to keep awake and to not feel so utterly, bloody miserable. Or not to feel anything at all. I felt like a mole because I never saw daylight, and I missed being outdoors so badly it felt like a claw was scooping out my insides. One day I couldn't get out of bed. I couldn't eat. I couldn't speak. I couldn't do anything. I was broken." He laughs bleakly, "I guess it's why they call it a breakdown. It never occurred to me before. Anyway it was over, and I went back home. It wasn't great for a while with Dad, but I survived and Mum's been amazing. She helped me no end. I wouldn't have survived without her or Estella."

"Estella?"

"She's given me free rein at Pencallyn. Uncovering the garden has been the best therapy I could imagine. Estella ought to charge, and put on mindfulness retreats!"

"So you work for your father now?"

"For the moment. He's put me in to project manage the farm conversion, but that's not for me in the long run. I want to work in horticulture, I always did, and I've applied for a City and Guilds course at Calmouth College. I'm really looking forward to it. I'm going to specialise in garden archaeology, and I've Estella to thank for that too. Before I met her I didn't think I'd ever look forward to anything again."

"That's brilliant," I tell him warmly. "Everyone should follow their dreams."

"I agree, and that's exactly what I'm going to do. It's been a long road to get here, though. Some days are better than others, but the black void is never far away. The trick is learning to recognise what triggers it."

"Yes. I think you're right," I say. "Thank you for telling me your story. It helps, if that makes sense. Knowing that we're all on a journey of some kind, I mean."

"You don't have to thank me. I wanted you to know the truth about why I'm here, Nell, and the truth about me too. I need you to understand why Estella's so important to me. She's might be old, but she's a true friend and a huge part of my journey to this point. Pencallyn's gardens and Estella have helped to heal me."

"She's a special person."

"She's incredible, and I don't think we even know the half of it yet. I mean, the way she was prepared to risk her life to save an enemy. Her kind of bravery is something else. I can't wait to find out more."

As Josh and I watch the red sun sink behind the rooftops of Calmouth, far more than our hands are linked. There's something between us which hasn't been present earlier. I like to think it's the understanding and peace which comes with true honesty.

I wonder if Estella ever knew anything like this or whether her story, like her best friend's heart, is far, far darker?

CHAPTER 26

Nell
The Present

When Josh and I return, Estella's sleeping and a nurse is checking her drip. I'm no medic but I can see she's weaker, a frail figure marooned in the sea of starchy hospital sheets, sailing further away from us with every moment. Estella's long white hair is spread across the pillow and her face, relaxed in repose, seems younger. If I squint a little, I can glimpse the girl she used to be, high cheekboned and slender and with a cloud of dark hair. Or is it Evie I'm picturing? It's hard to know where Estella ends and her adopted sister begins.

"We've given her a fair amount of painkiller. She's not likely to wake up for a while," the nurse explains. "You can be with her, if you like. She'll know you're there."

I sit beside Estella and take her hand in mine. She doesn't stir, but the slight pressure of her fingers on mine suggests she knows she's not alone. I wonder who she thinks I am: her mother? Evie? Violet? Or somebody else? There are names I have yet to slot into the story. Jay Miller, of course, and the mysterious and rather threatening Hamilton.

"Are you her next of kin?" the nurse asks Josh.

"We're friends," he replies. "I don't think she has any family left."

"Poor old thing. What a shame. She's lucky to have friends like you."

Josh shakes his head. "We're the lucky ones to have her."

We sit a little longer with Estella before the business of medicine trolleys and observations become our cue to depart. Josh drives us back to Pencallyn, on the journey pointing out many places from Estella's story. We pass Bury Barrow, where two girls had cowered in the grass as a dogfight raged high above, skirt the deep wood where a German plane had met its end, then turn into the lane leading to Pencallyn Farm. Josh slows to swing into the gateway and the No Trespassers sign is bright and bold. It's hard not to take its message personally.

"Do you want to have supper?" he asks. "I do a great omelette."

"I should bail," I say. Tired and a little emotional, the last thing I need is another confrontation with Martin Richardson. "I can walk back to the pub from here."

"Apart from the fact I wouldn't dream of letting you walk back alone, nothing Jen and Toby serve will compare with my omelettes. Trust me!"

"I do, but I don't think I'll be welcome!" I point to the sign.

Josh pulls a face. "Not the best PR for a bunch of incomers, is it? If it's the thought of Dad that's putting you off, he's in London with Mum."

"You're sneaking me in while you have the house to yourself? What are we? Teenagers?" I tease.

"Come on, live a little! I thought we could raid their drinks cabinet, invite all our Facebook friends over and trash the place. How about it?"

"You should have said so before. I'm up for that!" I laugh.

"I didn't think you'd be able to resist. But seriously, Nell, I'd love you to come for supper, I truly would."

"How could I turn down a Facebook party and an omelette?" I say. "Supper would be great. Thanks."

Josh parks the Defender. When he hops out and opens my door, taking my hand to help me make the jump down, I feel as though I've stepped into one of my own novels. The misfit heroine, the handsome troubled hero, the beautiful country house with sage paintwork and immaculate gravel, the Land Rover –if he wasn't holding one hand and my other clutching my satchel, I'd pinch myself.

"This is looking good," I say admiringly as I follow him into the kind of aspirational kitchen I usually encounter in glossy magazines. Although the far end is swaddled with plastic where the wall has been knocked down, there's no mistaking that the huge Aga, the giant refectory table and the full set of Le Creuset pans suspended from a massive rack are all hugely expensive.

"It's come on in the last few days. We're not far away from finishing now," says Josh, his voice muffled as he peers inside a vast fridge. "White, OK? Pinot?"

"Fine by me," I say. I won't mention that my usual choice is the nasty cheap stuff I pick up in the supermarket. Josh Richardson may love the simple life but he's very much at ease in these surroundings. I imagine he's grown up with kitchens you could fit an entire house into. Dad's terrace would fit twice in this one room. But although this room is impressive, I far preferred Dad's little kitchen. It might have been tiny but it was warm, and the small table had been perfect for the two of us. The walls had always been smothered in my school paintings, and although none of the mugs or plates matched each one had a story to tell. The chips in the china and the marks on the Ikea table were the history Dad and I had made for ourselves. They made our home feel like home. I have kept a chipped spotty mug and a faded Peter Rabbit plate, and I know they will travel with me wherever I go, cherished mementos of a happy childhood. But this perfect room, although beautiful, feels faintly unwelcoming. The bright ceiling lights don't quite chase away the shadows lurking in the corners, and I shiver.

Josh busies himself cracking eggs into a bowl and I lean against the Aga. Warmth soaks into my skin but doesn't chase away the chill of the kitchen. It's as though the cold isn't coming from the temperature at all but from a melancholy atmosphere. I recall Josh's comment about his mother not being happy in the house and how she hates being there alone.

Maybe this isn't my imagination after all?

"Is your mum happier with the house now?" I ask.

"I hope she will be once the kitchen's finished and the specialist team's cleared and sealed the well," Josh replies, flicking eggshells into a compost container. "It's going to be a striking feature, all lit up and in a range of colours, and ought to look amazing. Dad's really excited about it."

I think of the ancient well feet away from me and encircled by new walls which trap it inside a designer kitchen. A blinded eye, it will stare at the ceiling from now on, for ever shut away from the sky and the people who would make a mysterious pilgrimage to throw coins into its depths. Something about this makes me feel uneasy. It's my writer's imagination at work, of course, but if pressed I would have said the odd atmosphere in this room feels like grief. It's akin to the clawing sensation I have in my chest when I think about my recent losses. There are legends and myths here that are still powerful.

"Do you think there's any truth in the stories about the ley lines?" I blurt.

Josh looks up from his cooking. "What's made you come out with that? Estella's story about the sundial? She said herself she was only making it up to distract Evie."

"She said she was weaving old myths and legends into her own games," I correct. "It's what she does in *Mysterious Garden*, but there's an element of truth running through the fiction. The well and the sundial are meant to be linked by ley lines, aren't they?"

"If you believe in that kind of thing," says Josh.

I glance outside. The sun is low and the shadows bloom across the newly planted garden. Swallows stitch up the falling evening. Something shifts in the fringe of trees at the far end of the lawn, just a glimmer and nothing more than a figment of my imagination, but for a moment it seems a blond man stands there, staring at the house with unseeing eyes. I blink and he's gone. It was just the light, but if there were blinds I would lower them and shut the image out.

"Anything seems possible here, no matter how fanciful," I say.

"That's Cornwall's magic for you. I feel the same way, and, although it's going to ruin any hope I might have of appearing as a macho alpha male, I can't say I particularly like being alone in this room, either. The rest of the house feels fine but here?" Josh throws me a self-deprecating smile. "I'd say it feels unhappy in this room, and I don't blame Mum one bit for not being thrilled with having to live here alone."

"Is it the well?" I ask. "It's supposed to be sacred, isn't it? You said people were pulling the lid off."

"Actually, that hasn't happened for a few days." He pours the eggs into a pan, stepping back when they hiss and spit. Then he turns to me, looking thoughtful. "Come to think about it, all the funny business with the well stopped the day you came here."

"I don't think I can take the credit. I think your dad's sign may have something to do with it."

"Perhaps," says Josh. "Or maybe not. Could it be something to do with your family history, if Evie *was* your grandmother? We know the girls played here. Maybe you've awoken echoes of the past? Somebody's glad you've arrived in Pencallyn? Maybe Evie knows you're here?"

"What a woo woo idea!" I attempt a laugh, but could he be right? Does something recognise that I am here and searching for the truth?

Josh raises his eyes to the ceiling.

"Sorry, Nell! I had an out-of-body experience as I said that, I think! Hunger's probably getting to me, and exhaustion. I promise I'm not having a relapse of what we talked about earlier."

"I didn't think that for a minute. Anyway, I really hope Evie isn't my grandmother. I don't like the sound of her at all."

"I think she was forged in a hot furnace. A kid like her would have to have learned how to survive. She sounds clever and brave, even if her moral code was a little skewed. Besides, Estella loves her dearly. It's always Evie she calls for, isn't it?"

We chat a little more about Estella, then he dishes up the omelettes which we carry through to the snug. This cosy room, with its low ceiling, red walls and deep sofas, feels totally different to the kitchen. Lamps throw yellow puddles of light across the floor and there are no dark corners filled with creeping shadows. By the time I've finished my omelette, which is every bit as gooey and cheesy and mouth-watering as promised, I'm convinced I've imagined the strange atmosphere next door. As Josh said, it's been an intense few days.

After clearing away and making coffee, we spend an hour attempting to google Evie Jenkins but, apart from appearing on a list of children evacuated from St Margaret's Junior School in Bethnal Green in 1939, there's no mention of her. She had certainly never fulfilled her dream of becoming a Hollywood star, which makes me sad, and although we search as many records as we can think of, we don't find her. It's as though she vanished.

Jay Miller is another matter. He was in the army and should be possible to trace. Josh finds a charity called GI Trace which helps the children of American soldiers based in the UK during the war find their missing fathers. We read stories of men and women who discover long-lost siblings in the States and travel across the Atlantic to meet very elderly parents. The more I read the more I'm certain Jay Miller must be my grandfather. Everything fits. His age. His race. The fact he was stationed here in 1944. That my father was abandoned. There are countess similar stories, and everything falls into place with this theory.

"Do you think it's worth writing to them?" Josh asks. He's sitting on the floor, back against the sofa, with the laptop resting against his knees while I am curled on the sofa, warm and sleepy.

"Maybe," I say. "We have his name and we can find out which regiment was based here easily enough. There might be records of him deserting too – although it's interesting how many official documents seem to have been 'lost'."

"You have a suspicious mind," Josh says.

"I'm an author! People lose things for reasons in my experience. I did one of those Heritage DNA tests too, so if it comes up with a link to a shared relative that could really help."

"In that case I'm sure the answers aren't far away."

"As long as Estella can remember enough to help us find them."

"What if something happens to Estella? What if all my questions are making her worse?" I say, gnawing the skin around my thumb.

Josh shuts the laptop and takes my agitated hand, smoothing the sore thumb with his gentle fingers.

"Trust me, if Estella didn't want to talk to you then she wouldn't. She's old but she's strong-willed. I think telling you her story comforts her. Who else does she have to listen to her? I think you coming here has been a blessing because Estella can finally share her story with somebody who cares. My God, what must it be like to carry secrets for a lifetime and never be able to share them?"

"Awful," I whisper. My own secret was shared earlier and I feel lighter already. Then I frown. "Do you think Estella has secrets? I would have thought that was Evie's forte."

"Oh, she has secrets, I'm sure of it," Josh says. "I have one myself, actually, and unless I share it soon, I think I'll go crazy."

His beautiful mouth is smiling but his eyes are serious.

"What is it?" I ask, intrigued

"Come and sit here and I'll tell you," he says patting the floor beside him. "If I can find the words."

There are moments in life when you know everything is teetering on the brink. A delicate balance that will tip you for ever one way or another. A choice which sends a million parallel universes splitting away. My mum driving to the nursery one sunny May morning. Nanna Summers spotting Dad at the children's home. Violet choosing Evie from the other evacuees. Me sliding from the sofa …

We sit beside one another in silence. There's a stillness about Josh, a thoughtfulness and patience which must come from tilling the earth and waiting for green shoots to break through, but I don't possess that quality. I have to talk to him.

"What did you want to tell me?"

"Something you might not want to hear. Nell, but I have to say it. I can't not say it. I know we've not known each other long but there's something between us, isn't there? I can't stop thinking about it."

"What do you mean?" I ask. My heartbeat accelerates. Is Josh trying to say he has feelings for me? Do I want him to say this?

"I'm better at talking to plants than women!"

"And that's your secret?" I tease.

His fingers waltz across my cheek.

"I think that's glaringly obvious! No, what I mean is since I first saw you here, having a set to with my father, I've not been able to put you out of my mind. I can't stop thinking about you. About how much I want to kiss you." He smooths the curls away from my face. "Is that OK with you, Nell Summers? Is it OK for me to kiss you?"

I can't look away from his beautiful mouth. His heart-stopping face. His deep sea eyes. And the more I look, the more I know it's very OK with me. More than OK.

It's wonderful.

"Yes," I whisper. "Yes, it is."

The moment our lips meet my whole body tingles. It only takes a kiss, as soft as the brush of feathers, to know beyond all doubt that the parallel universe we've stepped into is the one I want to inhabit. The only one for me. And I also know I've been keeping a secret too, one so deeply buried I never even shared it with myself.

I wanted to kiss Josh Richardson too. Very, very much.

Now I've kissed him once, I'm not sure I'll ever be able to stop.

CHAPTER 27

Nell
The Present

I wake with a start. The weight of the duvet and the crisp newness of the cotton sheets are unfamiliar, as is the large sleigh bed in this low-ceilinged room. Light strobes through a gap in the curtains and shivering birdsong fills the air. I fall through the holes in memory's net, as hopelessly lost as Estella must so often be, and my heart drums with panic. This is not my simple London bedroom. The incense of salt and soil and leaf mould are a world away from fumes and stale food, and where I live bird song is never heard above the traffic.

I'm at Pencallyn Farm.

I've spent the night with Josh Richardson. Or rather, I've spent the night at his family home. I've only kissed Josh, an innocent thing in this age of Tinder and sexting and a million other things I don't have a clue about, yet it has been enough to make my entire world spin. It was a kiss which unlocked a chamber of possibility I'd believed was sealed for ever. A kiss overflowing with an inexplicable certainty the future is about to change. A kiss that spoke of shared hopes, the wonder of finding the very person you'd not even known you were searching for, and a kiss that opened the heart with a new blossoming of hope. As we'd kissed, mouths and hands exploring one another, the curve of a cheek and the soft nape of a neck were uncharted landscapes filled with possibility.

"Nell," I heard him gasp, my name melting on his lips. "Oh, Nell."

The warm fabric of Josh's shirt and the silken texture of his skin when I slipped my hands beneath to trace the swell of his muscles, made my senses reel. I drank in his scent, clean linen and lime and man, and felt dizzy. My fingers slipped into his silken hair, falling over his face as his lips nuzzled my throat, and then I was unable to focus on anything other than his skin against mine. Nothing mattered more than being as close to Josh Richardson as possible. This longing had come from nowhere, but I totally and utterly trusted it; everything had conspired to lead me to this point –

finding the pictures, my journey west, the links to Estella Kellow. All these were part of a bigger tapestry woven by a loom designed long ago for the sole purpose of stitching Josh and me into its pattern.

Was this Fate? If so, who were we to resist? Listening to Estella's tale, and seeing all around me the shadows of the past, reminded me life is fleeting and all we ever possess is the present moment. Carried forward on a tidal surge of longing, my response was primal and more intoxicating than anything I'd ever known. Thoughts and logic melted like ice in sunshine.

"Nell." My name on his tongue sounded exotic, as though I was someone else, someone alien to my old self and that he had just discovered. His hands cupped my face as he gazed into my eyes, his dark pupils a whole new universe I wanted to explore. Even my eyelashes ached for his touch.

"Nell," he repeated softly. "You're so beautiful. So wonderful. If we don't stop now, I'm not sure I'll be able to step away."

"So don't," I whispered.

He kissed my eyelids, the tip of my nose, my parted lips.

"There's no rush. This is special, *you're* special, and this should be perfect. Emotions are running high. I need you to be sure this is what you really want."

My blood was pounding in my ears. "I'm sure. How about you? Are you sure?"

He laughed. "I was sure the moment from I first saw you standing on the drive having a row with my father. I couldn't take my eyes off you, Nell, and haven't been able to stop thinking about you ever since – but that isn't the point! I want you to choose this, to choose me, and not just because of a moment of madness or a need to grasp life. Or even because the wine is strong. I need you to want this because it's right and it means something. For me, it's far more than some no-strings fun."

"You're saying you want more than one night?"

Josh raised my hands to his lips and kissed them. Stubble grazed my skin and I shivered as I imagined how this would feel brushing my throat, my breasts and lower …

"You're worth *far* more than one night," he said quietly. "So much more, Nell."

The mood had changed. It was still charged with need, but there was an intensity and a promise too. What was happening between us had shifted from a moment of passion, a distraction from the terror of peering into Time's transience, to a wonderful possibility. Josh was right; it had to be a choice made with a clear head rather than impulse's chance outcome.

"I can't think much about anything now. Dad, Estella, my baby, my family …" I shook my head. "It's overwhelming."

Josh folded my hands in his and rested his forehead against mine.

"*Exactly*, Nell! That's why, as much as I want nothing more than to make love to you until the sun comes up, I want it to be the right thing. I don't want our friendship ruined by regrets and awkwardness. Trust me, though, I'm using every ounce of self-control I have! This thing with Estella is emotional and I don't want to confuse anything. Maybe once it's over, when we have the resolution to her story and yours, we'll know exactly where everything is heading. Just as clearing bindweed and brambles will show us what's really beneath Pencallyn's garden, perhaps clearing all the questions will show you what you really want. You've been through so much – the last thing I want to do is put more pressure on you."

"I wasn't feeling pressured," I sighed. "I was feeling …"

I pause, stuck for the right word, and he grinned.

"Horny?"

I burst out laughing.

"Horny? Is the teenager in you back again?"

"This time I've channelled my inner Austin Powers!" he replied, waggling his eyebrows and doing a bad impression. "Oh, behave! Yeah, baby!"

Any awkwardness, any fleeting smart of rejection, evaporated. Josh kissed me softly before helping me to my feet.

"And I will behave," he promised, "but only until you're one hundred percent it's time not to."

I'd had to be content with this. Part of me was disappointed, but another part was grateful because Josh was right; feelings were running high. From sharing secrets, to worrying about Estella, to finding out about my family's past, the previous few days had been a crucible of high emotion. I liked Josh, I really did, but was this the time to start something new? Was I in the right space to do so? My heart said 'yes' but my head needed to agree. When a man like Josh Richardson gave his heart, he would do so mind, body and soul. Josh would love with everything he had and until the world stopped turning and the stars went out.

He deserved the same.

We'd cleared away, and because it was late Josh had shown me to one of the spare rooms. Part of me still hoped he wouldn't stop at the bedroom door, but he'd been a total gentleman. Then exhaustion, a full stomach and several glasses of wine had sent me into a deep sleep, and I didn't wake until the sun peeped over the tops of Estella's rampant trees.

So now, as I stand beneath the sharp jets of the en suite's rainfall shower, I relive the events of the previous evening, tentatively prodding the deepest parts of my soul to establish how I feel. Do I regret kissing Josh? Was it a mistake? Do I feel as though I've betrayed Andy? Do I feel awkward? The questions build with the lather of the shower gel, but the answer to each remains the same.

A resounding *no!*

Am I glad he stopped things going any further? As I towel myself dry, I must admit the answer to this question is complex. No, because the moment was wonderful and I knew what I wanted. Yes, because there's so much to think about without the complications of a fledgling romance. By the time I head downstairs I'm starting to agree with Josh and the garden analogy – I need to clear the ground first before I can contemplate planting anything new.

The builders are already on site and the farmhouse is no longer the peaceful spot of the previous evening but a hive of activity. Voices shout, a cement mixer rumbles and a delivery of wood is being unloaded. As I walk into the kitchen, I recognise Kelly's husband, Darren, chatting to Josh at the back door.

"Sorry," Josh says once Darren has departed with his instructions. "Work starts extra early when you live on site. We've a specialist team in today and it's going to be busy." He shuts the door and smiles at me, his beautiful green eyes as clear and gentle as ever. "How did you sleep?"

There's no awkwardness at all, and knowing this gives me a warm feeling, as though I've stepped into a patch of sunshine.

"Really well," I say. "I was out like a light."

"I thought you would be. The room was OK? Nothing upset you?"

I think I know what he's alluding to.

"It was great, and if you're asking me about atmosphere, I'd say it was peaceful." My hand steals to the crucifix. "It's just the kitchen which feels unsettled and sad."

"Exactly what I think. And how about everything else? Is all that OK too?"

I step forward and wind my arms around his neck.

"Everything's good," I promise. "Better than good. It's all wonderful."

Josh's hand rests briefly against the small of my back and I feel any tension slide away.

"I'm glad," he says. "So very glad."

I hold my breath hoping he's going to kiss me, but a second lorry arrives and there's a flurry of activity outside followed by a crash.

Josh grimaces. "That doesn't sound good. I'd better go and supervise. I'm not being a very good host, am I? I should have made you some breakfast."

"It's fine, I'll grab something later," I say. "I thought I'd head into Calmouth and find out a bit more about the Americans being based here. That might give me more information for the GI tracing people. I'll get to the hospital for visiting time."

"Good idea. Look, I'll be caught up here all morning but one of the lads can whizz you into town. I'll do my best to get to the hospital as soon as I'm free." He pulls me close and I feel his heartbeat beneath the fabric of his shirt. "I can't wait to hear what you find out, Nell. I really wish I could come with you."

"Me too," I say because Josh and I have become a team these last few days. It feels as though we've become Estella's surrogate family. To continue without him beside me feels strange.

I'm driven to Calmouth by Shane, all of nineteen and, judging by our speed through the high-banked lanes, either a frustrated racing driver or a lad with a death wish. As the journey unfolds, I still can't quite believe the events of the previous evening. Everything feels brighter and sharper today, the sun warmer and the blue of the sea deeper than I recall. Before, everything was muted. Dulled. Held at a distance. Today I feel as though I'm coming back to life after a long winter.

From an intellectual perspective, I appreciate I've been grieving. I've lost my baby, my marriage, my father and, unless I get writing soon, probably my career too. I have often felt as though I've been observing a woman called Nell Summers as she's been going through the motions.

Nell didn't tear at her hair or wail. Nor did she shun the outside world. Instead, she went about her business just as she'd always done. From signing her divorce papers, to burying her father, to putting away for ever the bootees and soft toys she'd purchased with such hope, Nell Summers did it all with a quiet resolution. She didn't complain, or at least not to anyone tangible although God was the recipient of many a late-night tirade. She waded through a mire of bone-grinding weariness. Previously simple tasks, like choosing what to wear or pushing a trolley around the supermarket, were insurmountable, and the world felt as though she was peering through the wrong end of a telescope. Nell Summers had learned that feeling anything hurt too much. Conducting life as though sealed behind Perspex was by far the safer choice. Feeling, loving and living were dangerous.

But Josh Richardson, gentle gardener of plants and hearts, has provided the perfect conditions to coax her back to life. As a seed needs light and soil and water, so she only needs time and understanding and patience from a wise soul with a tender touch.

Today the Perspex has gone. The telescope has been turned around.

I feel different.

I feel happy. Something has shifted. There are good things ahead, I just know it.

Shane drops me off at Calmouth Library, a large building in the centre of the town. Marble floors, high ceilings and a sweeping oak staircase harken back to a more glamorous age and, as I settle down with a selection of books, I wonder whether Estella and Evie came here. The past and the present overlap, and as I open my notebook I see two teenage girls, dark hair swept up in victory rolls, giggling as they dart in and out of bookshelves. They're older now, sixteen perhaps, and excited to see the handsome new arrivals driving their jeeps through the town. Was it in Calmouth that they first met Jay Miller? According the books I'm flicking through, a blend of locally published paperbacks and more academic tomes, this town was where the American army had first set up a camp. Black and white photos show grinning boys waving from lorries, posing for official uniformed portraits like Jay's, and relaxing on the base. Forever young, they are frozen in time on photographic paper, the twentieth-century equivalent of ancient bodies preserved in peat bogs or cast in volcanic ash.

I shiver. How is it possible such vibrancy and life can be cut short? It feels wrong. A blood sacrifice made on a foreign beach for a peace we take too easily for granted and pay lip service to once a year. How quickly a generation's loss can be forgotten and consigned to history. How swift we are to take peace for granted. I sigh and turn my attention back to my reading.

I love research. One of the best parts about writing my novels is digging into the background of my characters and uncovering their world. Each detail I unearth, be it as tiny as the type of lace used to trim a nightgown or as huge as an Act of Parliament forced through by a King to justify his lust, gives life to the book and puts flesh onto the bones of the people within it. When I write I see the past – the places they inhabited, the food they ate, the clothes they wore – and it's exactly the same for the world of 1940s Pencallyn and the daily mechanics of the army life experienced by the young man who's quite possibly my grandfather.

My hand flies across the pages of my notebook as I scribble down ideas, questions and observations. Hours are truncated into minutes. By the time the clock above the librarian's desk tells me it's past noon, my hand is cramped from writing and I ache from sitting still for so long. I flex my fingers and stretch. The world of the library has continued to turn while I've been lost in the early nineteen-forties. Students have arrived, spreading out folders and books in an imitation of work but in reality scrolling through Facebook and Instagram. My social media presence is another thing I've let slip since I lost my baby and my father. Instagram became a place where each image of a smiling infant or happy family is another paper cut of loss. Individually they are nothing. Cumulatively, I could bleed to death. My agent manages what's left of my online author presence, and if anyone misses seeing pictures of what I've had for lunch, I'm yet to know about it. Maybe I should take some pictures on my phone and post them? Drum up some interest in my next book? The problem is, my search into the past has now replaced my drive to tell a new story, and my new novel has stalled. I have a suspicion that until I manage to lay Jay Miller's story to rest, I won't be able to write a word.

As though sensing I'm thinking about it, my iPhone vibrates. It's a text from Josh to say he's running late and will meet me at the hospital, if that's OK. Touched by his concern, I send a quick reply saying the walk will do me good after a sedentary morning.

'Did you find out anything helpful?' he messages back and I pause. I've found out lots of background, and I have a clearer idea how life was in Pencallyn in 1943 when the Americans arrived, but Jay Miller is as shadowy as ever. He's not mentioned by name, which I supposed deep down was my hope, but remains as one of many young men who made the journey from the United States to England. The Cornish girls went crazy for the new arrivals because America was another world, glimpsed through movies, and the American boys had a glamour which made them impossibly attractive. In my notes I've written 'Evie wants to be an actress and loves Hollywood – possible reason why she would seek out Jay?' which is my sole hypothesis. It's not a lot to go on.

My research also covers the imported segregation laws and social tensions which the US army brought with it. Over one hundred thousand African-American soldiers came to the United Kingdom to fight alongside the Allies and were subject to the segregation laws. One locally produced pamphlet, written as part of a millennium history project, is filled with anecdotes from people who lived in the Calmouth area at the time, and their reactions to racial segregation. As I read about young black soldiers segregated from the pubs, being given menial tasks and some being abused in the street by their comrades if they dared to speak to a British girl, anger bites into my soul. It hurts to know what Jay Miller must have endured every day.

What my own family members probably had to bear …

Where I've made notes about this subject the nib of my pen scores into the paper. I've recorded the high number of mixed-race babies born in Cornwall and circled it in red, but what stands out most is a vile quotation I've stumbled across. Even writing it down for my research turns my stomach, but it gives me more insight into Estella's world than anything else so far. The ugly words are taken from a letter written to Anthony Eden by the then MP for Calmouth and Pendray. The MP's letter lists the reasons African-American soldiers should be sent back to north Africa, his main argument being, and I quote, that 'half caste babies' were bad for the country'.

Reginald Kellow. Estella's father.

Seeing his bile printed on the page in front of me makes my stomach heave. What kind of man would say such a thing? I already know Estella was afraid of him, and she's hinted that he hit Violet. How must it have been living with such a man? Especially if your best friend, one Hollywood-loving Evie Jenkins, was having a secret affair with a handsome black GI? At this point the notebook's page is covered in my ideas and theories. Had

Estella covered for Evie while she was meeting Jay Miller? Was she so afraid of her father that she betrayed her friend? Did Evie run away with my infant father because she was afraid of Reginald? Did Reginald Kellow throw her out? Or was it Violet, poor unremembered Violet whose memorial in St Brecca's is little more than an afterthought, who covered up for Evie? Or was Violet the one who had the affair with Jay Miller? Evie had called her a tart …

So many questions and, as always, no answers. The more I search into my father's story the more gaps I seem to find. It feels as though the truth recedes with every passing day.

I sigh so heavily that several people turn around. Flushing at their scrutiny, I text Josh back, telling him I've several more theories, before gathering up my belongings and returning the books. It's time to head into the bustle of Calmouth. The one person who can help me solve this mystery lies in a hospital bed on the far side of town, and with every minute that passes the danger of her story slipping away for ever grows greater. I can't hold my questions back much longer; she needs to give me some answers before it's too late.

The time has come to ask Estella Kellow what she remembers about Jay Miller.

CHAPTER 28

Estella
The Present

Time was folding like laundry. The past would be washed away as the tide once licked away the words Estella and Evie had carved into the sand with driftwood. Memories, like stories, are not linear and if Evie was here sometimes, sixteen and scornful as Estella struggled to keep up with her, this was as natural as the sun rising and setting. Sometimes Violet drifted past in a cloud of scent, on other occasions Alex sat on the bed, handsome in his sheepskin flying jacket, and teased her just as he'd done when she was a sickly child.

"I'm ninety-five not twelve, Ally," she'd grumble but there would be no reply. Time would telescope, hurtling her back into a present where her mind and identity were decomposing with her body and where the people of the past walked the landscape of memory. They were gone but soon she would join them.

Jay Miller never visited, and Estella had learned a long time ago not to hope for him. Wherever it was Jay went all those years ago must have been very far away indeed because he never travelled back – or rather he never had until the girl, Nell, had brought Estella his photograph. Now Estella saw him all the time. He was in Nell's smile and the sweet curve of her cheek. His laugh echoed in Nell's amused tones and when the girl smiled at Josh, Estella's breath caught to see the look of pure love she'd seen so many times before.

Nell Summers was a bridge between past and present. She was Jay's kin. There was no other explanation. But how? Evie had gone. Jay had vanished. How could there be a Nell? She couldn't exist. Had she imagined Nell? Was this yet another cruel trick of a dying mind?

During the rare times when lucidity swam Estella to the surface, and she broke through the meniscus of age and medication, she thought she glimpsed an explanation far more fantastical than anything she had ever written. It was so wonderful, yet so dreadful too, that before she could begin to grasp it the water weed coiled around her thrashing limbs and dragged her back under. Then the shining revelations were little more than ghosts gliding through the haunted corridors of memory.

She would close her eyes and give in to sleep. Dreams scarfed her days and veiled the truth. Maybe they always had? What were the games she had played with Evie if not dreams? And what was her friendship with Evie except another work of imagination as fantastical as *Mysterious* Garden? Their friendship had proven false. Evie had left. She'd abandoned Estella. She had broken her promise.

Estella felt as though she'd resided in the hospital for ever, prone on a hard bed like one of the marble effigies in St Brecca's and with consciousness lapping at the edges of her mind. Reality was as solid as the silver webs strung across the blackthorn by busy autumnal spiders, a delicate lacing she would never see again, and her story just a jumble of beginnings, middles and unknown endings. The magic came from finding the perfect order, but Estella no longer had the time for this, or the heart.

Yet the girl, this Nell with Jay's gentle touch and soft voice, seemed to believe there was hope. Like the seasons, she visited with a comforting regularity. Estella understood the leash of fascination was tightening around her neck to draw her back. Now Nell was saying she needed to know more. Her pretty face was troubled. Estella strained to hear what it was she said.

"I have to find out before …"

Nell didn't finish her sentence, but she didn't need to. Estella knew her time was growing shorter with each turning of the tide. She was at peace with this and able to slip into the past with increasing ease. At first this had been frightening. She had fought hard to tie up on the pontoon of the present but the effort seemed greater than the reward and so she let her moorings slip. She was too tired to fight. She was too tired to live.

"Estella, I really need you to try and remember when the Americans first came to Pencallyn," Nell said. Her beautiful blue eyes shone with determination. "I think it's the key to finding out the truth about my father's family."

Nell was young, young enough to believe the truth was a good thing. Estella toyed with warning her that sometimes the truth was best buried. Had it helped her to know what her father did to women behind closed doors? Had it been good to know Evie was capable of betrayal? Or that Jay could leave without a farewell? After the war the whole world had been given a glimpse into the darkness which slumbered within every human heart. Was this a warning? Or was it an invitation into depravity, given the right circumstances?

Estella swam for the surface, where the memory was within grasp. She wasn't sure she believed in God – it was hard to have any faith in a benign bearded deity when everyone you had ever loved had been taken from you – but she had the strongest conviction somebody wanted her to tell Nell all she knew. They wanted it so badly they were prepared to let her swim on. She was still here and she could still remember. She could tell her story to this young woman. It was the right thing to do.

"The Americans arrived in Pencallyn in 1942," Estella whispered. Her voice was as cracked as the rough greaseproof paper Cook used to wrap the land girls' lunch in. Nell leaned forward to catch her words.

"After Pearl Harbor," she said.

Estella nodded. It was impossible to explain the joy they'd all felt when America had stepped into the fray. With France and the Soviet Union invaded, and London, Coventry and Plymouth all but flattened, the likelihood of the Germans crossing the Channel to goose step across Britain grew stronger every day. But with the might of the United States on the Allies' side there was a sudden glimmer of hope. Hitler might have met his match in Uncle Sam.

By 1943 it was hard to remember a time when there hadn't been a war on, just as it seemed impossible Evie hadn't always lived with them at Pencallyn House. Although Estella did her best to manage the vegetable patch, the formal garden had long since been abandoned, while Evie did household chores – albeit badly. They still played Mysterious Garden from time to time, but as they grew older this beloved game felt as though it belonged in the past. They stopped leaving notes in the sundial and as the box hedges grew unchecked even the labyrinth no longer had the same appeal. It felt as though it belonged to the past.

"It's strange how something extraordinary soon becomes commonplace," Estella told Nell. "We were living through a war but we were lucky in many ways because Cornwall was more removed from the war than other parts of the country. We had enough food and we had a lot of freedom."

"But you lost loved ones," Nell said, a small frown making a valley between her neat dark brows.

Estella closed her eyes. "Oh yes, of course. Everyone did, and it was hell, but at Pencallyn we still had our chickens and milk and vegetables. There was the blackout and air raids and searchlights, but life was happy in many ways. After what happened to that poor German boy I was keen to become a military nurse, and Evie still dreamed of Hollywood, but we were too young and father expected me to stay at home with Violet. Not that *she* was ever there often once he was involved in his war work."

Evie had known what Violet was up to long before Estella had understood. As Estella grew older she had realised why Violet was subdued when Papa was home and why her makeup might be applied more heavily. How could she blame her stepmother for looking elsewhere for happiness?

"The Americans …" Nell prompted, and Estella nodded. She'd always known this part of the tale would arrive. Part of her longed to tell it but another part was afraid. By holding it close she was keeping it hers; setting it loose with words would mean losing sole ownership for ever. Yet her time was coming and Jay Miller's tale, so entangled with hers and Evie's, deserved to be remembered. Maybe Nell would find out what had really happened to him?

"When the Americans arrived in the village it was so exciting. They widened the roads and installed water mains, laid asphalt surfaces and drove their jeeps at such speed it made you giddy! We had no idea what to expect, of course. Cowboys and ten-gallon hats were about all we knew of Americans, and I don't suppose they knew quite what to make of us either. They seemed very tall and very handsome, and they flashed their money about, which my father certainly disapproved of – probably because he didn't have a great deal of his own at that point."

Estella could still hear Reginald's hectoring tone as he complained about the parties and gum chewing and most of all the African-American servicemen. He had called time and time again for them to be sent back to north Africa.

"My father had some strong opinions, some of them very unpleasant," she began, but Nell laid her hand over Estella's. How young it was. The skin taut and firm, not lined with blue veins or sprinkled with brown spots like her own. When did my hands begin to look like this? Estella thought. Like so much, she couldn't recall.

"I read what your father wrote about black GIs," Nell said gently. "And I know he thought mixed-race children, like me, would be detrimental to the British way of life."

Estella's heart broke that this beautiful, clever, *exceptional* young woman should ever hear anything disparaging about her, even something written a lifetime ago and by a very unpleasant man.

"The black American GIs had a hard time," she agreed. "There were more than a million stationed in Britain and they weren't treated at all well by the white officers, at least not from what I could gather. Some officers revelled in humiliation and cruelty."

Blond hair. Eyes empty as mine shafts. A heart as black as night. Her hand flew to her throat. How could Hamilton Mason still terrify her? He haunted the garden, where she never ventured, but he was long dead.

"The black GIs were billeted separately too," she continued. "They were given the worst jobs because they were regarded as inferior and not believed to be courageous. Educated and well qualified men, some even in medical school, would be tasked with laying roads or digging latrines simply because of the colour of their skin. They were in such trouble too if some officers spotted them talking us British girls. We liked them far better because they were polite and respectful. They never catcalled."

Nell's expression was grim. "Of course not. Back home in the US they'd have been lynched."

"Yes, I would imagine in some states that would have been so."

Estella heard a honeyed drawl. Confident. Entitled. Evil. Decades on, her skin still crawled.

"They weren't welcomed by your father, either," Nell said slowly.

"My father was not a nice man. I can't begin to tell you how afraid I was of him as a child. He ruled the house and he physically abused my stepmother, or so I later came to realise, and I've often feared my own mother suffered the same treatment. We were all scared of him."

"Even Evie?"

"Evie avoided him like a cat will skulk away from somebody it senses may kick it, but she did her best to thwart him when she had to. Oh yes. She wasn't afraid to do that."

"How do you mean? What did she do?"

Estella smiled. "All in good time, dear Nell. I thought we were talking about the GIs? Oh, so many memories of when they arrived. Where to begin?"

She could smell the Camel cigarettes she and Evie had learned to smoke, spluttering and coughing like old hags. Estella had never mastered the art of smoking, unlike Evie who, channelling her inner Rita Hayworth, was soon blowing smoke rings with ease. Even in her latest incarnation as a dried-up old spinster, Estella still felt the shiver of excitement when a handsome boy caught your eye and winked. Oh! What a time! Nissen huts popping up like deformed mushrooms. The strains of jazz floating in the night breeze. Concrete poured onto the beaches. The hammering of the pier into the cove. A road slashed through their garden like a brown wound in green flesh. Her first-ever taste of sticky tinned peaches. Ice cream powder. Kisses snatched beneath a star-sprinkled sky while a band played Glen Miller. It was so vivid and so immediate she was shocked to realise these memories were over seventy-five years old.

"I could tell you all about the first time Evie and I saw the soldiers, driving their jeeps along the lane by the farm," she offered. "Or when Violet took us Christmas shopping in Calmouth, and the Americans managed to wedge one of their vehicles in the narrow streets. They weren't used to our little Cornish lanes, so they had to fetch a mobile crane and winch it over the rooftops. All the Christmas shoppers gathered to watch, and we applauded when they succeeded. It was far better than the pictures, we all said."

Estella already knew what Nell needed to hear but after a lifetime of holding it so close she still wasn't ready to set it free.

"That's fascinating! I'd really love to know more about the soldiers who lived at the Pencallyn camp. I want to know about Jay Miller. What was it like when he was here?" Nell said. "What was life like for him and his friends?"

Estella exhaled. No more prevarication. It was time to pass her story on. She had waited a long time to do this and she needed to do it justice.

"They were little more than boys far from home and they must have often been lonely. Just boys missing their families and sweethearts and probably scared, too, because it was a dangerous time. Black and white, colour didn't matter to the Cornish. The locals opened their homes and hearts to the lads, and when the camp was built at Pencallyn it made everything so lively and so much fun. The local manor house was requisitioned for tank training and the woods there were out of bounds because they became a munitions dump. We had check points and roads built, and there were always exercises taking place. Evie and I would see the soldiers leave dressed for battle and return hours later all dishevelled and muddy. We were at war and we were often scared, especially when we thought the Germans might invade and my father said he would shoot all of us first, but at times it seemed like a game, a game where there were jeeps and tanks and dances and – for Evie at least – flirting."

"Evie flirted with the GIs?"

"Oh yes! She loved the glamour they brought with them. To Evie, well to all of us, they were the closest we ever got to Hollywood. And Evie was striking, Nell, she really was. They loved her."

Evie the swan. Estella still felt so proud; whoever would have believed the skinny urchin with lice and scabby knees would blossom into a willowy girl with a tumbling mane of jet-black hair and peaches and cream skin? At a glance they had still looked alike except Evie was all bones and elegant angles while Estella was petite and curvy.

"Those American boys couldn't take their eyes off Evie," she recalled with a fond smile. "She looked like Vivian Leigh, especially when she pinched Violet's red lipstick and wore her hair in victory rolls."

Nell grins. "I love the idea of you two dressing up and flirting with American boys."

But Estella shook her head, as quick to deny wrongdoing in her nineties as she would have been at seventeen.

"Goodness, not me! I wouldn't have dared, in case my father found out. Besides, by then we had two American officers billeted with us at Pencallyn and he'd all but made up his mind one of them would be a suitable match for me."

"And was he?" Nell's eyes were wide, and Estella realised she was already spinning a romantic tale about a young English girl and a handsome American officer falling in love against the background of war. They would be torn apart by the horror of D-Day and reunited in death after a lifetime apart. But that narrative was off key, like an out-of-tune piano, and it made

Estella shudder. What could be worse than being united with Hamilton Mason, in life or death?

"No," she said vehemently. "He was *not.* It was never him. He was never the one. There was only ever one man for me."

Nell leant forward; her hands clasping Estella's were a buoy that would keep her from sinking. But the bottom of the water was a restful place, and Estella had to fight the longing to slide into it. She had to make sure she told Nell everything, for once she sank back into forgetfulness she might never strike for the surface again.

"Let me tell you about the day I met Jay Miller," Estella said.

CHAPTER 29

Estella
1943

"Outrageous! Utterly unacceptable!"

Reginald Kellow's outburst made Estella jump. Tea slopped into her saucer and her knife clattered against the plate.

"What's wrong, my dear?" Violet looked as though she'd rather not ask the question; her husband's puce face suggested the answer wasn't one she'd enjoy hearing.

"This!"

Reginald Kellow brandished a letter.

"It's those bloody Yanks again," he barked, his moustache bristling with indignation. "They want to billet officers with us. Of all the damn nerve! I shall write to the Home Office at once and say no, of course. Haven't they had enough from me? My son? My land? And now the sanctity of my own home? What's becoming of civilised life? We may as well just invite the Germans to move in!"

"If they are officers, surely they should be fairly civilised?" Evie asked. Although her tone was light, and she looked as though she couldn't care less whether American officers stayed at Pencallyn or not, Estella knew that her blood sister's pulse was racing at the idea of handsome Americans under their roof. Although Evie had only recently turned sixteen, she flirted like a woman twice her age when there was a good-looking American to practise on.

"It's training for when I meet a rich man or a film producer," she'd explained to Estella. "Men are idiots, Stell, and if they think you're going to give them what they want they'll do anything for you. The trick is not to let them have it but think they might!"

By 'it' Estella presumed Evie meant sex – a bargaining chip in her eyes and one not to be squandered lightly. How Evie knew so much about all this was a mystery. Estella imagined Evie found all her information by watching films in the cinema, something she still loved to do whenever she could persuade Violet to take her.

Reginald Kellow looked at Evie askance. He was unsure whether she was asking a genuine question or being impudent, but Evie gazed back at him with guileless blue eyes. Estella was impressed; to hide her excitement so completely showed what an accomplished actress Evie was.

"Well, yes," he conceded, "but having them here will cause all kinds of problems. You mark my words."

A silence fell, punctuated by the ticking of the clock on the mantelpiece and the scraping of Violet's knife on toast.

"It's lucky they don't want to requisition the whole estate," Evie remarked. "I heard Treconnoc Park is a tank base now."

"Gosh, yes, it is," Violet confirmed. "I saw Jilly St Martin at Dizzy Poldeen's drinks do and she told me all about it. Bertie St Martin's utterly heartbroken. He says the grounds will never recover, and they've built roads everywhere. Can you imagine that here?"

Reginald Kellow could, and he shuddered.

"It's important I lead by example and show I'm prepared to do my bit for the war effort," he said, carefully replacing the letter in the envelope. "I shall write back this morning and say that we accept. In a time of war, we must all make sacrifices"

Evie caught Estella's eye over the table and winked. Then the family returned to their breakfast, unaware that life at Pencallyn, and everything they knew, was about to change for ever.

It was towards the end of October, the time of year when autumn slid into winter in a final burst of plums and golds and purples, and when ragged rooks huddled in trees to escape the sharp teeth of a nibbling easterly, that First Lieutenant Hamilton Mason and Second Lieutenant Lexington Boone arrived at Pencallyn House. Estella and Evie were in the pantry, a cool dark room at the back of the house, white walled and with marble worktops and a mesh-caged meat safe, and they were busy hanging up the onions they'd dug up from the vegetable patch. The air was sharp and vinegary from the pickles and preserves, and Estella thought how much she enjoyed the rhythm of the tasks and the way they were governed by the seasons. Her family's legacy was horticulture but until the need to work the land herself had arisen, Estella had had no idea how clever nature was or how much she enjoyed gardening. Four years into the war, Estella was something of an expert in understanding the soil; she had discovered what to plant and when, and how to rest the ground over the winter. She had also learned that she possessed the Kellow magic: weeding, digging, planting, thinning, pruning and harvesting came naturally to her. But it wasn't this way for Evie, and the girls often joked Evie simply needed to look at a plant for it to shrivel. Crows ate the peas she planted, her runner beans drooped, and her potatoes had blight. Estella didn't dare let her near the hens and pigs!

"How much more?" Evie asked, straightening up from her stacking, and rubbing the small of her back. Although there was a streak of dirt across her nose and she was wearing an old pair of man's trousers tied up with string, she still looked impossibly glamorous with her glossy red lips and a Hermes scarf 'borrowed' from Violet tied over her glossy curls. Estella, dressed in an old Liberty print dress, hessian apron and gumboots, and with her hair pinned on the crown of head with a bulldog clip, felt very dowdy in comparison.

"Just another box," she said. "Then we need to think about helping Cook pickle some of the beetroots."

Evie screwed up her nose. "Christ! We'll stink! Do we have to?"

"If you want to eat them," Estella said. Sometimes she was irritated by Evie, who tended to vanish whenever there was hard work to be done. Estella had lost count of the times she'd turned around to ask her friend something while they were digging the vegetable garden only to see Evie's fork lodged in the soil and no sign of her. "We're digging for victory, remember?"

"Are we going to asphyxiate the Nazis with onion fumes?" grumbled Evie. "Come on, we've been at this for hours. At least let's get a cuppa?"

Estella flashed her a look, just daring her to quit. "Not yet. We'll finish these first."

Evie pulled a face. "God, when did you become so bossy? They should send you to Berlin. Hitler would soon give up after ten minutes of your nagging!"

Estella ignored her and continued to twist onions together. Sometimes it was better not to rise to her friend's teasing. Besides, when Evie had her head down, she was a fast worker and just the kind of person you wanted beside you to get a job done.

The girls were finishing their task when the pantry door flew open. Violet stood in the doorway, flanked by two uniformed strangers. The American officers had arrived.

"Oh girls, there you are! I've been looking for you everywhere! I wanted to introduce you to our house guests, Hamilton Mason and Lex Boone! Gentleman, this is my stepdaughter, Estella, and our …" Violet paused as she sought to define Evie, for what was she exactly? A house guest? A friend? Adopted daughter? Estella saw Evie's jaw tighten.

"And our friend Evie Jenkins," Violet finished, a little awkwardly. "As you can see, we've been digging for victory at Pencallyn House!"

"That's a great thing, ma'am. I so admire your British spirit," said the shorter of the two men. His slow accent spoke of peaches and heat and sunsets and he smiled politely at the girls, but the taller man said nothing, his gaze roaming over them both with an intensity which made the hairs on the back of Estella's neck prickle.

She studied the American officers. Their names were a world away from the usual Ruperts and Henrys, and their ornate uniforms and perfect teeth appeared exotic. Both men were so broad-shouldered and muscular they seemed to fill the pantry. The tall man had hair so fair it was white against his sun-kissed skin while the other was dark-haired and pale. As Evie tilted her head to stare up at the blond man, Estella saw an expression cross her friend's face she'd never ever seen before. It looked like awe mingled with adoration.

"Hamilton Mason, ma'am, at your service," drawled the blond man as he took Evie's earth-crusted hand in his white-gloved one and bowed over it like something from a film. "Honoured to meet you."

Evie stared up at him, mesmerised. Estella supposed she thought she was Scarlett O'Hara to a real live Rhett Butler. How Evie loved that film! She must have known it word for word, and could speak with a perfect deep south accent if she chose. Watching her, Estella imagined her friend thought all her Hollywood dreams were coming true. She wouldn't be the first girl to have her head turned by the Americans; healthy and glowing, and with money at their disposal, they were a marked contrast to the British troops, and all the local girls were going mad for them.

"Our boys don't like it at all," Cook had told Estella over a bubbling pot of blackberry preserve they were taking it in turns to stir on the range. "One look at the Yanks and our girls are losing their heads. Giving them chewing gum and stockings and heaven only knows what else! It hardly seems fair, especially when they get paid more than our boys and haven't been in the war as long."

Like Evie, Violet certainly seemed taken by her new house guests. Already on first name terms with them, her cheeks were flushed and her eyes sparkled. She was probably planning drinks parties and soirées, thought Estella.

Wiping her earthy hands on her apron, she stepped forward and shook hands with Lex Boone. A second lieutenant, he was stockier than his companion and had a nose as freckled as a fresh bantam's egg. Estella could picture him fishing in a fast-flowing river or climbing apple trees, and had to stop herself because these were images straight out of *Huckleberry Finn*! Lexington Boone the Second, as he introduced himself, came from a city; it turned out that he was a wealthy man's son rather than a Tom Sawyer. She really must read a little more widely about the United States of America.

Lex turned to greet Evie, and Estella found herself looking into a pair of grey eyes, the exact hue of a stormy November sea and equally chilly. Just as little could entice her to jump into the water on a wintry day, so she wanted to recoil from the touch of this stranger's fingers, and it took all Estella's manners not to flinch.

"Hamilton Mason, ma'am," he said, and she wondered how she could ever have thought his voice was honeyed and warm when it dusted her skin with chills. Hamilton looked her up and down as though she was a horse he was considering buying, before adding, "It's a pleasure to make your acquaintance."

Hamilton Mason had the face of an angel. His features were perfectly symmetrical, the nose patrician and straight like that of a Roman statue. His white-blond hair was close-cropped to a shapely skull, and a smattering of golden stubble sprinkled his square jaw. Long grey eyes seemed to see into her soul and a wide sensual mouth spoke of pleasures she didn't yet understand. The US Forces uniform could have been designed purely with him in mind, showcasing to perfection lean hips and muscular thighs, the jacket clinging like a second skin to his powerful torso and the brocade gilding the strong set of his shoulders. Yes, he was striking but, like a piece of sculpture, as cold as marble.

"I look forward to getting to know you, Miss Kellow," he was saying as he raised her fingers to his lips. A warm tongue flickered across her knuckles in a serpentine kiss which burned like a brand. An image of a python flickered through Estella's mind. When he released her hand, it was all she could do not to wipe it on her apron.

Violet flashed the new arrivals a dazzling smile.

"Now you've met my girls, do let me show you to your rooms. My husband will be at home tonight and we'll dine at seven, if that suits?"

"Sounds just fine, ma'am," Hamilton replied. He didn't take his eyes from Estella and she felt as though it was her he wanted to devour. "I look forward to it."

Once the officers had departed, Violet's chatter carrying all the way along the corridor to the kitchen, Evie turned to Estella with a scowl.

"What was that about?"

"What?"

She crossed her arms and leaned against the work top.

"You know. All big eyes and staring up at him as though you were about to swoon. I saw Hamilton Mason first. He's mine."

Estella laughed but the sound withered on her lips when she realised her friend was serious.

"Don't laugh at me," Evie snapped.

"But you sound crazy! What do you mean, you saw him first?"

"What I said! I've never wanted anything for myself, Stella. Never. You have it all, and I don't care because I love you. But I want him. I want Hamilton Mason."

Estella was taken aback. This was the voice of the angry evacuee who had arrived covered in lice and filthy. It was the growl of the girl who'd wanted to leave a German boy to bleed to death. And it was the voice of somebody who was glaring at her as though they were mortal enemies and not blood sisters at all.

"You're being utterly ridiculous! I wasn't looking at him in any way at all. I was being polite and nothing more. You can have him. He's all yours."

"You promise? You ain't lying?"

Sometimes Evie's old patterns of speech slipped out, usually when she was under stress. When gardening she would turn the air blue with the sodding weeds, and when she had to stretch the chickens' necks for the pot (a job neither Estella nor Cook were able to face if Bert wasn't about) she'd order the bugger of a chicken to bloody sit still.

"I'm not lying. I promise."

"On the sundial?"

"Yes, on the sundial. We can go there right now, if you want?"

But Evie was satisfied. The scene of their old blood promise and many other games since, the sundial held a sacred significance for her.

"No, I believe you," she said. "You wouldn't lie on the sundial."

"I wouldn't lie at all!" Estella shot back, stung. "Not to you, Evie. We're blood sisters."

Evie regarded her for a moment.

"Yes, we are. We swore never to betray one another. On pain of death, remember?"

This wasn't quite how Estella remembered things, but the years between thirteen and nearly seventeen were long ones.

"I remember," she said. "But Evie, I don't think Hamilton Mason's somebody we want to be near. Something about him …"

Her words stalled while she searched for the right adjective.

"Something about him scares me," she finished lamely. This wasn't quite the word Estella was seeking. 'Scare' didn't come close to describing the cold dread she'd felt when the American officer had taken her hand. Nor did it convey the revulsion when she'd felt at the touch of his tongue against her flesh. Every cell in Estella's body was screaming at her that this man was dangerous.

"Don't be a goose," Evie said, tugging off her headscarf and shaking her hair free. "He's beautiful. I think he looks like a film star."

Estella couldn't deny it; Hamilton Mason *was* beautiful, but in the same deadly way a tiger was beautiful. Like a bright sun, he dazzled the vision and drew all eyes but would burn you to a crisp if you got too close. A man like Hamilton Mason knew his own power and wasn't afraid to use it.

Poor Evie wouldn't stand a chance.

"The moment I saw him I *knew* he was the one," she continued, dreamily.

"The one?" Estella echoed. "What do you mean?"

"That he's the one for me. The man I'm going to marry. Love at first sight."

Estella stared at her, dumbfounded. Hamilton was a total stranger. Evie liked to flirt with soldiers, and she loved dances, but never once had she mentioned marriage. Or love. She'd scoffed at *Romeo and Juliet.* As far as she was concerned Paris was a far better choice and Juliet an idiot. Since when had Evie Jenkins believed in love at first sight?

"Don't look at me like that!"

"Like what?"

"Like I'm a head case."

"I don't think that," fibbed Estella, "but I do think you've watched too many films. You don't know this man. He's much older than you and he's a total stranger."

"What's age got to do with it? I knew the minute I saw him, Estella, I truly did. I'd do anything for him to want me. *Anything*!"

As she spoke the sun slipped behind a cloud and plunged the pantry into gloom. Evie's face was shrouded in darkness, but this didn't hide the determined tilt of her chin and the light of devotion in her eyes. The room swam with shadows and Estella had the sensation that something very, very bad was coming. It was the same sensation of gathering dread she felt when contemplating the enemy lurking over the horizon. Menace was just a breath away.

Estella knew nothing good would come of Hamilton Mason's arrival, for her or for Evie. She would need to be on her guard.

CHAPTER 30

Estella
1943

If Reginald Kellow had reservations about opening his house to a couple of US Army officers, he soon forgot about them, and before long Pencallyn House became a byword for drinks parties, cocktails on the terrace and elegant soirées. The pain of seeing a road carved through his garden and fifty acres of land sacrificed to become an army base was soothed by glamour and the extra food the American officers brought with them. Reginald Kellow and Violet were soon invited to social gatherings across Cornwall, and once to cocktails at Daphne du Maurier's Menabilly.

Estella was turned inside out with envy. She'd devoured *Rebecca* and had loved the gothic twists and turns of the plot. In the haunting descriptions of the ruined Manderley she recognised the insidious power of nature now taking possession of Pencallyn's garden, while the unnamed narrator mirrored her own increasing fear of attracting attention. Evie, however, had been far more interested in the dark and dangerous Rebecca.

"Rebecca knew what she wanted, and she made sure she got it," was her verdict.

"But she was wicked and cruel," Estella argued, and Evie threw her a scornful look.

"Her name's the title of the book. Rebecca's the character the author cares about. She's the interesting one."

Estella thought how wonderful it would have been to meet the author and to ask her about this, but only her parents had been invited to Menabilly and there was no way either of them would be interested in a literary discussion. Estella was secretly writing her own book, a literary version of her beloved Mysterious Garden game, and she would have given anything to discuss it with the famous author and ask her advice. Violet had returned from the visit full of excitement about the grandeur of the house. Daphne's husband had been utterly charming, she'd said, and the grounds were beautiful! Fowey was simply divine! Frustrated, Estella had stomped off to the library to work on her own book without the input she was certain would make it a masterpiece.

She spent as much time as possible in the library, hidden in a window seat and tucked behind a curtain in case any unwelcome visitors might stroll by. There she would write and sketch until her hand cramped and her eyes hurt. A few weeks into the officers' stay she realised Evie was no longer curling up opposite with a book or joining her to wander through the tangled garden. She was absenting herself, drifting about the place in the hope of seeing Hamilton Mason, and Estella missed her company.

Once upon a time the girls had chatted late into the night, burrowed beneath blankets and whispering secrets, but although they still shared a room those conversations had faded away, and lately Evie had been turning her back after a brief 'good night'. She knew Estella disapproved of her fascination with Hamilton and, being Evie, was determined to punish Estella by shutting her out. Evie hated it when Estella disagreed with her.

The two girls were drifting apart. There was nothing Estella could say or do to change this. Evie watched people and stored secrets and frailties as a squirrel stashes acorns, and Estella knew she had noted Hamilton's interest in her during that first meeting. Any inklings of a preference now would be noted and considered a betrayal. Estella felt desperately sad. How she wished the Americans had never come.

Like *Rebecca*'s unnamed narrator, Estella's dearest wish was to be unnoticed and she made a concerted effort to avoid the American officers. She was horribly conscious of Hamilton's cool gaze resting on her whenever the officers joined the family for meals. It was hard to eat when those long grey eyes scrutinised her every mouthful, his gaze crawling over her skin like a rash, and harder still when she knew Evie was also watching her closely.

Unlike Evie, who was smitten, Estella's aversion to First Lieutenant Mason grew with every passing day. For a powerfully built man he had an unnerving habit of slipping silently from the shadows. He would come across her when she least expected it and feign surprise, but Estella knew he was watching her and picking moments when she was alone. He might pretend to be surprised but she wasn't fooled.

There was nothing outwardly untoward that she could complain about. Hamilton was always courteous and friendly. He would express interest in the book she was reading or ask innocuous questions about the garden, but the intensity of his gaze made Estella feel as if she was a delicacy he was about to consume. She had a terror he would bite into her flesh with his strong white teeth, flicking his pink tongue across her skin as he had that first day. He repelled her.

Yet Evie, feisty and clever Evie, was totally in Hamilton's thrall. To Estella she seemed like one under an evil enchantment. Evie didn't see how dangerous Hamilton was, but instead waxed lyrical about his golden beauty and made a fool of herself trailing after him in the hope he might notice her. 'Moonstruck' was how Cook described Evie's behaviour.

"It's puppy love," she told Estella one morning when, rather than helping with the daily chores, Evie slipped away to daydream. As Estella kneaded dough, she wished she was pounding Evie's strange obsession out of her head.

"It doesn't make any sense," she said, her words in time with her thumping fists. "She doesn't even know him. He's hardly spoken three words to her."

Cook laughed. "Love doesn't make sense, Miss Estella – you'll understand that one day. It comes from nowhere and there's no accounting for it or fighting it. You'll see."

Love seemed a strange thing to Estella; it didn't do women any favours. Look at Violet having to endure her father's temper. Then there was the disgraced land girl who got herself 'in the family way' and was discreetly moved on; and now Evie was behaving strangely. No, love was not something Estella Kellow wanted to look for, thank you very much. She was going to write books and paint pictures, and she wasn't going to answer to a man, especially since she was the heir to Pencallyn House. If she did fall in love, it would be with her dreamed-of soulmate – otherwise she vowed she would be a spinster. Evie could live here with her and when the war was over they would eat cake every day, write books and have a jolly marvellous time doing exactly as they pleased. As plans went it seemed a good one, or at least it had until Hamilton Mason arrived and Evie slipped under his evil spell.

"I won't fall in love," Estella said firmly.

Cook gave her an indulgent smile. "One day a young man will catch your eye and you won't be able to think of anything else. It happens to us all – even me. When I met my Bert, I thought I heard the angels singing!"

Estella found this hard to believe. Cook's red-faced husband, who did odd jobs around the estate when he wasn't propping up the bar in The Pilchards, was hardly the stuff of romantic novels.

"He's changed a bit," Cook admitted, seeing Estella's look of disbelief, "but he was a real dish once! You must admit Lieutenant Mason is so handsome – especially in uniform."

Estella was admitting nothing of the kind. There was a reptilian quality to Hamilton Mason which blocked out the golden good looks just as the clouds did the sun. When those cold grey eyes swept over her, she shivered, and not from longing or desire or any of the other old clichés either but from pure fear. Something about him that made her skin crawl.

"He isn't interested in Evie," was all she said, and Cook laughed.

"Well, we all know that, Miss Estella! You could have no eyes in your head and still see who *has* captured his attention!"

Estella's hands froze mid-knead. Clods of dough plopped onto the marble work top.

"What do you mean?"

"Bless you! Lieutenant Mason can hardly take his eyes off *you*, Miss Estella. I swear he'd gobble you up if he could. Mind you, a girl could do a lot worse. He's wealthy, by all accounts, and your father's very taken with him. It's a good match."

Estella grasped the worktop with her sticky hands to keep herself from crumpling onto the floor. If the servants had also noted Hamilton's interest it went without saying Evie would have seen it too. Estella wasn't sure what made her feel more filled with dread: Hamilton singling her out for attention or Evie feeling hurt. She would be furious too, and Estella knew her best friend well enough to realise when Evie could become savage if she felt slighted. It wouldn't matter to her if Estella had no desire to be the focus of Hamilton's attention; Evie would still feel betrayed. Although the floor was hewn from stone, it seemed to sag beneath her feet.

"Lord, look at you about to swoon for love," laughed Cook, mistaking Estella's horror for maidenly emotion.

"I am not swooning for love," Estella said through clenched teeth. "I'm not interested in Hamilton Mason. I know how Evie feels about him, and I would never, ever get in her way. She's my friend."

"What nonsense you speak sometimes, Miss Estella! Lieutenant Mason's a gentleman. He wouldn't consider the likes of her," said Cook. "I know you two are thick as thieves, but you're not from the same backgrounds at all. If it wasn't for this war your paths would have never crossed. You're a gentleman's daughter, but Evie Jenkins was a filthy guttersnipe when she arrived here. She isn't a match for somebody like him and she'll work that out soon enough, you'll see."

But Estella knew Cook was wrong. Once Evie put her mind to something there was no turning back. No change of direction. Nothing was too much effort. She would make winter posies to leave outside his room and at mealtimes her food would go untouched as she stared longingly at him. 'Mooning' was how Violet had once teasingly described it, and the look Evie threw her was so black it had taken Estella aback. Luckily Violet hadn't noticed. She was too busy giggling and flicking her hair to notice anything; but Estella, exhausted from gauging her father's dark expression and avoiding Hamilton's hungry eyes, felt undercurrents swirling around the dinner table as surely as they swirled around the rocks at the mouth of Pencallyn Cove. Sometimes she feared she might drown.

Despite his wife's flirting, Reginald Kellow thoroughly approved of his two house guests. They were well bred Southern gentlemen who came from old money and had attended West Point before taking up commissions in the US Army. They shared his own views on many things from opera to fine dining too, and most importantly for Reginald Kellow, the role of black servicemen. Lex was from an old Georgia family, his father was something important in the railroads, and he had no issue with the black soldiers digging the roads and doing the menial tasks. Hamilton's family owned a large plantation in South Carolina – built on slavery like Tara in *Gone with the Wind*, Estella presumed – and he made it plain he regarded the black soldiers he commanded as his inferiors in every way.

Estella lost count of the times she'd had to listen to the men discuss the inferior intellect of the African-American soldiers and conclude it was right they were assigned the labour and service roles. The more she heard, the greater her unease grew. She may have only been seventeen but to her understanding there didn't seem a vast difference between the philosophy her father was endorsing and Hitler's treatment of the European Jews. Weren't the Allies supposed to be fighting racial prejudice and persecution?

"One thing I've noticed here, and which I don't care for, is that the British don't draw a colour line," Hamilton remarked over dinner one dreary November evening. The American officers had been complaining about the Cornish weather, which had led to a discussion of what they missed about home. Estella found it telling that Hamilton missed the segregation laws rather than his family. The locals in the village hadn't been impressed by some of the attitudes they'd witnessed.

"We're all in this together, black, white or green with blue spots," was Cook's verdict. "Ivy Pendriscott has a lovely lad billeted with her. He's a medic and she says he's credit to his family. I don't hold with all this 'them and us' nonsense. It's Hitler we should be fighting, not each other."

But of course Reginald Kellow agreed with Hamilton: "It's outrageous," he nodded.

"I've seen nice-looking British girls going out with negro soldiers," Lex chipped in, and Hamilton scowled at this.

"I've seen those black boys dancing with British girls too and I've seen them kissing girls goodnight. We wouldn't allow it at home. I guess you British have different standards?" he said. "You don't seem offended by things we'd say aren't decent."

"Oh, trust me, Lieutenant, decent British people are certainly offended," Reginald Kellow said slowly. "It's as I've always said, bringing negroes here will pollute the population. Before we know it, the country will be littered with half-breeds."

Estella jumped to her feet. She couldn't keep silent a second longer.

"What a vile thing to say! They're people just like us, and we're fighting this war together! We should be thanking them."

"Hold your tongue!" Reginald bellowed.

"No! Not when you say things like that!" Estella cried. She was sick of them all and their ugly words, and she was bitterly ashamed of her father.

Violet's hands rose to her mouth. Evie's eyes were big circles of shock. Nobody at Pencallyn House ever dared speak back to Reginald Kellow.

"I said, hold your tongue!"

Estella's hands were shaking. She tucked them into the folds of her skirt.

"I can't," she said quietly.

"Then I'll rip it out by the roots!" Reginald lunged across the table, knocking over a bottle of red wine which pooled across the snowy cloth like spilt blood. Estella shrank back, tripping on her chair and slamming onto the floor.

"Darling, please, calm down," pleaded Violet. "Estella doesn't mean it. She doesn't know what she'd saying! She's just a child."

Reginald rounded on his wife. Spittle flecked the corners of his mouth.

"She's seventeen and she knows enough to keep her opinions to herself. I don't recall asking for yours either, madam."

Violet stared down at the table. She was white.

"Anyone else?" Reginald Kellow demanded, gazing round the room.

There was a time when Evie would have leapt to Estella's defence, their promise to love and protect each other stronger than any punishment, but now Evie didn't say a word. They locked eyes for a moment before Evie's slid away like butter from hot crumpets.

Something had shifted. The tight bonds of the promise were starting to fray.

"I think I need to keep a closer eye on the women in my family," Reginald said to his guests. "They seem to be picking up some very peculiar ideas. I apologise, gentlemen."

Hamilton looked sorrowful. "There's no need, sir. Emotions run high with ladies. Their tender hearts don't understand such complicated issues. Please don't think any more of it. Besides, there's nothing wrong with a bit of spirit." His eyes flickered over Estella and she glimpsed something so dark in their arctic depths that her fear of her father was as nothing: a childish terror of the monster lurking beneath the bed in comparison to the mounting horror of something far darker. Estella's dread was intensified when Hamilton added so softly only she could hear, "It makes the joy of mastering that spirit all the sweeter."

Estella didn't know a great deal about men, but she recognised the threat wrapped up in his slow honeyed tones. Her skin prickled.

"Get out, Estella," Reginald Kellow hissed. "I'll deal with you later."

Estella's punishment was not something she wanted to ever think about again. Her father's belt had stung, and she hadn't been able to sit down for days. She hadn't given him the satisfaction of tears, but it had been a close thing. The bite of leather against her skin had been savage and Reginald had given her ten hard wallops.

"I would have liked to have seen you strapped," Hamilton had whispered the next morning, pausing behind her chair as she sat down gingerly and tried her hardest not to wince. "What a pretty sight it must have been."

Estella's blood drained from her body and she'd thought she would pass out. His words made her feel tainted and grubby and oddly ashamed.

Evie had asked what Hamilton had said and Estella had made up something about the weather but she could tell her friend wasn't convinced.

"Don't you care that he said those things about the black soldiers?" she asked as a distraction.

Something flickered across Evie's face. For a moment Estella thought she had found a way to break the spell. The Evie she loved dearly was rebellious and brave and clever. She would hate Hamilton's ugly words. Estella was certain the real Evie was trapped beneath a sheet of ice and was banging her fists frantically as she fought to escape. Was there a small crack appearing?

"You can't agree with what he said?" she pressed.

"He's not from here," muttered Evie. She couldn't look Estella in the eye.

"Surely what he said was wrong no matter where he comes from? We're all equal."

Evie snorted. "Easy for you to say."

"What's that supposed to mean?"

"You're Estella Kellow. You belong here. You're one of the family. You've no idea what it's like for the rest of us. Are you equal to Cook? Or Dolly? Or the land girls? Or Bert?"

Estella didn't know what to say.

"Of course you're not," Evie continued scathingly. "I'm not your equal even though we try to pretend we're sisters. Everyone knows I'm the cuckoo in the nest. Don't bother to argue, Stell. I know what Cook thinks of me. And Dolly. And all of them. Your father's the most honest because he despises everyone."

"We *are* sisters! We're blood sisters!"

"That's a game. When the war is over where will I go? Do you think I'll stay here? Be a lady like you? Bollocks I will. It'll be off to a factory or a shop for me – but not if I marry a man like Hamilton. I can go to America and live a new life. I could go to Hollywood."

Estella could hardly believe her ears. "You'd leave Pencallyn? But I thought we were going to stay here and write books?"

"That's just a dream, Stell."

"It's not. I'll make it happen.

"You'd try to, but your father wouldn't let you," Evie said sadly. "I know how the world works, but I've met the man who can change my destiny for ever. I feel it here." She pressed her hand to her heart.

Estella felt ice seep through her blood. 'The man who will change my destiny for ever.' It was horribly prophetic, but she suspected that any changes brought about by Hamilton would not be for the better.

Just like the princess in their old games of Mysterious Garden, now consigned to childhood and the secret novel, Estella would have to work out a way to rescue her friend from Hamilton. Estella had promised to protect Evie, but how she would do this she had no idea. Hamilton Mason was dark and dangerous. He was the type of man who wouldn't think twice about taking advantage of a young girl's infatuation or forcing another against her will. When she recalled how he relished the thought of watching her being beaten, Estella felt queasy.

She would have to be doubly on her guard – for herself and her foolish, infatuated friend.

CHAPTER 31

Estella
1943

"The Americans are holding a dance at the schoolhouse tonight!"

Evie burst into the kitchen, a blast of chilly air swirling in with her, and put her basket of winter greens down with a thud. Her cheeks were flushed, and her blue eyes sparkled with an excitement Estella hadn't seen for weeks.

"You might look a little more interested," Evie grumbled, placing her cold hands on the range. "They'll have music and food and dancing. Everyone is bound to be there. It will be fun. Remember fun?"

By 'everyone' Estella imagined Evie meant Hamilton, and the thought didn't fill her with joy. The officers had been busy for the past few weeks, out on manoeuvres and exercises, and to Estella's relief scarcely present at Pencallyn. This meant she could drop her guard, and Evie was unlikely to do something daft. Estella had watched her best friend as intently as soaring buzzards scrutinised the ground for prey, and had become her shadow. There was safety in numbers after all.

"I'm not really one for dancing," she protested. Besides, what could be worse than having to jive and Lindy hop for hours with confident young men who thought a stick of Juicy Fruit and a can of peaches was enough to win them a kiss?

"But *I* am!" Evie cried, whirling across the kitchen. She was light on her feet and quick to learn the steps, and Estella knew she would love nothing more than to spend an evening dancing. Young men would queue up to throw her into the air and spin her around, and even better if one of them was Hamilton Mason. Estella suspected the officers wouldn't be interested in a dance arranged for their men, but Evie, unfamiliar with the hierarchies of public schools and the armed forces, wouldn't have thought of this.

Maybe a night out from under Reginald's beady eye wouldn't be so bad. Although Estella had been duly punished for her dinner table outburst, she was still in her father's bad books. Soon the fading blue bruises on her buttocks and the knowing glances Hamilton Boone cast her way were all that suggested anything untoward had ever taken place. Estella had learned to hold her tongue the hard way, and although she seethed at some of the conversations which took place over meals she decided she would pick her battles in the future. One day she would tell her father what she really thought of him. He was a bully and a racist. Hamilton might have the face of a god but he was no more than a younger version of Reginald Kellow.

If only Evie could see this. If only Estella could make her see it!

But Evie's thoughts were still on dancing. She shimmied over to Estella and threw her arms around her neck.

"Come on, Stella! Please? It's one dance. It'll be fun. You never know, you might meet a handsome American soldier!"

Estella rolled her eyes. "Unlikely."

"Highly likely, I'd say! Have you any idea how many of them there are here? Dolly's going mad!"

As the situation across the English Channel grew increasingly serious more American troops had arrived in Cornwall. Truckloads of young GIs trundled through the lanes, and warships were frequently anchored in the bay. Estella often walked Poppet through the woods and down to the creek, but barbed wire halted her passage to the water's edge, where camouflaged barges wallowed in the shallows like prehistoric beasts and the rampant undergrowth bristled with unseen creatures. Once she saw a stoat perched on a fallen log, staring at her with bright and inquisitive eyes. Estella wished she still had her old Box Brownie camera to capture this moment of stillness for ever. It seemed sad it had been confiscated in case she inadvertently took pictures which might help the Germans. Estella had protested she didn't even know any Germans, but her father insisted and so the camera had duly been handed over. The long sunny days of fun with Evie as they snapped pictures in the garden or at the old farmhouse belonged to another life.

The army camp at the top of Pencallyn Valley had tripled in size, swallowing even more of Reginald Kellow's land and necessitating further widening of narrow lanes. Rashes of canvas tents pimpled the fields while extra roadblocks were set up along the route into town. Estella became accustomed to showing her identity card and answering questions, but her father, who had owned the land for so long, found it infuriating. With the onset of winter, food was in short supply too, even in Cornwall, and the strain of being at war for five years was telling on them all. Tempers were frayed and everyone was tired. Maybe a dance was exactly what they needed. Estella wished she could feel a little more enthusiastic.

"All right, I'll go," she said and was deafened by Evie's squeal of excitement. She'd probably regret giving in, and would spend the evening sitting at the side of the dance floor wishing she was at home in the library writing her book – but it would be worth it to see Evie happy rather than obsessing over the clay-footed object of her affections.

The girls walked through the garden to the village. Although the blackout was down and the night inky, a full moon lit the way and cast shadows across the path. A frost was already falling, and the leaves and grass glittering as though dusted with diamonds. Nights like these were beautiful but dangerous, lighting the way for the German bombers, but this evening Estella tried her hardest to put the war from her mind. Tonight, she was seventeen and having fun.

Music drifted on the cold night air as the schoolhouse door opened and closed. The place was packed to bursting point. The girls were all dressed in their best frocks, hair swept into victory rolls and mouths slicked with red lipstick. Dressing up wasn't something they did often in Pencallyn, and this evening they had dug out their finery. Estella and Evie had raided Violet's wardrobe – she was away in Calmouth again, tearing away down the drive ten minutes after Reginald had departed for London. Evie plumped for a midnight blue dress which made her eyes shine like sapphires, and liberally applied lipstick and set her hair in rolls with a large one at the front. She looked at least twenty, which Estella supposed was the intention.

Estella had chosen a simple white frock, tied at the waist with a blue ribbon, and had left her hair loose. If she looked dull in comparison this was fine by her. Estella was more than happy to blend into the background because that way Evie couldn't accuse her of trying to steal anyone!

The music was loud and the room was hot. The chairs and desks had been stacked at the far end and the place was filled with couples twirling in perfect time to the music. The young soldiers looked dashing in their uniforms and swaggered across the floor with just the right mix of confidence and hopefulness as they asked girls to dance. There might be a war on, but for this one evening nothing mattered more than dancing and having fun. Evie, beaming from ear to ear, was quickly singled out by a handsome young man and whirled across the dance floor. Estella saw her scan the crowd hopefully but when there was no sign of Hamilton, Evie threw herself into the next dance, tipping her head back and giggling at partner after partner. Her flirting was fine by Estella, because Evie was far safer doing this than skulking around Pencallyn.

Sipping a glass of punch, Estella glanced around and felt pleased when there was no sign of the senior officers. The presence of several young black GIs suggested this was a gathering her father's guests wouldn't particularly enjoy, and Estella concluded it must be an evening arranged for the privates. The presence of the military police, stationed outside, would be more than enough to quell any trouble, and everyone seemed to be dancing happily. Dolly and the land girls were Lindy hopping with great gusto, and Estella was in awe of their grasp of the steps. Less time writing and more time dancing, she told herself. Then she could join in!

As she watched Evie throw herself into dance after dance Estella wondered how her friend kept going. Several boys asked her to dance but Estella said she was resting and they didn't seem to mind. They were polite and wholesome and suggested tales of log cabins and open spaces and apple pies, a life that was nothing to do with Germans and bombs and death. Tonight, the war was another world. Tonight belonged to the young people who would have to fight it tomorrow and who were determined to squeeze the pips out of each moment.

Every few moments a young man would slip outside with a girl, throwing his jacket across her shoulders as they headed into the cold air. Estella wondered how it might feel to find someone you wanted to be alone with, someone who made you forget the cold and the frost and who you wanted to pull close until you could feel the heat of their skin against yours and their lips were just a kiss away …

The punch must be stronger than she realised if she was thinking like this! Maybe she ought to get some fresh air. It wouldn't hurt Evie to have a rest too. She was looking flushed. Maybe they could stroll outside.

As Estella placed her empty glass on the windowsill it slipped from her grasp and shattered on the floor. Without stopping to think, she bent down to scoop up the sharp shards, when one sank into her right hand.

"Ouch!" Estella gasped, snatching her hand back and splashing bright red onto the skirt of Violet's beautiful dress. Closer investigation revealed a deep cut, about an inch in length, which bisected her palm. The sharp pain brought tears to her eyes. How stupid she was, Estella thought. What a silly thing to do. She ought to have fetched a dustpan and cleared it up properly. What on earth was she thinking of, attempting to pick glass up by hand? 'More haste less speed,' as Tommy would have said.

As more blood seeped from the wound, she clenched her fist, hoping to staunch the flow, but it trickled through her fingers and splashed onto the chalky floor. Estella cradled her injury in her left hand. She needed a cloth to mop up the blood. Maybe the ladies' room would have a towel? She would be able to wash it there too and make sure the wound was clean. As the music swirled around her and the heat pressed down, she swayed a little. Blood always made her feel a bit faint. Maybe she wasn't cut out to be an army nurse after all.

"Hey, that looks nasty. May I have a look?"

Estella looked up to see a young man peering down at her. His soft dark eyes were filled with concern and his hand was outstretched to take hers. Tall and broad-shouldered, he wore his military uniform well and was undeniably handsome with close-cropped hair the colour of molasses, a chiselled high cheekboned face and a cinnamon sprinkle of freckles scattered over his nose. Although this stranger was an American his accent was nothing like the slow and deliberate tones of Hamilton and Lex, but kind and gentle. Something about his voice, so musical and soft, instantly made Estella long to close her eyes and slip into it like a warm bath. Along with his shy smile it invited absolute trust.

As she held her hand out to him time was suspended like the mist over the valleys on chilly mornings, and Estella was a young girl again trying to capture a face from a half-remembered dream. She knew this man! She had seen him before all those years ago.

It was her soulmate.

He was real.

And he was here.

"It's so silly, but I picked up a piece of glass," she said, and her voice sounded as though it came from a long, long way away. "It's nothing."

The young man was gently unfolding her fingers and raising her palm to the light so he could study the injury more closely. His dark brows drew together in concentration and perfect white teeth bit his full bottom lip as he examined the cut.

"You're a brave lady. That wound's deep and it's going to need cleaning and dressing. Possibly even a stitch."

Estella was dismayed. "Are you sure?"

"I'm sure," he told her firmly. "I'm an army medic, Miss. I'm here in case any of the lads get into a scrap. Somebody has to patch them up, so I'm just here doing my job in case you're thinking this is a mighty strange way of plucking up courage to talk to a pretty girl!"

Estella's heart swelled at the compliment. She glanced down at her hand, so small and pale as it rested in his. It felt right there, as though it had rested in his one thousand times before. Perhaps it had in another life, because everything she was, everything she would ever be, knew him.

"Aren't you a soldier?" she asked.

"Sure am," he said, turning her hand backwards and forwards as he assessed the injury. "I was studying medicine at Lincoln University before I joined up. I wanted to be a doctor, but the war got in the way."

Estella was surprised "That's unusual for —"

"Unusual for a guy like me?"

Mortified, Estella looked at down the toes of her dance shoes.

"I'm so terribly sorry. I didn't mean to offend you. We have some American officers billeted with us and they gave me the impression such a thing wouldn't be usual."

"No offence taken, Miss. I guess it all depends on whereabouts in the United States you come from. It hasn't been an easy journey, but my folks always taught me a man follows his dreams and fights for them. I was also lucky enough to have a wonderful schoolteacher who believed in me. Miss Gray always told me to reach for the stars, so I did and," he flashed her a smile of such wall-to-wall beauty Estella was scarcely able to think straight, "here I am, a combat medic serving with the 320th. Private First Class Jay Miller at your service, Miss."

"I'm Estella," she said, unable to look away from him. Her throbbing hand was forgotten. "Estella Kellow."

Estella couldn't explain quite was taking place at the side of a busy dance floor and in the ordinary village schoolhouse with its smell of chalk and cabbage and mildew – but she knew she would remember this meeting for the rest of her life. She was drawn to Jay Miller in a way she had never imagined was possible. She had been waiting for him all her life, but until now she had never known who she was waiting for.

This made no sense. Private First Class Jay Miller was a stranger. He had been in her world for less than five minutes. He was a negro, a *black man*! Her father would forbid her from seeing him. He was not the sort of young man who would be deemed a suitable match for the heir to Pencallyn House. There were a million reasons why she shouldn't be feeling this way, but none of them mattered in the slightest; Estella felt as though she knew this man, and as soon as she saw him she had taken the first step onto a path strewn with obstacles and dangers.

Estella was trembling. The person she had always been and the person she'd assumed she would become unravelled with dizzying speed, and a new Estella Kellow took shape in less time than a beat of her heart. The world had for ever changed. How was it possible that until a few minutes ago she had no notion Jay Miller existed? How was such an existence possible when he was all she could see and her hand in his all she could feel? Everything from her father to Evie to the pain of her wound was forgotten in the wonder of feeling his skin upon hers.

She was home.

"You're called Estella? Like a star?" Jay Miller said. He shook his head wonderingly. "All my life I've been told to reach for the stars and now I understand why. You're Miss Star. It all makes sense!"

"Does it?"

Jay Miller nodded and the devotion in his gentle brown eyes snatched Estella's breath away. As his thumb skimmed across her fingers, she felt her stomach fold over and her eyes widened with wonder. He knew her too! He felt the same way!

"Oh, she doth teach the torches to burn bright," Jay murmured, and Estella was lost.

Romeo and Juliet. What could have been more appropriate? Destiny. Fate. Star-crossed lovers, and a father who if he saw them talking would want Jay Miller dead. If she'd needed a warning here it was. Everything was against them and Estella knew she should step away, but that would be impossible. She could no more do this than she could stop breathing.

While dancing couples twirled and jived and the moon rose over the schoolhouse, Jay Miller had become her everything.

CHAPTER 32

Estella
1943

"How does it feel?" Jay Miller asked, tucking the end of his handkerchief into the makeshift bandage. He examined it critically. "Not too tight?"

Estella wiggled her fingers. She would have endured twice as much pain to have met Private First Class Jay Miller.

"It's fine, honestly. I'm sorry to have been such trouble."

"It's no trouble at all," he said, still smiling at her and in a way, which made her tummy do roly-polies. "I can't say it's my best work, and my mentors at Lincoln would be horrified, but being in the army sure teaches a guy to improvise."

"Have you seen action?" Estella asked, fascinated.

"Not yet, but I will. They need guys like me to patch us up. For now, I'm kept busy at the medical treatment facility up at the Pencallyn camp. Your damp British climate is sure giving our boys lots of colds and chest infections."

Estella had heard this before. Lex and Hamilton were always complaining about the climate, although what they had to moan about when they were billeted at Pencallyn with log fires and warm feather beds was anyone's guess.

"Do you find it cold after America?" she asked politely.

Jay Miller laughed. He had a lovely laugh, low and contagious, and Estella's mouth curved upwards too.

"I'm from Pennsylvania so I'm used to proper cold in the winter! Deep snow and lakes that freeze, so this isn't too much of a shock. Anyway, I'm lucky because I've a billet in the village so I'm fine and toasty, not like some of my men. But you guys sure do get a lot of rain. I often take my boots off and expect to see webbed feet!"

"Cornwall is wet," Estella agreed and wanted to kick herself. Cornwall is wet? Was this seriously the best she could come up with when she wanted to know everything about Jay Miller, from his favourite play to his feelings about the war to his home life? She could have kicked herself.

But Jay Miller didn't seem to mind talking about the weather.

"It sure is a wet and windy spot," he agreed, "but there are wonderful things to compensate. I may never want to leave."

Estella's breath caught, certain he meant more, but Private Miller was busy adjusting her bandage.

"Anyways, we need to keep a little pressure on the wound to make sure it stops bleeding," he said briskly. "I think it will heal just fine. You may have a scar though."

"He jests at scars which never felt a wound," she said, and Jay's head snapped up.

"Hey! You know Shakespeare?"

"I know *Romeo and Juliet* pretty well."

"Ah," he said slowly. "Star-crossed lovers."

Their eyes met.

"I *love* that play," Estella said, "especially the scene where they meet for the first time."

He held her gaze. They both knew the conversation was working on another level.

"You know how that play ends," he said quietly.

Estella nodded. "The stars set it all in motion."

"So we can't escape our fate?"

"Would you want to?"

He smiled into her eyes. "Not any more," Jay Miller said.

The sound of the dance rose like the tide and Evie spun past, her eyebrows rising when she spotted them talking.

Estella raised her bandaged hand. With a roll of her eyes, Evie danced on.

"Miss Gray, the teacher I was telling you about, was crazy about Shakespeare," Jay Miller was saying. "We studied loads of plays and poems. I won the English prize one year and she gave me a book of his Sonnets as a prize."

"I love the Sonnets," said Estella.

"That book's my most treasured possession, after my mom's crucifix. I'll show you sometime, if you like."

So she would see this man again? It was terrifying how high Estella's heart soared at the thought.

"I'd like that," she said. "Yes, please."

"Is this boy bothering you, Miss?"

A GI, pimply-skinned and no more than twenty, stepped between them and a scowl corrugated his brow when he spotted Estella's hand in Jay Miller's. Estella felt him tense and, recalling some of Hamilton's dreadful comments, she dredged up every ounce of privilege and authority she possessed.

"Absolutely not. I've injured my hand and have been fortunate enough to be attended by an army medic. Without the assistance of Private First Class Miller, I dare say I would have bled everywhere. He's been an utter godsend."

But the young private didn't agree. He jabbed a finger into Jay's chest.

"You've no right touching her, boy."

Jay Miller didn't flinch.

"The young lady's hand has a deep cut," he said quietly. "The wound requires constant pressure in order to stop the bleeding."

"I said *let her go*," hissed the soldier. Several heads turned and Estella felt a prickle of alarm. When there was drink involved, situations could become ugly fast. She had to speak as though she expected to be obeyed. This had always worked for Tommy.

"Don't be so utterly absurd. If Private Miller releases my hand the bleeding will get worse," she said haughtily. "I'll probably faint from blood loss and hit my head, and that will be your fault for interfering in a medical matter. Unless you are a qualified medic. Are you a medic, Private?"

This tone, ringing with British upper-class confidence, stopped the young man in his tracks.

"No, Miss."

"Then I'll thank you not to interfere. Otherwise I shall make certain my father, who is a Member of Parliament, hears about it. And your commanding officer too." She sought for names but had no idea who commanded what battalion. The names she did know would have to suffice. "First Lieutenant Mason won't be happy either when I speak to him," she added. "He's a family friend."

Something flickered in the soldier's expression and he took a step backwards.

"There's no need, Miss. I was jus' trying to help."

"And I appreciate it, I really do," Estella said, "but as you can see it's most unnecessary. Now, was there anything else?"

Her dismissal was clear. Wrong-footed, the young man retreated into the crowd.

Jay Miller whistled. "Remind me not upset you, Miss Star. I almost feel sorry for the fellow."

"After he was so rude to you?"

"Hey, that's nothing."

"Nothing? He was vile. Surely, you're his superior? Especially if you were at university?"

Jay gave her a tired smile.

"Nope, I'm a Private First Class. Commissions for negro officers are limited, and since there were none available for me when I enlisted I'm a lowly combat medic. Suits me fine, though, because I can help the men this way. Besides, I could be Commander in Chief of the US Army and some folks still wouldn't see me as their equal, never mind take orders."

"But that's so wrong!"

"Yeah, but that's how it is," he said evenly. "Or how it is for now, at any rate. One day I hope things will change, but until then I'll put all my efforts into battling the Nazis rather than my fellow Americans." His eyes narrowed and she sensed a sudden change in him, a cooling towards her which made panic tear through Estella like a rip tide.

"Talking of my compatriots, is Lieutenant Mason really a family friend?"

Estella shook her head. "Oh Lord, no. Absolutely not. He has a billet with us. I don't even know why I mentioned him."

"Oh, I think you do," said Jay Miller. "And you're right; he's very dangerous. All the men are wary of him because has a mean streak as wide as the Atlantic."

"Yes, I know. My best friend thinks he's marvellous, though. Evie's obsessed with him."

Jay looked troubled. "She needs to be careful. He's …"

"What?"

"He's not honourable. Try to keep her away from him if you can."

"That isn't easy. She won't listen to me because she thinks he's wonderful."

"My Oberon, what visions have I seen?"

"More a case of 'Fair is foul'," sighed Estella, and they exchanged a look of mutual understanding which thrilled her to the core. She had never, ever met anyone like Jay Miller. It made no sense, and it defied all logic, but he was her other half. Her twin soul. Whoever would have thought it?

She scanned the crowd for Evie, but her friend was nowhere to be seen. Had she slipped out with someone? Or was she plotting a way to accidentally cross Hamilton's path? Estella hoped her friend would be careful. Jay Miller had only confirmed what she had known in her heart; Hamilton Mason was dangerous.

"You be careful too, Miss Star," he warned. "Mason's not a man you want to cross."

Estella waited for him to continue but Jay Miller didn't elaborate. Around them the music rose and fell, laughter and shrieks wrestling with the highest notes, as young people who knew they could die at any moment squeezed as much life as possible into every second granted to them. Jay's warning hung heavy in the air and made her uneasy.

Was this a premonition?

He loosened his grip on her hand.

"I think the bleeding's abating, Miss Star. How's it feeling?"

Estella flexed her fingers. The gash was throbbing less, but she missed his firm grasp mooring her to the woodblock floor. She was pretty sure it wasn't blood loss making her feel so lightheaded but the proximity to him, because whenever she sneaked a look at Jay Miller, she felt floaty and strange. Estella longed for him to take her hand again, but not here. Here, in the small village school, unseen eyes were watching and danger lurked in the shadowy corners. Who might report back to her father? Or tell Hamilton? Had she unwittingly put Jay Miller in danger?

"It feels much better," she said, feeling horribly afraid she might never feel her hand in his again. "Thank you."

"My pleasure, Miss Star," he replied. "My absolute pleasure. I think you're fit enough to dance. I'm sure the hand will hold up to it."

Injury dealt with, there was no longer a reason for them to be speaking. Estella pushed her hair back from her face. The room was still so hot, and she had no desire to dance unless it was with Jay Miller, but she didn't want cause him any trouble. Her insides knotted with frustration. She should be able to dance with whoever she chose. and so should he. At the very least, they should be able to talk without being harassed.

"I'm not one for dancing. It's not really my thing," she said.

"So, what do you like to do, Miss Star? Apart from quoting Shakespeare?"

"I like to write stories," she confessed. "I want to be an author. And I love painting. One day I'll write a book and draw and paint all the illustrations too. That's my dream."

"That's a great dream," Jay Miller said warmly. "Say, maybe one day I'll read your books and see your paintings."

"Maybe," Estella said, blushing. She couldn't believe that she'd just told a stranger about her most cherished ambition. It was because Jay Miller didn't feel like a stranger. He felt like her oldest and dearest friend.

Now she understood what Evie meant when she talked about being under a spell. She longed to draw Jay Miller. It was impossible not to look at this man without wanting to trace the firm line of his jaw or the outline of his mouth. Her fingers ached to pick up a pencil and commit his features to paper, or to draw her brush through water colours and watch his image flow onto thick cartridge paper. How would she ever find the right hue for the smooth brown skin, nightshade hair and those sherry-hued eyes flecked with warmest amber? The colours and the skills didn't exist that could do Jay Miller's beauty justice. If only she could stay here and talk to him all night!

"Well, Miss Star, your hand will mend real soon and I'm sure you'll pick up a pen in time," Jay Miller said. He paused and she knew he didn't want their meeting to end either. "Is there anything else I can do for you?"

His question was an invitation to do more than bandage her hand, and they both knew it. Danger was all around them, but this was their moment.

Another might never come.

Estella delved deep for courage. Who knew how long they had or what lay in store for Private Miller? Maybe tonight was the all the time Fate would give them?

"I'm feeling a little hot. Would you help me take some air? Just in case I faint?"

She saw amusement in his eyes.

"You're feeling faint, Miss Star?"

"Not at the moment but I may do from the blood loss," she improvised. "Wouldn't you agree?"

His mouth twitched. "Sure. It's wise to be prudent, Miss Star."

Star. The word on his lips was magical; a name as heaven-sent as he was. She loved him calling her by that name. Loved how it melted in his mouth.

Outside, cold air caressed her flushed cheeks. The moon had slipped beneath indigo clouds and the stars had been blown out. Cloaked by darkness, they strolled down to the barbed wire fence and past the pub to the place where Pencallyn House's garden began. It was here the Americans had bulldozed a road to their camp, and by day the butchered greenery had the appearance of a work of art slashed by a madman; at night it was an invitation to somewhere safe and quiet. It was the magical entrance to the mysterious garden of her childhood world and Estella knew every twisting path, pitch-black or not.

"Come on," she urged Jay when he faltered.

"This is private land, Miss Star. We've been warned not to trespass. It belongs to a local landowner."

"We're not trespassing! It's my family's garden," she said.

Jay Miller stared at her. "That's your family's land?"

She nodded and he laughed.

"Jeez, Miss Star! That's not a garden. That's a park!"

Estella giggled and took his hand, tugging him through the gateway. The path twisted through the looming rhododendrons, and skirted the thick bamboo. It wound past the open-mouthed gunnera and whispering giant ferns until it ended at the deep koi pond. By day it was possible to glimpse Pencallyn House from this spot, but in the blackout there was only the velvety darkness. Now and again the flicker of a koi flashed in the still depths, but otherwise all was still. Estella and Jay stepped onto the small white bridge and peered at their reflections floating in the inky water.

"It's like a Monet!" he breathed.

"We call it the Japanese garden. There are lots of plants from that part of the world. My family are collectors."

"What a place to bring an American. We're not too fond of the Japs lately," Jay deadpanned for a moment. "Hey, I'm just kidding with you, Miss Star. This whole darn war's awful but we can't blame the plants. We can't blame all the Japs either, any more than we can blame all the Germans or all of anyone for the godawful mess of it. People are people, and I have to believe there are more good ones than bad. I have to make sure this war doesn't stop me seeing beauty." He smiled down at her. "And this garden is beautiful, Miss Star, so beautiful. Thank you for bringing me here. Thank you for reminding me the world is wonderful and that the good in it is worth fighting for."

"Is that why you joined up? To fight for good?"

"I guess. I sure didn't want to see what's happening to the Jews happen to us and, trust me, the Nazis want that to happen everywhere. I must do my bit. I'm not a natural soldier but I am a good physician so maybe I can make a difference. I certainly hope so."

These were noble sentiments, Estella thought. Darling Ally hadn't been quite as civic-minded. He'd wanted to play his part, for sure, but he'd also liked his flying jacket, thinking it cut quite a dash and impressed the girls.

"My brother joined the RAF because he said girls like men in uniform," she said.

Jay Miller laughed.

"And do they, Miss Star?"

Oh! was this flirting? What ought she to say? What were the rules? Estella was flummoxed for a moment before she glanced at Jay Miller with his kind smile and gentle eyes. All uncertainty was gone when he smiled; she was simply talking to a Shakespeare-loving boy who had healing hands. The softly spoken boy who reached for the stars. The twin soul she'd recognised the very moment she saw him. There were no games or silly rules here. She was talking to Jay Miller.

"This girl likes *you*. The uniform really doesn't matter."

Although it was dark, she sensed Jay smile.

"And I like you too, Miss Star," he said.

There was a brief pause and the air shimmered with frost and promise. Estella knew this moment was the most significant of her life.

"May I kiss you?" he asked shyly.

"Yes," she whispered. "Yes, please."

In his eyes Estella glimpsed a new life and when Jay's soft lips met hers, she longed to live it so much that she ached. As her lips blossomed beneath his, she almost wept with the relief of finding him after a lifetime's search. The years of separation were over, and this first kiss spoke a language all of its own; it told of promises and dreams and the peace of coming home to a calm harbour. It was a kiss Estella already knew she would remember for the rest of her life.

"It's you," Jay whispered wonderingly when they broke apart. He traced the curve of her cheek with his forefinger and shook his head. "It's really you. My Star. I can't believe it. I never imagined this could happen."

He raised her bandaged hand to his lips and kissed each fingertip. The touch of his mouth turned her soul to flame.

"I wasn't expecting this, Star, I promise. I didn't walk outside with you thinking I'd kiss you. I never dared dream it since I'm —"

The worried words stopped abruptly when she kissed him again. Estella wanted her lips to tell Jay Miller everything that was in her heart and exactly what he already meant to her. As she felt his heart racing beneath his uniform, Estella knew he'd heard her soul's cry and understood that nothing mattered except finding one another.

"I never expected this either," she said eventually, "but it is everything. *Everything.* I don't care about anything else."

"But you're a lady. I'm a farmer's son, and …" his voice faltered, and Jay shook his head in confusion. "C'mon, you don't need me to spell out the rest? You must see that this will make your life so hard, Star, and I don't want that for you. I don't want you to have anything in your life which could make it difficult. I want nothing but the best for you."

"You don't get to decide what's best for me, Private Miller."

"The timing's wrong," he said and the conflict in his voice tore at her heart. "*I'm* wrong!"

"Stop it! You're *perfect* and so is the timing. Jay, I'm not an idiot! I know this makes no sense on paper. Of course I do! And I know exactly what the difficulties will be for us, but I don't care. You're here, we've found each other and I'm not wasting another second of time apart! Who knows how long we have? All we have is now. Please don't say anything else!"

He pulled her close and buried his face in her hair. Estella loved being in his arms. Loved the safety. Loved the closeness.

She loved *him.*

"I could be mobilised tomorrow, Star."

She shrugged. "A bomb could fall on Pencallyn. Anything could happen at any moment, but we have this time, don't we? Can't we live for now?"

His arms tightened. Lips kissed her temple.

"Yes we do, and if it all ends tomorrow, if I die in combat sometime soon, I swear I won't regret a moment because everything in my life has led me to this point. Has led me to you. I think I was meant to come to Pencallyn Cove."

"I think so too," she agreed. "It makes no sense, and it's come out of the blue, but I recognised it as soon as I saw you. I knew you, Jay. I feel like I've always known you."

"And I knew you too," he said quietly. "But …"

She pressed her finger against his lips.

"Don't. I can't bear it."

"Me too, Star, but we have to face what might happen. Time isn't on our side, that's for sure, but I want you now, always and for ever. That terrifies me because I sure wasn't looking for this. I wasn't looking for love. Not in the middle of a war."

"Love?" she echoed.

"I sound crazy, huh?" Jay sighed. "Too much, too soon?"

"No. Not at all. I feel the same way. Besides, we don't have time to take things slowly, do we?"

"But is it too fast? Like Romeo and Juliet: 'Too rash, too unadvised, too sudden?"

"All of those," Estella agreed. Unbidden, the line 'these violent delights have violent ends' rang through her mind, but she pushed it away impatiently. The war sped things up, and many people met and married within weeks these days; it was how things were when life was precarious, but even if she'd met Jay Miller in peacetime Estella knew she would have felt the same way. It defied all logic, but her heart already knew there would never be another man for her. It would only ever be Jay Miller.

She loved him and she wanted to show him she meant it.

"Come on!" Estella said, tugging his hand.

"Where are we going?" Jay asked.

"Somewhere special. Come on!"

Jay didn't protest, although the hour was late and she was leading him deeper and deeper into the garden, through the iced labyrinth and to the magic place where the sundial stood. Even during the blackout, and deep in the quiet of a winter's night, the spot had an atmosphere of coiled watchfulness.

Jay Miller glanced around uneasily. "Say, what's this place?"

"It's the sundial garden. It's supposed to have been important in the days of pagans. It's a special place to make promises."

"I'll have you know I'm a Baptist, Miss Star! Momma teaches Sunday school! We Millers are good church-going folk!"

"This is the closest thing I have to a church," Estella said. "It's a good place to make promises. Besides, I don't think there are going to be many rules we don't break."

Jay looked thoughtful. "You're right; love doesn't care about rules. The first of the Millers, my great-grandpa, was a slave from the South who fell in love with the plantation owner's daughter. Now her folks didn't approve at all, but my great-grandparents knew from the start they had to be together. There was never a choice. They were soulmates even if they came from different worlds."

"Like us," Estella breathed, wide-eyed. It was so romantic!

"I guess so. There must have been all kinds of dangers to face, but eventually they made it to the North, and they built our family home at Millers' Hollow. My mom's crucifix is meant to have belonged to my great-grandma. It's our family talisman, because it watched over them on their journey. She gave it to me before I joined up, so now my great-grandparents are watching over me."

"That's lovely."

Jay kissed her.

"Yes, it really is."

He looked around as he sought to distinguish the sundial from the shadows.

"So, you think this is the right place to promise we'll be true? Now, always and for ever? Sure, why not. I promise that already, Star. I'd promise it a thousand times. My heart's yours until the day I die and every day beyond. There's only you"

Estella stood on tiptoes to brush his mouth with hers. It was the most natural gesture in the world, as though she'd been kissing Jacob Miller all her life.

"Whatever happens, my heart is yours too; now, always and for ever. I promise there will only ever be you."

As the words fell from her lips, Estella felt the atmosphere ripple, and understood they'd made a vow as solemn as any spoken in St Brecca's and uttered before a priest. Something had listened to them. Something ancient had recognised the solemnity of their words.

No matter what happened, and whatever the war might throw their way, Jay Miller and Estella Kellow would never be parted. They were promised now, always and for ever.

CHAPTER 33

Estella
1944

Estella had once read how falling in love changed your life for ever, but until Jay Miller had come into her world she hadn't believed a word of it. Love had been an abstract noun, a device playwrights and poets used to drive narrative and heighten emotion. She loved Poppet. She loved Evie. She loved Pencallyn. She had loved Ally too, even though he was an annoying brother. Estella knew what love was.

Yet once Jay Miller entered her world, Estella realised her understanding of love had been so far removed from the truth it was scarcely recognisable. She didn't know how you could love a person you had only just met, but there was no other word to describe her absolute certainty that Jay Miller was her future. When Estella thought about her longing to be with him, the need to touch him, to kiss him, to feel his skin against hers, the love she felt was so overwhelming it drove away all logic and dissolved any doubts. Jay Miller was her soulmate. Race, creed and class faded away because he was all she wanted and all she needed. Now, always and for ever.

That Jay Miller felt the same way was not in question. Their love was equal. It was destined, and everything that Shakespeare, Keats and all the poets before, after and still to come promised.

"It's *you*," Jay had said in surprise, and Estella had laughed out loud because yes, it really was her. She was the star he had been reaching for. She was his other half, and this realisation intoxicated her like wine. Drunk with delight and dizzy with desire, she could scarcely think of anything else. Urgency flowed through her like molten lava and each time they met it grew stronger. All obstacles crumbled to dust before their love; the war, race, time – what did any of these things matter when there was a Jay Miller in the world?

This didn't mean they didn't need to be cautious; neither Jay nor Estella were so swept away by passion they weren't conscious of the dangers of their love. In some ways the war, that dark cloud on their horizon, also worked in their favour because amid the chaos it was easy for Estella to slip away and meet Jay in secret. Her father was often in London, Violet was rarely at home and the increasingly overgrown garden was perfect for hiding lovers. The only difficulty was Evie who, although still obsessed with Hamilton Mason, was sharp-eyed enough to spot any change in her friend.

Unused to having secrets from Evie, Estella found it painful to keep her happiness to herself. Joy bubbled through her like a spring and she longed to share her happiness with her best friend. There had once been a time when she would have confided in Evie instantly and could have relied on her help, but Evie's obsession with Hamilton meant her loyalty was compromised. Instead, Estella skirted around Evie's questions and threw herself into the chores by day and writing her book by night. She painted too, dark and menacing paintings where faces loomed out of greenery and danger lurked behind every leaf and ferny frond. If by some chance Estella painted Jay Miller's beautiful countenance into the flowers and the trees, then this was her own secret and these pieces of work were stored right at the bottom of her canvas pile.

Another complication was Evie's familiarity with the garden; there were no places Estella had kept secret from her friend. Although Evie showed no inclination to be out dog walking in the bad weather, preferring to haunt the house in case Hamilton returned unexpectedly, Estella could never be sure she wouldn't change her mind. Evie might follow her if she suspected something was up. It was sad, but Estella didn't trust Evie since Hamilton had arrived. So instead of confiding in her friend, Estella hugged her secret close to her heart and only allowed herself to dream when she was alone.

When she slipped away to meet Jay, Estella doubled back on herself or took a route which would quickly bore anyone shadowing her. It also helped that Poppet would instantly give away the presence of any followers. Even so, Estella and Jay decided to keep away from the garden, choosing to meet in the ruined farmhouse at the far side of the grounds. Always mindful of discovery, they didn't dare leave messages in the sundial, and Estella took to walking Poppet every afternoon. If Jay had leave, he would find her waiting and his smile of pure joy when he broke through the thick trees and spotted her sent something molten and wonderful racing through her blood. When he scooped her up in his arms and spun her around, she thought she would die of happiness. Everything in her world was brighter now he was in it. Everything was glorious.

The ruined farmhouse became their place; it was a haven in a world turned upside down and a refuge when life felt as tremulous as birdsong. Estella and Jay snatched every second greedily, for who knew how long they might have? They could have weeks, but it was equally likely each meeting might be the last. Nobody knew these days, when life was so uncertain. Their time together was counted down by an invisible clock and each moment was so vivid it was almost painful.

Jay never spoke of the army but Estella could see the troops were massing. There were more warships and practice exercises than ever, and she understood from listening to the wireless that tensions on the continent were increasing. Something momentous was building; she felt it in the excitement of young voices and in the rumble of vehicles driving down to the cove. Her heart was constantly quaking with terror for Jay Miller could be gone at any moment and the likelihood was he would never return.

Each time Estella stepped into the weed-strewn courtyard of the old farmhouse and found Jay waiting for her, maybe smoking a cigarette or reading a book, she was weak-kneed with relief. Poppet would hurl herself at him too, barking in delight and licking his face in pure ecstasy. Sometimes, though, weeks went by without Jay appearing at the farm. When he finally returned, he was thinner and his eyes were filled with sadness. Estella would trace the scratches on his limbs and kiss the bruises, but mostly she would hold him close, letting him fall into a deep and exhausted sleep. The time was approaching when the soldiers would surely leave Cornwall, but until that dark moment arrived Jay Miller was hers to cherish and love and comfort in this tumbledown ruin which was their world.

When Cornwall was in the grip of winter, they huddled inside the ruin and burrowed under the blankets Estella had carried over from Pencallyn. Curled up like dormice, they devoured books sneaked from the library; fat tomes of Shakespeare, yellow-paged Keats and well-thumbed novels which Jay read aloud, his fluent voice full of cadences she knew she'd never tire of hearing.

Once spring came, they spread a blanket on the grass and lay on their backs, watching the clouds drift by as they kissed and shared their dreams. Jay told her about his family home, a farmstead in Pennsylvania beside a lake as big as a sea and promised he would take her there after the war. He would stroke Estella's face, tracing the planes and contours with worshipping fingers as though trying to commit every detail to memory.

"Tell me about your home," she said to Jay one May afternoon when the rain pattered down on the patched roof and the air hung heavy with moisture. Estella was tucked in the crook of his arm and his words wove dreams of another life.

He laughed. "Not again, Star!"

"Yes, again! Tell me! Please!"

He pulled her close. "Remind me, how did it go?"

She elbowed him in the ribs, and he yelped.

"Ouch! Hey, what did I do to deserve that?"

"Stop teasing me! You know how it goes."

"I surrender! OK, once upon a time there was a small homestead set in the hollow of the hills, where the sun always shone and crops danced in the breeze. My family have lived there, at Millers' Hollow, for generations and they'll live there long after we're gone. The Millers are simple folk. We grow wheat, raise a few cattle and live a simple life, for sure, but it's a good one. There's something about sitting in the rocker on the porch, with a glass of lemonade and watching the red sun sink low on the ridge, that makes your heart glad. When we have children, they'll run in those old fields and sail on the lake just like I did. You'll love my boat, Star. She's small with a white sail and she races like the wind. We'll skip over the water in her. It's like flying."

Estella loved it when Jay spoke about the life they'd share when the war was over. She loved it that this was as real to him as the rain and winds of Cornwall. She pictured Millers' Hollow vividly, the small white house with the big arc of sky above it. Jay said England was cramped and until you galloped across the prairie or sailed on a lake as big as an ocean, you had no idea how vast God's earth was. Estella could hardly wait for him to show her.

She raised herself on one elbow.

"So, we're having children, are we?"

He kissed her nose. "Hell, yeah. Lots and lots. A whole tribe of 'em. I'll need to keep you busy while I'm tending to my patients!"

"And what will we do next?" Estella asked, although she knew the words off by heart.

"We'll moor our boat at the end of the boardwalk and stroll down the dirt road which crosses our land. We'll admire our tall crops while the children run ahead and dive in and out of the wheat. We'll fly kites, plant flowers and sit on the porch in our rockers and watch the sun sink. Maybe we'll take the boat back onto the lake and fish for our supper and watch the sunset from the water. My momma will teach you to make apple pie and I'll show you how to play baseball and draw a diamond in the yard. We'll grow old there with all our children around us. We'll be so happy."

"Will we?" she said, doubt curdling in her stomach. People would make threats. Men like her father and Hamilton would say their children should never be allowed to exist. Their love was fraught with danger.

Jay's arms tightened around her.

"We will. I promise. You're my girl, Star, and I love you. Never, ever forget that. Now, always and for ever. No matter what comes next."

Now, always and for ever. These were their words, words which she knew bound them together for eternity. How could she ever forget? As Jay's mouth met hers, Estella's hands cupped his face, pulling him closer as her tongue sought his and her body pressed closer. This need to be close to him grew stronger each day. It drove away all reason and laughed at all fear. Nothing else mattered.

"Don't stop," she said. "Please, Jay. Don't stop."

They had teetered on brink of desire before but always stopped short of making love. But Estella had decided this wouldn't be the same today. Today they would be close in every way.

It was their time.

Jay's hands gripped her shoulders and he gazed into her face with such love it made Estella want to weep. How could happiness and heartbreak chase each other's tails this way? Love and loss were hand in hand lately, each only real when holding onto the other, and she was starting to understand how heartbreak was the currency with which you paid for such joy. Trembling as she felt Jay's silken skin so close to hers and his heart beating against her breasts, Estella knew she would pay any price to know such a moment. She wanted this.

She wanted *him*.

"Listen to me, my Star," Jay said urgently, his voice hoarse with emotion. "There are things about to happen and when it all begins I'll have to leave you. I may not come back, Star. I need you to understand that could happen. You must be sure about this. You have to understand what could come next for us."

"I understand, Jay, and I'm sure," Estella whispered. Whatever came afterwards, she would have this moment; she would be as close to her beloved Jay as any human could ever be to another. Estella needed him, and she would die if he pulled away now.

"I'm sure," she said again. "Oh, my love, I've never been more certain of anything."

Jay moaned softly and, dipping his head, kissed her once more. Then he lay Estella tenderly against the blanket they'd draped over the flagstones and pushed into her as she arched to greet him. With the wonderful hardness of him inside her, and his strong arms holding her, Estella gasped with sheer amazement. As her eyes flew open with wonder, she saw his shining with tears.

"Oh, my Star," he gasped. "My beautiful, precious, Star!"

And Estella laughed out loud with pure joy and cried too, murmuring soft words of love and rocking him closer in a newly discovered rhythm that was all her body's own. Her spirit soared high above and gazed down at them in amazement, marvelling at the beautiful contrast of their skin; dark and light, yin and yang. They were mirror images, soulmates reunited in the most timeless and glorious way. Estella tumbled back down to earth, gasping as he pulled her on top of him, plunging even deeper into her as he cried her name over and over again. She showered his face with kisses as waves of pure delight broke over her, washing Estella up onto a beach of sensation where each nerve ending tingled and her heart felt ready to burst. Laughing and crying, she felt every tremor before Jay gasped and sank against her, shaking like a tree fern in a gale.

"Star," he whispered. "Oh, Star."

Estella held him close, dropping a kiss onto his forehead. She was awash with love and tenderness. Jay's eyes were closed, fluttering beneath the delicate lids, and she thought she wanted to hold him like this for ever, protecting and guarding him as he lay in her arms. Skin on skin and with their hearts beating in perfect time, Estella finally understood what all the writers had really been on about. This feeling, this overwhelming bliss, this utter completion was *everything*, and once you had discovered it you would do anything to hold onto it because you felt truly alive.

She lay her head against Jay's shoulder. They were different now. *She* was different now. She'd crossed a threshold and now so many things fell into place. Her father's odd choice of wife. Violet's frequent trips to town. Even Hamilton Mason's dark threats.

She shivered and Jay drew her against him, pulling the blanket over her.

"I love you, Star," he said. "There's only you for me."

"You too. So much. I promise there'll only ever be you, Jay. Now, always and for ever."

Estella knew beyond all doubt that she could never, ever give Jay Miller up. There would never be another for her. Ever. Even if Estella lived until she was an ancient old lady there would only ever be Jay.

Now, always and for ever.

CHAPTER 34

Estella
1944

The wonder of her love affair with Jay Miller aside, May 1944 would not be a month that Estella Kellow would look back on with any fondness. The weather was unseasonably cold and her friendship with Evie under increasing strain as Estella sought ways to slip away undetected. As though sensing something huge had changed for her best friend, Evie was her constant shadow.

"You're different, Stell," she remarked the day after Estella had first made love to Jay. "What's happened?"

Estella, dreamily staring at her boiled egg as she relived the magical hours of the previous afternoon, was jolted. Yes, she felt different in every way, but did she *look* different? The girl who gazed back her from the bathroom mirror looked the same as always; wide deep blue eyes, mane of dark curls and a pink rosebud mouth. Perhaps the mouth had been a little swollen from Jay's kisses? It certainly curved in a secret smile and her eyes were dreamy with happiness, but these were all such subtle changes. Estella had felt certain nobody would notice and nobody else had – apart from Evie.

She ought to have remembered how observant Evie was. Happiness was making her careless and she would have to be on her guard, Estella realised. She loved Evie dearly but her best friend was in thrall to Hamilton Mason and so couldn't be trusted. Who knew what she would tell him in exchange for a kind look?

"Nothing," Estella said. She picked up a toast soldier to dip into her egg, a nonchalant gesture which failed utterly since the shell was still intact.

Evie quirked a dark eyebrow.

"Clearly. Come on, Stell. Off your food? Day dreaming? Are you mooning over a man?"

"You're talking utter rot," Estella said, turning her attention to slicing the top off her egg. She was alarmed her friend was so close to the truth.

"Am I?" Evie said. "Don't think I haven't noticed how a certain person looks at you. I'm not an idiot. If there's anything going on, you should tell me. We're best friends, remember?"

Estella sighed, ripped from her happy musings back to the world of Pencallyn House where unspoken threats and simmering resentments dwelt everywhere lately. Although her days had been filled with happiness at her love for Jay, the unsettling presence of Hamilton Mason was still a nagging worry, like the throb of a boil that could catch you unawares, and when he was at Pencallyn his attention was trained on her with the deadly accuracy of a buzzard. Of course Evie had noticed. Although Hamilton's comments were innocuous, a polite enquiry into the book she was reading or a compliment on the dress she wore at dinner, the way he looked at her was far from benign. He staked a claim with each word, and danger lurked in his grey-eyed scrutiny like a sharp-toothed pike circling the depths of the lily pond.

"I've never thought for one instant you're an idiot," was all she said now. "How many times do I have to tell you? I'm not at all interested in Lieutenant Mason!"

"He's interested in you," said Evie bitterly "It's you he sees, not me. Girls like me are good enough to screw but we're not fit for anything else."

"You haven't …"

"Haven't what? Screwed him? Shagged him? Oh, don't be such a prude, Estella. It's just sex."

But Estella, who vibrated like a violin string at Jay Miller's slightest touch, knew it was far, far more than this. When the right man loved you, it was heaven on earth and made sense of everything.

You would do anything for more.

"Have you?" she repeated, feeling terribly afraid. Hamilton would destroy Evie. Her friend might think she was tough, but her heart was open to him, and vulnerable. A man like him would think nothing of breaking it for his own amusement. Estella recognised something ugly when she saw it.

"No," admitted Evie after a pause. "Like I say, he isn't interested in me, but he will be. You wait and see. I'll find a way to make Hamilton Mason notice me."

Estella no longer had any appetite. She pushed her plate away.

"Evie, please be careful. I know you think you're in love with Hamilton, but he isn't a nice man."

"Nice?" echoed Evie. She elongated the word, mimicking Estella's accent perfectly. Then the tone slipped, her own East End diction shining through as it often did when she was fraught. "Who gives a toss about *nice?* Where does nice get you? Did it get my ma anywhere? Or my gran? Or me? Aren't I always as nice as bloody pie? Do what I'm told? Follow you around like a shadow? Read my books? Say my prayers? Let Cook look down her nose at me because I'm just some urchin from the slums? I'm sick to death of being bloody nice! I'm a cheap copy of you and where has it got me? Nowhere!"

She swiped her hand across the table, sending eggs, toast and crockery flying. The teapot shattered on the stone floor.

"I'm sick of always being second best!" Evie yelled. "Do you hear me? I am *sick* of it!"

The two girls stared at one another without speaking. A ravine had opened between them and Estella had no idea how to bridge it.

When Cook returned her eyes widened when she saw the mess on the kitchen floor, but rather than scolding them, she burst into loud sobs.

"You've already heard? Oh girls! I don't know what to say. Those bloody Germans! When will it ever end?"

Estella glanced at Evie who shrugged one shoulder. United by confusion, the girls sat Cook down at the kitchen table and let her splutter and blow her nose until she had control of herself.

"Oh girls, here's me in pieces and you're being so brave, bless you," she sniffed. "Poor Mrs Kellow. What a thing. Despite everything, she didn't deserve it."

Estella took Cook's hand. Red and rough, it was a hand that had fashioned a thousand pies, chopped countless vegetables and was a part of life at Pencallyn.

"We haven't heard anything," she said gently. "What's happened to Violet, Mrs Tullis?"

Cook looked puzzled. "But the mess? I thought you must know and knocked the table in shock?"

"We had an accident," Evie supplied swiftly. "My sleeve caught the tea pot."

Estella never ceased to be amazed how readily Evie could fib. In the past she'd been impressed but today she was unnerved; what else had her friend lied about?

Cook's chins wobbled as she looked from one girl to the other.

"There's no easy way to say this; Mrs Kellow's dead. She was killed in a bombing raid last night in Plymouth."

These were dreadful words to hear, but as soon as Cook uttered them Estella laughed with relief.

"That can't be right. Violet wasn't anywhere near Plymouth last night. She was in Calmouth with the Pembertons. They were having a dinner party at Seaways."

Violet Kellow was great friends with the Pembertons. She was always racing off to visit them and often stayed the night. But Cook and Evie exchanged a look and suddenly Estella understood; she wasn't the only young woman slipping away from Pencallyn House to meet her lover.

Violet had never been visiting the Pembertons, had she? It was a cover for what she had really been up to. Evie had been right all along.

After this, events happened fast. The police came, respectful and with bowed heads, to tell them the grim details, and the vicar, who had heard the news, visited to offer his prayers. Estella trembled to think what her father would do when he found out the extent of Violet's deception. Would he blame Estella or Evie? Would he think they'd lied for Violet? Would he fly into a rage?

She felt sick with dread.

The facts of the situation were that Violet Kellow had been asleep in bed with her lover in one of the beautiful hotels on Plymouth Hoe when a rogue German bomber jettisoned what was left of its deadly load. There had been no air raid warning and the random bombing, coming after months of inactivity, was totally unexpected. Violet would have died instantly and in this Estella had supposed there had to be some comfort. Her lover had also perished and, although Estella neither knew him nor had even heard his name before, but knowing how wonderful it was to lie in the arms of the one you loved, she wept for him too. This man had made Violet happy, which was more than Reginald Kellow had ever done.

Estella knew even though her father would seek to cover up the truth, scandal would follow Violet's death as surely as night followed day. His anger would be terrible. Had he known his young wife was unfaithful? What would grieve him now wouldn't be the loss of Violet but her lack of discretion and the humiliation. Poor, foolish Violet! She'd paid a high price for marrying a man for status and seeking her happiness elsewhere, Estella reflected as she walked Poppet in the garden, and it was a sharp lesson in how not to live your life. Although she too was hiding the truth, as soon as the war was over Estella and Jay would tell the whole world about their love for one another. They wouldn't care who did or didn't approve. All that mattered was being together.

As always, Estella waited at the ruined farmhouse but there was no sign of Jay. After several hours had passed, Estella made her lonely way back through the woods, each step feeling as though her legs were manacled with iron. Unable to face returning to the house, she walked Poppet into the village, where there was great activity on the beach. When she approached the barbed wire barricade to see what was happening, Estella discovered that a new checkpoint had sprung up and she was turned away.

What was going on? Why were there so many men, and what were they building? Troops were everywhere and vehicles were parked all the way through the high street. Village life must be sorely curtailed, and the sunny days of picnics on the beach and swimming in the cove felt as though they belonged to another life. Estella dashed away more tears with the back of her hand, although she was no longer sure she was crying for Violet, before turning back to Pencallyn House. Her father would be on his way back, and there would be a great deal to arrange.

The realisation that Estella was now the mistress of the house started to dawn when Cook asked her what they ought to do about dinner. Poor Violet had only been dead for a matter of hours, but already the responsibility for Pencallyn weighed heavily on Estella's shoulders. She so longed to feel Jay's arms close around her and hear his warm voice promising all would be well. She needed to hear how blushing sunsets, rockers on porches and making love in a little boat beneath star-embroidered skies lay in wait for them. Estella had to hold onto these wonderful dreams and keep his love close to her heart. A marvellous life would be theirs once the war was over. Knowing this, Estella could endure anything.

She called Poppet to heel and turned away from the sea, still feeling uneasy. Then, steeling herself for what was to come, Estella began the steep walk back up to the house.

CHAPTER 35

Estella
1944

It was touching how many mourners made the journey to Cornwall to bid farewell to Violet Kellow. Although there were whispers in the village, and no doubt polite society was talking, St Brecca's was packed. Violet was popular, more so than Estella had ever realised, and the small church was filled with people from all walks of life. They were artists and shopkeepers, a milliner and a florist, old school friends from London and even colleagues from a Knightsbridge art gallery where she had once worked. As Estella chatted to them all, and heard stories about her stepmother's kindnesses, she was touched. Violet had made her mistakes, but Estella understood why.

Perversely the sun, which had hidden for most of May, decided to shine for Violet's last party, peeping out from behind the clouds like a debutante from behind a fan and bathing the churchyard in golden light. As the vicar conducted the memorial service, coloured rays kissed the worn stone floor, bright shards of light taking the place of the flowers Reginald Kellow refused to order. His anger was palpable, and although he would follow the rites of passage there would be little else for Violet. There would be a private committal and her name was to be left off the family memorial.

"She's fortunate to be getting this much," he snapped when Estella tentatively asked whether they could have a simple plaque. "If I had my way she'd be buried in a communal pit."

Estella hadn't mentioned it again but as she stood beside Reginald Kellow in the family pew she vowed that one day she would commission a memorial for Violet. It wouldn't be large, or filled with false sentiment, but it would be here in the church, and in years to come people would know there had been a Violet Kellow. She would not be forgotten.

A small wake was held at Pencallyn House and Cook did a sterling job of creating a buffet out of their limited rations and produce from the garden. There was tea and sherry and a cake made from all kinds of strange ingredients, which contained the household's entire sugar ration for the week. The guests made small talk but the awkward circumstances surrounding Violet's death created awkward chasms of silence and when the door finally closed behind the last mourner Estella was exhausted. Evie had slipped away hours ago, at about the same time Hamilton Mason made his excuses, and Reginald had closeted himself in the study with a bottle of brandy. Left to entertain the guests, Estella hadn't had a moment to herself. Her temples were thumping.

Estella returned to the drawing room and collected up the glasses and plates. Alone at long last, she tugged off her hat and unpinned her hair, massaging her head with her fingertips and groaning with relief when the tension slipped from her scalp. She slumped onto a couch, kicked off her shoes and wiggled her freed toes. She'd change in a moment and walk Poppet through the woods to the ruined farmhouse in case Jay was there. She hadn't seen him for ten days but with the increased military activity Estella was hardly surprised. Lex and Hamilton had also been largely absent, until today at least, and something was up. There had been talk of a 'big push', and whatever this might mean, Estella suspected it meant parting from Jay.

This thought was unbearable. Jay could promise all would be well as many times as he liked, but how could he be certain? Dread stalked Estella every day. Even sunshine contained the chill of snow. She so wished the war would go away. It ruined everything!

"Hey, the war brought us together, honey," Jay would soothe whenever Estella vented this frustration. "One day all this will all be history. Our grandchildren will learn all about it in high school and they'll come over to Millers' Hollow to ask us how it really was. What happened to us will just be papers and tests to them, you'll see."

She loved it when he wove stories about their future.

"And what will we tell them?"

Jay's answer would be to grin and pull her close, trailing kisses down her neck and across her breasts before his lips strayed to her belly and she melted with longing for him.

"Not about this, my Star, that's for sure! We'll tell 'em it was like old Charles Dickens says, 'It was the best of times and the worst of times'! We'll say we hadn't figured on finding love in the middle of it all, but that's what happened. They won't be listening anyhow because we'll just be old folks to them. They'll never believe we know about such things!"

Back at home at Pencallyn, Estella smiled as she recalled these sorts of conversations. When she was with Jay it was easy to push her doubts and fears aside; he had a way of making everything seem possible. There was no need to worry about the future when they were together because all that mattered was the present moment. Jay always said this was all anyone ever really had.

"Now, always and for ever," she said aloud, and her heart lifted at the sound of their special words – only to plummet equally swiftly when the door opened and Hamilton Mason stalked in, resplendent in full dress uniform. He closed the door behind him with a click and bestowed her with a chilly smile.

"Why, Miss Kellow there you are. I swear you look more lovely each time I see you," he drawled, iceberg eyes raking over her body. Acutely aware her tucked-up legs revealed suspenders and stocking tops, Estella sat upright hastily. Every nerve in her body was on alert.

"My father's in his study," she said, pushing her feet into her shoes and smoothing down her skirt.

Hamilton didn't move. "I'm not looking for your father, Estella. I think we both know that."

Cold eyes held hers and Estella couldn't look away. She was rooted to the spot with dread.

"I've waited far too long," he said softly. "I think I've been more than patient with your teasing."

Her head snapped up. "I beg your pardon? What teasing?"

Hamilton's cruel mouth snaked upwards.

"Oh honey, I think you know. All those looks. The coolness. The playing hard to get. It can stop now. I've spoken to your father."

"Me too," said Estella.

"Don't sass me. It's not what I look for in a wife."

"You think I would marry you?" Disbelief made her laugh, which was a mistake. His face darkened.

"I don't think you have any choice. Your pa's run this estate into the ground and unless a wealthy son-in-law comes to help him out, he'll have to sell up. I have the money and you have a nice property. He wants to do business and he says you'll comply."

Estella's heart was thudding hard beneath her black blouse. Was he telling the truth about the estate? Maybe. Or maybe not. A man like Hamilton enjoyed fear. It drove him.

"You're both deluded," she said. "I hate to break it to you, but slavery's been abolished. I'm not for sale."

But Hamilton laughed.

"That's what women always say. All of 'em are, for the right price. See, honey, I know what women are like. Especially you, Miss Prim and Proper. I hear you're not too picky with the company you keep so you can drop the act with me. A girl who lets a black man dress her hand and walk her home isn't fussy. What would your father say about that, I wonder? He'd have the boy horsewhipped."

Estella felt as though the floor had given way and she was falling into nothingness. Had the red-faced soldier from the dance said something? Unlikely and far too long ago. Had Evie said anything about Estella's disappearance from the dance hall? Evie hadn't been pleased she had been abandoned and forced to walk home with Dolly and the land girls, but she'd understood about Estella's injury. No, Evie wouldn't betray her. It was far more likely Hamilton had had spies at the dance.

And everywhere …

"You're talking nonsense," Estella said but she heard the tremor in her voice and so did Hamilton.

"Am I? I think we both know the truth 'bout that, but if you're a good girl I won't say anything to your pa. I think you and I can come to an understanding and I'm still inclined to make him an offer for you."

"I'm said I'm not for sale."

"Everything's for sale, darlin', just ask your father what loans are secured on this house and why he really married the woman we've just buried. I'd bet her folks wanted the same as mine; his class for their money. It's a simple enough trade and one your old man's happy to make, so be a good girl and do as you're told. You let a negro dress your hand, after all, so we know you're not picky."

Estella had never felt distilled hatred before, the kind which gnaws deep into the soul and rages through the blood like a storm surge, but she felt it now. Corrosive and biting, it flooded through her in a bitter tide.

"I'd rather have him dress my hand than let you anywhere near me," she spat.

Air hissed through Hamilton Mason's teeth and he strode across the room. Before Estella had a chance to flee, his hands were clamped on her shoulders and he was pulling her against him, holding her so tightly his fingers dug into her skin, and she could feel the hardness of him pressing against her thigh. His intention could not have been clearer. Although she flailed and twisted, Estella was no match for brute strength and when Hamilton slammed her against the mantelpiece and plunged his meaty tongue into her mouth, there was little she could do to fight him. She gagged, sickened by the invasion, and when he started to pull at the waistband of her skirt and ram his hand into her pants, she was truly afraid.

"No!" she gasped but Hamilton was encouraged by her protests and increased his efforts, driving a knee between her legs and thrusting her again and again at the mantelpiece.

No! This couldn't happen!

Estella writhed in his grasp, managing to turn her head away and free her mouth. Air flooded her lungs and she made a desperate break for freedom. Her hand grabbed at his wrist and she twisted it with all her might, but Hamilton just shook her off as though she was a fly.

"Take your hands off me!" Estella screamed as Hamilton Mason tugged at his breeches. His cock reared from a nest of dark hair, purple and angry, and she thought she would vomit.

"Scream all you like. Your father's halfway through the brandy, the staff have gone home and sweet little Evie is running an errand for me. Lex won't help you because we don't much like negro lovers where we come from, Miss Kellow. Scream away. Be my guest."

Merciless hands rucked Estella's skirt past her hips. She twisted in his grasp but Hamilton had pinned her against the fireplace and there was no escape route. The marble mantelpiece bit into her back and no matter how desperately she wriggled, there was nowhere to go. She was trapped.

Panic sucked oxygen from her lungs. Her skirt was around her waist. Hamilton grunted, pinning her with one hand as he pushed down his breeches. His focus shifted only for a split second, but it was long enough for Estella to seize her chance. Ripping her left hand from his grasp, her fingers stabbed thin air blindly until they felt the mantelpiece and brushed against what the memory told her they would find: the solid silver frame containing her mother's picture.

If Estella had ever needed her mother's help, it was now.

Estella snatched the heavy frame and swiftly brought it down on the side of his head with all her might. Into the blow she poured every drop of her loathing of his arrogance, her fury at how he played with Evie's feelings and her revulsion at the ugly words he dared utter about Jay Miller, a man worth ten million of him. As she dashed the frame into his hateful skull, Estella hoped it would smash like an egg.

"Jesus Christ! You bitch!"

Hamilton's grasp fell away from her body and he lurched onto his knees, gasping and clutching his head. Crimson blood flowered in blond hair, seeping through his fingers and splashing the uniform. Robbed of his brute strength and with his breeches around his knees, he was pathetic. He was pitiful. Like her father, Hamilton Mason was no more than a bully.

Estella replaced her mother's photograph and smoothed her skirt down over her stockings, and checked herself in the mirror over the mantelpiece. Her reflection possessed glittering eyes and flushed cheeks, but otherwise she appeared unscathed – even if inside she was quaking at her narrow escape.

"Don't ever touch me again," Estella said.

Hamilton glared up at her.

"You'll be sorry. You'll wish you'd said yes to me when you had the chance."

Estella looked back at the mirror, patted her hair into place, and looked down at him with a shrug.

"I doubt it," she said.

Estella turned on her heel. She didn't look back, but she felt Hamilton's eyes scorch into her back. She was shaken and close to tears.

If Hamilton Mason had been dangerous before, now he was deadly. He would want revenge. If this man found out about her relationship with Jay Miller, she trembled to think what he might do.

Estella knew she had put the man she loved in the most terrible danger.

CHAPTER 36

Estella
1944

The following day Estella had bruises on her wrists, and her shoulder ached from swinging the picture frame off the mantelpiece, but otherwise she was unscathed. Estella hoped Hamilton Mason felt as though a donkey had kicked him in the head. His vile words had gouged deep wounds in her heart, and she was glad to learn the officers had departed early. The idea of encountering Hamilton today was not one Estella relished. He would be watching her and waiting to pick his moment. Like a spider in a deadly web, Hamilton had been spinning a trap for months.

Was the Pencallyn estate really in debt? Estella imagined this was highly likely; exotic plants hadn't come cheap, and since the Americans had taken over the land the home farm hadn't been producing anything. It was also true that Violet's family were new money and had been thrilled by the match with Reginald – but would her, Estella's, own father really be willing to trade his daughter for financial gain and new specimens for the garden? Was that all she meant to him?

Glancing at him over the toast rack, Estella studied Reginald Kellow as he scowled at something he was reading in the paper and decided such a transaction was very likely indeed. Her papa had always loved his garden more than anything, and knowing this was enough to make her hate it now. When she inherited, maybe she would plough the whole lot up. Or let the lot go wild? What sweet revenge that would be.

"You're quiet, Stell," said Evie. "Are you feeling unwell?"

Estella shook her head. "I didn't sleep very well."

It wasn't a lie. She'd woken several times with a dry mouth and a racing heart. Estella desperately wanted to tell Evie what had happened with Hamilton, but felt oddly ashamed and as though she'd provoked him. This was nonsense, of course, but what if Evie thought Estella had encouraged him and saw it as a betrayal? Estella couldn't bear that. She needed to warn Evie what Hamilton Mason was truly like, but each time she opened her mouth the words shrivelled on her tongue. She wouldn't dare tell Jay either. He would be furious and want to protect her. Honourable and brave, he would be bound to speak to Hamilton, which would give their relationship away and place Jay in terrible danger.

No. It was far better if she kept her own counsel and steered clear of Hamilton.

This last day of May dawned bright and sunny. After breakfast, Estella worked in the kitchen garden and listened to the endless convoy of vehicles trundling down the new road to the cove. There seemed to be more and more activity with every passing day, and Cook was most put out since the road into Pencallyn village had been closed by the military, forcing locals to walk through the fields instead.

"I don't know what they're playing at," she grumbled as she hung up her coat. "There are jeeps parked halfway up the hill and tanks on the beach. And my shoes are covered in mud now. I don't know what things are coming to. My Bert's in the Home Guard, but even he can't tell me why I need to wade through filth!"

"Maybe it's to stop invading Germans?" Dolly suggested. "They'll all get stuck in our Cornish mud and give up!"

Cook laughed. "I'd like to see old Hitler goose step through that! His shiny boots wouldn't last long!"

Estella hadn't walked into the village for a few days, but after this conversation she took a detour before her usual visit to the farmhouse, pleading the excuse of walking Poppet. Sure enough, the beach was thrumming with activity and vehicles were lined up all the way from the schoolhouse to the pub. The entire shoreline was cordoned off now, so she couldn't get close enough to see what was going on, although it looked to her as though they were loading vehicles onto ships by means of makeshift jetties and floating platforms. When one of the Home Guard asked her to move away, Estella's suspicions were alerted.

Something was happening. Something big.

Jay was waiting at the farmhouse and, overjoyed to see him after so long, Estella soon forgot all about the activity on the beach and the dreadful episode with Hamilton as she gave herself up to the heaven of being in his arms. As they snuggled up beneath a blanket, Jay's fingers gently stroking her hair, Estella knew what pure happiness felt like. She slipped her hand beneath the rough fabric of his shirt and marvelled again at how warm and silky his skin was. It was as smooth as satin and she longed to kiss every single inch.

"I think something big's about to happen," Jay said, his lips against the crown of her head. "Something's coming, Star, and I don't think it'll be long until the war is over."

"When it is, I want to be with you all the time," she said. "Now, always and for ever."

"Do you mean that?"

"Of course I do!"

There was a brief pause and she felt him tense. Then Jay exhaled slowly.

"Then marry me," he said.

Estella's eyes widened.

"I mean it. I know it's sudden, but I also know there'll never be anyone else for me. I don't have much to offer you, Star. Hell, I know there are other guys lining up who could give you the world with a bow on it, but I swear to God they could never love you like I do. All I have, and all I'll ever have and be, is yours. I will love you until the end of time. Now, always and for ever."

"Now, always and for ever," she echoed.

"Is that a yes?"

"Of course, it's a yes! Of course I'll marry you!" Estella shrieked. She flung her arms around him. "Yes! Yes! Yes!"

"I don't have an engagement ring," he warned.

"I don't need one."

"You sure do. What kind of guy doesn't have a ring for his girl?"

"One who's miles from home fighting a war?"

"I can't be giving you Brits more excuses to think badly of us Yanks. Anyhow, I came prepared with something that might work until we can find one you like."

Jay delved into the pocket of his shirt and pulled out a small silver crucifix. Estella shook her head.

"That's your mum's!"

"I know, but she said since I'm the eldest it should be mine. It's part of the family legend. Remember? The two lovers who proved the whole world wrong?"

"Just like us."

Jay slipped the necklace over her head. "Just like us. Maybe it's a family trait? Did any of your folks marry crazily for love?"

Recalling Hamilton's sneering words about Violet, Estella shivered.

"I don't think so."

"Then you're the first." He kissed her again. "I love you, my beautiful fiancée. I'll spend the rest of my life taking care of you and making you happy, I promise."

They talked some more and made plans before, aware the hour was growing late, making their way back to the boundary. Estella wove her fingers into his, not wanting to let her new fiancé go. If she did, she feared she would never see him again.

Stop being stupid, she told herself sharply. It was superstitious to believe that bad feelings and premonitions were real.

"Will I see you tomorrow?" she asked.

"I'm hoping so," Jay murmured kissing her tenderly. "I love you now, always and for ever. No matter what, that will always be true. I love you, Star. I always have and I always will."

Estella didn't want to let him go. She knew how Juliet must have felt when Romeo climbed down her balcony. All the 'it was the nightingale and not the lark' business had never made any sense when Tommy had taught it, but now every beat of the pentameter was in perfect time with her own fearful heart. Estella longed to plead with Jay to stay for just a few moments longer but after one last, gossamer-soft kiss his fingers slipped from hers until just the tips were touching before he dissolved into the woods, lost from sight and out of reach. She stood willing him to return, but when seconds turned into minutes and all she could hear was the soft sigh of the wind, Estella knew he wasn't coming back.

She had the awful feeling she would never see him again …

Too much Shakespeare, she told herself sternly as she turned for home. Nothing would change between this moment and tomorrow. When Jay next had leave he would be here and, since his medical role allowed him to move freely between the camp and his billet in the village, she was certain to see him soon. It was the excitement of being newly engaged that was making her feel on edge, nothing more sinister. Her hand rose to touch the crucifix, and she smiled. It was the oddest engagement ring in history but it couldn't have been more precious.

Estella was almost back at Pencallyn House when she realised Poppet wasn't with her. Usually the little spaniel ran ahead, chasing unseen woodland creatures and following scents irresistible to a doggy nose, but this evening she seemed to have vanished.

"Poppet!" Estella called but there was no joyful answering bark or crashing of stumpy body through bracken. "Poppet!"

She peered into the darkness, but the shy moon was hiding behind clouds and the blackout made everything blacker. The dog was absent. Blast! Poppet must have picked up a scent and followed it back into the woods; she was a terror for doing that. The spaniel also adored Jay, rolling over in ecstasy when he stroked her, and she often tried to accompany him back to his billet.

"She'll be the one who gives us away," Jay had joked one evening when he had dragged the dog back to Estella, but this didn't seem funny tonight. Who knew what eyes were watching them or might have noticed Estella Kellow's spaniel following the young combat medic back to his billet? Several times Jay had feared he was being shadowed and Estella still made sure she meandered on her route to the farmhouse. They weren't safe.

The nature of their relationship meant they would always face danger.

"Poppet!" she called, into the darkness. "Poppet! Heel!"

But there was still no sign of the dog, so Estella retraced her steps to the ruined farmhouse, growing more worried. At one point she froze, thinking the crack of a twig and the rustle of undergrowth ahead were footfalls; Nature's betrayal of another presence in the night-time garden.

"Hello?" she called, but her mouth was dry and her words little more than a whisper. There was a scuffle in the darkness and Estella gasped. Someone was there. She might not be able to see them, but she could feel them.

She ran her tongue over her dry lips.

"Hello? Who's there?"

There was no reply. Whatever it was out there was hiding, tense and poised to flee. It was probably a fox or a badger, annoyed at having its night-time world invaded, but even so Estella was unnerved. The atmosphere felt odd – jagged – and the silence was weighted. Everything in Estella wanted to flee. There was something ugly here.

Something evil.

"Poppet?" she called again, and her voice shook.

Maybe the spaniel had run away to the village? Or perhaps she'd chased a fox and got herself stuck? This was highly likely because Poppet loved to follow scents. But knowing there was little hope of spotting a black spaniel without the help of a glimmer of moonlight or friendly beam of a torch, Estella returned to Pencallyn. She would have to wait until it was light, and search in the morning. Maybe Evie could help? They hadn't spent a great deal of time together lately; Estella hated how Hamilton Mason, with his thirsty eyes and chilly smile, had come between them. She had to put things right. She couldn't let him destroy their friendship.

The house was still when she let herself in. Although it wasn't late, ten o'clock at the most, her father's study was in darkness and only a dim bulb lit the hall. With the blackout down, the house swum with shadows, and every creak of her footstep on the floorboards was amplified. Cook had walked home; the land girls were in their billets above the old stables and her father must have gone to bed.

As she climbed the stairs, Estella tensed in case Hamilton or Lex were present, but no tell-tale light shone from beneath the doors of their rooms. They must be out, on exercise somewhere or maybe drinking in Calmouth, so there was no danger of coming across either officer. Estella had seen pure hatred in Hamilton's eyes and knew that next time she would not escape so easily. It was a dreadful thing to realise so fully that the enemy under her father's roof was as much a threat as the enemy they were meant to be fighting.

Musing this, Estella pushed the door open to the girls' bedroom.

"Eves, I've lost Poppet ..."

The room was empty. Evie wasn't curled up in bed reading or setting her hair in fat rollers at the dressing table. Although the bedside lamp was switched on, the pink candlewick bedspread was undisturbed, and Evie's nightgown was still laid out across the pillow.

Estella frowned. It was unlike Evie to slip away in the evening. She usually liked to read in the library or listen to the wireless – although she was really making sure she was indoors should Hamilton Mason return to his billet. A faithful hound couldn't have waited for its master with more devotion. Not that Hamilton seemed to appreciate or even notice her efforts. The more Evie fawned on him, the more he seemed to despise her, and the more Evie resented Estella for being the object of his unwanted attention.

Estella yawned. Everything about her life lately, from the strain of hiding her love for Jay to ignoring the whispers and gossip about Violet's death, was exhausting. Overcome with weariness, she undressed and tugged her nightdress on over her head, too tired to even brush her teeth. She kept Jay's necklace on, though, and as she drifted into sleep one hand was curled around it as she dreamed about the man she adored and the wonderful life they would share once the war was over …

It wasn't the thud of a shutting door but the crying which woke Estella. Huge sobs, dredged from a soul in despair, trawled the depths of sleep to rip Estella from her dreams and into wakefulness. For a moment she lay confused. The blackout blinds drowned the bedroom in darkness, making it hard to tell whether it was morning or night. As she became more awake, Estella realised Evie was breaking her heart. Evie never cried.

Never.

Estella switched on the bedside lamp.

"Eves?"

There was no reply, but from the huddled mound beneath the bedspread came a gulp. Muddy boots on the rug and her own red coat tossed over a chair suggested Evie hadn't stopped in the boot room when she arrived home but had raced upstairs in a terrible hurry. There was no sign of her usual pile of clothes shucked off by the bed in a heap, a habit Tommy had failed to break, which suggested Evie had dived beneath the covers fully dressed and in the manner of someone desperate to hide away as fast as she could.

Estella glanced at the clock. It was four in the morning. Had Evie only just come home?

"Evie?" she whispered again. "What's wrong?"

There was no answer except for a muffled whimper. Estella was alarmed. In five years of friendship she had seldom seen the other girl cry. Even when Evie had learned of her grandmother's death, she had remained dry-eyed.

Something truly awful must have happened.

Estella swung her legs out of bed and padded across the room, perching on Evie's bed as she had a thousand times before.

"Evie, talk to me. What's wrong?" An icy knife of fear sliced through Estella as she recalled the enmity in Hamilton's words as he'd sprawled on the hearth rug clutching his head. Surely not? "Has someone hurt you?" she asked.

Evie's answer was another gulping sob. She was curled up like a child, knees folded in against her chest and her thin arms wrapped tightly around them. When Estella tugged the covers back and the lamplight hit her face, Evie wailed and tried to bury her head in the pillow but not before Estella could see her face was cut. The fingernails of her hands were broken too, and dark with dried blood.

"What happened to you?"

"I fell."

Estella thought this had to be her friend's least convincing performance.

"No, you didn't. Someone's hurt you. Who?"

Evie dashed tears away with the back of her hand.

"No one. It was an accident. I was walking in the garden and I fell. It was stupid."

"At night? Alone? You fell and bruised your wrists? You broke your nails falling?" Estella wasn't buying it. "Was it Hamilton Mason, Evie? Has he hurt you? Tell me!"

Evie flinched. "Don't be silly. I slipped and fell."

She was lying. Usually Hamilton's name was enough to make Evie light up like a Christmas tree.

"I don't believe you, Eves. Look, if this is his doing, he can't be allowed to get away with it. We'll go to his commanding officer first thing and tell them and then —"

Evie sat bold upright. "No! I went for a walk and I slipped and fell."

"Don't lie to me. I'm not an idiot," said Estella.

But Evie hugged her thin body tighter with arms flowering with bruises that were an exact match for the cruel bite of a man's fingers. Estella stared. Did those bruises match her own?

"Leave me alone, Stell," Evie said.

"Never. We're blood sisters, remember? We promised to protect each other and to look out for one another. I love you, Evie, and I'm not going to let anyone hurt you. We promised, remember? We promised!"

Evie wept even harder, her whole body shaking with distress.

"I'm sorry, Stella. I am so, so sorry."

Estella pulled her friend into her arms, smoothing her hair back from her wet cheeks.

"You have nothing to be sorry for. Nothing! Do you hear me? I love you, Evie. Nothing Hamilton's done will change that. Nothing!"

Evie sobbed and Estella held her tightly, telling her friend repeatedly how everything was going to be fine because she loved her and would never let her down. As she wiped Evie's tears away with her thumb it was as though the distance which had opened between the two girls with the arrival of the American officers was no more than a bad dream. Their shared childhood, their secret games, the messages they would leave at the sundial, their solemn promise – all these were magically restored, and they were sisters once again. They held no grudges and they kept no secrets. As Estella soothed Evie she knew she would do anything to protect her friend. Anything. If this meant facing Hamilton Mason once more – if indeed it was him who'd hurt her friend – then so be it.

It was only once Evie finally fell asleep, exhausted from her torrent of tears, and the sky grew seashell pink that Estella realised Evie hadn't really told her anything. She still had no idea what had taken place or what had so upset her friend. Neither had she told Evie that Reginald was determined that she was to be married to the man.

As dawn broke, Estella felt desperately sad. Despite everything, it seemed that she and Evie did keep secrets from one another after all.

CHAPTER 37

Estella
1944

Estella, still on the end of Evie's bed, fell asleep in the early hours. When she woke it was past eight o'clock and there was no sign of Evie. The heap of crumpled garments had been tidied away and the bedroom door pulled to. If Estella hadn't woken up in the wrong bed, she would have thought she'd dreamed the entire episode.

Desperate to find Evie, Estella washed and dressed as quickly as she could. The house was unusually quiet and, judging by the empty dining room, the officers weren't present either. Nor had Poppet crept home, smelling ripe and with limpid eyes filled with remorse. Estella's heart sank. Everything felt odd, like a familiar tune played in the wrong key. When she learned from Cook that Fore Street was closed by a roadblock Estella felt even more unsettled.

"Something's up, mark my words," Cook said. "The Americans are ever so busy. The lieutenants haven't come home for breakfast and there's all manner of vehicles heading down the beach."

"Is Hitler coming?" Dolly asked, looking alarmed.

"If he is, he'll have some bother getting past all these blooming Americans," huffed Cook.

Estella stared down at her toast. Jay had said he thought something big was about to happen. Was the army mobilising? Were they to be parted? Would she ever see her fiancé again? She touched his crucifix and felt reassured. She was loved and protected. All would be well.

"Have you seen Miss Evie this morning?" she asked Dolly.

"No, Miss. Can't say I have."

"I saw her heading into the garden when I was on my way up. She looked like a wet weekend. Have you girls fallen out?" said Cook.

Estella pushed her plate aside. Something bad had happened to Evie, and instinct told Estella that Hamilton Mason was the cause of her friend's distress.

"No, we're fine – but Poppet's run off. I ought to go and look for her,"

Cook rolled her eyes. "That blooming dog. It'll be down in the village, I'll be bound. It follows one of the American boys about, doesn't it? One of the coloured lads?"

"I know the one you mean," nodded Dolly. "The doctor one billeted with Ivy Pendriscott? He's ever so handsome! Ivy's right fond of him and I can't say I blame her."

Jay was billeted with Mrs Pendriscott. Estella felt alarmed. If the locals were remarking on Poppet following Jay Miller, how could Hamilton Mason with his penetrating grey eyes fail to notice? Oh! Why hadn't she been stricter with her dog?

Worried, Estella set off to search the woods and garden again. She called and called for Poppet until her throat was raw, but there was no answering bark. By the time she arrived at the old farmhouse, Estella was close to tears. Poppet had never gone missing for this long. Something was desperately wrong.

The ruined farmhouse was deserted, but Estella had the oddest sensation she wasn't alone. The ragged cloths tied in the trees by the well fluttered in the breeze, but the place felt unusually quiet. There was no birdsong, Estella realised. This was what seemed peculiar.

"Hello?" she called. "Is anyone there?"

Her voice sounded thin and she glanced around nervously. She was being ridiculous, Estella told herself sharply. This was a happy place. Their happy place.

But it didn't feel at all that way today. It felt melancholy and despairing.

Estella crept into the ruined farmhouse. Nothing seemed amiss. Their blanket was neatly folded in the far corner and the pile of books was stacked beside it. Everything appeared to be exactly as they had left it, or so it appeared until Estella caught sight of a small book at the far side of the room. Pages splayed, it looked as though it had been thrown across the space and hit the wall hard.

Estella's blood froze. This was Jay's copy of Shakespeare's Sonnets, the cherished prize awarded to him by the teacher who told him to reach for the stars. He always carried it, and, after the family crucifix, it was his most precious possession. There was no way he would have left it here, and when they had packed their things away the book hadn't been on the floor. She would have noticed it.

Estella picked the book up, holding against her heart, which fluttered beneath her ribs like a bird trapped in a chimney. Something dreadful had happened here. Her nerve endings prickled, and she fled from the ruin, tearing headlong down the path and plunging into the woods. Estella tore along the familiar tracks until she broke free from the trees and stumbled back into Pencallyn's garden. She floundered past the bamboo, sliced her arms on razor-edged palm fronds and paddled through a foaming tide of cow parsley, but she didn't stop.

She was too afraid.

What had happened last night? First Poppet vanished. Then Evie arrived home in a dreadful state. Now Jay's precious book had appeared in the ruined farmhouse. Something malevolent was stalking them all. Estella's fingers caressed the book in her pocket, closing around the warm leather Jay's beloved hands had touched so many times.

"Jay," she whispered fearfully. "What's happened? Are you safe, my love?"

The rest of the day passed torturously slowly. Estella had planned to work in the kitchen garden, but when she realised she was pulling out her plants rather than the weeds she gave up. There was no way she could focus on anything with such worry twisting in her belly. On Estella's return Evie was in bed once more, pleading illness, and when Estella peeped into their room she was sound asleep, or giving a good appearance of being so. Estella had closed the door quietly. While Evie slept, she wouldn't relive the horror of what Estella suspected had happened to her.

Once the sun began its descent into the valley, Estella headed back into the garden to search for Poppet once more. Her red coat was missing, so she borrowed one of Alex's old sweaters from the boot room, and it was comforting to feel close to her brother as she burrowed into the darned wool. If only Ally was here, Estella thought sadly. He could have kept them all safe from Hamilton.

This time Estella didn't venture inside the ruin but sat in the courtyard watching the sunshine catching the leaves and dancing diamonds upon cracked paving stones. The patterns soothed her, and she drowsed in the warmth. Her imagination was running away with her, she decided. Jay must have dropped the book and, caught up in farewells, they hadn't noticed. There was nothing more sinister going on. Poppet would come home, thinner and muddier, and Jay would be here presently to pull her into his arms and kiss away her fears. It was all unrelated to whatever had happened to Evie.

So Estella sat and waited, as she had so many times before, but when owls began to screech and bats flitted in and out of the gaping eaves it was clear Jay wasn't coming. The empty windows of the ruin smoked with dusk and, more and more on edge with every solitary second, Estella abandoned her vigil with a heavy heart. She called for Poppet all the way home but there was still no sign of the spaniel and Estella's hopes faded with ebbing of the day.

Once home, Estella put the sweater back and decided to check on Evie. The door to the drawing room was ajar and she caught sight of Lex Boone deep in discussion with her father, a brandy balloon held loosely in his blunt fingers. Feeling uneasy, she ran up the stairs and straight into Hamilton Mason.

"Why, Miss Kellow," he drawled. "What a pleasure to see you this evening."

The lamplight caught Hamilton's square jaw, highlighting four livid scratches south of the wound she'd inflicted. His right hand was bandaged and resting in a sling.

Hamilton saw her glance and laughed.

"Trust me, this time the other party got what they deserved. They won't underestimate me again. Anyone who does that is making a big mistake because nobody insults me and walks away."

The implied threat was clear, and Estella felt icy with dread. Was he referring to her? Or poor shaken and bloodied Evie? But how could Evie insult Hamilton when she idolised him? Or was it Jay he was referring to? But Hamilton didn't know about her love affair with Jay.

Did he?

Hamilton stepped forward and, repelled, Estella shrank away. The newel post pressed against her spine.

"Worried about your lover? Or your slut of a friend? Blacks and whores. Nice company for a lady to keep." His face was so close to hers Estella could smell the taint of whisky and feel his hot breath on her skin. "But then, you're no lady are you, Estella Kellow? A lady doesn't behave the way you have. It's disgusting. Nobody decent would stand by and let it happen. I sure couldn't."

He knew about Jay. How, Estella couldn't say but he knew.

"What have you done?" she whispered.

"What was necessary. You British don't understand how these things are. When folks step out of place they have to be reminded." He reached out and grabbed her jaw, twisting Estella's neck and forcing her to look up at him. His top lip curled. "Why, I declare! You could have had me, and you chose Miller? There's no sense in that. You're soiled goods now, Miss Kellow. No decent man will touch a girl like you. I certainly wouldn't touch Miller's whore."

"He's worth a million of you," she said, jerking her head away, but his fingers only increased their pressure.

"Why, that's strange, because I'd say he's worth nothing. Dead men have no value."

Estella's legs turned to water. She caught the banister rail.

"What do you mean?"

But Hamilton simply gave her a malevolent smile and shrugged uniformed shoulders.

"What I said, dearest Estella. Now, if you'll excuse me, I must get back. Apparently we have a deserter to deal with."

He stepped past her, his arm pressing against her breast for a second, before continuing down the stairs. Estella slumped against the banister and watched him descend. Unable to move, her skin was tight with terror. Hamilton Mason could not have made himself clearer; he had done something truly dreadful to Jay and it was all because she had rejected Hamilton.

She was to blame.

Estella barely slept that night and bad dreams shadowed any fitful snatches of rest she did manage. Several times Evie cried out in her sleep before waking, sobbing and gasping. Estella climbed into her bed and held her friend close, stroking Evie's face until the girl calmed and her thin body stopped shaking.

"What is it?" she asked quietly. "What's wrong, Evie? Please tell me. Is it Hamilton? Has he hurt you?"

At just the mention of his name, Evie tensed, and Estella sensed her withdrawing deep into the dark part of herself. It was easier to prise limpets off the rocks than secrets from Evie, but Estella's suspicions grew even stronger, and with them her fears.

When Estella rose, her head was thumping and her eyes were gritty. Evie was subdued and picked at a piece of toast before offering to weed the kitchen garden. The cuts on her face were healing, but the bruises on her wrists and arms were the angry violet of a storm-filled sky.

"I fell," was all she said when asked, and Estella saw Cook and Dolly exchange knowing looks. Whatever the truth of the matter, Evie would not share it.

Not yet anyway.

"I'm going to look for Poppet," Estella announced. She unhooked the lead from the back of the door. "I'm going to try the village."

Cook passed her a wicker shopping basket and their ration books. "Pick up some food, Miss Estella – and cut through the garden into the fields to get to the village. There are roadblocks and checkpoints everywhere."

"The Americans are dead busy," Jenny said.

"Too busy for dancing these days," sighed Dolly.

Cook tutted. "Dancing isn't going to stop old Hitler, is it? What do you think the troops should do, my girl? Jitterbug over the Jerries?"

"Lindy hop over the Luftwaffe?" giggled Dolly. She sprang up and started dancing around the kitchen. "Those Nazis couldn't keep up. They'd all drop dead with exhaustion!"

Estella set off for the village. The amount of traffic rumbling down the woodland road to the beach seemed greater than the day before, as if every vehicle the Americans possessed was heading to the cove. She could see what was happening because she knew the secret tracks through the woods where it was possible to catch glimpses of jeeps and trucks and tanks carried on low vehicles. If she wasn't so afraid for Jay, Estella would have been far more curious, but this morning all she could think of was making certain he was safe. Hamilton was most likely toying with her, a cat playing with a mouse for his own sadistic pleasure, but she had to know for certain. And darling Jay needed to know he was in danger.

But there was still no trace of Poppet, and eventually Estella quit the garden by means of a hole in the fence she and Evie had made some years ago. Brushing off leaves and twigs, she emerged in the sloping field which led to the village. Since the army had closed the top of the lane this was the sole pedestrian access in and out of the village, and Estella had to show her ID card at two checkpoints. Rather than collecting the shopping, however, she turned into the narrow street opposite the schoolhouse to call at the small cottage where Jay had his billet. Perhaps Bill and Ivy Pendriscott could put her mind at rest.

Bill and Ivy were simple folk, Pencallyn born and bred, and Jay was fond of them. They had made Jay feel a part of their family, inviting him to the Methodist chapel with them on Sundays, and Ivy regularly corresponded with his family.

"Miss Kellow!" Ivy Pendriscott couldn't have looked more surprised if Princess Elizabeth had been standing on her doorstep. She wiped floury hands on her pinny and looked flustered. "Are you better? I do hope it wasn't a serious accident, Miss?"

Confused, Estella wanted to tell Ivy Pendriscott she hadn't been unwell, but no break came in the flow of chatter.

"Come in, come in. You look like you need a glass of water. It's a hot day for early June, isn't it?"

Distracted, Estella hadn't noticed the weather, but sure enough the sky was the same soft blue as a duck's egg and the sun shone brightly. The sea, snared in barbed wire and barricaded behind concrete, was sparkling, and bright beams glanced off the metal hulls of the warships moored off Calmouth Bay. Following Mrs Pendriscott into a tiny kitchen, Estella was offered a seat at a small table.

"We're at sixes and sevens here, I'm afraid, Miss. We're so worried about Private Miller, you see," Mrs Pendriscott continued. "My Bill and me, we don't believe what they're saying about him. It must be wrong, I said, because Jay was tending you. He'd not run away, I said. My, he's worked miracles. Your leg seems fine."

"My leg?"

"You fell up at the old farm, didn't you? A broken leg was what the officer thought when he came looking for Jay. Jay wants to be a doctor, you see, and he's an army medic. He's very clever, that boy. A marvel!"

"What officer?" said Estella.

"The dark-haired one billeted up Pencallyn House," replied Ivy, as though this was obvious. "Wasn't that how he knew you were hurt? What were you doing at the farm anyway, Miss? And on your own? Oh!" She flushed. "None of my business, of course."

There was a rushing sound in Estella's ears. A dark-haired officer from Pencallyn House had to be Lex. Why would Lex come here to tell Jay she was hurt at the farm? Her stomach lurched. Had Hamilton asked him to lure Jay into a trap?

"When was this?"

"About a quarter to ten, Miss Kellow. The officer asked me to give Private Miller his message as soon as he arrived back. I said it might be a while," Ivy smiled fondly. "He has a sweetheart, I think, because he's always whistling and looks all starry-eyed. 'Young love', my Bill always says, 'ain't it grand!' "

Tears burned Estella's eyes. Jay loved her so dearly, but she'd led him into dreadful danger. It would have been better for him if they'd never met.

"What happened next?" she said quietly.

"Well, as soon as Jay came home, I gave him the officer's message. He went running up the road before I'd finished talking. He looked in a dreadful state."

Estella wasn't surprised. If Jay believed she was hurt, he wouldn't hesitate to go to her side.

"He had that little dog of yours with him, Miss, come to think of it. She does love to follow him about," added Ivy. "It's like she knows him. Everyone laughs to see her. She sits outside my house some days!"

Estella closed her eyes. Oh, Poppet!

"We haven't seen Jay since, but sometimes the boys go out on exercise, so I didn't think any more of it. It was only when the military police knocked that I realised something was wrong. They said Jay was absent without leave," Ivy recalled with a frown. "I told them I was worried because he hadn't come home – but they didn't seem interested in anything I had to say, the cheek! So I told them to talk to the officer from the big house who could confirm what I'd said."

Estella knew Lex would deny everything. Jay would have no alibi and the military police would think the worst. It was dreadful.

"Then the lad billeted with Ellen Tamblyn told her one of the camp medics has deserted and there's a right hullaballoo about it. I know it must be Jay, but I don't believe for a minute he'd do such a thing. He's very proper, is Jay. I wouldn't have thought he was the type to shirk his duty or let his parents down when they're so proud of him. I would never have thought him a deserter —"

"Of course, he isn't! Jay believes this is his fight as much as anyone else's!" flared Estella.

Ivy Pendriscott's head tilted.

"Do you know him, then? Why exactly are you here again, Miss Kellow?"

But Estella didn't have time to talk and she rose to her feet.

"Thank you for the water, Mrs Pendriscott. I'll be sure to let you know if the officers tell me anything more. I'll see myself out."

Outside the cottage a fat sun was high in the sky, but Estella didn't feel its warmth. Trembling from head to foot, she didn't think she would ever feel warm again.

CHAPTER 38

Estella
1944

Estella left Ivy Pendriscott's cottage in a terrible state. Somehow, she managed to visit the butcher and the grocer and fill her basket with the week's rations, but this activity felt like a dream. The village was buzzing with activity; soldiers marched down to the beach, and jeeps and trucks were parked from the beach to the top of the hill. Planes flew overhead and the road through the wood was busy with rumbling vehicles. As the sun climbed higher the physical temperature rose in perfect time with the heating up of activity.

Estella deposited her groceries with Cook and, on the pretext of going foraging, plunged into the cool of the garden. Once out of sight she followed the new road to the army camp.

"I need to see whoever's in charge," she told the soldier manning the gate. She flashed her ID card and made sure she sounded as much like the Queen as possible. Americans loved a British accent, or so she had been led to believe. "I'm Estella Kellow, from Pencallyn House, and it's vitally important I see your commanding officer."

What she hoped to achieve Estella had no idea, but she had to try and speak to somebody official. She needed to make them realise Jay Miller hadn't deserted his post. They would help her. They had to.

"I'm sorry, Miss, but there's no civilian access to the base," said the GI. He was holding a gun and looked as though he wasn't afraid to use it if she took one step closer.

"But it's terribly important," Estella said desperately. "I think something awful may have happened to one of your combat medics, Private First Class Miller?"

"Miller?"

"Yes. Private First Class Jacob Miller. Do you know him?"

"Sure do, Miss. The MPs have been searching all over for Miller. First Lieutenant Mason's wild. Don't waste your time, Miss. Cowards like Miller want shooting."

"Private Miller isn't a coward!" Estella flared. "He's been the victim of foul play. I need to see your commanding officer! At once!"

But the soldier gave her a weary look.

"I'm sorry, Miss. You can't come through. That's orders. Talk to your British police if you have a concern. Now move along, please."

It was hopeless. There was no way Estella could make it into the camp, and even if she did succeed it was apparent nobody would believe her. The military police had already made their minds up about Jay.

"Something terrible's happened to him – please help me!" she begged, tears streaming down her cheeks, but a convoy of trucks was passing through now and her pleas were drowned in the rumble of tyres. Filled with despair, Estella walked back Pencallyn House. Her footsteps brought her through the labyrinth to the old place where the sundial slumbered, the half-forgotten centre of childhood games. Her hand brushed the rough stone, and the metal disc sliced by the sun was hot beneath her fingers. But there were no messages beneath it today.

"Now, always and for ever," she promised, the magic of the ley lines thrumming beneath her feet. "I'll find you, Jay, and I'll wait here until I die if I have to."

A breeze stirred the leaves and Estella whipped around. For a split second she saw a figure standing at the edge of the green depths, hand stretched out to her and eyes soft with sorrow.

"Jay? Darling? Is that you?"

But there was no answer and when she blinked there was only emptiness. It was a trick of the light – and for Estella one disappointment too many. Wracked with sobs, she crumpled onto the grass and wept until the shadow of the sundial stretched long and black across the garden.

That evening Reginald Kellow returned to London and Evie was nowhere to be seen, so Estella spent long hours trying to read; but it was impossible to focus when her every thought was for Jay. She shook with fear at what might have befallen him. Determined to confront the American officers, her ears were on elastic to hear them return, but by the time the longcase clock in the hall struck midnight it was clear Hamilton and Lex weren't coming back that night.

When Estella heard aeroplanes flying over Pencallyn House, she leapt to her feet with her heart racing. There were buckets of sand outside and water too – they were still prepared for a raid even if these were less frequent now – and she was on her way to the cellar when she realised these planes were flying out to sea. This meant they belonged to the Allies.

Something was happening!

She was about to run outside and look up at the sky when Evie flew in through the front door. She was wrapped up in an old mackintosh and holding Estella's missing red coat.

"We need to go outside. Come on! Something's up!"

Estella nodded. "Yes, I think you're right. Hey! Where did you find my coat?"

"Golly, I don't know. The boot room, I think. Never mind that, anyway. Come on!"

Another squadron of planes passed, low overhead. Their throbbing engines rendered all conversation impossible.

"Put your coat on!" Evie bellowed. "Something big is happening! Come on!"

Estella placed her book on the arm of the chair and shrugged on her coat. It was a clear night, and when the girls craned their necks skywards they saw an endless stream of planes heading out over the sea towards France. Some were towing gliders while others flew in formation, and all of them were pointed firmly in the direction of the Continent.

Estella gasped. She had never seen anything like it.

"What's happening?"

"I think I know!" Evie cried. "Follow me!"

"Where are we going?"

"Bury Barrow. We'll see it all from there."

"See all of what?" Estella demanded, but Evie had sprinted ahead. By the time she caught up Evie had clambered over the top Pencallyn gate and was running along the lane. Estella, never as fit or as fast, struggled to keep pace.

"The checkpoint's deserted!" Evie called over her shoulder. "They've gone, Stell!"

She was right. There was no soldier present at the usual place. Estella was used to showing her ID card these days and it felt strange to find the post abandoned.

"Wait for me," she cried, but Evie was way ahead and vanishing over the stile into what was now known as Dead German Wood. Above their heads planes were still swooping over Pencallyn and casting moon shadows onto the still warm earth. Estella hurled herself over the fence after Evie and ran up hill, her breath coming in painful gasps. When she broke through the tree cover, she understood why Evie had chosen this particular vantage point.

"My God!" Estella observed the bay in amazement. "What's going on? What are they doing?"

Evie's eyes glittered. "They off to invade France! Bloody hell, Stella! This is why they came here! They must have been planning it all the time. But where did all these boats come from?"

A flotilla of ships had assembled in Calmouth Bay, dark shadows lurking in the silvered water like mysterious sea creatures magically surfacing from mythology. There were so many vessels they must surely stretch from Pencallyn Cove to Calmouth, and even beyond to the Helford and Trebah. This was a war fleet waiting for the signal to set sail. It was an allied Armada poised to chase the invaders away from England's shores.

"They must have been hidden in the creeks," she said slowly. Now it all made sense: the roadblocks, the restricted access, the patrol boats. Cornwall with its hidden inlets, coves and creeks was the perfect place to conceal a massing fleet from prying enemy eyes. What better spot for secreting weapons and men to take the Nazis by surprise than this ancient haunt of smugglers?

"This is it," breathed Evie. "The Allies are pushing back! They've just been waiting for the right moment."

Estella nodded. Jay had told her the time was drawing near when his medical skills would be tested. He had hinted that a parting was imminent. He understood he could be asked to lay down his life, and had never shown the slightest doubt he was doing the right thing. How brave he was! How utterly impossible that he could have deserted. Jay Miller's whole life had been leading to very this night and playing his part in the fight against a regime he believed was truly evil.

Oh, where was Jay? What had happened to him? Down in the bay were men who could answer this question, and Estella was so afraid they would take their secrets with them. What if she never found out what had happened to him? She sent up a silent prayer for Jay and for all the young men who were setting sail for France – except for Hamilton Mason and Lex Boone. They could take their chances.

The girls stood in silence and watched the activity in the cove. As the moon peeked out of the clouds Estella saw hundreds of men moving in an endless stream along the pier and the embarkation platforms which stretched out to the ships. Little more than black smudges pressing forward into the darkness, it was sobering to think each dot was a young soldier stepping away from land and into the unknown. Estella could barely imagine what lay in wait for them across the water, and her heart ached to know that so many of these boys who were willingly crossing the gangplanks might never return. So much loss and so much sadness. How could anyone ever bear it?

As the stars traversed the arc of sky above them the activity on the beach gathered pace. Aeroplanes continued to fly over. Estella and Evie sat on the summit of the barrow and watched. It was the closest the girls had been for months.

As though sensing Estella's thoughts, Evie turned to her.

"I'm sorry," she said.

"For what?"

"For everything. For not keeping my promise to you. For not being a better friend. For not seeing what was right in front of me. I promise I won't let you down again, Stell. Not ever."

"Do you mean Hamilton?" Estella asked nervously because it was the first time Evie had willingly approached the subject. As when watching the wild birds in the garden, Estella was afraid any sudden movement might frighten her away.

Evie nodded. Her long dark hair swung over her face and concealed the cuts on her cheek.

"How can I explain? It was madness. I felt like I was like looking at the sun and I couldn't see anything else. Hamilton dazzled me, Stell. He was all I could think about. I could barely eat. I couldn't sleep. I've never felt anything like it. It was just like in all the books we read. He was Rochester and I was Jane!"

Estella understood, because falling in love with Jay Miller had felt exactly like this. Her appetite had vanished for weeks, she'd drifted through the days deep in wonderful daydreams, and lived for the snatched moments when they would be together. Yes, it was the wonder of first love Evie had felt – and how awful that the object of her affections was dark and twisted. Hamilton had warped the most beautiful of emotions into something stunted and ugly. whereas her own love for Jay had grown more beautiful with every passing hour.

"You thought you were in love with him," Estella said.

Evie hung her head. "Yes, I really did. He was like something from a movie. Handsome. Rich. American. Glamorous. I dreamed he would fall in love with me and take me away with him to Hollywood. I prayed for it. I wished for it. I thought he could make me somebody."

"But you *are* somebody already! And he didn't deserve you! He's not a nice man," Estella cried. How could Evie have failed to see this?

Evie's hands were tight knots in her lap.

"I'm not a nice girl, Stella."

More planes swooped overhead, so low the long grass rippled, and they could feel the wind from their wings. Once these had passed and the noise was distant, Evie turned to Estella and the expression on her face was despairing.

"I'm not like you, Stella. Inside I'm dark and mucky like the bottom of a deep pond. You can peer into the surface and think you see something glittery and pleasant – but underneath, in the depths where nobody ventures, it's another story. I saw that in Hamilton and maybe I recognised it. I thought he was damaged and needed understanding. I thought I could help him. I would have done anything for him."

"Anything?" Estella asked. A cold finger of fear traced a passage down her spine.

"Maybe not quite anything. I didn't tell him you've been seeing Private

Miller. I wouldn't do that to you, Stella. I'm not a sneak."

Evie knew? How? She and Jay had been so careful.

Hadn't they?

"How did you find out about Jay Miller?"

"I saw you at the dance when you cut your hand and he tended it," Evie shrugged. "I was watching. Then you vanished together, and I had to walk back with Jenny because you pushed off."

"Private Miller escorted me home. That was all," Estella protested, and Evie laughed.

"Please, Stella, stop treating me like an idiot. I know you, remember? Your face shows everything you feel. You're not like me – you can't act to save your life, and everyone could see the happiness coming off you in waves. You wore it like a bloody halo. The person who gave your feelings for Private Miller away was you, Stella. You betrayed your feelings for him with every smile! Every time you glanced at the scar on your hand. Every time you needed to take Poppet for another walk or kissed that crucifix. That's from him, isn't it? God. You really must think I'm stupid. You must have laughed at me."

"Of course, I didn't!"

"I always knew you were sneaking out to meet him, and I waited for you to tell me but you never did," Evie continued. "You took Miller everywhere. The old farm house. The gardens. The Japanese pond. You even took him to the sundial, and that really hurt, Stella. It was supposed to be our special place. It's Mysterious Garden, remember?"

"You spied on us?"

"It's your fault for shutting me out! You've never told me a thing. That was when I knew you could keep secrets from me. How could you, Stell? We're supposed to be sisters. You're meant to trust me!"

Estella couldn't listen to any more.

"How could I possibly trust you? You were infatuated! When I met Jay, you were so insanely jealous because you thought I might steal your precious Hamilton. If he glanced at me, you flew off the handle."

Evie's knotted hands tightened, and Estella knew she was fighting not to cry. But she felt she had to press on.

"Dear God, Evie! How could I have told you I was in love with Jay Miller when you would have done anything to get Hamilton Mason to notice you? None of us were under any illusion regarding how he feels about negroes, were we? You even agreed with him at times, and for all I knew you could have told him about us just for a kind look. Of course I couldn't trust you. You were obsessed!"

"I could have told him, but I didn't. I couldn't do that to you. Even though I was so jealous of you, I still loved you best. Even more than Hamilton."

"But why would you be jealous of me?"

"Because of who you are! Miss Kellow of Pencallyn House!"

Stung, Estella said, "I've never seen you as any different to me."

"You might not – but everyone else does."

"Rubbish! People sometimes struggle to tell us apart."

"Not since we were children. When they look closely it's clear who the fake is," Evie said. "Hamilton could see it. He had no interest in me, and I always knew that deep down. He wanted the real thing. It was always you he wanted."

Estella shuddered. "Trust me, I didn't want him."

"I knew that deep down, but it didn't make any difference because he wanted you and that bloody well hurt. All I ever wanted was for him to look at me just once the way he always did at you. Just once, Estella! Once!"

Estella shook her head. "Hamilton Mason's evil, Evie. Trust me, he really is. He tried to hurt me once and it would have been a lot worse if I hadn't fought him off. He would have …" She paused because a thrill of horror still ran through her when she recalled the dreadful incident. "He would have forced himself on me."

Evie's eyes widened. "Bastard. Is that how he hurt his head?"

"I hit him with my mother's silver picture frame. It stopped him."

"Bloody hell, Stella. He was wild after that. Why didn't you tell me?"

"I was afraid you wouldn't believe me," Estella said sadly. "I thought you'd think I had encouraged him. Maybe that is what you would have thought … You must believe me. I never wanted that man near me."

Evie swallowed. "I do believe you and I'm so sorry, sorrier than I can ever say. I'm sorry I didn't listen to you. I'm sorry I ignored all the awful things he said. I'm sorry I told myself maybe he was right even though in my heart I knew it was wrong. That makes me as bad as him, I think. Maybe I deserved what he did to me?"

Estella's head snapped up. The scratches. The nightmares. The shrinking in on herself …

"He didn't —"

"No. *No!* He said he wanted to meet me at the old farm, and I was so happy. So excited. I wore your red coat because he said he liked it, and I felt special for once." Evie's mouth twisted as she fought for control. "Anyway, he didn't want what I wanted. He only wanted me because I looked like you, so I ran away. I was scared because he was so angry, and I thought he would kill me, I truly did. He looked at me as though I was nothing."

Estella understood. She'd seen that rage and felt those cruel hands bite into her skin. Estella had no doubt Hamilton Mason was capable of the very worst atrocities.

"Afterwards, I hated myself," Evie continued. "I was taken in by him and I'd let you down. I was supposed to love you and protect you, Stella, but I didn't. I was jealous and angry and a bad friend. I betrayed you by putting him first. It's all my fault!"

"No," Estella said. "Nothing he's done is because of you. You're not responsible for that man's actions."

Her own rejection of Hamilton had been the catalyst, Estella now realised. He must have been plotting his revenge ever since, and lured Jay back to the farm on the pretext of being needed by her. He had planned to use Evie as a decoy – until she had spoiled his scheme by running away. Hamilton used Jay's love for Estella as a trap, and the moment Jay set foot in the ruined farmhouse it would have been sprung. Evie had accidentally become mixed up in something far more sinister and complex than she could have ever realised.

Oh! What had the officers done to darling, darling Jay? Where was he? Was he hurt? Or was it something worse? Knowing she had brought disaster onto him, Estella wanted to hurl herself into the water in despair. This was all *her* doing. Everything which had taken place was because of her rejection of Hamilton's advances. He'd warned her that no one insulted him and got away with it. Why hadn't she listened? Why hadn't she been more careful?

Evie, who never cried, was weeping bitterly. "Everything's ruined, Stella. Everything. I've broken my promise to you and I've let you down. I am so, so sorry."

More planes flew over. The growl of engines ricocheted across the valley, joining Evie in her grief. So much danger and so much aggression. No wonder they had been caught up in it, Estella thought.

"Whatever Hamilton's done it's not your fault," she said, taking her friend's hand. "This is *my* fault, Evie. I rejected Hamilton, and humiliated him, and he was furious with me. It was me he wanted to punish. He's a dangerous man and he knows how to manipulate people. I'm glad you escaped, and I hope Jay got away too and is hiding somewhere."

Evie said nothing. but a silent tear slipped down her cheek.

"I'm so scared for him, Evie. I think they might have really hurt him," Estella said.

"I think Hamilton's done something terrible," Evie whispered. "He was so angry. Oh Stella. I'm so sorry. We made a promise, didn't we? I won't betray it again. I'll never, ever let you down again."

The girls clung to one another while the warships in the bay began to pull up their gangplanks. Hamilton and Lex were down there, men who might have done something terrible to darling Jay. Deep down, Estella knew they had. It was the only explanation for his absence and the dreadful pain in her heart.

They may as well have ripped her heart out by the roots, for what was there to live for without Jay? How could Estella carry on in a world where he wasn't there to hold her? Where she couldn't hear his honey-sweet voice or feel the touch of his lips? How could she live with herself, knowing his love for her had led him into such dreadful danger? She'd thought the worst enemy was over the water when it was far, far closer …

"I'm scared, Evie," Estella said. "The military police say Jay's deserted, but I know he wouldn't do such a thing. We're going to be married once the war is over, and he'd never leave me, not willingly. What if Hamilton and Lex have really hurt him? They're dangerous."

Evie's gaze was trained on the activity in the cove.

"Trust me, Hamilton Mason and Lex Boone won't come back. I swore in blood at the sundial that if they pay with their lives for what they've done, I'd willingly give mine in return. I'll settle this score in blood. Retribution in this life and the next. What's happening now is happening because of my oath. Hamilton Mason and Lex Boone won't see another sunset. It's been sealed."

The intensity in Evie's voice frightened Estella. The hairs on her arms stirred.

"That's just a game," she whispered. "A childhood game."

"No. It's real. There's power in the ley lines and it's heard me. You'll see. Retribution is coming to Hamilton Mason and Lexington Boone. As surely as day follows night, it's coming."

As Evie said this the sun began to rise. The pen was poised to begin a new chapter, and as she watched the final soldiers embarking, Estella realised Jay Miller wouldn't return. She would have to spend the rest of her life without him.

Her hand slipped from Evie's and she drew her knees against her body, hugging them tightly. The world no longer felt solid. If only she had given in to Hamilton. If only she hadn't allowed herself to fall in love with Jay Miller.

"I'll make things right," Evie promised as the dawn broke and the pigeon-grey sea turned to gold. "It'll be all right Stella, you'll see."

But Estella knew her friend was wrong. No matter what Evie said or did or promised, life at Pencallyn would never be 'all right' again. She couldn't turn time back and restore her world to the way it had once been any more than these soldiers could turn back for the shore. Everything had changed, and nothing would ever be the same. None of this was Evie's fault. Jay Miller hadn't been punished for Evie's transgressions but for Estella Kellow's.

And Estella had absolutely no idea how she would carry this burden for the rest of her days.

CHAPTER 39

Estella
1944

Evie and Estella made their way home, and everything felt different. There was an unusual stillness at the entrance to the army camp. The habitual traffic, shouting voices and sense of urgency which had become such a part of everyday life vanished with the last stars as though the army's' presence in Cornwall had been little more than a dream. Only Estella's broken heart and the small crucifix around her neck proved there had ever been a man called Jay Miller who had loved her, now, always and for ever. Everything had a strange and otherworldly quality.

When the girls entered Pencallyn's boot room, Cook called them into the kitchen where the wireless was on and the entire household staff were gathered to listen to the BBC.

"Quick, girls, quick! Sit down!" she cried, flapping her hand at the empty chairs tucked beneath the table. "We've been listening to the radio, and you'll never guess what's happening? We're invading France! This is it! Time for our boys to have Hitler on the run!"

"Blimey, you two look like death warmed up," observed Dolly. She picked up the tea pot and sloshed stewed brown liquid into mugs. "Here, have a brew."

"You both look peaky," Cook agreed. Her eyes narrowed suspiciously. "What have you been up to? Have you been out all night?"

Estella and Evie exchanged a glance. Where to start?

"We've been up on Bury Beacon watching the troops embark," Estella said.

"There were thousands of them," added Evie, curling her fingers around the Cornish ware ceramic mug. "I'd no idea there were so many men here."

"Just think, Dolly, all those boys you never kissed!" teased Jenny.

"They set sail from here, did they? No wonder they've been practising getting on and off boats for so bloody long!" remarked Cook.

"And building that pier," added Bert.

"I'm glad I gave my Dwight a kiss when he asked! Hope it brings him luck," sighed Dolly.

"He'll need more than luck, poor sod," Beth said, her mouth set in a grim line. "Those dear, brave boys. May God go with them."

"There are two He won't be going with," Evie muttered darkly, but her words were lost amid the crackle of latest news from the wireless.

"We have reliable information that the combined forces of the British Commonwealth, the United States and patriots from occupied Europe left the British coast for France in the early hours of the morning," said the announcer. "A new phase of the Allied Air initiative has begun."

Cook and the others cheered, but Estella shivered. She couldn't help wondering what the young men would be facing when they landed on the French beaches. Jay had known a time was coming when his medical skills would be tested and had hoped his training was adequate for the wounds he would be called to tend. Yes, he was afraid, he'd admitted when she asked, but he was ready for battle. It was what he felt called to do, and he was prepared to fight shoulder to shoulder with his men.

Jay Miller was prepared to play his part in fighting the Nazis and to lay down his life for what he believed in. Estella knew there was no way he would have deserted. The man she loved hadn't run away from his duty. Although the departure of the Allied forces struck hope into the hearts of the British, it also filled Estella with a dark despair, for Jay Miller would never dream of abandoning his comrades when they needed him most. Hamilton Mason had done something dreadful. There was no other explanation.

Her heart breaking, Estella excused herself and went upstairs to lie on her bed. She drew the blackout down, turned her face to the wall and cried until there were no more tears left. The man she loved was already dead.

Jay Miller was lost to her. They had never stood a chance.

Later, when the scale of the operation became known, Estella was hardly able to believe over 160,000 men had left the coast of Britain to fight on the beaches of Normandy. More than 5000 ships and 13,000 aircraft had supported the invasion, and by the end of 6 June 1944 the Allies finally had a foothold in France. Jenny and Beth neglected their farming tasks that day, and Cook only served bread and cheese because the small household spent the day in the kitchen listening to the wireless as the news of the offensive unfolded.

Eisenhower spoke of the venture as a crusade, and in the evening the King made a moving speech calling upon the nation to renew the 'crusading impulse' with which they had entered the war. After the National Anthem had played, Cook made more tea which they drank quietly, all contemplating what might be happening across the water and what might become of the men they knew and loved. From the excitement of the morning the mood became subdued. Beth was thinking of all the handsome young Americans she had flirted with. Jenny's husband was in the RAF and likely to be involved in dropping troops farther into France, while Cook had a nephew serving in the Duke of Cornwall's Light Infantry. The price of freedom would be high.

Evie was still certain that Hamilton Mason and Lex Boone would meet a bloody end on the beaches of Normandy; having promised in blood at their old magical place she was convinced, although now a near-adult, that her wish would be granted. Both men would be punished, she said, and appeared to totally believe this. As the slow, sad days passed Estella looked at her friend and worried whether the dreadful events of that fateful June night had turned her mind.

'Little Miss Heathcliff' Tommy had once called Evie, and Estella's skin rippled with goose bumps at the memory. Hadn't Heathcliff taken revenge to the ultimate conclusion? Was Tommy's observation prophetic. or tongue in cheek? Estella wasn't certain, but she did know for sure there would never be another man for her. Meanwhile, Estella longed for Jay so terribly it was a physical pain. Even touching the small crucifix brought little comfort, for what was the purpose of a world without Jay Miller in it? Sometimes Estella would walk to the Japanese garden and stand on the bridge watching her pale face shimmer in the water below. Could she choose death and join Jay wherever he was now? Did she have the courage to be Ophelia?

Maybe. It seemed kinder to sink beneath the lilies and allow the water to close around her than to drown in an ocean of years without the man she loved. All that stopped her stepping off the little bridge was knowing how aghast Jay would be if he knew she was thinking this way. He'd loved life and he had loved her. Would giving up on living be a betrayal? Estella didn't know the answer to this. She only knew that the thought of death was a comfort. Friendly Death waited in the shadows. He was willing to take her hand if life continued to have no meaning, and each day that dawned became a feat to be endured rather than a joy.

As June yawned into July, Estella's misery grew. She couldn't eat and she barely slept. Constantly exhausted, she rose each morning feeling sick with despair. Simply dragging herself out of bed to eat a slice of dry toast and tend the kitchen garden or feed the chickens was an effort. Drowning in misery, Estella stumbled through the long, hot days feeling heavy and lethargic. What was the point of anything? Without Jay it was all meaningless. There was no joy. There was nothing to look forward to. Her novel gathered dust, her watercolours dried up and she couldn't focus on reading. Everything was pointless.

Evie, however, seemed to rally. It was as though the departure of the

Americans, and her belief in the power of the sundial, was enough to banish the spectre of what had happened to her that night. As her bruises yellowed and the cuts healed, so her nightmares also lessened. Hamilton and Lex were long gone, and with each passing day Evie's strength grew, in direct contrast to the waning of Estella's. The girls didn't talk about the events of early June, but Estella knew Evie understood the heaviness of her loss. Sometimes their gazes would lock, and each would know the other was back in the night-time garden, forever trapped in a maze of alternative routes and choices; but they always were left with the same outcome. All they could do was hold one another and cry. On other days the girls would walk down the service road, now abandoned by the Americans, to the barbed wire frill of the deserted beach. Here they would sit in silence and watch the sun dance on the water. Their closeness had returned and once again they were best friends with no secrets and no need to speak. Both understood the horrors the other faced each day, and the unspoken sympathy was a comfort. Their love for one another wasn't the same as it had been before the Americans had arrived at Pencallyn, but now it was deeper, and tested. Stronger too, fired in a crucible of fear and suffering. They had been through the worst life could throw at them.

Or so they believed.

At night Estella cried into her pillow, Jay's book of the Sonnets tucked beneath it, and slept with her fingers curled around the crucifix. She would trace the scar on her palm as she recalled Jay tending it, and sit in the window seat for hours staring out to sea yet seeing nothing. During the day she trailed listlessly through the grounds, wandering along paths she and Jay had followed but, mosaicked with memories, the garden was becoming a place she struggled to find pleasure in. Who knew what had really taken place here? Let the paths grow ever more tangled, Estella thought. When she inherited, she would allow nature to reclaim the entire place and choke the past. The specimen garden that the Kellows had cherished for generations was fast becoming a place she feared and even hated.

Similarly, the old farmhouse, once her refuge, was not a place Estella wished to revisit. Although she sometimes skirted the ruin, she felt uncomfortable. There was a strange atmosphere there now, and a sense of melancholy she'd never noticed before. Once Estella thought she glimpsed a blond man lurking in the trees and she had frozen in terror before realising this was no more than a shard of sunshine. Even so, Estella had hurried away. There was nothing for her at the ruin without her beloved Jay.

As July progressed, the weather becoming hotter and rampant plants digging their green talons into the asphalt of the Americans' road, Estella felt increasingly exhausted. Sometimes she could hardly crawl through the morning. As August grew closer, Estella felt no better. Was the heat? Or was she ill? Could you die of a broken heart?

Once morning, at the tail end of July, Estella was sitting on the edge of her bed and trying to recall the symptoms of her old childhood enemy, rheumatic fever, when she was overwhelmed with nausea. Before she could stop herself, she was retching into the wash bowl until her sides ached.

"What's wrong with me?" she gasped, holding onto the washstand while the room swayed.

Evie, brushing her hair by the window in the hope of catching what little breeze there was, stared at her.

"I think I might know," she said slowly.

Estella wiped her mouth and sank onto her bed. She felt as though she could sleep for a thousand years.

"What do you think it is?"

"No, it's impossible – unless you're the Virgin Mary? Immaculate conception and all that. It's probably a bug. Let me fetch you some water."

"I'm not the Virgin Mary, Eves."

"I was being silly. It's probably something you ate. I'm not sure it was really beef last night. I bet it was horse. Or whale. That'd make you puke."

"I mean, I'm not a virgin."

Evie's mouth fell open. "You're kidding?"

Estella gave her a weak smile. "No. I'm not kidding."

"You've gone to bed with him? *You*?"

"Yes, *me*. Why's it such a surprise? I'm not a total prude, you know! Jay and I were going to be married."

"Oh, bloody hell," said Evie. "Couldn't you have waited until after the war?"

Estella was stung. "I love him, Evie, and I'm so glad I didn't wait. I don't regret a second I spent with Jay. Not one second. I'd do everything all over again if I could."

"You're pregnant, Stella. Up the duff. Bun in the oven. Do you understand? You're having a baby. Didn't you notice any signs? The curse stopping? Feeling tired? Nausea?"

Estella stared at her. Evie was speaking but her words made no sense. It was like listening to another language.

"I thought all those things were to do with being unhappy."

"I think they've got more to do with being pregnant," Evie said.

Estella couldn't speak. Her hand was resting on her belly where, all curled up safely and in secret, Jay's child was sleeping. Now everything made sense. Lucy, the land girl who'd got 'into trouble', had been unable to face breakfast. This was what had first alerted Cook to her predicament. She'd been tired, too. It seemed unbelievable to Estella that she hadn't made the connection, but since Jay had vanished each day felt like wading through molasses. Estella had assumed it was grief which had made her feel like this.

"It isn't going to go away," Evie said when she failed to reply.

"I don't want it to go away!" Estella cried.

She was carrying Jay Miller's baby. How incredible! Estella was frightened but she was also thrilled. Wasn't this proof he hadn't abandoned her but, just as he had promised, would love her – now, always and for ever? This child was a part of him. It was his to love and, now she knew it was here, his baby would become Estella's whole reason for existing. She had been born so this child could live.

But Evie was looking worried. Dark brows meeting, and palms pressed against each other, she began to pace the room.

"When I lived in Bethnal there was a woman people went to see if they had an unwanted baby. She'd sort it all out for a payment or some food. There's bound to be someone like that in Calmouth. I can ask around, and since you've got money it shouldn't be too hard to sort."

Estella was appalled. "I'm not doing that!"

"Fine. There are things you can do yourself, but I'm not sure how easy it is. We can get some gin easily enough and I can fill the bath right up with hot water if no one's watching. There's herbs, too, we can find but if we get them wrong it could be dangerous or even kill you, so I think the best way is to see if there's somebody in Calmouth. It's not easy and it's going to hurt, but don't worry; either way, you can get rid of it."

"It's not an *it,* it's a baby! My baby!" Estella cried. She wrapped her arms around her body and glowered at her friend. "I am *not* getting rid of my baby. Absolutely not."

It was incredible, this rush of love she felt for her unborn child. It was primitive and wild and wonderful, and already Estella knew she would do anything to protect it. Jay had sent this baby to comfort her. He loved her now, always and for ever, and now she felt this great love for their child too.

"Oh, bloody hell," said Evie with an eye roll. "This isn't going to be easy …"

Estella had known a difficult path lay ahead for her and Jay, but now she was filled with purpose. There would be whispers and ugly words, but she and Jay had always understood this would be the case because not all folks would see that their love went beyond race and skin tone. They'd dreamed of the children they would have one day, a couple of boys to help on the farm, Jay had thought, and a pretty daughter with her blue eyes and good looks to make him an over-protective father! Estella had thought their dreams were lost for ever, but now she could see a baby in her arms or a chubby toddler running through the garden. Maybe even a five-year-old fishing in a glassy lake with his doting American grandpa? In her best daydream Jay would return; he had been sick in the sanatorium and had lost his memory. He'd be such a kind husband and a proud father. They'd walk hand in hand through the orchard at Millers' Hollow, watching this little one run about and living the life they'd dreamed of …

"What will your pa say?" said Evie, looking worried.

Estella imagined Reginald Kellow would want to kill her with his bare hands.

"I don't care what he says." At least her voice sounded defiant and confident, even if inside she was wobbling like one of Cook's trifles. "He'll have to put up with it."

"Oh yes," said Evie. "I can see that happening, all right. Especially when it comes out black as the ace of spades. He'll be thrilled."

"I don't care. I'm keeping my baby," Estella said, crossing her arms. "We'll just have to think of a way."

"*We?*"

"Yes, *we*. You promised to help and protect me, didn't you? If you really meant it then here's your chance to prove it!"

Evie sat down heavily on the bed. "Of course I meant it. Fine. How far gone are you?"

Estella thought hard. "Two months? Maybe three?"

Evie counted on her fingers. "Baby's due in March. I reckon we can keep it a secret until Christmas. After that it'll be tricky because you'll show, and we'll need a doctor for the birth. Let's hope your father is away on war business and Cook doesn't twig. You'll have to have a sudden relapse of rheumatic fever and stay in bed a lot."

"Will that work?"

Evie grimaced. "It's going to have to, isn't it? What a bloody mess."

"You might be a little more excited, Eves. It's a new life. A whole new person. Tiny, of course, but still here. It's wonderful!"

Evie raised her eyes to the ceiling. "It's a nightmare, more like."

"Not to me," said Estella. "I love him already."

"Oh, bloody hell. And it's a boy, is it?"

It was the strangest thing but as she said this Estella felt a little fizz of something deep inside. It was probably nerves but she liked to think her baby was saying 'Yes! I'm a boy! Hello, Mummy!'

'Hello, you!' she greeted him, silently. 'Hello, baby! Hello little Jay!'

Evie, catching the look on her friend's face, shook her head despairingly. "We'll work something out between us somehow," she said. "I won't let you down again, Stella. I'll do whatever it takes to keep this baby safe. And that's a promise."

CHAPTER 40

Estella
1945

Estella slept on a mattress of soft sand beneath a deep ocean. Her head pillowed by weed, she drifted with the tides and floated away the hours where it was warm and still and safe. Occasionally she caught snatches of conversations, but the voices bore little meaning in her watery existence. Sometimes gentle hands raised her head and held a glass to her lips, but her eyes were too heavy to open and the current of lassitude too strong to resist. Life above the surface felt little more than a dream. She didn't know how long she slumbered but as the darkness began to retreat and the ocean seeped away, she was beached on a strange shore. Something was wrong. Very wrong.

Panic knifed Estella into wakefulness. She kicked the weeds away and broke for the surface. Her hands felt for the dome of her stomach, magical home to the doubling of self, but felt only loose flesh.

The baby was gone. He had left her.

Terrified, she tried to sit up, but there was no strength in her body. Floundering and desperately striking for shore, Estella thrashed her limbs against the sheets. The room was out of focus and her heart thudded against her ribs.

He wasn't here! Her baby was missing!

Estella's stomach was free falling; the little passenger beneath her heart had disembarked.

"Where is he? What have you done with him? Where's my baby?"

Her voice was a croak. How long had it been since she'd spoken?

"Evie?" Estella whispered. "Evie? Where are you? Where's my baby?"

But the room was empty. Evie wasn't there.

Estella blinked against brightness of a sun-filled window. Rose-pink curtains hung from a gilt pole, plump cushions were strewn across the window seat, and the bed was a vast four poster affair. This was Violet's old boudoir! Why was she here? Estella could even smell the lingering notes of her sweet perfume and she shivered. Was Violet's sad ghost lingering too? Her hand stole to touch Jay's crucifix for comfort, but it was no longer around her neck. Like her baby, it had vanished.

Estella cried out in distress. Why was she here? Where was her baby? What had happened to him? Was he dead? Was she dead? Was this Hell? It must be, for being ripped away from her precious one was the cruellest torment.

"What did I do that was so wrong?" she whispered, and her voice was as soft as the sucking of shingle in the shallows. "All I did was fall in love."

There was no answer and the room began to spin. Estella sank into the pillow. Overcome by despair, she longed for the whispering sea to call her back and pull her under once again. In the pink caves of her eyelids she could relive what little she remembered of the time before. She had to piece the memory fragments together, otherwise something would be lost. Her hand fluttered to her belly but there was no joyful somersaulting or butterfly hands pressing against her flesh. Where was the baby? Think, she told herself. Think!

The secret pregnancy and keeping Jay's baby. That was the link. That was the start. Go back to the very beginning.

In her naïvety Estella had thought it would be easy to conceal her pregnancy. Who at Pencallyn really noticed what she did? Cook was sharp-eyed, but she was worried about her nephews and was busy running the house with a skeleton staff. Tommy had been sent to Egypt and was unlikely to return. Reginald Kellow was increasingly busy in London. Dolly had recently joined the WVS – but Jenny and Beth might twig if Estella came down to breakfast and threw up. As it turned out Jenny's husband was killed in Normandy and she left Pencallyn House to return home, followed shortly by Beth who was, Cook whispered, 'in the family way'.

"I dread to think how many silly girls have got themselves into trouble thanks to those American boys," she tutted. "Not the sense they were born with! They deserve all they get, if you ask me."

"*Nobody* did, actually," snapped Evie, and Cook brandished a wooden spoon at her.

"Don't think I'm not keeping an eye on you too, young lady!"

Evie and Estella exchanged a look, both thankful Cook's beady eye was trained on the wrong girl. Estella was already wearing her skirts loosened, and her breasts felt twice the size. So far nobody had noticed and her absence from the breakfast table had been explained by Evie snatching a couple of slices of bread and cheese and saying they were starting work early in the kitchen garden. By the time the harvest was in, Estella was over the morning sickness and wanting to eat everything in sight. Once the autumn arrived baggy jumpers and slacks concealed her belly and with the growing tensions in Europe there were more important things to focus on.

Estella cherished the time when the baby was her and Evie's secret. She loved telling him about his father and Millers' Hollow. America became her promised land, and Estella whispered stories about lakes as big as oceans and wheat which rippled like an inland sea. Estella vowed she would go there and do all the things she and Jay had dreamed of when they lay in each another's arms listening to the rain pattering on the old slate roof.

Many times, Estella began a letter to Jay's parents but she was never able to get beyond the first two lines. How could she tell them she feared their son was dead? They deserved to hear news like that in person rather than in a letter. Her hope was that when the war was over and she presented them with their grandson – for Estella was certain her baby would be a boy with his father's heart-stopping smile and beautiful dark eyes – there would at least be some joy within the sorrow. She would put her letter aside and rest her hand on her belly, whispering to the baby how much he was loved and wanted.

As excited as she was about her baby, Estella was sad too. It was astonishing to feel the baby move and see the outline of a heel press against her belly. How she wished she could have shown Jay. He would have shared her joy and held her when she was afraid. As a medic he would have been able to explain everything. As her lover he could comfort her and soothe her fears. She and Evie gleaned their scant knowledge from books, and Evie's old life in the East End, where women regularly gave birth without medical intervention, but it would have been reassuring to have spoken to an expert.

One afternoon, before she became too ungainly to manage the steep and narrow staircase, Estella ventured into Pencallyn's attic. When she and Alex had been younger this dusty space had been a place of wonder. Filled with treasure, to their eyes at least, the attic had been a new kingdom to explore. They raided the boxes of old clothes for dressing up and made dens out of moth-nibbled blankets and ancient tent poles. Once Evie had come to Pencallyn, the attic enjoyed a renaissance as the girls played there when ceaseless rain drummed upon the roof and the whole garden drooped beneath the onslaught of a gale.

Estella hadn't set foot inside the attic for a long time, but it was the perfect place to hunt for baby clothes. She wasn't disappointed, and when she staggered back down the stairs her arms were piled high. There was an old Moses basket and a beautiful blue blanket that must have belonged to Alex. She wondered who had put all these things up here; had her mother carried them up and lovingly put them aside as treasured mementos? Or had one of the nursery staff been dispatched to attend to the task? Estella felt sad she would never know. As the baby in her belly grew, so did Estella's need to talk to her own mother.

She rested her hand on her rounded stomach.

"I'll always be there for you," she whispered to the baby. "I love you now, always and for ever."

As the months progressed and Estella slowed down, Evie became more resourceful. Her acting skills were utilised when she dressed as Estella and headed into Calmouth when there was official business to do with solicitors and the bank. When Reginald Kellow came home, she was so convincing in her description of the stomach flu Estella had contracted that even Estella almost believed she was ill. It was utter bliss to have a week in bed without the need to pretend she was anything other than heavy and slow. Luckily her hair and skin glowed, and her bump was neat and small, but Estella hated deceiving anyone.

But as she approached her eighth month Estella began to realise the grand plan hadn't gone beyond concealing her pregnancy. Hiding a birth and a baby was something very different. Estella had read voraciously in order to prepare herself but the more she learned the more she realised two young girls wouldn't be able to manage alone. They needed help.

They needed adults.

"I saw lots of women give birth when I lived in Bethnal," Evie said defensively when Estella raised the topic. "I know what happens."

"So do I," Estella replied. She'd seen enough foals and puppies born to have a fair idea about the mechanics, but this was something else altogether. "Won't we need a midwife? Or a doctor?"

"How can we get one of those? The secret will be well and truly out. No, we're going to have to deliver the baby ourselves. We'll need towels and hot water and other stuff."

"Other stuff? Like what, exactly?"

"Oh Lord, Stell! Carbolic soap? Baby clothes? Antiseptic? Linen clouts? And you'll have to keep the noise down if it happens in the day. We can't have Cook thinking you're being murdered."

"This won't work. I'm going to need a midwife," Estella said, chewing her thumbnail. Her stomach was turning itself inside out, and the baby was jigging about in unison.

"You can't have one. We have to do this alone, remember? If we tell anyone they're bound to split on us – and then what?"

"What if there's a problem and something goes wrong? I don't think we can keep the birth secret, Evie. We can't hide a baby! And what if my father comes back home?"

Evie looked troubled. "The baby will be here by then. It'll be too late for him to do anything."

Estella's felt a cold stone of fear sink right down to her toes. Reginald Kellow would no more accept a fait accompli than he would accept a mixed-race grandchild. She clutched Evie's arm in terror. "He'll make me give the baby up. You know he will. He'll have it taken away from me.

Don't let him take my baby away, Evie! Don't let him!"

"Of course I won't! I promise I'll never let your father anywhere near your baby!" Evie said staunchly. "I'll die first!"

Estella, thinking wildly, said, "I'll go to America and have the baby there, at Millers' Hollow. Jay's parents will take me in." At least she hoped they would. What if they were as horrified by the idea of her as Reginald would be at the notion of Jay? Then what would she do?

"Don't be so ridiculous," Evie said. "You're eight months gone. There's no way you can travel to America. Besides, in case you hadn't noticed there's a war on. Ships are being torpedoed in the Atlantic. It's far too dangerous."

Evie was right; it was. Although Estella longed to flee there was no way she would risk the baby's life.

"So, what do we do?"

"Is there anyone we could go to? Anyone you trust?"

Estella thought hard. "No."

"Godparents? Aunties?"

"None that I can think of."

"Bugger," said Evie. "We'll have to come up with something ourselves. Somewhere you can go to have the baby. We could swap names and pretend you're me. I'll go into town and see if anyone knows where Beth went to have her baby. That might help us make a plan."

Evie's trip to Calmouth paid off, because she had managed to find two of Beth's fellow land girls. Over afternoon tea she discovered Beth had gone to Lockett Hall near Bristol, which had been sequestered as a maternity hospital. Beth had apparently worked for her keep – unlike the wealthy young ladies who had gone there to rest before and after giving birth. Most of these mothers went on to give their babies up since they had been born in secret. The idea of doing this would break Estella's heart. She couldn't imagine how awful giving up your child would be. It would kill her.

"Never," she promised her own baby silently. "I will never give you up."

"You've got the money to do this," Evie told Estella.

"I have if I sell a few pieces of jewellery."

"Sod that," Evie said. "I know where your pa hides his cash. I'll make sure we get some. It's the least the old bastard can do after the way he's treated everyone. All you need to do is say we're going away to visit an old school friend. Nobody will ask too many questions here. Then once we're safe, I could be the one who gives birth according to any records, so nobody will trace you."

Estella was thinking as fast as she could. Lately any kind of cognition felt like wading through treacle.

"And afterwards?"

"Afterwards we'll write to Jay's parents and find a way of getting you to

America. This war can't go on much longer, surely? Everyone says Hitler's been on the run since D-Day."

It wasn't the greatest of plans, but it was better than nothing and Estella had been reassured. As soon as Christmas was over, she and Evie would pack up and catch the train to Bristol. After this the plan was a little hazy but Estella was beyond caring about logistics and details. All that mattered was making sure her baby was born safely. Once he was in her arms, she would work out the rest.

Now, frightened and alone, Estella stared up at the ceiling of Violet's bedroom and felt overcome by this deluge of memories. These events had been mere weeks ago but already felt as though they belonged to another lifetime. Her heart clenched with pity for the two girls who naïvely believed they could conceal a pregnancy, plan a birth and a passage to America. They were little more than children themselves, and the whole venture had the feel of one of their old games. It was Mysterious Garden played for higher stakes than they could have ever dreamed. Their confidence in their plan and Estella's determination to contact Jay's family had turned out to be their undoing.

It was such a silly mistake to make, but as the weeks passed, and her time grew closer, Estella had grown increasingly frantic. It was all very well for Evie to tell her everything would be fine, but nebulous reassurances were no longer enough. The baby, somersaulting and dancing inside her, needed more than vague hopes; he needed structure and certainty. He needed grandparents. He needed a home. He needed family.

Estella had fetched paper and ink and written once again to the Millers. Her pen flew across the page as she told them how proud they ought to be of their son, but stalled a little as she attempted to break the news of Jay's disappearance. In the end she simply said she was having Jay's baby, due in late January, and very much hoped they would be pleased. Then she addressed the envelope, tucked the letter inside and placed it on the table on the hall for Evie to post when she next went into Calmouth.

This was her big mistake.

Perhaps the strain of concealing her pregnancy and the exhaustion accompanying the final months had stopped her thinking clearly. A letter like this should have been handed to Evie, not left lying around for anyone to come across. What had taken place next was still hazy, but Estella did recall her father bursting into the kitchen later that evening.

"Slut," he spat. "Filthy little slut."

He yanked Estella from her seat and shook her like a rag doll. As he showered her with vile insults, she knew denying the truth was pointless; her sweater strained against her distended belly and her condition was obvious.

Cook's hand flew to her mouth. "Oh, my goodness!"

"So, it's true," Reginald Kellow spat, holding Estella at arm's length as though she disgusted him. "With Miller? You're carrying a half-breed? I should fling you onto the streets and let you starve."

"Daddy, please —" Estella began, but Reginald Kellow shook her even harder. Her plea only enraged him further.

"You're no daughter of mine!" he snarled as he thrust her from him. "You disgust me."

Estella lurched forwards and the toe of her shoe caught in the uneven flooring, pitching her with full force onto the stone. Immediately a white-hot sword sliced through her belly and she doubled up as the blade stabbed her again and again. She could hear an awful screaming, a dreadful sound which was torn from the soul, but it was a while before she understood that this keening came from her. Cocooned in a world of pain, all Estella could do was clutch her belly and ride out each wave of agony.

Cook was at Estella's side. "It's all right, Miss! Keep calm. I'll send for Dr Trevenna."

"You will do no such thing," Reginald Kellow said, and his voice seemed to come from far, far away. "There'll be no doctors called to Pencallyn. Not a word of this is to be spoken outside of this house. I don't want her shame tainting our good name."

"But she needs help, Sir!" Cook pleaded.

"No doctors," Reginald Kellow repeated coldly. "And if so much as a word of this is mentioned beyond these walls then you and your husband will find yourself without positions. Do I make myself clear, Mrs Tullis?"

"Yes, sir," whispered Cook. "Very."

"Good. Get her upstairs, will you? I can't stand the sight of her."

Through a haze of pain Estella watched her father's brogues step away. The kitchen floor was cool against her cheek and she wanted to close her eyes and sleep. She felt as though she would never move again, that she would die from the terrible pain that was slicing her in two. Cook tried to haul her to her feet but to no avail, and as the pain grew worse the room began to telescope in.

"Jay," Estella sobbed. "Jay! Where are you?"

But there was no answer – and after that there was nothing …

She frowned. There must have been something else, because her baby was gone and since the sun shining through the window was higher and brighter than before, some time must had passed. Estella heaved herself up onto her elbows, wincing at the dragging pain in her abdomen, and cleared her throat.

"Evie? Evie? Where are you?"

Her voice was a croak, but somebody heard and the bedroom door opened. Estella's heart lifted briefly before she saw her father leaning against the door jamb. His eyes were narrowed, and so cruel that she shrank back.

"Where's Evie?"

"Don't waste your breath. She's gone."

Estella stared at him, not understanding. "Gone where?"

Reginald Kellow stepped into the room and loomed over her. His face was so close Estella could see the tributaries of broken veins across his cheeks and each wiry grey hair in his eyebrows. His loathing was palpable.

"To the devil for all I care. She's deceived me in this matter too, and run away with Violet's pearls. When the police catch up with her, Evie Jenkins will swing. She's just another of your stepmother's foolish mistakes and, as I always say, bad blood will out."

"Evie wouldn't do that. She wouldn't leave me," Estella whispered. She looked over her father's shoulder, expecting to glimpse her friend in the corridor, because there was no way Evie would abandon her. Evie wouldn't break her promise.

"She left without a backward glance. You could have bled to death while you birthed your bastard, but Evie Jenkins couldn't have cared less. She didn't stick around to know whether you lived or died. She's gone, just like your worthless Miller," Reginald Kellow's gloating voice was laced with cruelty. "Where are they now when you need them most? Gone. Like your son."

Estella's brain was whirling. She wanted to turn on the searchlight in her memory, for how could she have had her baby without remembering? Her arms ached to hold him and her heart, already broken, was in smithereens.

"Where's my baby?"

Reginald Kellow ignored her question.

"Evie Jenkins didn't care you could have bled to death. She simply saw an opportunity to rob us when our backs were turned. Just as Miller used you like the slut you are. You're a fool, Estella. Miss Toms was wrong; your intellect is nothing to be proud of."

Estella knew he was aiming to wound her – it was what her father always did. Jay had truly loved her, of this she had no doubt, and so did Evie. And as for Evie using Estella's illness as an excuse to steal? This made no sense for Evie could have robbed the Kellows any time she chose. She knew where the money was kept. She knew the combinations to safes. She knew everything.

She always had.

"What's happened to me?" Estella said. "Papa, please! Where's my baby?"

He studied her for a moment and then shrugged.

"You went into labour and apparently the birth nearly killed you. You lost a lot of blood and then you had a fever. Mrs Tullis took it upon herself to fetch a midwife – she's been dismissed for that – and the midwife thought you'd die. It might have been better if you had, than live with this shame, but she'll keep your secret, no doubt, and they've both been well paid to keep their mouths shut. Nobody will know about your bastard."

Poor Cook had been dismissed for trying to help her? Estella tried to swing her legs out of the bed, wincing at the dragging pain in her abdomen and collapsing against the pillow once more. She felt so dreadfully weak and so very afraid.

"You said I had a son. Where is he? What have you done with my baby? Who's looking after him?" Her heart began to beat wildly. "I want to see him!"

Reginald Kellow ignored her.

"Once Miller had what he wanted, he deserted just like the coward he is. It's as I always said: his kind have no morals and no backbone. He slunk away like a rat. Just like Evie. You're abandoned. You're soiled goods, Estella, and I'm ashamed to have a daughter like you."

Estella's hands were tight fists beneath the counterpane. Jay was true and brave and honourable, but she would not rise to her father's taunts. She'd seen him do this before to Violet, and what he wanted was a reaction. Reginald Kellow relished seeing his barbs meet their target. She had to be smarter than him because she was no longer just fighting for herself. Estella uncurled her right fist and studied the thin whisper of a scar etched on her palm. This was as real as Jay's love. She had to hold onto this knowledge. Theirs was a love so real it had become a child, and nothing mattered more than the baby.

Their baby meant *everything.*

Estella raised her chin. She was a mother. A parent. Reginald Kellow held no authority over her. He was a vindictive and bitter man who bullied women and servants. His cruel words would bounce off her. Her heart swelled with such love for her child she could barely hear the words he continued to hurl at her. They were bubbles of sound popping to nothingness like the soap bubbles she and Evie used to blow in the garden. Harmless. These words couldn't hurt her because no matter what her father might say, what lies he told, she knew that Evie, like Jay, wouldn't willingly abandon her. She would be waiting nearby or have gone to fetch help. Evie would sooner die than break her promise, and this knowledge filled Estella with courage.

"I'd rather have Jay and Evie as my friends than a father like you," she said. "I'm proud of them and I'm proud of my child. I will never regret him. Never. He's everything to me."

Her father did not reply. Encouraged by his silence, Estella pressed on.

"I want to see him now. I need to see my baby."

Reginald exhaled and gave her a thin smile.

"Very well. When you're dressed, I'll take you to see him. Make sure you wear your coat and hat."

"My coat and hat? Why do I need those?" Estella asked, confused.

Her father's eyes glittered with malice and, too late, she realised she had blundered right into his trap. Their conversation had been nothing more than a cruel game of chess.

"Because it'll be cold in the graveyard," Reginald Kellow said.

CHAPTER 41

Nell
The Present

Estella's eyes close but her whispered words hang in the air like the trail made in the sky by sparklers.

It's some tale. My own skills as a writer pale into insignificance in comparison to the story woven by Estella Kellow, but what else would I expect from the author of *Mysterious Garden*? Love, hate, jealously, bigotry, betrayal, lust, anger, revenge; the full gamut of emotions is woven through her story and the intricacies of character and plot crafted with a dexterity I dream of. I can picture Calmouth and Pencallyn as they once were, and so vividly; I'll never view these places in the same way again. I will always see them through her eyes. Dead Man's Wood. Bury Barrow. Pencallyn army camp. The Richardsons' farmhouse. The tangled garden. The old school-house where Jay Miller dressed Estella's hand. I glance down and a lump fills my throat when I see how her open fingers reveal a palm traced with the faintest scar of a long-ago wound.

I wait for Estella to say more, to tell me her father was lying, and the baby lived. Was her little boy secreted away with a woman in the village? Ivy Pendriscott who had so loved Jay? Or the loyal Mrs Tullis? Perhaps Evie stormed into Pencallyn and told Estella it was all lies? I am avid for more, and my hands grip the side rails of the hospital bed.

But Estella doesn't speak. This pause doesn't mean anything, I tell myself. There have been plenty of these already, and her narrative has been punctuated with intervals where she slipped into sleep. Each time she wakes Estella picks up a thread of her tale and follows it through to weave a different pattern, or unravels it to reveal an unexpected knot. The afternoon has wandered by in tandem with the meandering of Estella's story, and I'm not ready for the story to end. I pour water from the plastic jug and hold the glass to her lips when her voice cracks. I smooth the sheet when she clutches it in her sleep. I sit beside her and listen.

In keeping with her fragmenting memory, Estella's narrative arrives in pieces. Snatches of past events blow through her recollection as the seeds from a dandelion clock are scattered by the wind. I can't catch them, but I watch where they settle and wait to see if anything will grow. What is fact and what is confusion it's hard to tell at times, and when she dozes I wonder whether she's travelling back in time to check a detail or ask a long-lost friend to remind her about something. I watch her frail chest rise and fall, and hope she's in Jay's arms or running through the garden with Evie. Where do we go when we dream? What shadowlands do we inhabit?

I have cobbled together a collage fashioned from memories and now I'm starting to build a design which makes sense. With every twist and turn of the tale I've felt more and more convinced Jay Miller must be my grandfather. and at one point it seemed Estella could be my grandmother. Excitement cartwheeled in my stomach at this. I have family. Blood family. Here in this room is my own grandmother! I know where I come from! I know why I write stories. Why I have blue eyes. Why I feel drawn to this place. Why Dad loved gardening and boats. I have the answers to the questions my father had never managed to ask before his time ran out. I have the last pieces to complete the puzzle of who Sam and Nell Summers really are.

Or I'd thought I did until Estella said her baby had died. Now I'm adrift again.

I uncurl my hand from the rail and take hers. The bones are bird-frail and the skin little more than tissue paper blotted with inky bruises.

"What happened to your baby, Estella? He didn't really die, did he?"

Her eyes flicker open. They are milky with age but the grief in them is as sharp as it was when she was a young girl. I recognise that raw and biting misery; it is the pain of a mother without her child.

"He died, Nell," she says and so softly I lean forward to catch her words. "He didn't survive the birth, and I nearly died too. Massive blood loss, or so they told me. There was no doctor, you see, and the midwife was no more than some wise woman brought in from Bodmin Moor. Cook had gone, and the girls and Evie too. There was no one else to tend us."

Grief corsets my throat. "He really died? You're certain?" So Estella's *not* my grandmother? And Jay Miller is nothing to do with Sam Summers? If these links are nothing more than projection on my part, then it's as though I've been bereaved anew. Grief-stricken and lost, I've chosen to see what I wanted to see and have made connections where none exist. Maybe Lou was right; I need counselling, not a wild goose chase.

A tear trickles down Estella's wrinkled cheek.

"I'm afraid so, my dear. He's buried at the edge of St Brecca's churchyard. There were no proper burials for illegitimate children then, so my little one sleeps all alone and just into hallowed ground. My father's influence was able to grant him that at least."

"That's awful!"

"It was a different time. People saw illegitimacy as a shame on the whole family. You must know how many girls in my situation had to give their babies up."

I nod. I've read countless records and listened to recordings of elderly ladies weeping as they relive the desperate choices they were forced to make. My father's own mother, whoever she was, must have been one such woman.

"But the Church shouldn't have punished you," I say helplessly. I hate to think of the young Estella I've come to know trailing sadly through the tangled garden to sit by an unmarked grave and weep for her lost child. It enrages me she couldn't have the dignity of a proper funeral.

Then I wonder – is it really Estella I'm angry for, or is my anger about my own loss?

"It was complicated in those days. My father controlled the living of the parish," Estella explains. "The rector wouldn't have wanted to defy him. Goodness, I had a hard enough time persuading the next incumbent to allow a small memorial for Violet, and my father had been dead a good while by then. He was a powerful man and people feared him. My baby has a special place full of wildflowers and butterflies. I like to believe Nature looks after him even if I can't."

I recall to my visit to the church with Josh. It feels as though it took place a very long time ago.

"I saw Violet's memorial. And I think I saw the place where your baby's buried. Is it at the far side? By the footpath?"

"It is. I used to walk up from Pencallyn and visit him all the time, but it became harder as I grew older. I hope he doesn't wonder where I went." Another tear slides down her cheek. "I hope he doesn't think I've forgotten him. I promise not a day's passed when I haven't thought of him or his father. I've missed them every moment of my life."

"It's a beautiful spot," is all I can say.

"I think so too. But I didn't see it on the day my father told me my child had died. The shock must have been too much, because I don't remember anything after that. I was very ill, and I didn't want to carry on for a long, long time. I couldn't believe Jay and Evie had left me and that I'd lost my baby too. Life seemed too cruel to bear."

"I sometimes think so too," I say, and my own tears fall now as I let myself grieve for my father and the precious baby I never held. "Life hurts too much. It is too much. How can we ever bear it when everything is so painful?"

Estella Kellow squeezes my hand.

"My dear Nell, life is a precious gift. Every second is to be lived. I'm old, my time is at an end, but I have been so blessed to have had this long."

"Blessed? But Estella, you lost Jay. You believe he was murdered. You lost your baby. Evie went away. Violet died. Your brother. Your parents. So many losses. How did you bear it? How is all that loss a blessing?"

"I was blessed to have known them at all," she replies. "Yes, sometimes life feels impossibly hard and you don't know if you can bear another second – but trust me, each second is a gift. To have loved, and to know true love, is the biggest blessing we can ever receive, and I would live every moment of pain a thousand times over for a second of the joy of loving Jay Miller and knowing he loved me in return. Oh, Nell, don't you see? Love and loss go hand in hand. Each only becomes real when holding onto the other, and pain is the currency we pay for happiness. You're young and there's a wonderful life ahead of you, my dear. One day you'll be old like me, and what more can you ask than to know that you loved and were loved in return? What more can any of us want?"

Estella's right. I mustn't let love slip through my fingers like water. If I find it, and I think I have, I must be brave enough to recognise it.

"Nothing more than that," I say.

"Love takes many forms. I loved Evie. I loved Tommy, who came back to look after me and saved me from despair. I loved Cook too – and, once my father had passed away, she and Bert returned to us at Pencallyn House and stayed until they died. Love is always here, Nell, and often found where you least expect it. Sometimes it arrives when you're not looking for it. But you've already discovered that, haven't you?"

I wipe my eyes with the heel of my hand. Estella's right. I loved my father and I loved my baby. I loved Andy too, and I love him still as a part of my journey. There's Lou and Antonio. My writing. There are new friends waiting to be made, and Josh Richardson with his warm green eyes and shy smile.

Perhaps. Either way, Estella's right; life is a gift and one denied to so many young men and women of her generation. My father lived to the full, and although he knew pain and sadness he still brimmed over with love and kindness.

For the first time in longer than I can remember I feel lighter. I feel hopeful. My journey to find my family may have come to a dead end, but maybe this doesn't really matter?

Estella falls asleep again and I sit quietly, checking my phone. It's been on silent all day, and a heap of emails and messages clamour for attention. There's an email from my agent asking after the progress of my book, which I think I'll reply to later since I haven't touched my novel for days, and a WhatsApp from Lou asking me to call her when I'm free. There's also a text from Josh, apologising for not being at the hospital. Apparently, there's an issue at the site and he can't leave.

'It's fine. I'll catch a bus back,' I type, and moments later the phone vibrates with his reply.

'Catch a cab and come to the farm as soon as you can. It's important x'

He's signed his message off with a kiss and I feel ridiculously pleased. Nell Summers, I scold myself as I slide the phone back into my satchel, you're acting like a fifteen-year-old with crush!

"Nell?"

Estella's awake but her voice is weaker.

"I'm still here, Estella."

"As am I," she murmurs. "For now. So, where were we?"

"Evie disappeared when you'd given birth," I prompt. "What happened to her?"

She sighs. "I never saw her again. She never wrote or contacted me. I always expected her to come back. She'd promised to be my sister and I knew she didn't take that vow lightly. I often thought I might see her on the screen or the stage, but as far as I know she never became an actress. I even went to Bethnal Green, but her old home had been flattened in the Blitz and nobody I spoke to had heard of her. Evie Jenkins just vanished."

"I can't believe she would have left you."

Estella's mouth trembles. A lifetime on, the loss is still painful.

"My father said she had stolen jewellery and maybe she had. She took my crucifix."

Oh! The necklace!

I reach to my neck and unfasten the crucifix. I've no idea how it found its way to Dad, but I do know where it belongs. I place it in Estella's hand, the silver chain caressing the silver scar, and she closes her fingers around it with a cry of joy.

"I never thought to see this again, and after all this time! How wonderful! Where did you find this?"

"It was left with my father at the hospital."

"With your father? How very odd."

"I know. How did he come to have it and those pictures? Who was the young woman who took him to Bristol? Was that woman Evie?"

"I don't know, Nell," Estella says wearily. "I don't understand it."

"Did Evie have a GI boyfriend too? Could my father have been her child?"

Estella regards me with frustration.

"Maybe? Who can say? All I know is that she ran away. She left me and it was the hardest time of my life. I didn't think I'd get through it."

I squeeze her fingers. "But you did."

"Yes. Tommy came back and helped me through the darkest time. My father lost his seat after the war and he took to drink. He drowned, you know, in the Japanese garden, and I often think he meant to do it. He was a man who'd done some dark things and he'd fallen into huge debt and he seemed haunted by his past misdeeds. I used to hear him yelling at people I couldn't see, and it scared me half to death, although it was just the drink."

Even though the hospital room is hot, I shiver.

"I inherited everything, of course," Estella says, "but there was no money left. That was when Tommy suggested I should publish *Mysterious Garden.* It was a success, as you know, but the rest of my story is quite dull. I suppose I became what people call a recluse. I didn't want to leave Pencallyn."

"Wasn't it painful there with all those memories?" I said this because I couldn't wait to leave the house Andy and I had shared. I didn't dare open the door to the room we'd so hopefully called the nursery. When I shut the front door for the last time it was with a huge sensation of relief.

"Pencallyn's my home. I'm part of the place. It's made me who I am, and it's a world of imagination and of dreams and hopes. Nightmares too sometimes – but you learn to live with those. Yes, I have let the gardens go, and in that decision there may have been a little bit of petty revenge because it would have pained my father. But if I weren't to live at Pencallyn, where would I go?"

"America? Millers' Hollow? You must have made enough money to travel the world."

"Ah, but wherever you go you always take yourself with you," she says. "Besides, what was there for me at Millers' Hollow without Jay? I was closer to him here, and my baby was sleeping beneath the grass at St Brecca's. How could I abandon my little one? I always had a tiny hope Jay might return, that Hamilton had locked him away somewhere and he would escape and come back for me, but deep down I knew this was no more than a dream. Anyhow, I'd promised I would wait for him, so I have. How could I break my promise?"

"Now, always and for ever," I murmur, and Estella smiles.

"Of course. I found my soulmate, Nell, even if it was for a short time. How lucky am I to have known such love! Don't be sad, my dear; Jay and my baby are waiting for me. It won't be long before I see them again. I'm not afraid."

I take her hand. "They're going to set your hip. You'll get better and there's still time to find out more. There's lots of things we can try. We'll find out how the crucifix reached Bristol. I'll trace Evie. I'll tell you what happened."

"No," she says. "Not now. There's no need."

Her eyelids flutter shut. The skin is translucent, revealing the delicate green and blue mapwork of the veins beneath, and heartbreakingly fragile.

"I'm so tired, Evie," she murmurs. "It's been a long day and I'm tired. Let me sleep a little. We'll play later."

Her breathing slows. I kiss her soft cheek and brush wisps of white hair from her face. Estella's hand still clasps Jay's crucifix. Seeing it there comforts me. It's as though a part of Jay is here too, watching over Estella during her final hours.

"You rest," I tell her. "You'll have all the time in the world for playing soon."

She's asleep, her dreams transporting her back to a time when she was young and in love and happy. The last chapter is almost told.

Estella Kellow's story is drawing to an end.

CHAPTER 42

Nell
The Present

"May I have a quick word?"

One of Estella's doctors, an older man with kind eyes, stops me in the corridor.

"Michael Yeale, lead orthopaedic surgeon." He holds out his hand and I shake it. "And you are … ?"

I try to decide what I am to Estella. "Nell Summers. I'm a family friend."

"Ah, yes. I understand Miss Kellow doesn't have any family, but I've seen you visiting her with your partner."

I flush. "You mean Josh Richardson. He's her neighbour."

"She's very fond of you both," Yeale says. He pushes his glasses up his nose with a forefinger and smiles, a sympathetic smile born of experience and which says he understands what he is about to disclose won't be easy. "I wanted you to know we've made a decision to set Estella's hip tomorrow."

"Isn't that risky?"

"At her age and with her heart condition, I'm afraid so, but she's done very well this far. In fact, she's exceeded all our expectations."

I think about the stories Estella has shared with me. A sickly child who survived rheumatic fever. A brave girl who tried to save an injured enemy. A young woman who defied convention and an abusive father to be with the man she loved. An elderly lady who cherishes the memories of her lost loves. She's brave and tenacious, and I'm honoured to know her.

"She's an incredible person," I say, close to tears. "A real fighter."

"Indeed she is, and she deserves a chance to have her hip put right. We certainly can't leave her like this indefinitely. I plan to set it tomorrow, theatre space willing and all that, but I must warn you the procedure isn't without risk. She may develop an infection, or the operation could be too great a strain on her heart." He pauses to allow the matter-of-fact words to sink in. "So I'm afraid you need to be prepared for the worst."

"I'm not sure I know how to do that," I say, and the consultant sighs.

"No," he says. "I don't think anyone does."

I leave the hospital and step into the warm sunlight of the late afternoon. I'm dazed, as though I have awoken from a long and heavy sleep, and the world feels as though it's rushing by at a pace I cannot comprehend. Estella's story hangs over me like the remnants of a vivid dream which on waking feels more tangible than reality. As with a traveller in time, catapulted forwards from 1945, the world outside her narrative seems too loud and terribly bright. Cars are fast. People are loud. Time is racing by. The world seems to have sped up.

Estella Kellow's time is running out. The lapses between the snatches of retelling have stretched out, elongating with the pools of sunshine seeping across the floor of the hospital room. I have seen her strength fade and her attempts to step over the cracks in her mind become more distressing. She stumbles frequently, grasping for names or words, and I'm afraid I might never find her again. The sinkholes of her memory will collapse and take Estella with them. Not only Estella but also Evie and Jay and Hamilton and all the others, names long forgotten, and faces erased by time, but people who can't be lost so long as she remembers.

Stories keep people alive. Estella has passed her story on to me, a fellow storyteller, and the people from her past live on in my imagination. I'm not sure what I will do with them, or what I've achieved by coming to Pencallyn, but I know there's more to be written and a narrative link I can't see. I need to work out what this is, and I need to do it quickly.

A cab pulls up outside the hospital and I hop in. My head is full of Estella's story, and as the car crawls through the early evening traffic I lean back against the seat and close my eyes. I must have drifted into a doze because when my phone buzzes from the depths of my satchel it makes me jump. It's Lou calling. Fascinated by what I've told her of Estella's story so far, she's probably dying to know what else I've found out.

"Didn't you get my message?" Lou demands when I answer. "I've been staring at the phone waiting for you to call. I thought I'd combust!"

"And hello to you too," I say mildly. "I've been in the hospital visiting Estella."

"Oh yes, of course. How is she?"

I stare out the window at the undulating road and soft swell of fields on either side. The car climbs up out of the town, and behind me I catch a glimpse of blue water and endless horizon. Ships sailed over that horizon carrying young men, so many of them who would never return. Some didn't deserve to return and took their dark secrets with them …

"Nell? Are you still there?"

I tug my thoughts back to the present.

"Yes, sorry. I was thinking. She's tired, Lou, and so weak. I don't think it'll be long now."

"I'm sorry, Nell. I know you're fond of her. Did you manage to find out anything more?"

"A little."

"Anything about Jay Miller? Has she mentioned him?"

All my life I've told Lou everything. We don't keep secrets from one another, but I do need to keep Estella's story to myself just a little longer. Pencallyn House and the people of the past are so real I want to keep them this way until I've had time to untangle the threads and see what sense I can make of everything.

"Yes," I say eventually. "He was based here. Estella knew him."

"Oh my God! I knew it! She must have had his baby! Sam was their child!"

"No. That's not possible."

"Yes, it is. That's why I've been desperate to talk to you. Don't be mad at me, babes, but your Heritage DNA test results came back today, and I couldn't help myself – I had to open them."

"Lou!"

"I know, I know," she says sheepishly. "I shouldn't have looked, but I thought I'd pop! I had to see so I could tell you. I'll scan the whole thing in and email it over when I'm home. Guess what it says?"

"That I'm of African descent mixed with Caucasian? I can look in the mirror and tell that."

"No, that's not it. Obviously that information is there with all kinds of percentages – you're 6% or something Italian too – but that isn't what I wanted to say." I hear a rustle of paper. "The Heritage team give you the details of other people related to you and are already working on their family trees so you can link up and get started. It's all about sharing research, apparently, but you won't believe this!"

"What? What won't I believe?"

Lou pauses. She loves a theatrical moment.

"Tell me!"

She giggles. "OK! I won't keep you in suspense. There's loads of Americans listed for you to contact, and they're all looking to research into their family trees. Tonnes of them, Nell, with the surname Miller! It's all there in black and white, no doubts whatsoever! You *are* related to Jay Miller because now you've got the DNA evidence. He has to be your grandfather and if you wanted to find family, I'd say you've hit the mother lode, girlfriend!"

I can't speak.

"There's Casey Miller Johnson from Illinois, Trey Miller Junior from Chicago, Michelle Miller from Pennsylvania," Lou is reeling off names from a list. "Trenton Miller the third from New York State – and those are just a few! Your grandfather had lots of relatives. Christmas might get expensive!"

I don't understand what I'm hearing. It's impossible.

"But Jay Miller died without children."

"Except he didn't, did he? You're related to him through Sam. I'm staring at the evidence," says Lou. "Jay Miller has to be your grandpa, and I bet when you start to go through some of these others, some'll turn out to be cousins."

I'm beyond confused. Surely Estella would have known if Jay'd had children, and from what she's told me he wasn't the type to play the field.

"It's not possible."

"It is," Lou insists. "Unless by weird chance another Miller relative happened to come by the UK and have a baby in 1945? Which I think we can agree is even more unlikely. You're Jay Miller's granddaughter, and he must have had a child. It's the only explanation.

"Estella Kellow told me today she did have a baby with Jay Miller but the baby died," I say. The words knife me each time but Lou gives a little squeak of triumph.

"Bingo! I think you'll find it didn't die at all and your Estella hasn't been entirely truthful. I bet she gave the baby up for adoption. Lots of women did that back then."

I recall Estella's face as she retold the story of her baby's birth. Her hands had covered her wrinkled face, tears trickling through her fingers, when she described waking up in a strange room to the terrible realisation her baby had gone. Evie was the actress, not Estella. There was no way this pain was an act. It was real, and I recognised it.

"She wouldn't have done that. Estella's mourned her baby every day since she lost it. It died in labour and she was desperately ill afterwards. She never even saw her baby." My throat tightens. "Trust me. There's not a lot worse than that."

"Oh, Nell. I'm so sorry."

I claw back control because this is not about me and my child. This injustice, this old cruelty, is Estella's grievance and a wrong I want to right for her.

"I'm OK," I tell her. "It hurts, it will always hurt, but I'm OK, Lou. I really am."

Lou knows me and she knows to move on.

"So, Estella gives birth but doesn't remember a thing and when she wakes up the baby's gone. It's possible they gave her something strong, laudanum maybe, to knock her out, and removed the baby. Would her family have done that?"

I think about Reginald Kellow.

"Oh yes. I'm sure of it."

Lou is morphing into lawyer mode. I picture her face settling into a serious expression as she starts to build her case.

"What evidence did Estella have that her baby was dead? Did her friend tell her, this Evie? Was there a funeral?"

"Evie vanishes from history at this point. Apparently, she stole a necklace and did a runner. That's what Estella's father said."

"So that's his side of events," muses Lou. "Maybe it was self-preservation. Or was Evie trying to help Estella by attempting to get the baby to safety – presuming it hadn't died? After all, Estella only had her father's word for that. How trustworthy was he?"

I feel a tingle of excitement. "Not trustworthy at all – but, oddly, she didn't think to question him."

"Well, she wouldn't have if she'd just been through a traumatic birth-giving, drugged up on God knows what. So let's think back and get some details. Have you seen the baby's grave?"

"There's no grave. There's just a spot by the far hedge."

I hear a pen scratching on a pad. Lou will have her glasses on as she makes detailed notes in her small neat handwriting.

"No headstone? No official plot? No burial record?"

"I wouldn't think so. The baby was illegitimate and not something to draw attention to. I think Estella's father had it buried quietly."

"Hmm," says Lou. "Or not."

The cab is on the Pencallyn road. I stare at the wide seascape and as the waves roll towards the land, unstoppable and relentless, so questions and possibilities surge towards me. Estella's allies were out of the picture, the midwife was hired from out of the village and sent packing, so only Reginald Kellow remained to tell her what had happened. Without her best friend and her lover, Estella's spirit must have been utterly broken. Her baby was missing and there was a grave as evidence, so why would Estella question anything?

"People lie," Lou continues. "Trust me, they do it all the time, and for far less of a motive than covering up the birth of an illegitimate mixed-race child. My theory is Estella's father had the baby removed and told her it was dead, so she never tried to find it. That would be the last thing he would want. Imagine his face if a mixed-race heir came back to claim his precious estate!"

I flick my eyes up to the taxi's rear-view mirror. My reflection stares back.

"Yes," I say. "Imagine that."

"That's what happened. I'd put money on it," Lou concludes.

Is Lou right? Is this what happened? So much of it makes sense yet, there are still pieces in the puzzle which don't fit. Where and why did Evie leave? How did my father come to have the pictures and the crucifix? Who was the young woman who lost her life bringing him to safety?

And this is when I realise: there aren't missing *pieces* to the puzzle – just *one* missing piece. A piece shaped just like Evie Jenkins, the girl who had promised she would do everything in her power to love and protect Estella. A girl who having failed once would rather die than betray her friend a second time. A girl who had sworn to protect her best friend with her life. She would do anything to protect the baby too, wouldn't she?

I'm about to share this theory with Lou as the cab swings into the drive of Pencallyn Farm and brakes sharply to avoid the police cars which block the drive. The farmyard, still in my mind a deserted spot where Estella and Jay made love and read poetry to one another, is bristling with activity. Policemen have wound tape across the drive, two men in suits are deep in conversation with Martin Richardson and a white tent has been erected at the edge of the extension.

Josh! Is he all right? This cold wash of dread at the thought of anything happening to him tells me all I need to know about what this man has come to mean to me.

"I'll call you back," I tell Lou, unfastening my seatbelt and almost tumbling out of the cab in haste. I must make sure the man I'm falling in love with is safe.

I need to find Josh.

CHAPTER 43

Nell
The Present

"Sorry, Miss, but you can't go past," the policeman says.

I'm standing beside a tape cordon which closes off the drive to Pencallyn Farm. Even when I stand on tiptoe, I can't see Josh anywhere. Builders are gathered around in huddles, but their tools are downed and the diggers have stopped. What's happening?

"This is my friend's house," I say. "Josh Richardson. May I go through and find him?"

"I'm afraid not. This is a crime scene," replies the policeman.

"Is everyone safe?" I ask – but what I really mean is is *Josh* safe? Instantly I'm ready to think the worst. It's as though I'm on the top of a cliff and poised to jump. Terror has his hands in the small of my back and is ready to push.

"Nell! Nell!"

Josh emerges from the kitchen area and waves. More relieved than I can say, when he ducks under the police cordon I throw my arms around him.

"Are you all right?"

"I'm fine," Josh says, folding me into a warm hug. "Absolutely fine. I've been with Mum. It's been quite an afternoon."

"I saw the tent and the cordon and I …"

I swallow. What did I think? That something awful had happened here once more? Hamilton Mason returning from the grave? Estella's story has affected me far more than I realised.

"And you thought the worst?" Josh asks softly.

"Yes. For a moment I did, and I couldn't bear it."

He takes my hands and kisses each finger. His eyes never leave mine.

"I'm sorry, Nell, and pleased too, if that makes sense. Pleased you feel that way, I mean. Not for giving you a scare. I should have called rather than send a text, but Mum and I have been talking to the police for ages."

"What's happened? Has your dad throttled a trespasser?" I try to joke but Josh hardly smiles. There are dark shadows under his eyes and his jaw his tense.

"For once it's not what he's done. It's what somebody else did and quite a while ago by the look of it. It's been quite an afternoon here."

The building work has halted. Darren and the other builders are unusually quiet.

"What's happened?" I say but somewhere deep down inside I already know. My hand slips from his and rises to my mouth. I think I may throw up.

"The well clearance team found human remains. I can't take it in. One minute everything's going great guns, the next everything's stopped and the police are sealing off the site. It's like a bad crime drama."

The well. Of course. It was always the well. The lid which kept being removed. The atmosphere of unhappiness. A flash of blond hair in the trees, the prickle of a malevolent gaze crawling across my skin. The unrest which Josh remarked had lessened since I've arrived. The well has finally given up its dark secret and Hamilton Mason's evil deed has been uncovered after nearly eighty years.

"Jay Miller," I whisper.

"What?"

"They've found Jay Miller. He was here all the time."

The photo of the laughing girl by the well was a message. I didn't understand what it meant until this moment, but whoever took my father to the children's hospital knew far, far more than she had dared let on. With her she carried the clues to the identity of my grandfather and his resting place. So it's no coincidence I'm here. My grandfather has been waiting for me to find him.

"I don't understand," Josh says. "How can you possibly know that they've found him?"

"Estella told me more of their story this afternoon." I want to tell him everything, but we're interrupted by detectives needing to speak to Josh, and Estella's tale will have to wait. I slip my hand into his and we pass through the cordon. Sarah Richardson is still talking to the police.

"It's just horrible. To think all the time a body was down there! I've always hated this place and now I know why. Oh, Josh, there you are. DCI Hambly, this is my son and — ?"

"Nell Summers," Josh supplies. "Nell's a friend of Estella's."

"Not only of Estella it seems," says Sarah with a watery smile. She dabs a hanky against eyes the same deep leaf green as her son's. "I'm sorry not to meet you under happier circumstances, Nell."

I smile back. Sarah is beautiful. Like her son.

"Could you talk me through the events of the afternoon once more, Mrs Richardson?" Inspector Hambly's pen is poised above a notebook. "You were supervising the work on the well, I believe?"

"That's right. The team arrived around lunchtime. They're experts on well clearing, you see, and my husband booked them months ago. Martin was so keen we had the well made into a feature in our kitchen."

DI Hambly looks up. "But you weren't?"

"It's supposed to be a holy well, but I always thought there was something odd about it. When the clearance people began work, they retrieved all kinds of junk. There was even a dog's skeleton."

Poppet! Dear, loyal, lost little Poppet. I see Estella searching for her pet, calling until her throat is raw, and am broken-hearted. To me, the naughty little spaniel was alive until only a few hours ago. To discover that she too was tossed into the well like rubbish is dreadful.

"A dog?" The detective looks surprised.

"Sacrificed to pagan gods, I expect," Sarah says, her nose crinkled with distaste. "They still believe all that stuff here. We've had all kinds of trouble with trespassers who want to see the well." Panic chases across her face. "Oh! Do you think one of them did it?"

"The remains aren't that recent, so it's unlikely."

"Anyway, the workmen had been excavating the well for over an hour – they lower a worker in and haul things out – when the lad working down there began shouting. The team pulled him up at once when he said there were human remains in the well. My son is our site manager and he called the police at once. What a dreadful thing. Maybe whoever it was fell down there by accident?"

"With the wall around it, I think that's unlikely too, Mum," says Josh gently. He turns to the detective.

"Have you any idea how long has the body has been there? I assume we're talking a long time rather than months?"

"It's usually hard to say without running tests in the lab but because this individual had military ID on him, we've a good idea of who he is and when he was alive. Those dogtags are comprehensive, so I won't be compromising any investigation by telling you he was here during the Second World War. The victim appears to have been an American GI."

Josh's eyes meet mine and I will him not to say a word, because we'll be sucked into a quicksand of bureaucracy if we mention Jay's name. There are still too many unanswered questions, and the mystery of how my father arrived at the hospital is yet to be solved.

My theory is that it was Evie who had taken him there. There's no other explanation. She must have been the girl who was killed crossing the road. Was she keeping Estella's baby safe? Or had Reginald Kellow paid her to abandon the child? I like to think Evie had more integrity and kept her promise to Estella, but I also know she was a survivor first and foremost. She vanished from history at that point, which would stand to reason if she had been knocked down, but also she was a consummate actress. Amid the chaos of war, it's possible she adopted a new identity and lived a long life under a different name. There's a breadcrumb trail for me to follow, but some of the pieces have been nibbled and it feels as though something important is still missing.

Maybe Evie never intended to abandon the baby at all but was keeping him safe. What if she was keeping her promise? What if the hospital was a red herring and she was never headed there at all? What if she was just passing it, and making for the docks and America?

"You were right. They've found Jay Miller, haven't they?" Josh says once Detective Hambly has moved on. We're still holding hands and I tighten my grasp. I don't want to be unmoored just yet.

"I think so. Yes."

"Christ. How bloody, bloody awful. The poor boy. I can't stop seeing him as he was in your picture, Nell. He was so young."

We're at the boundary between the Richardsons' land and Estella's. By unspoken agreement we climb into Pencallyn's lost garden.

"I think he was murdered," I say.

"Makes sense. I can't imagine he ended up in the well by accident."

"No, and I'm pretty sure I know why he was killed and who by. If I'm right, Estella's my grandmother and my dad was the baby she had with Jay Miller."

Josh whistles. "That's some theory. I've never heard any rumours about Estella Kellow having a secret child."

"Well you wouldn't, would you? Not if it was a secret!"

"OK, I asked for that – but you appreciate how it is in a small village. Somebody always knows something."

"Not if they were all kept quiet," I say. "There's more, lots more. I've got lots to tell you."

Josh pulls me close. "And I want to hear it, Nell, I do. But first, there's something I want to say to you. Something that belongs in the present and hopefully the future, rather than the past. It's something I knew the first time I saw you arguing with my dad, and it's something I knew for absolute certain when I saw you again this afternoon. I know the timing might be off with what we've learned, but that's also shown me how uncertain life is. Not a minute should be wasted or taken for granted."

I think of Estella and Jay who lived every precious moment they'd been granted and during a time where death and danger were constant companions.

"I agree," I say, and I know they would have said the same.

Josh presses my hands against his heart and lowers his head to mine. His lips are just a kiss away.

"I'm falling in love with you, Nell Summers. I didn't look for this and I never expected it and I must tell you how I feel. I'm in love with you."

I look into his eyes and realise I didn't need to hear these words. Josh's feelings are in his smile. His touch. His kindness. His sea-deep eyes. I've always known.

"And I feel the same way about you."

"You do?"

"I do. I'm in love with you too, Josh Richardson."

'Now, always and for ever' I add in my heart, and when he kisses me I know it won't be long before I say these words out loud.

"Now let me tell you the rest of Estella's story," I say after a while.

"I think this is the perfect time to hear it," he says.

We push through the tangled garden and as we walk I retell Estella's narrative as best I can, although this takes some time because we keep stopping to kiss, marvelling at how easily we have crossed the gulf from friends to lovers. I'm deeply saddened by the discovery at the farm, and reliving Estella and Jay's romance while threading our way along paths and tracks they would have known adds piquancy to the tale. They knew this racing of the heart and the singing of the blood, they would have felt the same shivers when fingertips brush and tingle with the delicious anticipation of knowing what lies ahead once night falls and the moon peeps above the horizon. Time blurs, past and present overlapping, and we could be my grandparents.

"So that's it," I conclude as we wind our way past giant bamboo, rampant and glorious after nearly a century of neglect. "Estella says her baby died and Evie deserted her, but I don't believe that's what happened."

"Neither do I, especially not if the DNA test's anything to go by."

"It's definitive according to Lou, and I'm related to all those Millers. It can't be a coincidence."

"So, let's imagine Estella's baby lived," Josh says thoughtfully. "Evie gets him out of the house and away somehow – whether at Reginald Kellow's bidding or off her own bat we don't know – and then what?"

I recall the story Nanna Summers used to tell me.

"Then she manages to get the baby to Bristol. He's got some bits and pieces with him, the crucifix and pictures, but not much else because —"

"Because she isn't intending to leave him anywhere! The abandonment theory's wrong. What if he was sick and she was taking him to the hospital for help?"

"Or she wasn't even going to the hospital but somewhere else entirely?"

We look at each other.

"Bristol docks," Josh says. "I bet you anything. She was trying to get the baby away to safety. She was going to take him to America."

"It's a good theory except for one thing – the girl who was knocked down kept saying she'd failed her son. Nanna Summers said she wished she and Grandpa could have told her she didn't fail him at all. Oh, Josh, I've got this all wrong. I've collected a load of coincidences and made them into the story I wanted to hear. The girl who took my father to Bristol died saying she'd failed her son. Evie would never have said that."

Josh frowns. "That isn't what she said, though, is it? Not exactly. You told me she said, 'son fail'."

"Yes, but it means the same thing."

"But what if it doesn't? What if that wasn't what she said at all and whoever was with her for those last few minutes misheard? What if what she said didn't make sense to them?"

"What do you mean?"

"Nell, what if she didn't say 'son fail' at all? What if she said 'sundial'?"

My mouth falls open. Of course! The sundial. The girls were obsessed with it.

"Oh my God! That could be exactly what she said. It was meant for Estella. Evie could have left her a message at the sundial because that was what the girls used to do when they were young. It was their special place where they made their promise all those years ago!"

The sun is lower and the woodland floor shifts with shadows and speckled light as we enter the heart of the garden. The old paths were smothered a long time ago, but their ghostly echo can still be glimpsed beneath moss and grass and thistles. It's an eerie spot and I shiver.

"It feels like the well," I whisper.

"Yes. Those girls were onto something, I think. Watch your arms," he warns as we fight our way through briars.

I'm scratched and bleeding, but I don't care. I spot the sundial first and when I see it is still keeping time, the shadow slicing the metal plate, I feel a pang of nostalgia for two little girls who had played here so long ago, and also for my long-ago self, curled up in my grandmother's lap as she reads me a tale of magic and mystery. No wonder this place feels familiar; I've seen it many times before.

"*Mysterious Garden*," I whisper, running my hands over the warm stone of the sundial.

"What's this inscription?" Josh bends over, peering at the weathered engraving. "*Silens loquor.* Aha! All those miserable hours of studying Latin have come in useful after all."

"What does that mean?"

" 'Though silent, I speak.' It's a message. It must be. Where would Evie have left it?"

"The girls hid notes in the sundial, at least that's what Estella said."

"How did they do that?"

I pull a face. "She didn't tell me that part."

"Handy,' says Josh. "OK. Let's figure it out."

We study the stone ornament. Weathered and velveted with lichen, it seems to study us too, and the hairs on the back of my neck stir. I can't shake the sensation that unseen eyes are watching us from the dense trees. Hamilton? Evie? Jay? All of them? None? I can't tell.

"It can't be hard if young girls could do it," Josh says. "Maybe something slides?"

"The base?" I crouch down, but there's nothing unusual there. Some tiny red insects scatter but little else.

Josh leans over the metal plate. His hair swings over his face, the colour of beech trees when the sun catches it, and he pushes it behind his ears impatiently.

"What about this? The surface seems loose. I wonder …"

He wiggles the metal plate. The bolt at the far end acts like a pin, and as the plate shifts it reveals a hollowed area beneath. Probably originally designed as a bird bath, it's the perfect place to leave a note or a hide treasure.

Josh straightens up and smiles. "I think that's what Evie meant, don't you?"

I can hardly believe my eyes. Inside, and nestled on a bed of withered leaves, is a rusty tobacco tin.

"Go on," says Josh. "It's for you."

I'm motionless. My mouth is dry.

"It's for Estella."

"Yes, technically, so you're going to tell her what it says – and soon, too, from what you've told me."

He's right. I think of Estella, tired and frail in the hospital bed. I hear the hiss and suck of her air mattress. I see the shallow rise of her chest. The sands in her hourglass are running low and she hasn't long to hear what Evie needed to tell her.

I grasp the tin with shaking fingers. Although the sun is warm the metal is icy to the touch and when I pop the lid open a puff of ice-cold air chills my hands. Inside is a folded piece of paper, age-stained and fragile but of unmistakably high quality. I unfold it carefully, terrified the precious document will turn to dust in my hands like something from a fairy tale – or maybe it will crumble to ashes for my daring to meddle? Evie had believed in magic and pagan lore and curses. Fortunately, neither happens and I'm looking at a page crammed with italic script, the words close together as though the writer needed to make the most of all the space she could. Some parts are smudged as though tears had fallen and blurred the ink, and in places the nib has scratched the surface deeply or underscored a word several times. The writer has signed her name with a flourish:

Evie x

"Is it her?" Josh asks.

"Yes. Oh, Josh, it's really her!"

I scan the letter. The writing's hard to decipher, the cramped hand a study in urgency, and the story it tells so painful I can hardly bear to read it. Hearing Evie's voice after all this time is as shocking as looking into a mirror and seeing your reflection move of its own volition.

Once I've finished reading I pass the paper to Josh, unable to hold my tears back any longer. My heart is breaking for Estella and poor, poor Jay, but most of all for the lost little baby – my wonderful, gentle, and dearly missed father.

CHAPTER 44

Evie
1944

"It's a boy, sir," the midwife said.

Evie pressed her ear to the study door. A seasoned eavesdropper, she had no qualms about listening in to private conversations, especially when they involved her beloved Estella. She would do anything to keep her friend safe. Anything.

There was a loaded silence. Although she couldn't see Estella's father, Evie knew his face would be puce and a fat worm vein would be throbbing in his left temple. He must have been hoping the baby would die. Bastard.

"The mother's not in such good shape, sir," the midwife continued, a note of nervousness creeping into her voice. "I've dosed her with laudanum and done my best to disinfect any wounds, but the birth was hard and she's lost a lot of blood. It would be wise to call a doctor."

Reginald Kellow's voice was cold. "No doctors."

"Sir, she could die!"

"I said *no doctors!*" The roar from the other side of the study door made Evie's feet leave the ground. "No doctors are to be called. If you go against my wishes, you'll never work again. Do I make myself clear?"

There was no reply. Evie assumed the midwife was struck dumb with fear. Her own stomach was churning. Without the attention of a proper doctor Estella might not survive the night. Evie had seen such things happen when she lived in Bethnal Green. What could she do? The house was down to a skeleton day staff since Cook and Bert had been sacked. Who would help Evie now? Who could take the terror away? Who could undo the dreadful damage caused by her stupid, pathetic feelings for Hamilton Mason?

A man now she hated. A man she hoped would have died in agony.

At night Evie still woke up with her heart thudding, and the remnants of bad dreams haunted her every day. After what Hamilton had done to Jay Miller, the man Estella loved, how could Evie look her friend in the face again? Now Evie had a secret so dreadful it could never be shared, and it would eat away at their friendship like a canker. Everything was ruined.

She wished Hamilton had killed her too.

Coming to Pencallyn had softened Evie. It had shown her a world where she could slough off the skin of her East End self and become somebody new. She could watch and learn, her quick mind grasping knowledge at lightning speed and her natural talent for mimicry enabling her to lose her accent and melt into the new landscape. If this had been all there was to her new life, she would have navigated it easily, but her love for Estella changed everything. At first Evie had tried to hold onto her anger, wanting to hate Estella for being everything she was not, but she had been taken aback by the kindness of her new friend. Like a rip tide racing across a beach, Evie's resentment was swept away by love.

It had taken someone special to do this, to make her feel love for the first time, and this person had been Estella. She had become the mirror held up to Evie, reflecting beauty and grace instead of a loathsome image. The new life at Pencallyn was a chance to be reborn and leave ugliness behind, and Evie had tried. But there was still a deep seam of darkness running through her and at times it broke through to the surface.

Yet Evie loved Estella with all her heart. Sometimes that love was twisted by jealousy and the knowledge she was the false coin to her best friend's gold, but she adored Estella. They were sisters. They were everything to each other, and Evie wouldn't let Hamilton Mason destroy that. She hoped he'd paid a thousand times over in Normandy.

She hoped his end was agony.

Evie had cursed him at the ancient place where powerful energy lines bisected. She knew the old magic would hear her plea and come for him. When the ships sailed away to France, Evie knew he wouldn't return, and she was pleased. Whatever horrors awaited Hamilton on the grey beaches of Normandy were nothing in comparison to what he deserved. Nothing.

Yet even in death he was triumphant. This secret was like a splinter, so she would never share with Estella; it would start an infection Evie knew would poison their friendship. But how could she tell her friend? How could Estella still love Evie if she knew it was all her fault Jay Miller died? Evie's fault this baby didn't have a father? Estella would hate her, and Evie couldn't bear that. No. It was better to keep quiet and let the infection of self-loathing consume her than to lose her best friend's love.

As she listened to the midwife describing Estella's precarious health, Evie's thoughts spun back to an early June evening in what felt like another life. She'd been so hopeful as she'd contrived a meeting with Hamilton. If only she could step back in time and stop herself! Draw the line at the secret kiss he'd bestowed on her in the pantry or the rare embraces behind the old coach house. Fool that she was, Evie had believed a night-time tryst would be romantic and seal their love. She'd been able to think of little else.

Oh! How Evie wished she hadn't gone!

"Meet me at the old farmhouse at ten," Hamilton had whispered into her ear as they passed in the dining room. His hot breath against her skin had made Evie's pulse race. "Wear the red coat so I can recognise you, and don't tell a soul."

Evie had been too excited to eat her dinner and had slipped out of the house under the cover of darkness, almost bumping into Estella, who was returning from meeting that soldier of hers. Estella was keeping secrets, and this hurt, but now Evie would have a secret of her own! And what a secret! An officer for her, not a lowly private, and maybe a whole new life in America! Evie had known it was simply a matter of time before Hamilton noticed her. Once they had kissed, maybe done even more if Evie decided to let him make love to her tonight, Hamilton would be hers. This was how it was in the films and plays she loved. Estella's warnings were no more than sour grapes, because Jay Miller didn't like him.

As she made her way to the farmhouse Evie had done her best to ignore the small voice telling her Hamilton's comments about black servicemen were wrong. She tried to convince herself he came from a different culture and by the time she was at the ruin she nearly believed it.

"Hamilton?" she'd called feeling nervous. "It's me. It's Evie."

She smoothed Estella's coat over her hips and patted her hair. Pinned in a victory roll, Evie thought it made her look at least twenty. She hoped the scent stolen from Violet many months ago smelled nice and he liked the stockings she'd worn especially. Evie wanted him to want her as much as she longed for him.

There was a rustle in the darkness and then a hand was clamped over her mouth.

"Shh, it's me."

Hamilton Mason released her, and Evie giggled with relief.

"You scared me to death," she said. Her legs felt wobbly and she stepped towards him, waiting to be encircled in strong arms as all the films and books promised. Would he ravish her now? What would it feel like? Would it hurt?

But Hamilton seemed in no hurry to hold her.

"Your hair's wrong, honey. Estella wears it down," he said, tugging at pins until the elaborate style was undone. Strong hands fluffed her hair and moved her head back and forth as though she was a doll. "That's better. You could almost pass for her."

Evie was confused. "Why have you done that?"

"I want to settle a score and I need your help. You do want to help me, don't you Evie?"

"Yes," Evie said cautiously. "Of course I do …"

Something about this felt wrong. Evie's nerve endings were jangling and instinct was telling her to flee. She ignored it. She'd waited months to be alone with Hamilton Mason. She'd dreamed of this moment.

"Good girl," he said and ran a forefinger along her cheek. To her surprise, Evie didn't shiver with lust but felt uneasy and as though something unpleasant had brushed against her. "Mr Kellow isn't too happy his daughter's been keeping company with Private Miller. He wants the boy given a warning he won't forget."

Evie's eyes widened.

"Surprised I know?" Hamilton said. His pupils were dark and dangerous, and Evie's head spun.

"I didn't think anyone knew about that"

"You do, Evie. I'm hurt you didn't tell me. That wasn't very friendly, was it? Not when we're friends. Friends shouldn't keep secrets. That makes folks feel betrayed and when folks feel betrayed, they get angry."

He gripped her chin and Evie gasped. This wasn't the Hamilton she usually saw. That man flattered Evie; told her she was a lady. He was charm personified, and she adored him. Was Hamilton an actor too?

"It isn't my secret to tell," she said.

"It's as well I had Miller followed," Hamilton said. "Your friend's disgusting, carrying on with the likes of Miller."

The mask slipped and something ugly looked out through Hamilton's eyes. How had she never noticed they were as cold and as bleak the winter sky? Evie tried to twist her head away, but his grip was like a vice.

"Estella isn't disgusting," Evie hissed. "She loves Jay Miller."

"Where I come from, carrying on like that it isn't decent behaviour."

"You're not there now. You're in Cornwall," Evie said. She began to struggle but Hamilton tightened his hold.

"Let me go!

"Oh honey, don't make such a fuss," Hamilton drawled as Evie twisted in his grasp. "I hate you keeping a secret like this from me, and from Estella's father too. Hell, can you imagine what he'd think if I told him you knew? He'd send you back to the slums, and wouldn't that be a pity? How would you survive? What would you do?"

It was as though he had found a window into her soul to peer at Evie's darkest fears. The thought of being sent away from Pencallyn and Estella was her greatest terror, and she knew Hamilton was right; if Reginald Kellow knew she'd concealed Estella's relationship he would send her packing.

She stopped struggling.

"Don't tell him. Please."

"Hell, that's a big favour you're asking," Hamilton said thoughtfully. "I'll need one in return. Oh, not that!" He laughed, catching her shocked expression. "Do you really think I'd lower myself to screw a street urchin like you? I want you to keep your clothes on. They tell me you're a mighty fine actress and I have a role for you. Play it right and I'll keep quiet. Get it wrong and you'll be out on your ear."

Then he told her exactly what he wanted, and Evie thought she would throw up. Jay Miller was on his way to the farm, coming because he believed Estella was there, and injured. Hamilton wanted Evie to pretend to be Estella and call Jay into the ruin. Evie could guess what would happen next. Hamilton wanted to teach Jay a lesson for touching a white woman, one he'd wanted since he'd first seen her. Hamilton had never wanted Evie. Of course not. It had always been Estella.

Evie was afraid. For all his wealth and manners Hamilton was no different to the East End thugs. He was dangerous and violent. Cunning and cruel. How had she been so blind? Estella had seen through him from the beginning. But jealousy had blinded her to the truth, Evie realised miserably. She had been an utter fool.

"Once Miller's here you can go," Hamilton said. "Make sure you sound like Estella. Otherwise I may forget you didn't want me to tell Reginald Kellow you've been keeping his daughter's lover a secret."

Evie was on the brink of telling Hamilton to forget it when three GIs and Lex Boone arrived, and she realised that things were deadly serious. They took her coat off, to drop it in the yard, laughing that Miller would see it and come inside where he would get what he deserved.

She felt sick to the stomach. This wasn't Hamilton settling a score. This was an ambush. Even though she was afraid of Reginald Kellow's anger, Evie knew she had to do something. Thinking fast, she decided to pretend to go along with their plan and then yell to Jay Miller that he had to run.

"Fine, I'll do it," she said with a shrug. "What do I care about Miller anyway? He's got it coming. Just make sure keep your word."

She was quaking inside, but Hamilton couldn't tell because she sounded so calm. As far as he was concerned Evie would do exactly as he asked. She would too – until the moment came to warn Jay.

"Jay?" she called, and in her best impersonation of Estella. "I'm in here! Help me!"

"That's perfect."

Finally, she heard footsteps running towards the ruin. Hamilton pressed her arm and she cried out in pain.

"Star? Darling?" she heard Jay call and the tender concern in his voice made her heart twist. "Sweetheart, where are you? What's happened?"

He was in the doorway of the ruin, lean frame silhouetted against the indigo sky as he peered into the darkness. All he cared about in the world was reaching Estella, and this was when Evie understood that Jay Miller loved Estella just as much as she did. No – more! He would never betray her.

"Run, Jay!" she yelled, pushing past Lex and sprinting towards the door. "It's a trap! Estella isn't here! Run!"

Hamilton grabbed her by the hair, yanking her back with such force that she screamed. Evie's hands flailed and when her nails raked his cheek, he hit her with the back of his hand, knocking her to the floor.

"You bitch!" Hamilton hissed, driving a boot into her ribs with such force Evie thought she would vomit. "You'll regret this!"

"Get out, Jay!" Evie gasped. "Run!"

But Jay Miller didn't run or turn away. He walked into the farmhouse and faced Hamilton as though on parade. Shoulders squared and head held high, he looked his senior officer in the eye.

"Let her go, Sir," he said.

Hamilton laughed. Three soldiers melted out of the darkness and blocked the doorway.

"Or what, boy?"

"Or you won't be a gentleman, Sir. This isn't her fault. Let Evie go. This is just between us."

"That's where you're wrong, boy," Hamilton said. "This is between every man who's had one of your kind touch a woman of his. This is about you not knowing your place."

"I know my place, sir," Jay said quietly. "Let the girl go. This is nothing to do with her."

"You ordering me about? Now that sure is stupid, boy."

"Insubordination, I call it," Lex chipped in. "You need teaching a lesson, Miller. Time you were made an example of."

Evie wasn't ever sure quite what happened next. Her head was spinning from the smack when she fell to the ground, and she was struggling to breathe after the kick in her ribs. She heard a dog bark and Hamilton cursing, followed by the crack of a pistol and a yelp. As everything blurred there were shouts and grunts and the thump of fists slamming into flesh.

"C'mon Miller," she heard Lex jeer. "Say you're sorry for touching what ain't yours. Say you'll leave Miss Kellow alone."

"He won't apologise," said another private. "He's a stubborn son of a bitch. He's not sorry."

"Is that so?" Hamilton asked. "He touches a white woman but he's not sorry? Hell, that's a cryin' shame. Sounds like he needs another lesson to me. Let's see what he has to say."

Her eyes accustomed to the gloom now, Evie watched Lex drag Jay into the middle of the room. He was bloodied and bruised but his chin was raised, and his eyes brimmed with courage.

"Say you're sorry, boy," Hamilton repeated, his voice low and menacing. "Say you'll never lay your filthy hands on Estella Kellow again. Say it!"

Jay's throat contracted. His quiet courage shamed Evie.

"No," he said quietly. "I won't."

"No? You're saying no to me, boy?" A muscle twitched in Hamilton's jaw. "Say, I don't think you understand. You ain't stupid, are you? Let me explain. You've no right touching a girl like her, and I think it's time you realised what happens to boys who don't know their place."

"I know my place," Jay said. "It's to serve in the US Army. It's to be a decent human being. It's to marry the girl I love."

"Love?" Hamilton sneered. "Marriage? You're overstepping the mark. You sure is uppity! Time we reminded you exactly where your place is!"

Evie heard flesh smashing into bone and curled herself up tightly, sobbing. Jay Miller was being beaten and there was nothing she could do. She was too afraid. After a few minutes the sound abated and all she could hear was groaning. As she opened her eyes, swollen with tears, she saw the huddled Jay slumped at Hamilton's feet.

"Sure she'll still want you now? Because you don't look too pretty any more, boy," Hamilton mocked. "I'll keep her warm for you, don't you worry. I've a good mind to see if Lex will help me. A girl like her who'll screw the likes of you will screw anyone. She's trash."

Evie had no idea how Jay Miller found the strength but somehow he was on his feet and his fist found Hamilton's jaw.

"She's everything!" he grated, his voice full of passion. "Don't you dare speak that way about Estella! You're not fit to say her name!"

Hamilton roared with rage, his hand clamped protectively against his face. "You'll wish you'd never done that! Where I come from this is how we deal with boys with attitude! Shall we show him, Lex?"

"Time we did. He's slow to learn," Lex drawled.

There was a tussle and the sound of boots hitting skin. Jay cried out and Evie flinched with each yelp of pain. If they didn't stop, they were going to kill him. She tried to clamber to her feet, but one of the other soldiers pushed her back onto the hard floor and the whole place roiled.

"She's been with you, which means she's trash," Hamilton was panting, each word punctuated with a kick. "Say it! She's trash! She's a slut!"

Jay cried out in pain but he didn't say a word, and Evie knew he would rather die than betray Estella. He was brave and loyal. How easy it would have been to crumple and give in! He must know they would hurt him ten times more badly if he didn't.

Jay Miller, Evie realised, loved Estella with all that he was and all that he would ever be. He would die for her.

"Estella's everything," Jay gasped, clutching his side. "I love her. Now, always and for ever."

It was as though these words, coupled with his refusal to be cowed, unleashed something dreadful in Hamilton. He flew at Jay with a roar of fury and the other soldiers followed suit. Fists flailing and boots stamping, they rained blows and kicks onto Jay's prone body repeatedly until Lex grabbed Hamilton by the shoulders and hauled him off.

"Easy, man! You're gonna kill him!"

"He deserves it," Hamilton spat. "On your feet, Miller. Come on."

But Jay Miller didn't stir. Lex prodded him with his foot. "Miller. On your feet, boy! Get up!"

There was still no movement.

"I said, get up!" Lex tried to sound stern, but doubt wobbled his voice. "Miller? Miller?"

Evie's heart was a tight knot of dread.

Lex crouched down and touched Jay's neck, recoiling and stumbling backwards as though burned. "Jesus Christ! He's dead! We've killed him! Shit!"

Hamilton rolled Jay's unmoving body over with the toe of his boot. "Hell, so we have. I think Kellow can consider Miller properly warned. He won't be dressing young ladies' hands or touching any part of 'em again, that's for sure."

Evie thought she would throw up. So Reginald Kellow had sanctioned a beating because he'd heard how Jay Miller once dressed his daughter's hand? She'd always known he was a nasty old bastard, but this was something else …

Lex rounded on Hamilton. "A warning was what Kellow wanted. Teach him not to think he can talk to British ladies, he said. He didn't say to kill him. Shit! What are we going to do? This is murder."

Hamilton fell silent. In the darkness of her hiding place, Evie trembled. She'd witnessed a murder, so what would they do to *her*? And if Reginald Kellow discovered she knew about his involvement … He would have her killed; of this she was certain. Evie's heart was banging so loudly she thought they would hear. Would she be next? Would it hurt?

"We'll be court-martialled," said one of the privates. His voice shook with fear.

"They'll shoot us," whined another. "I didn't sign up for this. A bit of fun. Put Miller in his place you said, Sir! You never said we were going to kill him."

Lex had started to pace.

"Shit! Shit! Shit! What are we gonna do?"

Hamilton Mason rounded on him. "Not panic like women for a start. Keep it together, for Christ's sake! This is between the five of us and it goes no further. Nobody else knows we were here this evening, and nobody needs to know."

"Kellow knows," Lex said.

"He won't say a word. If he does, he's finished too."

"What about her?" asked one of the GIs, pointing at Evie.

Hamilton laughed scornfully.

"If she opens her mouth, she can go the same way as Miller. We'll have Kellow on side to hush her up. He's a Member of Parliament so he can pull all kinds of strings. Maybe she'll steal something. People get put away for that."

Evie thought she might faint with terror because Hamilton meant every word. She'd seen exactly what he was capable of.

"You'll keep your mouth shut," Hamilton told her softly. "Because you lured Miller here, Evie Jenkins, which makes you an accessary to murder. Everyone knows what you are, and they won't be surprised. They've all seen you panting for me like a bitch on heat too, and Estella will hate you. You'd be hanged. Trust me."

"I'll keep mum," she whispered, her entire body shaking. "I promise."

"So, what do we do with him?" Lex jerked his head at Jay.

"We can't leave him where he'll be found," said another GI nervously.

"We get rid of it," Hamilton said softly. "The dog too. We'll put them where nobody will ever look."

"You mean bury 'em?" Lex sounded doubtful. "Have we time? And what if the military search? Won't they look for him?"

"Not if they think Miller's deserted. They won't bother wasting time on him," Hamilton said. His calm voice and swiftness of thought were truly chilling. As she lay on the hard floor Evie wondered how she had ever thought him beautiful. Now he sickened her.

"Where do we put him, then?" Lex asked him.

"There's a well in the courtyard. Should be nice and deep so nobody will find him there. Not for a very long time, anyhow, and by then we'll be long gone."

There was murmured agreement followed by grunting as they picked up Jay's body. The moon bobbed out from behind a cloud to illuminate his bruised face. The beautiful brown eyes seemed to stare straight at Evie, filled with unbearable sadness and reproach. It was a sight she knew would haunt her dreams for ever.

"I'm so sorry," Evie told him silently. She bit her lip hard to seal in sobs, and tasted blood. "I'm so sorry I was too scared to help you, Jay! I'm sorry I was a coward. I'm sorry! I'm sorry!"

She'd returned to Pencallyn that night and she had kept quiet too, at first because she was afraid of Hamilton, but later, once he'd gone and as time passed, because it became harder and harder to tell the truth. She told herself Jay was dead anyway, so what good would it do if she spoke up? The chances were he would have died at Omaha too, so what real difference would a confession make? How could Stella cope with a secret pregnancy if Evie wasn't on hand? She needed Evie. And how could Stella cope if she lost the man she loved and learned her best friend was to blame? It was best for everyone if Evie said nothing.

Outside the door of the study with one ear pressed to the crack, listening to Reginald Kellow berating the midwife, Evie reflected: the lies we tell ourselves, she thought. Back in the summer, the truth would have made all the difference in the world, because Estella would have known she and her baby were not safe at Pencallyn. How had Evie ever thought otherwise? How had she imagined she could protect them? Estella might die now through lack of proper medical care, and who knew what Reginald would have done to the baby?

She'd broken her promise to protect and love Estella. She was a bad and faithless friend.

Estella's labour had been long and hard, and even Evie, who'd watched her gran deliver many babies, had been shocked. Estella suffered dreadfully as her small body struggled to deliver the baby. Evie and the midwife had done their best, but by the time Jay Miller's son took his first breath Estella Kellow was close to taking her last.

"Internal bleeding," the midwife observed darkly. "She needs a doctor, if you ask me. You'll need to prepare yourself because it's not looking good."

Estella's head lolled and her eyes were closed. Evie's heart corkscrewed with terror.

"Her father won't let me call one."

"And now I know why," the midwife said wryly, her eyes flicking to the makeshift cot fashioned from a drawer where they'd placed the baby. Against the snowy linen his skin was as smooth as mahogany and his thick thatch of hair jet black. They'd fed him cow's milk mixed with sugar and he was sleeping with his little rosebud mouth open and his face screwed up as though already trying to puzzle out the world. It broke Evie's heart that Estella, who loved him so much, hadn't been able to hold him.

"He's perfect," Evie snapped. She had loved this baby instantly because he was Estella's but also because of Jay Miller, brave and loyal Jay Miller who'd stood up for her when he could have chosen to save his own neck. Evie closed her eyes and pushed the memory of that dreadful night into the deep place where all her dark thoughts went. Dwelling on it would do nobody any good. She'd make sure she didn't let Jay Miller down for a second time. Evie Jenkins would protect Jay and Estella's baby with her life. She would give her life for him if she had to.

"If you say so," said the midwife. She threw bloodstained towels into a heap and wiped her hands on her apron. "There's plenty like him being born these days, that's for sure, although not normally to girls like your friend. No wonder her father doesn't want word getting out. He's paid me well to keep my mouth shut and it's a shame he won't pay a doctor to do the same."

Evie laid a hand on Estella's forehead. It was burning hot.

"How can I help her?" she called to the midwife, already on her way out of the door to see Reginald Kellow. "Please! What can I do?"

The midwife's pudgy face was grim.

"Pray. And if all else fails get the poor child as far away from this place as you can."

Evie trembled as she stood outside the study. She knew better than anyone what Reginald Kellow was capable of. Danger was stalking Estella's baby already.

"I won't have that child here," Reginald said softly. "Get rid of it."

"Rid of it? What do you mean?" asked the midwife.

"Exactly what I what I say. Tell me, is it weak? Sickly?"

"No! He's a bonny baby."

"Shall we say he isn't? You will be compensated handsomely."

"I can't … I won't …" stuttered the midwife. Evie heard her backing towards the door. "No, sir. I won't be party to anything like that."

"If you won't I'll find someone who will. I don't care where it goes. I want rid of it."

Evie fled at this point, tearing up the stairs as fast as she could. She had to get Estella's baby to safety. There was no time to waste.

She had a vague plan. She would take the baby to America, to Jay's family. They would surely help. Estella had the address, and crossing the Atlantic could be no less precarious than staying here, for who knew what Reginald Kellow might do or what contacts he had? She'd get to Bristol and find a berth. She'd leave a note for Estella somewhere Reginald would never look. The sundial, of course! Yes, that was the perfect hiding place. She'd write to Estella and explain her plan. Her friend would be bound to look there when she discovered Evie had left. It was their special place, and they had always used it for leaving secret messages.

There was no time to waste. She would take a few pieces for the baby, pictures perhaps and the precious family crucifix to prove to the Millers this child really was their grandson. She'd take Estella's picture of Jay, in case they still didn't believe her, a postcard of Pencallyn to show where they came from, and a photo of Estella. The only image of her friend that Evie could find was a faded shot taken one long-ago afternoon at the ruined farm. It showed Estella laughing and carefree, and Evie thought the Millers would like to see this. The well was in the picture, and although it now sent shivers down her spine Evie decided this was a part of the child's heritage too, however dark. One day when the war was over and the child was returned to Estella, Evie would tell them both the truth. Then they would make sure Jay had a decent burial rather than the wildflowers she'd tossed into the well with a muttered prayer. She would put everything right.

And that was a promise too.

As she whirled around the bedroom, snatching up clothes and stuffing them into a holdall, Evie admitted her plan was vague. She had little knowledge of caring for a baby, but there must be people who could help with milk and clouts. This plan was all Evie had, and there was not a minute to lose. The midwife was right; the baby wasn't safe at Pencallyn. Evie hated to leave Estella, but one day her friend would understand.

She had some money, but not enough to reach America. So she rummaged through Violet's room, where Estella lay as still as any effigy in St Brecca's, and took her ID card, a bracelet and string of pearls from the dressing table. This was family jewellery, so it wasn't stealing, she reasoned. It was the baby's inheritance, and if selling it paid for their passage to America and keep for a few months, then so much the better.

Evie changed into a smart suit of Violet's, pushed her feet into court shoes and slicked her lips with scarlet gloss. Hair pinned up beneath a hat and with a broach at her throat she must look at least twenty. Hooking the gold chain strap over her shoulder, she pouted at the mirror. This was going to be the acting role of her life and she had better bloody pull it off. This really was life and death.

"I'm Mrs Evelyn Jenkins. This is my son, Henry. I'm off to visit my parents in Bristol because Papa's ill. What a rum thing in the middle of a war and with my baby so tiny!"

Hmm. More pathos. She tried again with a sob in her voice when she mentioned her father. Yes. Better. Men loved the knight in shining armour stuff. Or they did with women like Estella. Girls like Evie were thrown back into the gutter where they came from.

"Any of you divine boys have a light? Oh! Thank you, angel!"

Yes. This would do. She had the privileged arrogance off to a tee. Nobody questioned women who spoke like this. Doors would open everywhere, and she'd be in a cab and on the train to Bristol in a heartbeat. Nobody would link Evie Jenkins from Bethnal Green with a smart young mother with pearls. She'd dump her ID once she was in Bristol and booked on an army boat to the States. She and the baby would vanish into thin air, and Reginald Kellow would never trace them.

Bag packed, Evie fetched writing paper and a fountain pen. Setting herself up at the girls' old dressing table, she wrote to Estella and poured out her heart. Gradually the letter became a confession and Evie wept bitterly as her pen flew over the surface. She described the terrible events of Jay's death, begged forgiveness for her part in it and swore to keep her promise.

'I'll protect your baby with my life,' she wrote, and the tears fell faster, splashing onto the paper and blotting the words: 'I promise I will keep him safe. I love you, Estella. My sister, my twin, my everything xxx'

She blew her nose and placed the letter in an old tobacco tin of Bert's which the girls had once used to keep their messages dry. It didn't take her long to run through the garden and leave it safely in the sundial. As she swung the metal cover across and tightened the pin to hold it in place, Evie whispered once again the old promise to love and protect her friend. When Estella was better, she'd be certain to visit the sundial, and she'd know her baby was safe. Evie didn't know whether Estella could ever forgive her for keeping the truth about Jay's disappearance a secret, but she couldn't conceal the truth any longer. There could be no more secrets between them.

The midwife must have fled Pencallyn because on Evie's return there was no sign of her. Some clouts were left for the baby and several bottles of milk but otherwise it was as though she had never existed. If the woman was wise, she would have left as fast as she could and would do her best to put the unhappy events at Pencallyn House out of her mind.

Evie tucked the clouts and bottles into her bag before adding the baby clothes Estella had liberated from the attic. Anything else she needed she would have to find later. Estella slept heavily through all this activity, not even stirring when Evie kissed her hot cheek.

"I love you, Stella," she whispered. "I'm so sorry I haven't been a better friend. I'll guard your baby with my life. I promise."

There was no reply, so Evie swallowed back more tears and turned to pick the baby up from the box. He was so fragile, and she was terrified by the immense responsibility of him. This child would depend on her for everything. She couldn't fail him.

"I've got you," Evie whispered as she wrapped him in the shawl and held him against her shoulder. "You're going to be fine, little Jay. There's a fantastic life waiting for you, you'll see."

The baby whimpered to begin with, but then settled against her as though he sensed safety lay in her arms. He smelled of milk and sleep and delicious newness. Evie's heart melted. She loved him. She totally and utterly loved him and she would do anything to protect him. Anything.

"We're all set, little one," she said. "Auntie Evie's going to take you to meet your grandparents in America. Are you ready?"

Evie paused. Was she ready to leave Pencallyn? Perhaps. In her heart she had always known this day would come. Then, taking one last look at Estella and with her heart breaking, Evie Jenkins slipped out of Pencallyn House for the very last time.

CHAPTER 45

Estella
The Present

"Can she hear us?" The hand holding Estella's tightened, anchoring her to the earth as though its owner sensed she longed to drift away.

Nell. That voice belonged to the beautiful young woman with the wide periwinkle eyes, slow sweet smile and determined nature. Nell, who was the best of her and the best of Jay. Nell who was the best of that darling baby Estella had loved and lost. In this white halfway place, all the tempests of life were no more than childish fancies and she wanted to laugh out loud with the wonder of understanding everything. A lifetime spent missing her baby was a price Estella would pay a thousand times over because it meant there *was* a girl called Nell Summers. Nell was at the heart of the *Mysterious Garden*. The riddle led to her.

Dear Evie had paid a high price. Evie's mistakes were more than forgiven, for without Evie there would have been no Sam Summers, and Estella would not be holding hands with her beautiful granddaughter.

Her granddaughter! It was so incredible. She had a granddaughter. Her precious baby had been a father! The wonderful father Nell loved and missed so very much. To be given this gift was more than Estella deserved. More than she could have ever hoped for. Fate was kind after all.

Nell, Estella thought dreamily. The girl she had mistaken for Evie on the day she slipped and broke her hip. How ironic she hadn't seen what was right under her nose! She and Evie had always looked alike, but it wasn't Evie she'd thought she had seen. It was her long-ago self!

The truth had been there all along. She just hadn't looked in the right places. If only she'd revisited the sundial and hadn't closed the past off. Before she had been brought into this white place of peace Estella would have been distraught by this revelation. She would have wept and raged at the lost years. The idea of another woman having brought up her beloved child would have been unimaginably painful. Estella would have howled and torn her hair and screamed until her voice was in ribbons, yet in this white room she felt nothing but thankfulness. Her child had lived, and Estella was filled with gratitude towards the people who'd loved and cared for him. Without the Summers, and the events unfolding as they had, there would have been no Nell. Without Nell the circle would never have been complete.

"Does she know?" Nell whispered, and there was a catch in her voice. "Do you think she heard?"

"I think so, sweetheart. We have to hope so."

Josh, Estella thought. This second speaker was Josh Richardson. Gentle Josh who had magic in his hands, coaxing life from the barest earth and the rockiest soil, and whose quiet honour and kindness reminded her of Jay. Josh and Nell. It was perfect. Estella would have smiled if her lips had been willing but they, along with the rest of her, were so tired. How she longed to sleep.

Soon she would, and so deeply …

"She missed my father throughout her entire life. No mother should be denied time with their child," Nell said sadly, and Estella's heart went out to her because she recognised the pain of a mother without her child. Nothing she could say would ever sooth such rawness. It hadn't left her after more than seventy-five years, yet she wouldn't want it to, because at the heart of that pain was love. Estella knew she would make the same choices all over again because Jay Miller was the love of a lifetime.

Estella longed to reassure Nell she'd heard everything. Evie's letter had transported her back in time, and what a blessing to hear her dear friend's voice after so long. Although weary to her bones, Estella had listened to every painful and marvellous word. Syllables had slipped and slid, consonants were carried by currents and words washed over her in a torrent, but Estella had listened to them all. Like the shifting of the earth's crust they shattered and reformed her landscape, tossing her into a churning sea of revelations before washing her up on an alien shore. She lay on the sand gasping, her fingers clawing at scattered fragments of meaning until slowly, like shells and sea glass strewn along the shoreline, these sparkled and became a new landscape.

A new world.

She had a granddaughter. She had a son. Nell and Sam. Sam and Nell. Her little loves. Her dear ones. Her family. Her world.

Estella tried to hold onto the names. She wanted to tuck them close to her heart and hold them there, precious treasures to pore over, and she wanted to dance and sing and tell the world. Her child had lived! She hadn't let Jay down! Their baby had been under the same blue sky. Her father had lied.

Their precious baby had lived.

"If she knows, do you think she's angry?" Estella heard Nell ask. "Evie could have told her the truth way back about what had really happened to Jay. She could have given Estella closure."

Estella wished she could speak. She longed to explain that when you were in this special place, this new hinterland where it was calm and white and full of love, you didn't feel anger any more. All the tangles of human emotion and knots of grievance were smoothed away and all you felt was compassion. Evie just did what she'd thought was right. It was all anyone could ever do.

"Evie was a frightened child," Josh said gently. "She must have been traumatised after what Hamilton did, and realising Reginald Kellow had all but sanctioned murder must have been terrifying! Evie was a kid, Nell. They both were."

Estella floated on the sound of his voice. It was so gentle. So kind. So tender. Josh Richardson understood, and she had been right to trust him. She had been right to believe in Evie too, and hold fast to the certainty her friend would have never willingly forsaken her. Evie had made mistakes – but how frightened she must have been of Hamilton and of revealing what she knew. And how right she had been not to let Estella's baby remain at Pencallyn!

"But what about Reginald Kellow?" Nell pressed, and Josh sighed.

"He's certainly culpable and a product of his time. Men were the acknowledged head of the household in those days, and their wives and daughters had to obey them. If nothing else, history shows us how racism and bigotry allow people to justify the worst kinds of behaviour. No wonder he drowned himself. Posterity won't look kindly on him, and neither will the police. The same goes for Hamilton Mason when they reopen the case."

"But it's too late for justice. They've been dead for years," Nell said.

"Yes, but the record will be set straight and the truth will be told," Josh replied. "They can't hide their deeds behind a good name or a distinguished war record. They'll not be remembered fondly."

"Everyone will know Jay Miller was brave and loyal." Nell's voice had a determined note Estella recognised – and she was certain her solicitor would too! Like her, Nell would see things through. She was the best of them all. Jay would live on, and live well, through her, while Hamilton and Reginald rotted, their good names tarnished for ever by their ugly deeds. That was justice. It was revenge – if revenge was what she wanted. Now Jay and their baby were found, Estella was at peace; anger and vengeance were emotions from another life. Although new to the white land, Estella understood so much more than she ever had before. She couldn't forgive her father or Hamilton, but it was not for her to dole out punishment. Their ugly deeds would not be forgotten, and Estella suspected her father's death had been driven by far more than financial pressures. The world would know the truth at last; Jay Miller had died bravely and loving her right until the end. He was at peace too.

There were footsteps. The familiar squeak of rubber soles on floor. Beeping machines. The pressure of a cuff on her arm. The dear nurses could check and fuss all they liked; it would make no difference. There was a heaviness in her chest she knew of old and Estella welcomed it. It was time.

"How's she doing?" Josh asked.

"I'm afraid there's no change," came the reply. A nurse, Estella thought, and one whose soft tone suggested she'd seen people enter the white room before and knew they seldom returned.

"What does that mean?" Nell said.

"It's been twenty-four hours since she left theatre and she hasn't come around. I think you should prepare yourselves."

Theatre to Estella meant plush red seats, gilt paint and swishing curtains but most of all Evie putting on plays and dreaming of fame and fortune. But all her dreams were cut short, her heart crushed by Hamilton and speared with guilt. Oh Evie! Estella cried soundlessly. I've missed you! I forgive you for everything! And you saved him, Evie! You saved my baby! Thank you!

Emotion exploded in her chest like a mine. Estella gasped, blasted backwards by a sudden force which blew the door to the white place wide open. A face swam above her, blue eyes wide and filled with worry.

"Nell," Estella whispered.

"Estella? Grandma?"

"Grandma," she echoed, and her voice sounded like the rustle of dry leaves "Yes, Grandma."

There was a high-pitched whine followed by beeping and the thud of feet. Hands on her chest. A rattling trolley. A sob. The white room heaved, tipping and rolling and pitching Estella into a long corridor which turned as colour kaleidoscoped through. It was like nothing she'd ever seen, and to her amazement she was running, jumping swathes of scarlet and bathing in glorious sunshine yellow. There were hues and shades she'd never seen before and she laughed with sheer wonder.

Still laughing, Estella realised she was now in Pencallyn's formal garden. The grass was the greenest she had ever seen and the sky so blue it hurt her eyes. Everything was so vivid. So alive. Yet this wasn't the garden as she'd last seen it, but rather the garden as it had been in the days before the war. The hedges were clipped, the gravel paths were raked to mathematical perfection and each flower bed brimmed with jewel-hued blooms. At the centre of all this glory was the sundial, the dear and silent guardian of old magic and long-kept secrets. A woodpigeon's song trembled from deep within the woods, the salt-kissed breeze stirred the roses and a young girl danced in the clearing, her dark hair flying as she bowed to an imaginary audience.

It was Evie!

Estella's hands flew to her mouth. They were smooth and white once more. When she touched her hair it was thick, hanging to her waist in long ebony curls, and she stepped towards her friend with an easy tread. All her aches and pains had gone. Had it all been a dream? Had she never grown old after all?

Then Evie turned to face her, and Estella no longer cared about what was a dream or what was real.

"There you are at last Stell!" Evie cried. "You took your time!"

"Evie!"

Estella's real voice was back! As clear as a stream, it no longer cracked or faded as she chased her thoughts around. She was herself again! Overjoyed, she threw her arms around her dear friend's neck and held her tightly.

"Do you forgive me?" Evie asked.

"Of course, I do! Oh, Evie! I've missed you so much!"

"I've missed you too. We all have, and we'll never leave you again, Stell. Promise on the sundial! Look! Everyone's here to see you."

And then Estella realised there were other people in the garden too. Oh! Cook was here with Violet, and over there was Ivy Pendriscott chatting to Tommy. Now she looked closer she realised the garden was teeming with people. There was Ally in his treasured RAF uniform and deep conversation with a blond young man who waved and called '*Danke!*' There were more faces, more people, and names flew through her mind of dear friends long lost but never forgotten. Beth. Jenny. Bert. Mama. Dolly. Old gardeners and young lads who'd left Pencallyn to join up never to return – they were all here and so well and happy! She'd missed them all terribly, and Estella thought she would burst with happiness to see them again. They must have been here all the time.

"Come on!" said Evie, tugging her hand. "Let's play Mysterious Garden! Poppet wants to!"

And here was dear little Poppet, jumping up and down and barking with delight as her plumy tail became a blur and her pink tongue lolled. Estella hugged the spaniel tightly. Dear, loyal Poppet who'd defended Jay with her life …

Oh! Jay!

Estella scanned the faces. Surely he was here too?

"Where's Jay?" she asked Evie. "Isn't he here?"

"Of course he is!" Evie replied. "He's been waiting for ages. He wants you to go with him."

Estella's heart leapt. "I can go with him?"

"Oh yes but be warned – you may never want to come back."

"I don't care about that! I want to be with him!" Estella cried. "Oh, where is he, Evie? Where has he gone?"

"Nowhere, silly! He's been here all the time." Evie pointed into the trees. "Look, there he is! See? He never left you."

Estella peered but it was hard to see because the trees were melting and the garden dissolving. The greens bled into one another like the watercolours she used to spill onto wet paper, and they mingled with the sky. The ground was no longer carpeted with grass but solid and cool. Looking down, Estella saw her bare feet were young too, and pressing prints into soft sand.

She was at Pencallyn Cove.

There was a boat in the shallows, a small vessel with a white sail, and standing in the prow was a man. He had his back to her, but Estella knew him at once. She would know him anywhere.

Estella started to run, and now there were no barriers to bar her way and keep them apart. There was no barbed wire. No warning signs. No pillboxes. Or barrage balloons. The beach was as it always had been; the wet and wormcast sand rippled under her soles, and the water sparkled in the sunlight. The glare was so bright it was hard to see where the silver sand ended and the water began, and she shaded her eyes with her hand, squinting into the brightness as she splashed through the shallows. The man held out his hand and she saw his warm brown eyes, the wide curve of his generous mouth and the close- cropped hair outlining the pure lines of his beautiful head. He was proud and strong in his uniform, and every bit as handsome he'd been all those years ago.

"Jay?" she said wonderingly. "Is it really you?"

"It is, my Star," he replied, and his voice thrilled her because it was as caramel soft and delicious as it always had been. "Are you ready to sail away with me? Across the sea to the place where there are lakes like oceans, seas of wheat and an old white farmhouse with a rocker on the porch?"

"And we fish in the lake? And our children play in the fields and chase chickens? And your mum helps me make apple pie?" Estella recalled, and Jay tipped his head back and laughed.

"Oh yes, all of that! Why, our boy's already there and waiting for you. Are you ready to sail over the horizon?"

Estella thought her heart would burst. Was she ready? Of course, she was! She'd waited a lifetime to meet their child. Her arms had ached for him every day since he was born.

"I've been ready my whole lifetime," she said.

Estella held out her hand and Jay kissed each finger before lifting her into the boat which danced beneath her feet, as impatient as a horse longing to gallop.

On the shore her friends were waving and cheering. Jay smiled down into her eyes and when his lips met hers Estella knew she was truly in heaven. Paradise for her would always be wherever Jay Miller was.

"Ready?" he asked.

"All my life," Estella said.

Already the horizon seemed closer and the deep ocean was a glorious blend of blue and turquoise. This new world was full of wonder, and she couldn't wait to explore it with him. To love him. To share their family. To be together now, always and for ever, just as they had promised. Jay unfurled the sail, and a warm wind swelled the canvas, dancing them across the water, and Estella laughed with sheer delight because leaving everything behind wasn't difficult at all. It was easy.

As easy as breathing out.

EPILOGUE

The Present
Nell

It's early summer. Months pass with the turning tides, and the following June finds me at Pencallyn Cove. I can't imagine leaving. Cornwall is a place easy to fall in love with and impossible to turn your back on. Once it's in your heart it's there for ever, just like the man whose hand I hold as we walk along the tide's edge with shingle peppering our bare feet.

Waves break onto the sand with an eternal rhythm; Nature's metronome measures out the months and years and centuries. There's a comfort in this; loss and loneliness come to pass because that is the way of it. I miss my father, and I'll never forget my lost child, but being happy with Josh, tilting my face up to the sun and smiling when his lips graze my cheek, doesn't mean I love them any less. I only have to glance at the echoes of the past to be reminded just how lucky I am to walk along the beach with the man I love. So many didn't have that chance. So many lives were lost.

This newly minted June morning is sunny and Pencallyn's beach teems with visitors making the most of the weather as Cornwall returns to life after winter's hibernation. Gift shops reopen, shutters dusted off and unlatched, while café owners place signs in the street to tempt tourists inside with the promise of cream teas and pasties. Carousels spin and postcards wobble. Buckets and spades are claimed eagerly while long-suffering crabs are scooped out of rook pools. Children shriek when cold water kisses bare feet, colourful towels and windbreaks dot the sand like sprinkles, and sailing boats slice across the bay.

It's a peaceful summer's morning and impossible to imagine it could ever have been any other way – yet if I narrow my eyes against the brightness the air shivers and a thousand memories rise with the tide. The cracked concrete embarkation jetty rears above the waves like a mythical sea monster, and rather than children running along it to tumble into the waves, I see a column of young men stepping onto ships which ride the swell and tug at their moorings. The soldiers follow orders, faces set and serious because months of drills have led them to this moment. They understand only too well what's waiting for them across the water.

Today's pleasure craft gleam in the brightness and for a moment their hulls seem to be the iron grey of warships gathering in the depths. High on the cliffs, where long grasses hula dance and seabirds nest, abandoned pillboxes slumber. Smothered by ivy and choked by briars, they are the forgotten remains of a time when this shore was a war zone and for a while Britain stood alone against a powerful enemy. Facing inland and above the swell of shorn fields is a deep green wood where the soil sometimes gives birth to metal shards of a long-lost enemy plane and where locals still never venture after dusk. The past has echoes; if you listen carefully it whispers to you. In Cornwall the veil between past and present is thin and as delicate as gossamer.

Estella. My father. Jay. Evie. My baby. None of them are far away. Nothing is ever lost. Nothing is ever forgotten.

I gaze over the glassy water. It feels impossible that seventy-five years ago this beach was deserted after years as a hive of military activity. Seventy-five years ago, the Battle of Normandy began. Men from all walks of life gave their lives so I can watch children play freely here. Although the passing years may have erased those men's faces and crumbled the defences they abandoned, the courage and sacrifice of people like Jay Miller and Alex Kellow will never be forgotten. So many lives lost and such unimaginable horror on the beaches over the water. So much heartache as their losses were mourned by their loved ones. Cornwall's wartime history must never slip from sight. The stories and sacrifices must be remembered.

"It seems impossible, doesn't it?" Josh says. "All the activity here stopping overnight, and the fight to liberate Europe taking place over the horizon."

I think of Estella and Evie watching the troops leave. Of Estella's broken heart and Evie's dreadful burden. Of Jay's belief that it was a fight which encompassed good and evil, right and wrong, and a cause he was prepared to die for.

"They succeeded, though," I reply quietly. "We have this because of them."

"We'll never see a generation like theirs again. Estella was the last."

I lean against him. "I wish I'd had more time with her."

It's been hard to find and lose my grandmother. Estella never fully regained consciousness, but I'm certain she heard every word we said to her. Her passing was so peaceful; Estella exhaled slowly, as though reaching the end of a long journey, and smiled. I like to think she'd seen Jay Miller and Evie.

Poor Evie. I hope she knows she did save my father and keep her promise. If it hadn't been for her, I wouldn't be here. She made mistakes but she put them right – and what more can any of us hope to do than that?

"Do you think Estella would be pleased?" Josh asks. He looks worried and my heart squeezes with love for him. I never expected to meet somebody else, let alone share my life with them, but sometimes Fate takes you by surprise – and how wonderful that it does. Every day I wake up with Josh beside me feels like the first time. The wonder of finding him never lessens.

"Pleased about Pencallyn House or us?"

He draws me against him. "Both I guess, although I was thinking of Pencallyn and the garden. Would she have wanted all this? Have we done the right thing?"

After Estella had passed away her solicitor contacted Josh with the surprise news that she had left everything to him. Pencallyn House, the gardens, her royalties – it was all his. Josh was stunned and horrified in equal measure, but he was the perfect choice. Clever Estella! Josh is honourable and true, and loves the garden; Estella knew he could be trusted to do the right thing with her legacy. Josh tried to say no, arguing I should inherit as Estella's sole surviving relative, but the will was watertight; the estate either went to Josh or it was to be sold. Although Josh's father had put the farm up for sale there were plenty of other developers keen to snap up land in Cornwall, and the garden could be lost for ever. Estella had been very canny, for how could Josh ever allow such a thing to happen?

He accepted the bequest on the provision Pencallyn House and garden became a registered charity with a board of trustees, including myself, set up to run it. This way we could work to restore and preserve the garden. Josh has plans for the hydrangea valley, the Japanese garden, the labyrinth and the magnolia walk, and is so excited. It's the restoration project of a lifetime.

Once my father's estate was settled, I left London and moved into Pencallyn House, where Josh and I have worked on the plans for the garden. My novel morphed into a fictionalised account of my grandmother's life story, and last month my agent sold it for a good advance which will go some way towards helping us set up a tearoom. While I was writing through the winter and spring, Josh worked in the garden with a team of volunteers, and gradually the original design emerged from the briars and ivy. There are so many green treasures within, and I've discovered I like working with the plants, finding a peace amid nature I'd never known before. Country life suits me. Lou thinks I've gone mad, but she gets twitchy if she's ten feet away from a tube station. I've told her my new passion for gardening and rural life is my Kellow heritage.

My Miller heritage is something I'm working on. The DNA test links me to various branches of the family, but although it's wonderful to be part of something bigger, this no longer matters as much as it did. I'm Nell Summers. I'm an author. I am Sam Summers' daughter. Josh Richardson's partner. A director of the Pencallyn Garden Trust. I am many versions of myself, and I am a part of what we're building here. This is where I belong.

One day I'm going to travel to America and visit Millers' Hollow and sail a boat on a lake as big as an ocean and watch the rippling seas of wheat, but all that's in the future. When I lost my baby, and when my father died, my anchor slipped. I drifted until the river of events carried me downstream and gently bumped me against the banks of roots and love. Josh and Pencallyn are my family now, and this is my place. I've moored in a peaceful harbour.

I am home.

"Estella might not be thrilled you've chopped those massive leylandii down," I tease.

"She only let them grow so tall to annoy Dad, and she'd be delighted I've upset him by turning the lot into firewood. No wonder he thinks I'm having another episode!"

"Be honest, that's really why you did it?"

He laughs. "Guilty as charged. But I've planted some native hawthorns and elders there instead."

"But in answer to your earlier question," I continue as we leave the beach and walk through the village, past the pub where I stayed all those months ago and towards the lower entrance to the garden, "I think she'd be proud of what you've done. It was never the garden itself Estella disliked, but what it meant to her father and all the painful memories it held for her. She left the property to you because she knew you would protect it."

"I think Pencallyn can take care of itself. We're its guardians now, and it will be here long after we're gone," he says thoughtfully. "This is just the beginning, Nell. Pencallyn will live on, and the people who've lived here won't be forgotten.'"

He's right. With its connection to the author of *Mysterious Garden* and the tragic love story of the young GI and the daughter of the house, a story which hit the media when Jay Miller's body was found, there is already huge interest in Pencallyn. When we opened for the first time, deliberately choosing 6th June, we could hardly believe how many visitors descended on us. I think we're in for a very busy summer.

"One day we'll be as big as Heligan!" I say, and I'm only half-joking because I truly believe in Josh's vision for Pencallyn. It's a lifetime's work, but there's nowhere else I'd rather be and nobody else I'd rather spend my life with. I can't wait to see what unfolds. Life is, I've realised, not a gruelling feat to be endured but a gift to be treasured.

The bottom gate into the garden is unlocked and we pass through. The feeling of being watched is gone; now his dreadful secret has been revealed the restless shade of Hamilton Mason is exorcised. His role in the murder of Jay Miller has been recorded for posterity and investigated by the US military. His name will go down in infamy and with it those of Lex Boone and Reginald Kellow. The question mark over Jay Miller's conduct and the accusations of desertion have been removed, and the case, now so cold, is closed. When the truth came to light , the hold Hamilton Mason's evil deeds had on the garden faded. He has no power here. The same is true for

Reginald Kellow, who died a bitter man; legend has it that he drowned himself in the Japanese pond, but he may have slipped, because Estella never elaborated. I wonder whether a vengeful ghost with blond hair and eyes like glaciers enticed him there and whispered in his ear that he should step into the deep water? This is my imagination at work, but who knows … ?

Jay Miller was laid to rest in a private service at St Brecca's. He shares a plot with Estella, and although there were only a few of us present at the service, it was beautiful and peaceful. As I listened to the timeless words, I recalled the many memories Estella had shared with Josh and me. The first meeting with Jay at the dance. His smile in the moonlight. Fingertips skimming trembling skin. Stolen kisses. The lost nights of a magical summer when life could be snatched away at any time. I'd thought about how Estella loved only Jay Miller for her whole life. She had known he was her soulmate and her one true love. When it was time, and the old words had been uttered, I stood at the edge of their grave and poured the crucifix into the darkness. It was right it should rest with them, just as it was right they should rest together.

Hand in hand, Josh and I climb through the garden. Deep shadows pool the path and above the leafy roof are speckles of blue sky. No visitors are permitted here so we have the place to ourselves. Time feels suspended. It could be 1939 again with two girls playing in the labyrinth. Or perhaps the strains of Glen Miller drift on the breeze and it's 1944? If time is a curtain, does it part occasionally so we can peek through?

Can they see us? Does Estella know Josh and I have come together with her legacy and with our hearts? Do two little girls glimpse a man with fox-red hair and a dark-haired woman, and pause, wondering who has intruded into their Mysterious Garden?

Maybe.

It's certainly imagination that as we step out of the shade into the sundial clearing and the light dazzles me, I see a handsome young soldier holding a dark-haired girl close. In the dancing light, she smiles at me over his shoulder and I smile back.

My grandparents. My family.

Josh's fingers tighten on mine.

"Nell," he whispers, squinting into the brightness, "do you see …"

The sun bobs behind a wisp of cloud and there's only an empty garden, lichen-furred sundial and the pillow-soft quiet.

Josh passes his free hand over his eyes.

"I thought I saw … no. It was just a trick of the light and some wishful thinking."

"Maybe," I say softly. "But maybe not."

As we stand hand in hand the sun peeps out once more, filling the clearing with bright light. I won't see Estella again. Not here, anyway, and not in this life. Her story has been told. The wrongs are righted and lost loved ones restored, and the past has been laid to rest. Pencallyn and what remains of Estella's family are safe, and my heart tells me this is farewell. She can rest at last because the long-ago promises made in this spot have been kept. Love lives on.

I turn to Josh, the man I love now, always and for ever, and know everything has led to this moment and to the heart of the mysterious garden where he has been waiting for me all along. There is a pattern, although we can't always see it, and a perfect design amid the chaos. Most of all, there is the promise of love.

Now, always and for ever.

"Let's go home," I say.

The End

NOTES FROM THE AUTHOR

The Promise is a novel that came from nowhere and from everywhere. I was walking on the coast path, which hems the Cornish creek where I live, when I noticed remnants of the Second World War lying just beneath the tangled undergrowth and shifting mudflats. It was as though the past had overlapped the present and suddenly I saw the crumbling shells of abandoned pillboxes, ruin of a Home Guard station on the cliff and the ivy-smothered Nissen huts in Cornish farmyards. The past was just over my shoulder; if I turned around fast enough, I might catch it. These remains of the recent past are as much a part of Cornwall's past as skeletal tin mines, weathered standing stones and ancient Celtic crosses. The seed of an idea was planted, and a story began to unfold.

Researching and writing this book has consumed me for almost a year. In some ways it's been a challenge because the narrative involved issues I was facing at the time of writing. At times Nell and Estella's stories made me revisit some very tough situations and emotions of my own, but during others the narrative flowed so easily it was hard to keep up. Many people, from my immediate family to acquaintances, had memories to share about the war and their own stories to tell, and these began to weave themselves into the novel. As always, the landscape of Cornwall was a huge inspiration, as well as the myths and legends which are engrained in this ancient and mysterious landscape. These find their way into the story with the ley lines and the landmarks which can be found along them from St Brecca's Church to the sundial.

Nell's story is exceedingly personal, as I lost my own father while working on this book. Many times while writing it I found I was in tears and at times art imitated life in a way that I can't quite explain. Some of my father's memories of being a child during the Second World War are found within the story, and I owe him a big thank you for talking to me at such length and when he felt so unwell. His tales of gas masks, odd food and rationing gave me an insight into what that time was like for a child. Like my father, Estella and Evie grow up during wartime, and the memories remain with Estella until the very end of her days.

Nell's other loss, that of her unborn child, was also something I wanted to explore. Unlike the loss of a father it is one that's hard to speak about and is often accorded little space or acknowledgement. This loss of a child forms a bond between Nell and Estella, and is another reason why Nell's search for her father's roots becomes so important.

Although grief and loss are key themes of *The Promise*, love, hope and the continuation of life have equal importance. The ending of the story is a promise too – one of a new landscape and a future for Nell. Life is precious and every moment is to be lived, a message that Estella does her best to convey. It's through Nell that Estella and Jay Miller live on and his story can be told. The metaphor of Pencallyn's garden returning to life in Josh's hands reiterates this idea.

Pencallyn House and village are based on the wonderful Trebah House and Garden and the National Trust's Glendurgan, both found on the Helford where many American troops were based during the war. It is here where many preparations for the D-Day landings took place. I spent several days in this area exploring the gardens and immersing myself in the atmosphere. The specimen plants and sub-tropical gardens are incredible, and these are juxtaposed with concrete on the beaches, remains of embarkation piers and widened roads, all of which stand testament to the ugliness of war. Cornish creeks and beaches were out of bounds during the war years, and the stories of wartime life in Cornwall in the book are all taken from eyewitness accounts and memoirs.

A book like *The Promise* requires a great deal of historical detail, and I spent a lot of time on research in order to immerse my wartime characters in the world of the past. This is one of the parts of writing I really enjoy, and I'm always fascinated to see what lies beneath the surface of things I take for granted. Learning about the 'friendly invasion' of the US army was a revelation, and the character of this sleepy part of the world must have really changed during that time. Life was uncertain and love affairs blossomed under the pressure of time and danger. Heartbreak and loss were never far away and marriages often took place after a matter of weeks.

Some accounts of these times were wonderful to hear, happy memories from elderly neighbours of excitedly watching planes fly over. Others, like eyewitness accounts of the institutionalised racism towards the African-American GIs, were very distressing. As described in the novel, the US Army was run along Jim Crow lines and the Cornish were unimpressed by this – most people feeling everyone was 'in it together.' I read many accounts and anecdotes that are hard to reconcile or understand. The ugly attitudes voiced by Hamilton Mason and Reginald Kellow are, sadly, taken from real-life accounts: one Cornish MP did indeed write to Anthony Eden about the African-American soldiers in his constituency, and the vile words Estella's father uses are based on that letter. One elderly lady wrote an account about how a young African-American GI stopped in the street to ask for directions. He was beaten up in front of her by fellow soldiers for daring to speak to a white woman. Over seventy years on, she was understandably still upset about this incident. With this knowledge it's not hard to appreciate that the risks that Jay and Estella take to be together were very real. There are many accounts of couples like them who were able to make a life after the war, and wonderful anecdotes from their own children. Similarly, there are also many very sad stories of women forced to give their babies away, and children who spent years searching for their absent American parent. There are far too many to mention here, but Sam Summers' experience is not unique.

Jay Miller's experience of life in Cornwall and the prejudice that he faces at Pencallyn House is based on many accounts of young men like him. As a character, Jay Miller is a mixture of the accounts I found of African-American men who came to Britain during the Second World War, as well as the stories of the families who gave them billets and grew to know them. One lady, like Ivy Pendriscott in the book, stayed in touch for years with the family of the young man who had lodged with her. When he died in Normandy, she grieved for him and wrote to his mother to tell her how proud she should be. Another young man was studying medicine at university and became a combat medic who served with bravery and valour on the beaches of Normandy. I used these accounts, historical details and a little dash of imagination to create Jay Miller and to imagine how he might feel about fighting a war that must have seemed very far away from home. Writing Jay's final scene was very hard, and I cried a great deal. Jay is brave and noble and kind; he gives his life to protect Evie and never betrays his love for Estella when offered an escape. His qualities live on in his son and in Nell. I wanted Jay to feel real to the reader and for it to be clear why Estella loves him now, always and for ever. When Estella died, I wanted him to be waiting for her as he had promised. This scene was very important to me, and I know it's been key to my own coming to terms with loss.

In this book I've taken many anecdotes and eyewitness accounts of life in Cornwall during the war and woven them into the narrative. I was also lucky enough to have a diary that my granny kept during the Blitz, and this gave me a real insight into how the war became a new 'normality'. My granny talks about how people called Churchill a 'warmonger' but when my grandfather, who worked before the war in a metal factory designing filing cabinets and office furniture, came home and said he'd been asked to design gun racks for trucks, they realised he was right and that war was coming. My granny was pregnant with my uncle at that point, and he was a small child during the Blitz; she never seems to have been afraid but simply got on with daily life. She writes about how hiding under the kitchen table during bombing raids became something they grew accustomed to. In the wartime sections of the book I've tried to create a sense that normal life did carry on, and how children knew nothing else.

Londoner Evie Jenkins would have experienced some of the same events my grandparents did, and she is a character who fascinates me. A tough city kid, Evie's world collides with Estella's when the war brings her to Cornwall. She's bright and lives on her wits and is a survivor. There are many stories of evacuees who came to Cornwall, and I managed to listen to some accounts that were recorded a few years ago for a BBC Living History project. Some children had a marvellous time, many staying in touch with their Cornish wartime family for the rest of their lives, but others had a less positive experience. How out of place they must have felt, and homesick too. Evie's reactions to the food, smells and shock of country life are taken from these accounts – as are the dirty clothes and bad table manners. The close friendship she forms with Estella and the promise they make at the sundial are central to the plot. Evie is fiercely loyal but has a dark side too, which both draws and horrifies Estella. She's the shadow side of Estella in many ways – but her promise, and her refusal to break it, are ultimately what means there is a Nell Summers to tell the twenty-first-century story.

There's so much more I could say about this book, but that would take up another novel's worth of words! I've heard so many stories, I've spoken to so many interesting people and I've learned more about local history than I had ever expected. I've visited quirky museums and stately homes, and heard stories from people who lived through the Second World War. It's been a contradiction, the hardest and the easiest book to write, but it has also been cathartic. It's my way of keeping wartime stories and memories alive after those who remember them have left us.

Ruth Saberton
June 2019

I really hope you have enjoyed reading this book. If you did, I would really appreciate a review. It makes all the difference for a writer.

You might also enjoy my other books:

The Letter
The Island Legacy
Chances
Runaway Summer: Polwenna Bay 1
A Time for Living: Polwenna Bay 2
Winter Wishes: Polwenna Bay 3
Treasure of the Heart: Polwenna Bay 4
Recipe for Love: Polwenna Bay 5
Rhythm of the Tide: Polwenna Bay 6

Magic in the Mist: Polwenna Bay novella
Cornwall for Christmas: Polwenna Bay novella

Escape for the Summer
Escape for Christmas
Christmas on the Creek
The Season for Second Chances
Rock my World
Hobb's Cottage
Weight Till Christmas
The Wedding Countdown
Dead Romantic
Katy Carter Wants a Hero
Katy Carter Keeps a Secret
Ellie Andrews Has Second Thoughts
Amber Scott is Starting Over

Pen Name Books

Writing as Jessica Fox

The One That Got Away
Eastern Promise
Hard to Get
Unlucky in Love
Always the Bride

Writing as Holly Cavendish

Looking for Fireworks

Writing as Georgie Carter

The Perfect Christmas

Ruth Saberton is the bestselling author of *The Letter, Katy Carter Wants a Hero* and *Escape for the Summer*. She also writes upmarket commercial fiction under the pen names Jessica Fox, Georgie Carter and Holly Cavendish.

Born in London, Ruth now lives in beautiful Cornwall. She has travelled to many places, but nothing compares to the rugged beauty of the Cornish coast which never fails to provide her with inspiration for her writing. For the latest on Ruth and her writing you can also follow her on social media.

Twitter: @ruthsaberton

Facebook: Ruth Saberton Author

Instagram: Ruth Saberton Instagram

Web: www.ruthsaberton.com

Printed in Great Britain
by Amazon